THE
LOST
SWIMMER

THE
LOST
SWIMMER

ANN TURNER

**SIMON &
SCHUSTER**

London · New York · Sydney · Toronto · New Delhi

A CBS COMPANY

First published in Australia by Simon & Schuster Pty Limited, 2015
First published in Great Britain by Simon & Schuster UK Ltd, 2016
A CBS COMPANY

1 3 5 7 9 10 8 6 4 2

Simon & Schuster UK Ltd
1st Floor
222 Gray's Inn Road
London WC1X 8HB

www.simonandschuster.co.uk

Simon & Schuster Australia, Sydney
Simon & Schuster India, New Delhi

A CIP catalogue record for this book
is available from the British Library

Paperback ISBN: 978-1-4711-7674-6
eBook ISBN: 978-1-4711-5309-9

Printed and bound by CPI Group (UK) Ltd, Croydon, CR0 4YY

Simon & Schuster UK Ltd are committed to sourcing paper
that is made from wood grown in sustainable forests and support the Forest
Stewardship Council, the leading international forest certification organisation.
Our books displaying the FSC logo are printed on FSC certified paper.

For my parents, Margaret and Dick Turner,
with love and gratitude

'Everything flows and nothing abides,
everything gives way and nothing stays fixed.'

Heraclitus c. 535–475 BC

1

The sand was washed clean today, stretching wide at low tide. I ran along the glistening shore thinking of something I'd read last night: that you could travel a thousand miles and never notice anything. I suspected that this was as false now as when it was written by a Greek philosopher in the fifth century BC. Surely powers of observation would eventually take hold?

Two parrots were swinging upside down, a blaze of red and blue, sliding beaks and claws along a tree root that erupted from the stark ochre cliff. They swirled upright and bobbed about in a crazy dance, then one suddenly bit the other and flew off screeching in an ear-shattering blast as Big Boy, my border collie retriever, torpedoed from the shallows in a black and white streak and snapped at my heels. Years ago we'd rescued this shaggy giant from an animal shelter; now that the kids, James and Erin, were away at university in Melbourne, Big Boy was my reason for fitness, my daily coach.

The low rays of the sun tingled my skin as I scanned the ocean, a burning sapphire glowing with the promise of a long, hot summer on the Surf Coast. Hugging around the base of Victoria, this stretch of bush and beach lay exposed to dangerous storms off Bass Strait. But today there was no fierce swell; the waves rolled in gently, crystal clear. And yet for all the pleasure this morning gave, a hard fist gnawed deep inside my gut, clenched and pushing and out of control.

Heart pumping, I pounded up the cliffs through the moonah trees, resistance in my muscles making me aware of every one of my forty-seven years. Slamming through the pain, minutes later I rounded the bend to where our weatherboard home perched atop a steep drive, one massive glass door peering out like a Cyclops to the bleached timber deck. The house floated in a pale eucalypt haze, as if it might untether at any moment and drift away.

On the kitchen table a note lay bathed in sunshine. *Sorry, couldn't wait, see you tonight xxx*. Carelessly scrawled, unlike my husband Stephen's usual meticulous handwriting. He must have been in an extraordinary hurry. My stomach kicked again as I strode to the bathroom, stripping off my sweat-stained clothes and dropping them on the floor. I caught myself in the mirror, shoulder-length dark blonde hair plastered to my face, blue eyes clouded with frustration. What was so important that meant he couldn't wait? As water pounded my skin I cursed. Although I'd been an archaeologist for twenty years and a professor for five, this was my first stint heading the School of Classics and History at Coastal University, whereas Stephen, an economics professor, had led his department twice. I was used to sifting through dirt for fragments of the past, writing about the daily life of lost cultures and supervising my students, but dealing with the problems of colleagues, often urgent, was challenging. We were under pressure from budget cuts and I desperately needed Stephen's advice on several issues.

Suddenly I heard a volley of barks rising to a crescendo of growls. I stilled beneath the water, listening for Big Boy to stop, wondering what had set him off. When he escalated into frantic yelps I leaped from the shower.

The dog's claws were scratching like razors, raw against the glass. I wrapped my towel tight and peered out.

A kangaroo and her tiny joey lingered in the shadows at the edge of our lawn.

'Shh, it's okay.' Relief flooded through me but Big Boy's yelps grew more hysterical. Slipping my fingers beneath his collar I banished him into the depths of the house, and then I crept back and watched as the mother began nibbling tender shoots and the joey, tentative at first, bit down on the sweet blades. The kangaroos moved slowly through the dewy grass as they grazed. The mother had a fluorescent tag in her ear and a red band around her neck, on which BONNIE was written in large black letters – she was part of the local mob being tracked by a university study. The joey looked up shyly. Bonnie tensed and rose to her full towering height. Strong and proud, she stretched almost two metres from the ground. Our eyes locked and she became instantly still.

Bonnie had never been this far down the hill before. Her gaze was calm, alert, full of trust.

In a flurry of upside-down crumpling the joey fled into his mother's pouch, a wisp of tail the only clue to his existence until he righted himself and his perfect little head popped out, peeping back, emboldened. Bonnie turned abruptly, her powerful legs propelling her and her son silently up the hill in seconds.

Amid the tranquility I realised I was late for work.

2

'It's a matter of integrity. He conducted the interviews without ethics approval, the start of a long, slippery slide if we let him get away with it,' I said to the members of the Faculty of Arts Ethics Committee.

'But he's only twenty-four.' Douglas McCall, his tiny head protruding from a floppy brown suit giving him the appearance of a vulnerable turtle, fixed me with rheumy eyes. 'He meant no harm and he doesn't need this setback.'

'I'm concerned that he misled vulnerable women,' I countered.

'You're always trying to save the wrong ones, Bec,' McCall growled in a fatherly manner.

The rest of the committee, clearly divided, sat mutely. 'Could the Dean rule on this perhaps?' asked McCall.

Our Dean of Arts, Professor Priscilla Chiton, blinked once and then leaned forward, speaking softly so everyone had to draw towards her. Cornflower-blue eyes, stylishly cut blonde hair and a designer suit in the finest linen added to her complete authority. I'd known Priscilla for years – she was a French historian. In the early days we were friends. Now, we usually never agreed on anything.

'I'm with Rebecca on this.' Priscilla's mellow voice floated across the room. 'I'll be referring it up to the next level. It's completely unacceptable to carry out interviews for a PhD without ethics approval, particularly when the subject is the views of female prisoners on corrupt police.' Priscilla stacked her papers, banging them on the desk as she rose to indicate the meeting was over.

The worn chair, foam hanging out like honeycomb, with a wonky tilt I'd grown to love, met me with a sigh as I sank into it.

'How did you go?' Melinda Hoppen raced in eagerly, piercing me with cat-green eyes. In her early life Melinda had been a model, part of the Chelsea set. Her looks hadn't faded and she stood out here, a style icon even now, with a crop of thick brown hair, tall, perfect figure and an agility that defied her sixty-odd years.

'Priscilla was really supportive.'

Melinda dropped a heavy pile of papers on my desk. 'Watch your back if she's nice.' She walked out dramatically.

My email bleeped – more than fifty new missives had arrived

in my absence. I scrolled through. Oliver Yeats, an Australian History professor, was bitterly protesting about moving to a smaller room – he was due to retire the following year and we urgently needed his space to squeeze in several post-docs. This would be hard, confronting as it did the end of his less-than-spectacular career and the downward spiral of this decent man's awful path to irrelevance. Trappings. The world was full of them. Western societies and our need for grand spaces and trinkets to carve out our place in the social order fascinated me. I set up a meeting with my poor friend knowing his displacement was inevitable, then turned to the papers Melinda had brought in and began signing authorisations, granting the wishes of so many colleagues I felt angelic.

'There's a group of staff to see you, Bec.' Melinda stuck her head through the doorway and lowered her voice. 'They say it's urgent.'

My three most trusted allies filed in. Robert Fleming (American Revolution) was a huge bruin of a man, Constance Fitzsimmons (Early European) was beanstalk thin with a shock of red hair and Rachel Levine (Jewish Studies) was my dear friend, small and impeccably groomed.

'We've heard that Priscilla's made a complaint about you to the Vice-Chancellor. We want to go and see him,' Robert burst out. 'I was talking to Priscilla's assistant, that dreadful Amber, who let slip.'

My neck stiffened in horror. 'I should've guessed something was up when Priscilla was sweet today,' I said. 'She's an absolute disgrace.'

'She's been white-anting you right up to the top,' said Rachel.

'I rang around and found she's been lobbying members of the Council as well as the VC.'

'This is terrible,' said Constance. 'What are we going to do? I'm worried if we go to the Vice-Chancellor, that lot will just close ranks like they always do.'

'And Priscilla's upped her attack on Josie and Pam,' said Rachel.

I drew in my breath, frustrated. Josie Sweeney (German History) and Pam Edwards (Ancient World) were in Priscilla's sights and were both about to go on maternity leave. I'd been protecting them and had just sent Priscilla detailed performance reports that showed how valuable they were.

'Have you seen Josie?' boomed Robert. 'She waddled in yesterday about to drop the baby, and when we tried to send her home she wouldn't go. She was too nervous about her job.'

'Is she here today?' I said.

'Yes. I've never seen anyone so stressed,' said Constance. 'She burst into tears when I asked how she was.'

'I'll speak to her. I know her blood pressure's through the roof. At least Pam's stayed at home,' I said.

Everyone went quiet.

'Hasn't she?'

Rachel looked at me evenly. 'Not since she received the letter inviting her to take a package and leave by the end of semester. It came this morning while you were at the meeting. Josie got one too.'

'The letters expressly state they're not allowed to talk to you and must go directly to Priscilla.' Constance paused. 'They're intimating you're not our Head anymore.'

I tried to speak but nothing came out. Stephen had warned this job could get political, and after eighteen months I thought I was getting the hang of it. Now I'd landed in the middle of a minefield: it would be humiliating if I were removed as Head and awful if I couldn't look after the people I cared about.

'It will be all right. We'll see to it,' said Rachel firmly.

I tried to order my thoughts, and then finally I spoke, more calmly than I felt. 'Thanks so much for coming, I'm very grateful. I'll fight my own battle for now, if that's okay. But Josie and Pam are in real danger and we need to support them in every way possible.'

The group slowly murmured assent and began to file out. Rachel was the last to go. She hung a warm arm around me and squeezed tight. 'Just be careful, Bec. This may be worse than you think.'

I attempted to calm myself with deep breathing as I crossed the campus but it only made me dizzy. Flags proclaiming the merits of Coastal University hung in a line of honour. Their soft tick-ticking against poles sounded like yacht sails. Yachts that could be shipwrecked.

The day was becoming a scorcher and students had melted away. My steps echoed as I strode into the startling new building that rose like a silver tsunami where the Dean awaited in her million-dollar digs.

Amber, a Machiavellian sandwich of a person, smiled sweetly and ushered me straight through to where Priscilla sat typing intently on her computer. I took a seat opposite.

'On the comfy chairs,' Priscilla didn't raise her eyes. I repositioned myself in a leather chair, sea-blue to match the watery expanse below that stretched to the horizon.

'I'll just be a minute.' Fifteen passed, and the tapping of fingers on keys became a volley of bullets. Finally I gave in.

'I do have other meetings, Priscilla.'

She looked up, feigning surprise, and joined me in the plush chairs.

'Yes, I did send those letters this morning and I did mean the implication that your School is without a Head,' she said without prompting.

'But you can't just stand me down like that.'

'Then you'll need to prove you're worthy of the position. It's come to my attention that you've been undermining me left, right and centre to anybody who'll listen. I'm not going to lie: your gossip hurts, Rebecca. Personally and professionally. Did you really think it wouldn't get back to me? Whatever actions I've needed to take – and they haven't been easy, but in the current economic climate we've no choice – there you've been, thwarting me, taking up the fight to our colleagues. I'm not alone, many people are sick of you.'

No wonder she'd been nice this morning. Like a cat with a mouse. 'I'm here to talk about Josie and Pam,' I replied, keeping my voice steady.

'I've reviewed the paperwork. Neither has fulfilled the most basic requirements,' said Priscilla. 'Not even one refereed journal article in three years.'

'But they're each lecturing in four subjects – more than they should, because we're so short staffed. And they're both flat out writing books and have family responsibilities.'

'Books that don't have Research Council money.'

'They have publishers, which is no small feat in this climate.'

'They need research grants. You know how important that is to our quality review; if we're not placed highly our rankings will go down. That affects us all.'

'When they publish, that'll count in the quality review.'

'Promises aren't enough. They've had their chance. In any event, you're drastically over-budget and prancing around as though that's meaningless. Because you won't take the necessary steps, I'm going to have to. And if you're not careful, that will include replacing you with a Head who'll do the job. Take this as an informal warning.'

My stomach lurched. I took a conciliatory tone. 'Priscilla, Josie and Pam are hard-working members of staff. They're fantastic teachers and their courses attract significant numbers of students, which actually helps our financial position.'

'You know I can't force anything. They're voluntary redund-ancies.'

'So, they can say no?'

'Absolutely not. It's your job to persuade them to go.'

'But it will just make our budget situation worse if we can't offer some of our most popular subjects.'

Priscilla checked her watch. 'I have another meeting.' She walked to her desk. 'Oh, one more thing.' A flicker of a smile touched her rouged lips. 'You and I will be undergoing medi-ation. The Vice-Chancellor has suggested it to see if we can resolve our differences.'

Defeat. Utter defeat. I'd been the last one standing; now all five Heads of School in the Faculty of Arts would be in mediation with Priscilla. The room was stuffy and as my blood drained, Priscilla stood waiting for my response. I didn't lift my head, staring instead at her designer sandals, in blue and white leather of the finest quality. I could feel Priscilla's hands making pincer movements.

'What's wrong?' she said, looking down at her sandals.

'They're an unusual colour. I've never seen a blue quite like it,' I commented and walked out, leaving Priscilla studying her footwear.

By the time I slumped back to my office, one of my brightest PhD students, Carl, had arrived for his monthly meeting. I fought to banish the awful prospect of mediation with Priscilla as he spoke passionately about a dig on Lefnakos, an idyllic Greek island he was due to visit this European summer. I had been, and I shuddered at the memory. Several years ago, the day after I'd flown out, the place had caved in, killing five tourists and two archaeologists; I felt incalculably sad for them. I'd been working in the very spot of the collapse, sitting just a day before in my tiny air-conditioned tent, with all my high-tech equipment for analysing the constitution of the glass fragments that were painstakingly dug from the soil and handed over like fragile babies to have their secrets slowly revealed. One of my closest friends, Burton, had been badly hurt. He now got around in a wheelchair, his once-powerful legs crushed and useless, and had moved to Crete. I hadn't been back and was uneasy about Carl going, even though the area had been reopened and declared safe. It was a freak accident, unlucky, one that could happen anywhere at any time. Yet I still didn't want him there.

Carl had stopped and was watching expectantly.

'You know my feelings about that dig.'

He said nothing, letting the silence stretch, a code he'd developed with me over the years.

'Anyway, why don't you leave what you've written and we'll set up another time? I'm a bit distracted today, so please forgive me.'

'Is there anything I can do to help?'

'No, just keep writing like you are. That helps.'

Carl flushed with pleasure and hurried out. He'd deserved better.

Big Boy padded onto the deck. Where was Stephen? This was so unlike him. Leaving early. Not mentioning that he'd be late. And tonight, when I really needed him, he wasn't answering my calls. The dog started whimpering, gazing with come-hither eyes. I ignored him and took a large gulp of wine. It was my favourite time of evening, when the patch of sky through eucalypts morphed into a deep blue that washed to violet then rich purple as yellow-crested cockatoos screeched across high above like soft-winged puppets.

But Big Boy was a master at expressions that went straight to the heart. I grabbed his leash and we struck out for the beach.

The sea shimmered silver in the dusk, a smudge of pink glowing in the fragile clouds on the horizon. There were a few surfers on the breakers, as sleek as seals in their wetsuits. Big Boy galloped happily beside me. I wondered if my job could be at risk after two solid decades at Coastal, rising up the ranks from tutor to lecturer to senior lecturer, associate professor and finally professor, each promotion hard won through sacrifice, travelling constantly between semesters to digs in Greece, writing in every snatched moment, losing time with my children I could never retrieve. I had tenure, and post-grads came because of my reputation. I was supervising fourteen PhDs. My publication and grant records were impeccable. I'd written five books in the area of cultural archaeology, edited several collections and had articles in all the major international journals. I was a Fellow of the Australian Academy of the Humanities. Surely Priscilla couldn't ignore that I was an asset?

And yet her attack was so strident, so confident.

Rounding the bluff I pounded along the wild ocean beach. Pale aquamarine waves crashed to shore, sending up a haze of ghostly droplets, frothing white as they heaved back into the rocks – outcrops that lurked beneath the surface, stretching for miles, in days gone by tricking vessels that had sailed unwittingly into trouble, foundered and broken up. Loved ones who had never come home, taken by the sea. I knew the dull ache, the gap that could never be filled. The cruel consequences.

Not for me to be another lost soul. I would fight Priscilla and win.

3

'What's this for?' Stephen said as I hugged into his tall, strong body, warm and reassuring. His dark eyes looked down at me from beneath a flop of black hair, tanned skin and soft, neatly trimmed mustache and beard that showed no hint of grey; he glowed with health. His aftershave was newly applied and I breathed in the usual soapiness. It was his habit to swim after work; when the kids were teenagers they'd all go together, racing home afterwards for hot showers. These days if Stephen was busy he'd skip the swim but he still liked to throw himself into the shower and freshen up for dinner, a trait I found endearing.

'Why were you late?' I asked as Big Boy barked happily about us. 'Didn't you get my messages?'

'What's wrong?' He brushed strands of hair from my brow. 'Tell me about it.'

'Over wine. What's for dinner?'

Stephen looked helplessly at the empty stove. 'I'm sorry, I completely forgot it was my turn.' Flashing an apologetic smile he made a quick retreat. 'Let's go out?' he called, climbing the stairs two at a time. 'We can grab a meal at the golf club.'

'I haven't got time, I need to work tonight,' I called back, annoyed.

'I'll cook something simple, then. How about a casserole? Would you mind getting it started? I just have to make one phone call.'

I slopped meat into Big Boy's bowl and thumped it down. He looked up, alarmed. I tiredly chopped onions and within minutes they were sautéing in a deep pan, their scent pungent and so homely I could almost hear the orchestral riff of the six o'clock news that was forever entwined with my mother's cooking.

After I put the casserole in the oven, I went out to the deck and poured another glass of wine, reminding myself to sip slowly or there'd be no work done after all.

A shadow crossed the light and the door slid open. 'So, what happened today?' Stephen's voice cut softly into the silky air.

'That sociopath Priscilla is on the warpath.'

Stephen flinched.

'Oh, don't be like that, for goodness sake,' I retorted. 'Just hear me out.'

'I've been listening to angry people all day.'

'Priscilla's trying to sack us all!'

'That's ridiculous. What on earth's happened?' Stephen leaned back in his chair. He was wearing a pair of loose shorts, and his soft blue cotton shirt was half unbuttoned. His dark eyes focused on me with concern, their astute intelligence radiating.

'She's gone to the Vice-Chancellor about me,' I said.

Stephen grew still. 'Why?'

'She's claiming I'm incompetent. And she's making me have mediation with her like the rest of them.'

Stephen took the bottle and poured a large glass.

'You've forgotten to fill mine.' I tapped his arm and wine slopped everywhere. Stephen cursed.

'Has she spelled out on what grounds she's basing this?' he asked.

'Not really – except to say that I gossip. And that I'm too soft. And some nonsense about being over-budget, which still doesn't make sense.'

Stephen wiped up the spilled wine in one deft movement. 'She has no right,' he said. 'I'll speak to the Vice-Chancellor. This must be nipped in the bud.' He stood abruptly. 'Thanks for putting the dinner on. Promise I'll cook tomorrow.' He kissed the top of my head and went inside.

I watched him fondly as he moved about the kitchen, tossing together a salad. Then suddenly he returned and, bending down, lifted me in his arms. His fingers brushed against my skin as he lifted my dress and manoeuvred me into the house, smothering my lips with his own, which were wet and hot and tasted of wine. 'Not now,' I said softly, 'I'm not in the mood.'

'You looked so beautiful sitting there. I just don't want you to be worried.' His hands and lips worked their way over my tense body, smoothing knots of muscle, calming my jaded nerves. Slowly I started to let go.

'We'll sort it out,' he said and a familiar surge of attraction jolted through me. 'You'll be okay.'

My mind went blank as he flipped me around and kissed down my spine, each burning impact fervent and rough. His breath was hot on my neck and his aftershave smelled of orange blossom in spring. I found my body falling back into his, responding ever more forcefully to his touch. Soon I was caught in a fever, with a thirst that couldn't be quenched but was continually satisfied.

The next morning he'd left early again. Another note peered up from the table. *Enjoyed last night. Enormously! xxx*

Last night had been unusual: not the same old marital routine. It was as if Stephen had been exploring my body for the first time. Although it had been a welcome distraction from my troubles, something wasn't right.

I itemised my contact with him: nothing out of the ordinary until these past days – the leaving early, coming home late. A dead weight ran through my veins.

Surely I wasn't imagining it? The raw intimacy of last night had been genuinely different.

The campus was humming with students, cooler weather having flushed them out. Melinda looked up expectantly as I entered.

'Something you need from me, Mel?'

'Just a nice cup of tea. And a holiday.' The last said with unusual emphasis.

'You'd really like to go on holiday? But you never go on holiday.'

'I was thinking of New York. People say it's vibrant and I love the architecture,' she smiled shyly, her lips sensuous beneath immaculately applied lipstick. 'You know how I always read travel books? I think it's time to get back out there.'

'Well, just let me know when you've firmed up your dates and I'll arrange it.'

'I was hoping it could be in the next fortnight?'

'So soon?' My heart sank. 'It'll be tricky putting things in place that quickly.'

'I just feel . . .' Melinda's eyes teared up in a very un-Melinda-like way. 'Frankly I feel the Faculty's falling to pieces and there's nothing I can do about it.'

I reached out a hand but Melinda sat down heavily and started shuffling papers. 'I was around in the fifties when people were witch-hunted for all sorts of things. In the sixties I partied so hard I didn't notice anyone but myself. In the seventies I never really became a feminist but I always admired those women.'

I had no idea where she was heading. I perched on a corner of her desk, interested.

'You know that my husband and I split up ten years ago?'

'I remember it was just after I met you.'

'And I really felt then I was too old to do much, now I was on my own again. But I . . . I see so much going on here . . .' Melinda delicately brushed away a tear and, reaching out with trembling hands, picked up a letter. 'You don't deserve this, Bec.'

I read the details of my first mediation session with Priscilla, set for next week.

'It's demeaning and that letter is just full of lies,' said Melinda.

There was nothing much new from yesterday's meeting except a warning that formal action might be taken if I failed to attend and that the focus would be on my communication and leadership skills.

'It's okay, Mel. Who knows, maybe I'll come out a new and improved person?'

'You don't need improving and you haven't got time.'

'It's a gross waste of money and Priscilla's a hypocrite, I agree. Cutting staff, cutting budgets and yet she pushes all this rubbish.'

Melinda was looking at me with pity.

'Well, I'm made of sterner stuff than that,' I continued firmly, 'I'll just do what she says. Better that she picks on me than someone weaker.' I stuffed the letter into my pocket. 'What's annoying is that I'd planned to stay home and write that day.'

I was working on a book about Santorini in the seventeenth century BC and was in the middle of a chapter on the volcanic eruption where people had fled from their settlement in Akrotiri. Many items had been found at the settlement, either forgotten or left in haste; my favourite was a gold ibex figurine hidden inside a larnax, a clay chest. The little ibex, which looked like a child's impression of a goat mixed with a baby horse, stood in relaxed repose. The gold was pure with a sublime lustre. It was likely his owners had run high into the hills and only then realised that their most precious possession had been forgotten. After the eruption Akrotiri was buried in lava, houses entombed, the ibex waiting patiently for millennia until it was again cherished. But its precise use was lost in the mists of time. What was its significance?

'You're not going to think badly of me are you, like a rat abandoning ship?' Melinda's voice cut through my thoughts.

'Never. Email me the details and I'll sign off and send it to HR. Won't New York be cold at this time of year?'

'Freezing. I want a change of everything, including the weather. I'm hoping it'll be cloaked in snow.'

'And how long are you going for?'

Silence.

'Mel?'

She suddenly looked old. 'I was thinking until the end of next semester.'

'But that's a lifetime!'

'I have enough leave owing. I want to travel around, catch up with friends in Seattle and San Francisco. I thought you could get Justine in here? She'll watch your back. I've run it past her and she said she'd wrangle a temporary transfer from Politics.'

'Really? Well, I guess . . .' Melinda looked desperate. 'I'll call her. I'm sure we'll be able to make this work for you.'

'You're a brick.'

I smiled, doing my best to hide my concern. What would I do without her?

Their bellies stretched in front of them like two boulders. Pam Edwards, rushing straight from an Ancient History lecture, wore a body-hugging T-shirt and tapered trousers to accentuate her impossibly long legs; she matched these with killer stilettos that gave her the height of a giraffe and was accessorised to the hilt with chunky jewellery. Josie Sweeney was decked out in the traditional hide-all smock over bare legs; her feet reclined in Birkenstocks. Their faces were alike – both tragic.

'She's sent us another letter.' Pam passed it across.

Josie's voice was a whisper. 'It's so awful, being made to feel worthless. My husband and doctor think I should take the package.'

'You might feel that now, but when you're home alone with your child you may want this place, at least part-time in the first few years, which we can manage,' I replied. 'You're anything but worthless. You know how highly the students rate you. And the way through our trouble is to get more enrolments, not keep shrinking the department out of existence.'

Josie nodded, sniffing back tears. 'I've always loved coming to work.'

'My family want me to leave too,' said Pam as she rubbed her belly. 'I've become unbearable around the house. I'm screaming at everyone. I'm really worried what I'm doing to our baby. Ooh!' A smile split her face. 'He just kicked!'

Josie thrust out a hand. 'I can feel him, there's another one!'

'Little bugger,' chuckled Pam, her hand on her belly noticeably lifting as he kicked again. 'I reckon he's going to be a footballer like his granddad. Or a horse. I do really want to stay,' she added, looking at me with pleading eyes. 'I'm thinking of going to the union.'

'Priscilla says the next round won't be voluntary,' said Josie.

I quickly read the letter, trying to quash my feelings of inadequacy. There it was in black and white: the threat of forced redundancies if not enough people took the voluntary packages. 'Get the union to speak to me. We'll coordinate our actions,' I said.

Pam nodded but I could see she didn't mean it; she didn't believe I'd be an asset.

'We'll get through this,' I said.

Troubling irregularity found in accounts. Urgently need to meet.

I sighed as I re-read the email from Alison Wishart, our School Administrator. Alison had been seconded across from Architecture after I became Head, at Priscilla's insistence, the Dean claiming I lacked experience with money. To Priscilla's annoyance, Alison and I had grown close and I relied on her when it came to budgets.

Come straight over, I shot back, and she arrived minutes later in a luscious yellow dress with black stripes. She looked like a bee – and a rather angry one.

'There's a very strange account that's been opened in Athens,' buzzed Alison as soon as she sat down. 'Do you know anything about it?'

'No. Athens . . . why would we have an account there?'

'Well, that's what anyone's going to ask who looks at these books. And, Rebecca – it would appear that you've approved this account.'

'What's it for? Why on earth would I have signed off on an

Athens account? I can be a bit preoccupied when it comes to paperwork but surely I wouldn't be that vague?'

'It's like it's written by a drunk. Sorry, not casting aspersions . . . but listen to this: "Account for food and wine and accommodation and wine/travels."'

I quickly scanned the printouts. One was a bank statement in the name of Coastal University School of Classics and History with a very large deposit and multiple small withdrawals.

'Embezzlement is what it looks like.' Alison peered over the rims of her fashionable glasses with a frosty stare. 'I'm going to have to report this to Faculty straightaway. You can't just go opening accounts overseas in the university's name.'

'Oh God, Alison, can't we get to the bottom of it here? That's all Priscilla needs, ammunition against me that makes it look like I'm party to fraud – and hedonistic fraud at that. There must be an explanation. For a start, if someone was trying to hide that sort of thing they wouldn't be so explicit, would they?' I looked up, seeking her approval.

Alison stiffened. 'I don't know, there've been a few irregularities I've picked up. This one's just for a great deal more money. And Athens as the location is unacceptable.'

'Who's accessed it?'

'It would appear to be Josie Sweeney.'

'But Josie has nothing to do with anything Greek.'

'That's exactly what I thought,' said Alison. 'Whereas . . .' She paused and her face bloomed. 'Your work is generally based in Greece, isn't it?'

'Oh, maybe I do understand . . .' I said, as a thought occurred.

Alison waited in tense silence as I shuffled through more of the paperwork.

'Pam Edwards took a student tour to Greece in January last year in semester break to study pre-historic Hellenic culture. We had a lot of older students sign up and we hoped it would be a money-spinner. In the end we only broke even, but people had a great time – and who knows, we still might get some endowments or donations from the happy alumni.'

'Imbibing a lot of Greek wine, by the looks of it.' Alison's voice dripped with disapproval.

'Anyway, Josie went with Pam to help wrangle the students, and she was also interested in the itinerary.'

'I'm not surprised.'

'Okay, so they, we – I – made a mistake. This separate account shouldn't have been opened, should it?'

'Absolutely not! What were you thinking, Rebecca? You know all finances have to go through the central system.' Alison's flesh was now as red as a tomato.

'I'm sorry, I do recall now. Pam told me she'd set it up in the way it had been done before and I didn't check what that meant. I just approved it. Which means there must have been other accounts like it in the past.'

'Not my problem. I'm only going back one financial year, thank the Lord.' The last muttered under her breath.

'Do we really have to report this? Can't we just clean it up? It wasn't fraud, just an innocent mistake. No one was hurt.'

'I'll think about it.' Alison scooped up the papers and flew out.

Her dangerously noncommittal answer showed me that Alison's allegiance was not as strong as I'd thought. No doubt she'd run to Faculty to ensure she wasn't implicated in any manner.

I felt a wave of fear as I imagined Priscilla's response.

4

It was mid-afternoon and the tide was out as I ran on the hard sand, Big Boy lolloping beside me, salty, misty droplets swirling off the crashing sea. I tried to force thoughts of Alison and Priscilla from my mind; I needed to focus on the surprise party I was holding tonight for Stephen's fiftieth birthday – but that only made me more apprehensive, because when I'd sent the invitations ages ago, I'd included the Vice-Chancellor.

All morning I'd been cooped up. After reading the Saturday newspapers Stephen and I had each gone into our study to write. He thought the evening's activity was going to entail chasing a comet, due to be visible in the dusk sky, and then dinner with the kids. He had no idea what really lay in wait, especially because his actual birthday wasn't until next week.

The wind was buffeting as I ran towards the bluff, over slimy reef rocks that smelled deliciously of ocean tides. A young woman dressed in a vivid orange sari stood waist-high in the churning water beside a man stripped to his Y-fronts, a formal three-piece-suit on top. Laughing and hugging as a grey wall of waves rose behind, the orange cloth stood out boldly like a beacon as another be-suited man photographed them. He chuckled as he took the shot – two frail, loving humans about to be engulfed by the sea, captured forever in their hope.

Be careful! It's dangerous! I wanted to call. Just last month, two Indian students had drowned a little further up the coast. But the trio was engrossed, another photo underway, the photographer now wading into the turbulent water. They were wildly happy. I stopped and hung my body down towards the sand, taking a breather until they finally came out safely onto the beach.

I resumed my run, bounding through leathery piles of kelp to the bay side of the bluff. The sea here was much more placid, friendly waves capped with white tips of salty froth, small sailing craft bobbing as though viewed in a painting. Children in wetsuits frolicked in the shallows; surfers further out rode the swell.

A kite-boarder took off, his rainbow-coloured sail catching the wind, filling up, and he was away, surfing over the waves, roaring along the shoreline, his muscular arms hanging tightly to the crossbar as he was swept effortlessly along. One minute he was close to shore, the next he was a dot on the horizon. Then he'd catch a wave and come zooming in again. I thought of Stephen. He used to windsurf but had stopped about ten years ago when he'd hurt his back. The kids had been teenagers and he hadn't wanted to be incapacitated. He'd always insisted on taking his turn with them, ferrying them around, letting me get on with my work. I smiled as I remembered our first date here at the beach when I was twenty-two and he'd tried to get me to windsurf, but I'd refused. When he realised I wouldn't go in the water he was kind. Later, he didn't want me to go into my dark house alone, walking me to the door, waiting until I'd turned on the lights, then heading chivalrously back to his car after a soft, lingering kiss. The next date I'd invited him in and we'd been together ever since. I desperately wanted tonight to go well for him.

As I puffed up the cliff path the windsurfer was a distant speck out to sea. At the main road I clipped the leash onto Big Boy and we waited for a break in the line of gleaming cars making their way along the coast. As I crested the hill, the golf course lay below. To me, the sight of the mob of Eastern Grey kangaroos hopping among the golfers was always surreal. About a hundred roos were scattered around the fairways, and it was miraculous that they avoided being hit by the potentially lethal golf balls. The kangaroos loved grazing on the short sweet grass of the greens, and many a visiting golfer had been terrified as they hit up. But somehow the kangaroos, even the joeys, moved just in time to avoid the ball.

Inside the spacious clubrooms, airy floor-to-ceiling windows gave expansive views to the emerald course. I was surprised to see that tonight's decorations for Stephen's party were horribly minimal – a few balloons and some tacky bunting. My son James approached. At twenty-three he still had the pure skin and rosy cheeks of youth, but his body was tall and fit like his father's. His fair hair and blue eyes came from my side. Sweet and thoughtful, he was studying dentistry and lived in a flat in Melbourne with two old schoolmates. James was a good scholar but could be a shocking judge of character.

'Is this too daggy, Mum?' He forlornly held up a limp bunch of blue and red bunting. 'I think Klair got it at an op shop,' he whispered. 'I'm so sorry. I thought she'd be up to it but clearly she isn't.'

His girlfriend Klair, who a year ago had spelled her name with a C, made a beeline for us. Gaunt and Goth with white powder and black robes, she was in her early twenties, trumped up and full of herself. 'So, you've come to help?' she demanded.

'I can't stay,' I replied. 'I need to keep Stephen occupied.'

'Oh.' Klair didn't hide her gormless disappointment. 'We're running late – James and I slept in. Big night out, you know how it is.'

'You'll be fine,' I said, trying to stay positive. 'We're cramming lots of people in and we'll dim the lights.'

'It's four o'clock already,' said James.

'I'll phone Melinda and see if she can get here to help,' I said and James nodded, relieved. 'Just do your best,' I kissed his soft hair – it always reminded me of emu feathers – and kept a smile on my face as I dialled Mel's number. My mind was ticking in double-time as I waited for her to answer. If she couldn't help I didn't know what I'd do.

Erin, my daughter, twenty-one and happily living on campus in Melbourne studying law, had come early to organise the music.

Her deep blue eyes and impish face dropped when I broke the news that there was a change of plan. She stood up trailing electric cables, her delicate hands wrapped tightly around a power cord, strangling it. She had been excited to be tonight's DJ.

'Darling, I know it's not fair. It's just all I could think of to save this mess. Melinda's nephew is a professional DJ who comes with a huge lighting set-up. And we're desperate for that, given the lack of decorations. I've asked him to use your tracks as well as his own.'

'Just because James stuffed up with his stupid pretentious girlfriend shouldn't mean all my hard work goes to waste. I'm out of here, then. There's no point staying now.' Her slender body slumped in on itself, tearing my heart. She bit back tears as she kicked the cables violently into the corner.

'I'll make it up to you, I promise.'

Erin shot off.

'Where are you going?' I tried to follow but she wrenched her arm away from my grasp. 'Please stay?'

'I'll be where I'll be, if you really care,' she snapped cryptically and hurried through the doors to the outside world.

The last vapours of pink hung in the air like fairy floss and a gorgeous blue, rich and vast, flooded the sky. The wind had mellowed to a soft breeze; the evening was going to be clear and mild, perfect for comet hunting. I'd chosen my attire carefully – I couldn't look too fancy or the game would be up. My new dress had a gorgeous cherry-blossom print and smelled faintly of jasmine and gardenia. It was short, low cut and rustled as I walked, making me feel young and light. Stephen's white shirt, rolled at the sleeves, glowed; with his navy trousers, and jacket slung over his shoulder, he had a nautical feel. He draped an arm around me, then suddenly crushed me close and kissed me passionately.

Through the dusk I could see our neighbour Clarkey watching from his verandah; I felt like a china doll on show. I broke off the embrace and slipped into the passenger seat of Stephen's shiny new car. The leather made a satisfying sigh and embraced my legs sensuously, giving me an unexpected deep thrill.

'Let's go,' said Stephen with undisguised excitement.

We'd done this years before, when the kids were very young and a spectacular comet was visible. We'd left James and Erin with friends and taken off along open country roads to view the heavenly apparition. Alone, just the two of us with the universe. I'd been worn out at the time and temporarily getting away had been remarkable. I hadn't expected to become enthralled by the comet but its majestic tail and white, bright centre had entranced me. It was one of the most memorable nights I'd ever had. Could we recreate it?

The car hummed down the driveway and we waved to Clarkey, who gave a friendly wave back. We were off, part one of the plan unfolding seamlessly. The first star of the evening twinkled pale, growing clearer by the second.

As we drove towards the beach we could see a crowd gathering in the darkness of the river mouth. Kids ran squealing, a lone woman's voice soared in an eerie song, and strumming guitars echoed across the water. We parked and Stephen opened the sunroof, placing us as if within reach of the ever-darkening sky. More stars were peeking out and time felt suspended in breathless anticipation.

Silence was spreading as we walked hand-in-hand to the river. Small schools of fish darted in the current, shimmering in rippling pools of light from the boardwalk. I scanned the horizon at the point the comet was due to make its appearance. Empty. Through the centuries, comets had often inspired fear. Harbingers of doom, strange visitors foretelling events, usually of the ill variety.

I squeezed Stephen's hand.

'I wonder what it'll look like?' he said grinning, anticipation bringing out the young boy. The music grew louder as we walked onto the beach where the river met the sea. The crowd was large, about two hundred people. There was a hedonistic feel and yet no one was drunk or out of control. People were content. Clearly these observers didn't share the dark superstitions about comets, celebrating instead the theory of comets as life givers, bombarding the planet billions of years ago and providing water and carbon, changing everything.

Suddenly the murmur in the crowd turned to a roar as the comet appeared on the horizon. It moved quickly as it hurtled through space and time, its brilliant white ball luminous, trailing translucent silvery feathers of light. Its core transformed to glow a deep, rich red as its effervescent tail shimmered brightly against the inky sky.

Its perfection was overwhelming.

'Hop in!' Stephen said.

With great effort I peeled my eyes from the celestial traveller and realised with a jolt that we had walked back to the car. Stephen opened the door and I slipped inside. Seconds later we were away, chasing the comet, which now shot from one side of our vision to the other as we twisted along the ocean road in pursuit. Stephen let out a cry of delight. His eyes gleamed as he navigated the road and simultaneously looked up at the comet. He was on full alert, completely lost in the moment.

The heavenly apparition danced and played across the sky. There one minute, disappearing the next, then back again, now a brilliant golden orb trailing sparkling silver threads. Although I knew that its nucleus was ice, gas and dust, its coma burning bright a dense cloud of water and gas, its luminous tail nothing but smoke-sized dust particles reflecting the sun's light, the joyous comet seemed far removed from such mundane explanation. It was unique, alive, profoundly vivid. It burst into the heavens and simultaneously exploded in my mind, a messenger breathing promises of higher planes, of absolute union with the sky and one another. It was both spiritual and other, random and yet perfectly positioned as it played hide-and-seek in the dark orb above us.

Stephen put a burning hand on my arm and pulled into a shadowy, empty car park. He urged me outside, down a steep, sandy path towards the throbbing ocean. The comet was passing in an orderly path to the north. It seemed slower, more refined. And absolutely familiar.

'Dinner can wait,' said Stephen. 'The kids won't mind.'

The kids, I thought – James with his girlfriend problems, Erin's fury with me. We lay down on the sand and watched the comet, waves crashing in the dark, and I felt a sudden shock. What if the heavens opened and revealed with a roar the force of all dark omens foretold by comets? As Stephen drew me to him, ghastly possibilities whirled and snapped through my mind. He kissed me tenderly, and I wanted to ask why he was suddenly so physical, but this was going to be Stephen's big night; perhaps he was only lustful because he was turning fifty, trying to keep age at bay? After all, there was nothing bad in our marriage; it was easier now the kids had moved out. Over the years Stephen had taken far more than his share of looking after Erin and James while I was away on digs. He'd always encouraged and supported me in my work but I'd been a burden, stretching his kindness, leaving him to deal with the children's resentment of my absence.

Now all that was behind us and we had freedom in our daily routines. We both loved our academic research and were absorbed in our writing. It was a good time of life.

But tonight things felt blurred, disturbed, and the comet's bloody nucleus made me feel that awful things could happen. Perhaps I didn't pay enough attention to Stephen. Did I take him for granted after twenty-five years? The abyss of night sky was deepening, infinite and empty, choking me, making my heart race out of control as I fell into the rhythm of our two bodies. In one startling moment I remembered all the horrendous pain and deaths of those I'd loved. My mother's dreadful, shuddering breaths, the long gaps in between that went on for hours, days, before the death rattle. 'She died in peace,' we said. It was no such thing.

The inevitability of passing away when sickness took hold and there was no more that could be done by medicine or intervention. The gaping hole when my brother fled, unable to cope.

Stephen's breathing was rapid now, shuddering breaths of his own. Had he done this recently with someone else? Was he about to destroy our family as surely as death? Could it be my fault?

The ocean pounded. And the horror of my father's death, losing the person I'd loved most in the world to the angry sea reared before my eyes, his figure disappearing, beyond reach. Never to be reunited with his family.

Gone.

The sky was black and shimmering with stars when the comet departed. Panicking, I checked the time. We were late.

As our car purred up the long driveway, tall gums cast looming dark twins on the tarmac and the clubrooms appeared suddenly around the bend, lit up like an ocean liner at sea. To my relief festive lights festooned the deck creating a magical fairyland in which a swarm of shadowy revellers partied. Loud music thumped into the still bush night.

'Someone must be having a function,' said Stephen. 'I hope we can get in. I guess the kids would have phoned if we couldn't?'

'I'm sure it's okay.'

I let him lead me across the car park, placing my arm through the crook of his. As we funnelled down to the restaurant the whole area became alarmingly quiet. In the adjacent gambling room, the sound of poker machines grew to a relative crescendo; as we moved away, I felt like I might choke from the suspense.

'The music's stopped, how odd,' said Stephen.

'SURPRISE!'

It was classic and clichéd as our friends applauded and cheered. Stephen was taken completely off guard. A huge banner was strung across the room, *HAPPY BIRTHDAY STEPHEN – FABULOUS AT FIFTY!* Dazzling lights played on the crowd as the music roared back to life.

'Happy birthday for Wednesday, darling.' I brushed against the starched coolness of his jacket and kissed him. As happiness creased his eyes I loved him so much it hurt. I still felt raw from the comet but my fears seemed less rational now.

Then, as I led him into the throng of well-wishers, we both saw her.

'What's she doing here?' asked Stephen darkly.

5

Stephen marched like a man possessed to where Priscilla stood sipping champagne, wearing a simple black evening gown, a single diamond gleaming on a silver chain above her plunging neckline. I felt suddenly like a bird that is too gaudy or the kid in the daggiest frock at the party. What *was* she doing here? I glanced around the wall of guests trying to work out who her date might be.

'I'm astonished you've come,' said Stephen. Priscilla stepped back in surprise. James made a beeline for me and I stopped him gently, desperate to hear Priscilla's reply.

'Happy birthday, Stephen,' Priscilla purred, reaching out a flawless hand that glistened with a translucent aquamarine cocktail ring. Stephen declined to shake it.

'Does this mean you're going to clear things up with my wife?' he said.

'We're all friends and colleagues,' she replied smoothly. 'How are you, Rebecca?'

Stephen's anger intensified and he glanced at me. James watched us all, confused, as other guests pretended not to notice.

'I think it's highly inappropriate you're here given the situation,' Stephen said to Priscilla. 'You might like to reconsider your night's entertainment.'

I was astonished by his candour, out of character for a natural diplomat. Priscilla blushed and it seemed momentarily like she might break down. It occurred to me how often a bully was cowardly when confronted by someone they felt was stronger and more powerful.

Around us the mood was buoyant, the music loud and energetic and the lights as grand as Paris by night, if a little more Tokyo neon. The Vice-Chancellor, Patrick McEwan, tall, grey-haired and paunchy, strode up and clapped Stephen on the back, nodding hello to me. 'I hope you don't mind that I brought a guest?' He draped his arm around Priscilla. 'Sonya's away researching in Japan for a month. I decided it was time I stopped going out alone but I forgot to change my RSVP to two.'

'Of course not,' said Stephen, shifting uncomfortably. I knew that he'd tried to meet with Patrick during the week to discuss Priscilla's complaint about me, but Patrick had been unavailable.

'Pretty good bash you've got here,' said the Vice-Chancellor.

'Would you like another?' Priscilla took Patrick's glass. 'And Stephen, you don't even have a drink. I'll soon set that right.'

She sashayed off to the bar. 'And one for you too, Rebecca,' she called back.

Patrick leaned closer to us and James discreetly stepped back into the crowd. 'I invited her to clear the air. I think the mediation should go on. Let nature run its course. Priscilla has her own methods of leadership, which I respect.' He tapped my arm. 'Don't worry, the university values you, Rebecca, it'll be fine.'

'Thanks, Patrick, that's reassuring to hear,' I replied. Stephen leaned in and mumbled something unintelligible to Patrick, who laughed.

Priscilla returned with the drinks and Patrick whisked her off to the dance floor. She'd brought me champagne and Stephen a martini, something he drank only rarely, on special occasions. How did she know? As Stephen was called across to a group of friends and I went to follow, James drew me aside.

'Mum, I really do need to talk to you,' he implored.

'Sorry, darling, what is it?'

'I've had a humungous row with Klair. She was disgustingly rude about you and I told her to get stuffed.'

I tried to take in what he said but I was too preoccupied.

'You're not listening!' James spotted Klair advancing and dashed away.

'Happy now, darling?' Klair swayed drunkenly in absurdly high black and red stilettos covered in a design of cobwebs and bats. She was wearing a sleeveless version of her dark goth robes, displaying tattoos of more cobwebs with red-back spiders, and skulls. She settled against me. 'What a shame you hated my decorating – I always thought we could have been friends.'

'You never know, we still could be.' I smiled. 'Want to dance?'

Klair paused, put one hand to her brow then tottered off. I downed my champagne.

'Did you see who our tormentor's here with?' Robert Fleming planted two kisses on me, one on each cheek. 'My God, parading her power! What chance do any of us have?' He lowered his voice. 'Priscilla emailed me this morning, complaining about student numbers in American Revolution. She's micromanaging now. She's out of control.' Pam waddled over, pregnant belly huge in a tight-fitting purple dress, looking like she might topple face first. She jingled with chunky silver chains. 'I wouldn't have come if I'd known that bitch Priscilla would be here!'

'I didn't invite her, she gate-crashed,' I said, accepting another champagne from a passing waiter and drinking it rapidly.

'And I can't even get plastered and pretend it's not happening,' groaned Pam.

Rachel came up, sparkling in a black dress and gold jewellery. 'The nerve of the woman. What's she playing at?'

'Dad seems pleased!' said Erin as she joined us, radiantly happy, dressed provocatively in a white cotton dress the size of a tea towel that showed off her youthful good looks. The muscles in my neck relaxed as I saw that she'd snapped out of her anger.

'This is my daughter, Erin,' I said proudly to Pam and Robert, and they both shook her hand. Rachel kissed her warmly, having known her all her life.

'Excuse us,' said Erin and led me gracefully to the dance floor, where she shimmied and dipped in perfect rhythm to the music. I fell into the beat as she clasped my hands and swirled us around. As we swept across the floor heads turned. Usually

I hated being the centre of attention, but tonight it felt surprisingly good. I hoped Priscilla was watching with envy. Erin led confidently, twirling me like a whirling dervish. The lights whipped by.

Stephen flicked past in the corner of the room, then Klair, walking weirdly in her impossible stilettos. Where was my poor son? It took a few moments to realise I was losing balance. When the fall came, it was spectacular. First the legs, bending as they snapped earthwards; my arms splayed out and Erin's strong hands darted in to no avail. I heard a gasp from the crowd, even above the decibels of the music. Then I was trying to get back on my feet, aware of a sharp pain in my ankle but trying to ignore it. Melinda miraculously appeared, lithe in a sleeveless black top and black trousers, making simplicity stylish as only an ex-model could. She helped Erin take me across to the refuge of a chair.

I waved to the peering, gleaming sets of eyes. 'I'm fine! I'm fine! Nothing broken except my pride! I've heard it comes before a fall!' The pain was so excruciating I was worried I'd chipped a bone. I now prayed that Priscilla hadn't been looking.

'That was awesome, Mum! I'll get us some sustenance.' Erin patted me on the shoulder and happily trotted off.

Melinda was feeling my legs in a confident, no-nonsense medical manner. My head exploded as her soft, caring hands reached my right ankle. 'Any of these friends of yours doctors?' she asked.

'Only the academic variety, I'm afraid.'

'Well, that's useless,' Melinda muttered, 'as always.'

'Can I help?' Erin had returned with a kind-faced youth

about her age, who wore an expensive cotton shirt and tailored trousers that made the most of a body battling puppy fat.

'Jeremy's a doctor, Mum,' she said proudly.

I was surprised – he barely looked old enough to be out of school.

'A med student,' he smiled. 'Third year. Where does it hurt?' He squatted at my feet and I pointed to my ankle.

Erin put her hands on Jeremy's shoulders in a familiar, intimate way and I realised that I'd been too preoccupied to ask if she was bringing anyone to the party. It struck me it was the first time she'd had a boyfriend without telling me.

Jeremy gently felt my ankle, which was swelling like a balloon. 'Ice,' he muttered, and looked up. 'Ice, compression, elevation,' he recited. 'I think it's just a mild sprain.'

'I might sit out the next dance.'

'And the rest,' he replied. 'I'll see if there's a first-aid kit here.'

'Thanks, Jeremy. So, where did you two meet?'

'Pub chess,' replied Erin, grinning. 'Jeremy always wins. We'll get you that ice.' She led her beau off to the bar.

'Doctor Jeremy's just a kid,' said Melinda, green eyes burning with worry. 'Do you think we should see a grown-up?'

I squealed as Stephen ambushed from behind and lifted me airborne in a rugby tackle.

'Careful! She's just had a nasty fall!' Melinda, always the protector.

'I know! I just wanted to check you're okay.' He planted a sloppy kiss on my neck.

'I'm fine,' I said, not wanting to worry him. 'You're blind drunk, already!'

'Why not? I'm never going to turn fifty again!' Stephen hailed a waiter and passed me a glass of wine. 'To take the pain away.' He kissed me again and weaved his way onto the dance floor, waving as he was swept into the heady mass.

'I could drive you up to Geelong to the hospital?' said Melinda.

'Thanks, Mel, but it's okay.'

I sat down in agony. Melinda pulled up a chair to rest my leg on and then perched beside me. I knew she'd keep watch over me the entire night. Jeremy returned with supplies: he bandaged my ankle tightly and Melinda held the glass of ice to the swelling as Jeremy went off to dance with Erin.

'I'm going to miss you, Mel.'

'The time will fly.' She smiled. 'Although it's crawling at the moment. I just can't wait to be on that plane.'

We watched the crowd in companionable silence as I tried to ignore the pain that was now shooting up my leg. As the music beat a tribal rhythm and silhouettes shimmied through the tangle of technicolour lights, it seemed both an eternity and yet not that long ago that I'd been at dancing classes as a teenager, where I'd spent a great deal of time avoiding boys with sweaty palms and heavy feet, many of whom were fishermen's kids like me.

The years dissolved and I wondered what all the soul searching and competitiveness had been for. To what advantage? And what end? It was how identities were forged, money made, conversation with strangers had. But was someone who had done nothing public or notable any poorer? To achieve happiness and generosity of spirit, these things mattered. To garner wealth and fame – or at least in academic circles, be known and respected – did it really amount to much, was it worth the countless hours poured into one's identity? With universities changing, becoming as much about business as the acquisition of knowledge, we were all under such pressure with time. Expected to teach and publish in ever-greater, ferocious quantities, pressed to breaking point. Why were we all going along with it? Was it only out of necessity?

And always on the horizon, the trappings of wealth hovered inescapably. I gazed at our friends dancing the hours away; jewellery flashed, dresses flitted, well-fitted suits and beautiful shirts plucked out for the occasion. For a brief moment, it all meant nothing. I listened to the chatter enveloping me; academics talking endlessly about each other, the eternal conversation that was a pleasure and curse of our profession. So often inward-looking and gossip-based, it somehow nurtured and fuelled our passion to gather knowledge and help make sense of an increasingly senseless world.

I spotted Priscilla through the crowd and suddenly I seized on the cocktail she'd given Stephen. Had Geoff the barman suggested it? Or had I witnessed a knowing confidence in Priscilla? Was she the reason Stephen had been staying out late? I remembered when we were friends what good company she could be, witty and generous. I thought that side of her had disappeared as she'd manoeuvred up the ranks. People change, but maybe not – strip back the layers like a dig, and the original can still be there. I felt nauseous at the thought of her flirting with Stephen.

I scoped every female in the room. If there was a woman, was she here? Did she really exist? My head whirred with possibilities.

Maybe Geoff simply had a martini ready for Stephen. He knew his tastes, and Stephen *was* the guest of honour. Priscilla had been very quick in fetching the drinks – there hadn't really been enough time for one to be made from scratch.

Exhaustion was overtaking me and, as I grew numbed by wine, the evening started to implode. Like the dust in a comet's tail. Star dust. Galactic dust. Solar dust. I was drifting into oblivion when something caught my eye and my stomach dropped.

In the far corner of the room, Stephen and Priscilla stood talking. There was an intimacy as their bodies inclined towards each other, like they were drawn together in a magnetic field. As if sensing they were being watched, they suddenly stepped apart.

I blinked, hoping I'd just imagined it. They walked off in different directions and Stephen led Erin to the dance floor.

'She's gone, Mum.' James's distraught voice hauled me back.

'Who?'

'Klair.'

I held out my arms and he crumpled into me. 'I'm so sorry,' I whispered as I kissed his emu-feather hair and inhaled his raucous aftershave.

'I hadn't realised how completely tasteless she was until today,' James said bleakly.

'We were all stressed. Maybe she'll feel differently in the morning, sober?' I hoped that Klair wouldn't change her mind, and I knew James was destined for someone so much better. *Someone like me*, I thought, and caught the words just before they exited my wine-stained lips.

'Luckily I'm not that keen on her,' said James.

'I thought you were?'

'Well, not really. Not now. You never liked her, did you? Why am I such a fool, Mum?'

'She wasn't our favourite . . .'

'Who was?'

'The one you're going to meet next.'

James gave a mock punch to my jaw and I mock bit his fist. I really was drunk to be behaving like this in public. And when I looked up, there was Priscilla, with the Vice-Chancellor.

'Just wanted to thank you for a lovely party, Rebecca,' said Patrick. I rose, trying not to show the searing pain I felt in my ankle.

'Many thanks,' smiled Priscilla and winked. She sashayed off into the night with Patrick. As I watched her taut, athletic figure in the black dress I imagined her with Stephen and then forced myself to stop.

6

'I trust you won't find this too confronting, Rebecca.' Priscilla tapped me on the arm as she intercepted me in the doorway of Coastal's plush Counselling and Wellbeing Centre. My skin shrivelled. 'Thanks again for the delightful party,' she said. 'I hope you and Stephen weren't too worse for wear the next day?'

'We all had a great time, thanks.' I sounded like I was the guest and she was the host. 'How many sessions are you planning for us?'

'That depends on how it goes. The other Heads and I have got rather into a pattern. People find it helpful. It can be open ended.'

'Welcome, ladies,' said Vincent O'Shannessy, the mediator, a bone-thin, demure man in his early sixties with a thin slick of sandy hair combed over a pale scalp. One of the few psychologists who had survived a recent restructuring of the Centre, he led us into his office and gestured towards the armchairs arranged in a trio. Priscilla took the one with the view of the glittering coastline, O'Shannessy plonked in his commanding seat and I was left to limp around to the one facing the wall. I had tried to prepare for the session, forming my arguments, but Priscilla was far more experienced given she was in mediation with all her Heads, which made me nervous.

'I'm going to leave it pretty much to you two,' announced O'Shannessy, 'but I'll come in and pick up the slack and tackle if required.' He chuckled.

'Thanks for coming, Rebecca,' said Priscilla. 'I thought I might get the ball rolling by asking you to talk about why you've been so hostile towards me?' She eyed me with a steely gaze that was not in the least friendly, and her sudden mood change caught me off guard.

'I'm just concerned with some of the changes taking place. I don't think they're good academically or for the welfare of the staff.' I wished I could ask if she was having an affair with my husband. When I'd questioned Stephen after the party he claimed he couldn't even remember talking to Priscilla, that he was drunk and had probably just been civil because she was Patrick's guest.

'It seems that you're deeply unnerved by change. And change is inevitable, I'm afraid,' said Priscilla coolly. 'If you want to continue at Coastal and thrive, I think we need to analyse why you feel defensive rather than excited by the possibilities the future holds.'

'The thought of sacking people unnerves me and I hope it always will.' *Who are you sleeping with, Priscilla?*

'Change management involves tough decisions. Perhaps you're not ready for that level of responsibility. Where would we be if no one was prepared to act decisively for the best interests of the university? Back in the dark ages and falling off the league tables rather than steadily rising through the ranks.'

'But surely it's possible to take staff on the journey with us as willing companions, not scared for their lives?' *If you're sleeping with Stephen I will kill you.*

'Melodramatic. See what I mean, Vincent?' said Priscilla. And she hadn't even heard my thoughts.

O'Shannessy shifted in his chair.

'And people have lives,' I continued. 'Not everyone can publish at full capacity every year. Particularly those who are pregnant or have young families.'

'They make those decisions. I chose not to have children. That's a choice free to anyone. People are mollycoddled these days. How tough did you find it when you were young?'

'Okay, so it was hard.' Had Priscilla really decided not to have children or was it because of her perennial relationship troubles? *You'd better not be sleeping with Stephen.*

'Academics shouldn't expect an easy ride. And you shouldn't be so busy wanting everyone to be your friend,' Priscilla said evenly.

'I just seek to be fair.'

'You're not fair to me.'

I sighed. 'I'm just trying to look after my staff.'

'Well, you're not succeeding. Lisa Clements, for one, is very discontented.'

Lisa Clements was an ambitious and very average military historian who never had a good word to say about anyone.

'It's hard when you protect the dead wood while others are working their hearts out,' said Priscilla.

'That's the last thing I'm trying to do!'

'You need to think about that.'

'It would help if there was more transparency. If you could show me and the School Executive Committee a detailed budget we might understand why you need to make so many cuts.'

'I've given you all that material.'

'Could you go through with me line by line, then?'

Priscilla burst out with a startling, coquettish laugh. 'Darling, I haven't the time. I'll get Alison to assist you.' She gave me a piercing look, which made my heart beat a little faster.

'Is there anything else you'd like to add while we're talking budgets?' Priscilla said, and O'Shannessy sat forward.

I sat back. 'No. Not today.'

A flicker passed between them and I weighed up if I should raise the Athens misunderstanding. But before I could, Priscilla was talking again, and she spent the rest of the session giving a charming rendition of the importance of flexibility and the nature of responsibility. I focused on her blue and white sandals, intrigued by their colour: the cornflower blue of her eyes but with a tinge of mauve.

I said nothing more, except to agree I would meet with them next month.

*

The glossy travel brochure shimmered in the sunset, my large gin and tonic fizzing as I eased into a deck chair and sent the tart, juniper-berry liquid slipping down my throat. Flicking through pictures of glamorous hotels and sparkling Amalfi coastline I had a surge of longing. I'd been invited as keynote speaker to a conference in Venice and Stephen had been asked to give a paper at a finance conference on Capri. We were planning to combine a magnificent European holiday around our engagements.

We'd fly to Athens – Stephen's first visit – where I'd spend two days taking him around my special places before we'd head to Crete, for a night, for me to catch up with friends. Then we would move on to Italy for a week to relax like Jackie Kennedy and the sixties jetset by the clear waters of Positano, where I had a date with destiny: to conquer a painful memory of an awful, snaking road hanging high above the ocean – a road my mother had been too afraid to drive when, with my younger brother John, we went on holiday trying to escape the horror of Dad's drowning. I was a teenager at the time, fifteen and miserable. I had always intended to return, drawn to succeed where my mother failed – in some small way it would pay homage to my father, who had always encouraged me to never be beaten by anything.

From the Amalfi coast we would ferry over to Capri and spend three days at Stephen's conference; then back through Naples where we'd catch the train to Florence for a couple of nights in a city full of happy memories we had created over several visits. Finally, we'd arrive in Venice where I'd speak on the gold of Macedon and the jewellery of the Minoans and Etruscans at a prestigious cultural archaeology conference.

Our duties complete, we would fly to Paris and spend eight days in Stephen's favourite city, one we knew well and never tired of visiting.

And then we'd come home, having reignited our love in the most romantic places on earth. I felt queasy as I thought again of the possibility of Stephen having an affair. Perhaps I should confront him when we were overseas, far away from her? Although if it was Priscilla, she'd sent an email to the Faculty stating she'd be in Paris doing research on semester break and our time there overlapped. I hoped it was only coincidence – she was a French historian after all. And I still couldn't believe Stephen was seeing someone else. I knew that I could have an overactive imagination.

In the brochure I came to the pages on the Veneto region and the Serenissima. There was the Grand Canal: I could still remember emerging exhausted from the railway station on a hot summer's day when the kids were young, for our family to be met by a shimmering expanse of pale green water filled with frenetic activity, beneath a golden haze. Large vaporetto churning the tourist masses to their accommodations, sleek water-taxis plying their trade with gleaming wood and plush upholstery, the only noise a seafaring purr and clunk and splash. We had all fallen madly and exquisitely in love.

Returning in a steady rhythm of years I had manoeuvred my way onto the advisory board of an elegant glass museum on the island of Murano. I knew Latin well and could understand Italian. My spoken skills were less confident, not much better at first than my schoolgirl French, but after a while I became fluent enough to get by. My task was to help verify the age of the ancient exhibits through an analysis of their chemical properties, assisted by state-of-the-art equipment. Over time I made friends with the local glassblowers, whose arms were as thick as trunks from keeping aloft the long pipes through which they exhaled their creations; their appetite for food and wine and company was of Olympic proportions. As often as possible, Stephen would accompany me; we'd try to squeeze in a visit between conferences or research trips, and we'd take the kids when we could. I yearned to see my friends again and to escape the daily dramas of Coastal.

When I finally tore myself from the enchanted images I had the energy to work on my paper. Writing about jewellery and arranging a PowerPoint presentation of luscious photographs absorbed me. Big Boy padded into the study and stretched at my feet.

'Careful or I'll squash you.' He paid no attention.

The last streaks of pink faded from the vast orb of sky outside my window. I kept writing feverishly. It was a welcome distraction from the humiliation and frustration of my first mediation session. Surely what I was doing now was the point of my job, not kowtowing to Priscilla's mad obsession to slash and burn and crush? I made a mental note to set up a time with her to explain the Athens expenditure. Safer to clear it up than let it fester.

As the night wore on, Big Boy sauntered away and I heard him crunching on his biscuits. An owl hooted forlornly in the distance and two tawny frogmouths swooped from the nearby telegraph wire to catch insects in the glistening air. The ocean throbbed softly, echoing around the hills; there was a low-hanging mist, dulling the sharper sounds and lending an impressionist quality to the landscape, a trickster light, one that could hide a myriad of ill-begotten deeds.

Suddenly a hand grasped my shoulder and I jumped.

'It's only me,' Stephen said. 'Sorry I'm so late. I presume you ate already?'

'You'll give me a heart attack. No, I've been working.' With surprise I noticed it was eleven o'clock. 'Where have you been?'

'I got caught up at a seminar. We went for drinks and it turned into dinner. I meant to ring . . . but clearly I wasn't missed.'

His dark hair was dishevelled and he seemed hot.

'Who was at the dinner?' I asked.

'Just my PhD students.'

I looked at him, trying to decide if that was the truth. His eyes were calm and friendly.

'Can I tell you about my hideous session with Priscilla?' I said.

'Can't it wait? I'm exhausted and I have a dawn meeting.' Stephen planted a quick kiss on my cheek. 'Promise I'll hear all about it tomorrow night.' He kissed me again. 'You look so pretty when you research,' he said and headed into the bedroom.

I went back to work and tried to fend off my disappointment that Stephen hadn't phoned. He'd been like that when we'd first met at university. He'd say he'd turn up somewhere and then would completely forget. In the first year of our marriage I'd sat waiting night after night, dinners going cold in the oven, finally forcing mine down. I'd worried he'd been in an accident and I'd never see him again. I could still remember my fury towards him for treating me that way and towards myself for being so weak. Before Stephen, I'd been independent; after marrying him I'd transformed into a useless appendage. Later, I realised some of my feelings were hormonal when I discovered I was pregnant. And with the arrival of James, things had changed – so many nights Stephen was the one who'd get up to settle him or bring him in for a feed. He'd put up with the exhaustion and helped me get as much rest as I could. By the time we had Erin, Stephen was the best father I knew, a complete partner: fun, reliable, my best friend, my confidante.

And now I was mistrusting him, setting myself on a difficult, painful path. I'd never suspected him of being unfaithful before, so why start now? Outside, a kangaroo thumped through the grass on the hill high above. I rose stiffly and went to the bedroom, where Stephen was already asleep. I turned off the light, plunging the room into black ink, and returned to the study, battling a swift injection of fear that I might no longer be the most important woman in his life.

I worked until dawn.

7

The second mediation session was in progress and O'Shannessy was observing proceedings with a distinct lack of interest. I was growing to detest the man, who today had slipped tight leather espadrilles over bare feet and was dressed in fawn trousers and a cream shirt. By the way he was looking at Priscilla when she wasn't watching, I gathered he was developing a crush.

'I've dropped morning tea to save money, Priscilla,' I said.

'Morning tea was disbanded years ago in most departments,' she snapped back.

'The Fellows liked it and as you know, they can be very good donors.' I didn't mention I was planning to instigate an informal lunch with them instead.

'See how she has an answer for everything?' Priscilla turned to O'Shannessy.

'Hmm,' he mumbled, 'go on,' flicking an approving glance at Priscilla.

'And your research?' Priscilla seemed genuinely interested. 'How's that coming along?'

'Fine. Thanks.'

'How are you finding the time to write?' Said with a flirtatious lilt of amazement for the benefit of O'Shannessy, who gave her a little smile and chuckled.

'How does anyone?' he asked.

'It's harder since we have to fit in these sessions, actually,' I replied.

'Does that make you feel angry?'

'What if it did? It doesn't interfere with how I run the School.'

'Lisa Clements tells me your mood's been rather dark of late and that you've snapped at several people.'

'Then Lisa's wrong.'

'How so?' Priscilla's head tipped to one side like a budgerigar, her blue eyes genuinely concerned.

'It's been busy with Melinda away, and the admin staff are having to adjust. Perhaps that's what Lisa's referring to?'

Priscilla shrugged. 'Put it this way, if you are having problems, here's the place to air them. In a supportive and sympathetic environment.'

I had to wipe the smirk off my face.

'I saw that. Immature.'

'Oh for God's sake, Priscilla.'

'That's better. Let's really talk. Until we do, these sessions will just go on and on.'

'Is that why every Head is still in mediation?'

'Have you spoken to them? You know that's forbidden.'

'No.' Although goodness knows I'd tried. They were all terrified into obedience.

'So, let's get back to your research. You're writing a paper on the gold of Macedon?'

'I'm focusing on the Late Classical and Early Hellenistic periods.'

'And why gold? Is it wealth that interests you?'

'It's the uses of gold and the meaning in all facets of society I'm exploring. The period of Alexander the Great when Macedonian soldiers brought back spoils from the East.'

'Gold jewellery fascinates you?'

'It does – as a signifier of power and an enduring status symbol. I'm also looking at the gendered responses to jewellery and extending my analysis to the Minoans and Etruscans.'

Priscilla glanced down at my bracelet, gold with inset rubies. 'Did you get that on one of your research trips?'

'Stephen gave it to me.' I felt a surge of warmth as I remembered how he'd bought it off the Internet for my birthday.

O'Shannessy sat forward.

'I'm guessing it's Hellenic,' said Priscilla, gently lifting my wrist to take a better look.

'It's a reproduction from the fifth century BC. A classic Cretan design.'

'Do you collect jewellery? It seems to me from what you wear around the place that you have quite an extensive array. Is it one of those areas where your passion for research spills out into the real world?'

'Most of it has been given to me.'

'Really?' Priscilla leaned forward casually but her eyes scrutinised me. 'That could make an interesting journal article,' she said, sitting back and crossing her legs. 'The effects of research on scholars and those around them.'

The thought of Priscilla with Stephen hit me with a thud. *Has he given you jewellery?*

O'Shannessy scribbled on his large notepad. I tried surreptitiously to see what it said but his writing was illegible, I suspected intentionally.

'We'll take up from here next time, shall we,' he said. 'Good work both of you, today.'

I didn't see how, but I rose and shook his hand. 'Thanks.'

I drove away fast. The session had been definitely odd. Why was Priscilla quizzing me about my research and jewellery? Could it somehow relate to the Athens account, which still no one had raised? When I had asked Alison Wishart if she'd mentioned it she was noncommittal and had walked away. I hadn't found the courage to ask again, and I held on to the hope that it would just blow over. In the scheme of things it was an insignificant matter.

I turned the car into a nearby cove, glad to be away from Coastal, and walked down a path ragged with sharp-edged marram grass to a tiny yellow wedge of beach, where I sat watching the shimmering, glass-calm sea as the sun pounded in from the horizon. In silhouette I could see a new pontoon had been anchored a little way out. Rumour had it that money had changed hands with local counsellors to allow it to be floated there. A figure, lean and sleek, suddenly rose from where it had been lying on the boards. As it turned languorously, I saw that it was a woman in a white bikini. She dived into the sea and swam to shore with strong, confident strokes, emerging to shake salty droplets as she ran up the beach to a towel.

'Hello.'

Startled, I realised she was talking to me. To my horror she approached.

'Not swimming?'

I shook my head. As she looked down I tried to guess her age. Early thirties, perhaps. Dark hair was slicked about a glistening face. Her eyes were the colour of honey, generous lips carmine, nose slightly aquiline. Even in the harsh light I could see that she was unnaturally pretty, not typically so but with a symmetry and strength that flowed. She would photograph well. The classical quality to her chiselled jawline would have sat comfortably in a Minoan palace. She would have been beautiful in any century, any millennium.

'The water's wonderfully cool,' she said. 'You hot?'

'Stinking hot.'

'Then why not go in? Strip off. There's no one else around.'

I laughed loudly, splintering the air.

'I take that as a no?'

She bent and held out a tanned arm towards me. 'Sally Chesser.' We shook hands, hers cool from the water. 'I know who you are,' she said. 'I've read your books. Archaeology is a passion of mine.' With a touch as light as gossamer she brushed against my arm, an informal, warm gesture. 'You come often but you never swim.' She casually registered my surprise. 'I've seen you several times,' she said. 'I like to sunbake in the sand hills.' She cast a glance to the dunes behind us. 'With the snakes.' She chuckled, full and hearty as her eyes danced. 'You on lunch break?'

I nodded.

'I've been to a couple of your lectures. On the jewellery of the Minoans.' She paused. 'They were quite good.'

I rose. 'Time's getting on.' They'd been excellent lectures; I didn't appreciate her faint praise.

'You still at Coastal?'

'Yes,' I replied blandly.

'Nice to meet you, Rebecca Wilding!' she called as I strode away. I waved without looking back. This beach had been my secret place, the escape that replenished my soul between interminable meetings.

Not as secret as I'd thought.

The next week the summer rain came on suddenly. It was pelting down like cats and dogs, as my mother would have said. The air smelled of ozone, steam radiating from the tarmac in white puffs as I raced across the car park. I hadn't brought an umbrella.

'God, you look like you've been swimming,' cried Justine, who was filling in for Melinda. She gave a toothy grin as I charged for the refuge of my office. 'You're dripping! I'll have to get a mop!' She grabbed a small gym towel from her drawer. 'Here you go.'

I took it gratefully and went to my desk.

Justine followed on my heels. 'The Dean's been here looking for you.'

I glanced at my watch. It had just gone past eight a.m.

'I know,' said Justine. 'I asked if it was urgent but she wouldn't answer.'

'I'll call her.' I handed back the towel, panic rising. It was highly irregular that Priscilla would come here. Trying to appear casual I shut the door, which Justine opened again immediately.

'Let me know if there's anything I can do to help?'

Priscilla picked up on the first ring. 'Oh good, it's you. Come straight over.'

'There's something I've been meaning to tell you,' I blurted as soon as I entered her office.

Priscilla looked up at me, seeming genuinely upset. 'Rebecca, Alison Wishart has mentioned the Athens account, if that's what you were about to say.'

My heart sank.

'Sit down.' Priscilla sighed, her body somehow diminished, shorter, thinner, and achingly tired. This wasn't what I'd expected at all. Where was the triumph, the ah-ha moment that she'd finally got me?

I perched on the edge of a leather chair. Priscilla pulled hers close and lowered her voice, even though there was nobody around.

'Let me hear everything, please.'

'I signed off on something I shouldn't have, but it's okay,' I said. 'No one got hurt. No one did anything wrong.'

Priscilla's eyes sharpened. 'I said please tell me everything.'

I shrugged. 'I'm sure Alison's brought you up to speed. It was an accident, it won't happen again. And I'm truly sorry. I guess you were right, I'm not that good with figures.'

'Don't waste my time. It's better if you come clean now, Rebecca.'

Too late it dawned on me that something was seriously amiss. 'I'm not sure what you're asking . . .' My voice tapered off. Priscilla's expression was one I'd never seen on her before.

'Rebecca, we've found huge irregularities. Signed off by you.'

'I have no idea . . .'

'There's a forensic accountant coming in.'

'Okay . . .'

'I'm telling you this off the record, so please don't mention it to anyone. You're being investigated for alleged serious misconduct.'

I started to shake, unable to control my buzzing hands. 'But there must be some mistake?'

'I've gone over the accounts myself in great detail. I couldn't believe it either. I know we often don't see eye to eye but I've never thought of you as an embezzler.'

'Embezzler! Oh, Priscilla.'

'I genuinely hope for your sake – and your family's – that you can explain the situation. Professor Margaret DiStasio will run the investigation. Do you know her? She's in Medicine.'

'I've heard of her, of course. Her research into mental health.'

'She's a very fair person. I requested her myself.'

Was I imagining it or was Priscilla being sympathetic?

'But I've done nothing, Priscilla,' I said, trying to make sense of it. 'Truly. I'll help with the investigation in any way I can.'

Her cornflower-blue eyes pierced me, as though sending a laser through my façade into the core of my essence. I gazed back openly to show my innocence.

'It's your signature,' snapped Priscilla, as if reading my thoughts. 'Like a rat crawling uphill; I'd know it anywhere.'

I exhaled. This sounded like the old Priscilla. For a moment her usual sharpness relaxed me.

'I'd cancel that overseas trip if I were you,' she added.

'Absolutely no way. I've worked long and hard for this leave, and the Venetian conference is really important. I'm keynote speaker. I'll be fully contactable. Besides, I'm not guilty of whatever—'

'Alleged fraud,' she interrupted.

'If I was I'd probably stay, wouldn't I? Protest too much, try to cover my tracks? But as I'm not, I plan on going.' *And there's no way I'm letting you alone in Paris with Stephen.*

'I can't stop you either way,' she said matter-of-factly. 'The investigation's out of my hands. But when you get the letter from Margaret DiStasio you'll realise just how serious this is.'

I drew in a breath and found myself unable to exhale. Dots swam like tadpoles in my eyes.

'Breathe.' Priscilla reached out and touched me, and I let go of the air. 'Now breathe in,' she said. I obeyed.

'I really don't want to see you found guilty,' she said quietly, and I felt my world tip upside down. Surely none of this was happening. Surely I'd wake up soon and take Big Boy to the beach.

Outside the sky darkened to gunmetal grey. An ear-splitting clap of thunder shook the room followed by a sulfurous flash of lightning. Rain smashed down.

'You'd better wait here until it stops,' said Priscilla. 'You're going to need all your strength. These investigations are never pleasant.'

I asked Justine to keep everyone away, to not disturb me under any circumstances. I turned off my email, and brought up the accounts. At first I couldn't see any discrepancies. The Athens account made me cringe but it had been a genuine error and was, other than that, quite legitimate.

Figures scrolled in front of me. I found it difficult to concentrate but forced myself to focus. More accounts, more numbers. Nothing looked wrong.

I went out and made a cup of coffee. As I returned Justine had a pile of documents for me to sign. I took them into my room and read each thoroughly before blessing it with my approval.

The end of the day was racing towards me as I went through the financial statements again. And then I found it. An account: 'Athens 2'.

'Who are you?' I said aloud.

It held a series of small transactions – everything under ten thousand dollars. Money in, money out. Presumably it had been set up by Pam for some reason for the January student trip. It was irregular and I couldn't remember signing any authorisation, but it didn't seem enough to have placed me under investigation for serious misconduct.

I kept searching the accounts, but try as I might, I couldn't find anything else that looked out of place.

*

The unforgiving sea churned, sheets of rain sweeping ashore like an army of ghosts as I sat watching from my car. Somehow I'd managed to leave work without alerting anyone to my distress. I was lucky Melinda was away – she alone would have seen through my act and wrenched the details piece by piece, all the while soothing and ranting how unfair it all was.

It was only six o'clock but darkness was already falling, a deeper grey on grey as thoughts battled in my mind. Could I face Stephen tonight? Could I ride the whole thing out without him knowing? Could he find the irregularities that I seemed to be missing? But then again, I'd always hated how arrogant he was when it came to financials and me; the last thing I could bear was to be patronised. In any case I felt stupid and incompetent to have let the first Athens account be opened, and I was nowhere close to working out what the second account was all about.

I'd been part of investigations, on the other side, the interrogator, the seeker of truth. I knew DiStasio would talk to colleagues in my department, but everyone would have to undertake the strictest confidentiality. It was feasible that I could sort it out and Stephen need never be aware of it.

Out at sea, a light bobbed lonely on the horizon, frail and unreachable. A sharp tapping on my window jolted me, terror gagging my throat as I realised I was not alone in this isolated place.

Drenched hair plastered over her face, Sally Chesser grinned and shouted above the storm. 'Let me in!'

Automatically I leaned across and opened the passenger door and she ran around.

'What on earth are you doing out in this?' I said.

'I was walking and got caught. I thought the weather was clearing. Lucky you were here, I didn't think anyone would be.'

Neither did I. Inwardly I cursed.

'You okay? You look a bit fragile.' She touched my arm with a lightness that surprised as it soothed.

'How do you know that's not my normal state?' I countered.

'Is it? You didn't seem that type at your lectures or the last time we met, but how would I know?'

I shrugged and offered nothing. Into the silence I suggested I give her a ride somewhere. 'Where is your car, anyway? Or do you live nearby?' This tiny cove was away from houses, so I was surprised when she answered in the affirmative.

'About ten minutes. Work, not live.'

'Oh, what do you do?'

'I'm a lawyer.'

'Solicitor? Barrister?' Maybe Sally Chesser had been sent by the gods after all. 'Do you practise industrial law?'

'Family law. Why?' She was suddenly alert, like a hawk peering at a small bird.

'You must be cold.' I started the engine and turned up the heat. The blast of air made the car instantly cosy and the dash-board lights twinkled reassuringly. 'Direct me?' I looked across to Sally and she seemed so young in her dampened state, barely over twenty.

'What's wrong?' she said.

'Nothing,' I smiled. 'You'll be glad to get home.'

'And you? What were you doing down here?'

'Thinking.'

'I get that. I've been known to do the same.' She laughed,

a carefree, lyrical burst that was infectious. 'Wouldn't want to do it too often,' she continued gaily. 'You never know where you'll end up!' She looked out to the bleak road, trees bent into question marks in the wind, no lights. 'It's desolate, isn't it, when the weather's bad. It's hard to believe that civilisation's just around the corner.'

Minutes later I dropped her outside a tiny office that was in darkness.

'Are you sure you'll be okay?' I looked around at the isolation of the place. 'You wouldn't get much passing foot traffic here.'

'It suits our clients. Often when they're divorcing they want to be out of sight. Especially when everyone knows each other's business around here.'

Perhaps Sally could be useful? Although my work problem wasn't her area, she seemed smart and might be a good, objective listener with a sharp legal mind.

'Come to lunch?' I asked and Sally's face lit up.

'Wouldn't miss it for the world.'

I pulled a pen and paper from my bag and we scribbled down our phone numbers, exchanging details, and then I watched as she ran around the back of the building through the pelting rain. I waited until a light came on, but none did. Should I go in and check? Just then, a car appeared at the end of the driveway and sped towards me. Sally tooted happily and drove off in the direction from which we'd just come.

I couldn't help but wonder where she lived – and where she was going on this stormy night.

8

She was a vision in white from top to toe as she shimmered through a blue eucalypt haze in the heat of the lazy afternoon.

I wrestled with Big Boy as he danced and strained on the balcony, a writhing cacophony of barks and yelps.

'Who's this baby?' cried Sally as she planted a kiss in the air near his nose. Big Boy backed away whimpering, then quickly changed his mind and jumped up for more. Sally brushed a second kiss between his ears and then stood to pass a generous bowl of jewel-bright salad to Stephen as I introduced them.

'I have champagne too!' Sally plucked a glistening bottle from her pearly canvas tote as she entered the kitchen. 'I love you,' she crooned to her new canine admirer.

'He doesn't drink,' deadpanned Stephen, and Sally flung her head back and laughed – a little too loudly. White retro jewellery, chunky and flamboyant, sat well against her tan. Her eyes today flashed amber and her glossy hair had been cut in short, fashionable layers. Stephen's gaze made my heart sink.

'What a gorgeous house,' Sally said, scoping the room. There was a fizzy eruption as Stephen popped the cork and filled the glasses, which we raised in a toast.

'To friendship,' Stephen said unexpectedly.

'To friendship!' We clinked our glasses merrily.

'Delicious.' Stephen studied the bottle.

'Bought in a wine cave in Provence.'

'We go to Paris all the time but we've never been to Provence. Always meant to. What's it like?' he asked.

'Not what I expected,' replied Sally as I led the way outside to where I'd gone to some effort in setting a table. My mother's antique tablecloth, faded linen with extravagant blousy roses, flapped like a butterfly beneath vintage plates and glasses.

'Wow!' Sally picked up a gleaming spoon. 'Georgian silver.'

'My mum's. She was a collector.' I remembered the void she had tried to fill after Dad's death, wandering around shops, buying antiques and any other beautiful objects she could find, displaying them through our house until there was no room left.

'Your mother clearly had taste,' said Sally.

'Did you have any difficulty finding the place?' I asked abruptly.

'None at all.' Sally sat down and breathed in the air dramatically. 'I love that tang of salt. Perhaps we can go for a swim later? I brought my togs.'

'I'll join you,' Stephen said. 'Bec doesn't swim.'

Sally looked at me curiously. 'Is that why you don't go in? I could teach you.'

'She *can* swim. She just doesn't,' said Stephen, and Sally frowned.

'I don't like it.' I shrugged. 'Now, tell us more about Provence?'

'If you're on the fast train you don't see much, just a bit of greenery,' she said. 'You need a car, which I didn't have. The villages I did go to were sweet but not as evocative as I'd fantasised from reading a million books before I went. How about you? Any travel plans?'

'We're off to Greece and Italy and Paris in semester break,' I replied. 'I'm counting the days. We haven't had a holiday for ages, have we, darling?' Stephen's face clouded and my stomach kicked. 'You're looking forward to it, aren't you?'

'Of course. Can't come soon enough.'

Even Sally could see he was lying. I felt as if he'd struck me.

'You'll have to bring us photos of Provence. Maybe we'll go there next,' he said to Sally.

'Deal.' She flashed a slow smile that was dreamy and seductive.

'Let's put the barbecue on,' I announced, rising. Stephen followed obediently.

'I'll just be a sec,' I murmured and went inside to fetch the bowls of dips and bread I'd spent the morning making.

'What's his problem?' I said to Big Boy as he sprawled at my feet. 'I thought Stephen wanted to go overseas?' Big Boy cocked his head and whimpered. Looking out, I saw Sally hovering near Stephen at the barbecue, deep in discussion.

As I returned she was saying, 'But capitalism always re-invents itself!'

Stephen started to reply but clammed up as I approached.

'What Marxist theories are you two cooking up?' I said as I deposited a platter of steaks beside Stephen, their marbled flesh glowing deep red. He blinked, as if it were the first time he'd seen meat.

'Stephen was just filling me in on the stock market.'

'Oh? What about it?' I arranged the dips on the table.

'Just how uncertain it is these days,' Stephen muttered.

'Even I can see it's still jittery – and I don't really follow it,' said Sally. 'Stephen has some elaborate theories.' She gave him a playful look. 'You should back your judgement.'

Stephen chuckled. 'Never.'

'Stephen's far too wise to gamble,' I said. 'Aren't you?'

He didn't meet my eye. 'It's not gambling, it's investing.'

'Do you dabble?' asked Sally.

'No.' Stephen and I answered as one.

'We leave that to others,' I replied. 'I'd prefer Stephen stick to theories. One day we might get an investment property – but stocks are too scary.'

'You know that's ridiculous,' bridled Stephen. 'You read the bad stuff and focus on it. Sally's right – capitalism's resilient.'

'I have a few shares. Maybe we can exchange notes?' Sally grinned.

'Maybe,' said Stephen, 'when Bec's not looking!' He winked at me. Was this another secret? Had he been buying stocks without telling me?

'What would you do if you won ten million dollars?' said Sally suddenly as we settled into lunch.

Stephen topped up the glasses with a ruby-red shiraz. 'I might buy a boat – always wanted one but they're a money drain.'

I stared at him. He knew my feelings about boats. Was he deliberately trying to rile me?

'I'd look after my family,' he continued smoothly and leaned across to gently touch my knee. 'Buy this one the diamond ring I couldn't afford when we were married.' His face stilled. 'And see that the three people I made redundant this week were okay.'

'What three people?' I said, shocked.

'I finally persuaded Jim and Lucy and Ellen to take voluntary redundancies.'

I watched him as if he were a stranger.

'I know. That's why I didn't tell you.' Stephen turned to Sally. 'We've both been fighting to retain good staff but ultimately I had to make cuts.'

I fought back the words that wanted to surge forth. Better to save it for later when we were alone.

'You think I sold them down the river,' he said, meeting my eye.

'Economic realities don't go away,' said Sally. 'It clearly hurt you to do it.'

Stephen nodded, drained his glass and poured more with a steady hand. I wanted to cry. Stephen was becoming like the rest of them, the countless Heads of School through the university who were folding without a fight. And disturbingly he hadn't discussed it with me. Until last week he'd been encouraging me to stand firm, and that's what I thought he'd been doing too –

using his vast intelligence to think of ways to create income streams rather than just cut and slash and throw valued staff out onto the street. What had changed?

'What would *you* do if you won ten million dollars?' he asked Sally.

'Travel first class forever. I often go overseas to conferences and I have to fly economy. I hate it. It would be bliss to turn left as I walk onto the plane. And I'd acquire some fine antique jewellery. Bec could advise me.' I didn't smile and she blushed. 'Sorry, did I say something wrong?'

I pulled my mind back to the conversation at hand. 'Pardon?'

'So, what would you do?' asked Sally lightly.

'I have no idea,' I replied.

Sally laughed and tossed her head back gaily. 'We'll have to seduce you into the world of consumerism. For someone who writes so eloquently on jewellery, I'm surprised you're not hankering after some beautiful things of your own.'

'It's cultural history I write, not sales catalogues,' I replied somewhat tersely. 'Truly. Finding treasures in a dig. Absorbing them in museums. That's more than enough.'

'Don't believe you,' replied Sally flirtatiously.

'Nor I,' said Stephen. 'You've always liked what I've given you.'

'I have.' My eyes suddenly welled up. 'I love that jewellery.' *Because I love you. Please don't grow distant.* I quickly blinked the tears away. 'And I'm always grateful to accept more. You got me, Sally,' I laughed. 'I do love beautiful things.'

*

Eucalyptus pods plopped from above, dislodged by cheeky gang-gang cockatoos screeching like rusty hinges as they feasted in the torpor of late afternoon. After Stephen had shown Sally around the garden that he had single-handedly rescued from weeds to turn into a peaceful native haven, we dispatched a second bottle of wine before we ambled to the beach. Big Boy's tail bobbed like a feather duster as he ran ahead.

I felt the warmth of the sand as I watched Stephen and Sally rise in a clear green crest then disappear into a frothy haze, tumbling through the breakers. Our drenched black and white bundle jitterbugged in the shallows, barking as they emerged, racing back as they swam once more into deep water to rise and ride the crystal swell again.

As the mellow day merged to evening a pink glow engulfed the remaining straggle of beachcombers.

Was Stephen seeing another woman?

Stephen and Sally bodysurfed in on a wave. He seemed unusually relaxed with her. Was Sally his lover? Were they acting out a macabre game?

I shook the thought away. Perhaps I was just jealous that Sally hadn't stayed with me. Irrational, seeing as it was hot and it was she who had been eager to swim.

She showered me with salty droplets as she ran up to her towel and smiled so sweetly I wondered how I could have held any dark feelings. 'Come for a walk?' She reached down and took my hand, hers cooling mine, and pulled me up. We left Stephen and Big Boy cavorting in the surf and I decided to show Sally a well-kept secret.

'Wade through here.' Lifting my dress I walked up to my thighs in the aqua water at the far end of the beach. 'Careful of the rocks.'

Sally squealed as she stubbed her toe. 'I'm okay – lead on,' she said.

The swell was strong, the surf tugged, slapping slimy tendrils of kelp against our legs as we picked our way carefully over submerged boulders. 'Are you all right? It's not far.'

'Is the tide coming in or out?' Sally sounded fearful.

'Out. It'll be shallower coming back.' I turned and she smiled tentatively. 'Give me your hand.' She clutched so tightly I wondered whether I should be bringing her here.

The waves were rougher as we rounded an ochre outcrop and the hidden beach came into view.

'You don't swim but you'll brave this?' shouted Sally.

'Never said I was rational.' I gripped her hand and led on. 'Almost there.'

Just near the shore I stepped into a deep hollow and stumbled. Briny water gushed into my mouth as I floundered, trying to regain my step. Sally reached under my arms and lifted me up in one smooth movement. Trying to control a surge of nausea, coughing and spluttering, I staggered out onto the beach.

'Sit down.' Sally ushered me to dry sand, studying my sudden panic. I breathed deeply and forced myself to smile serenely. 'I'm fine.'

Sally nodded, concerned, then glanced around at the towering cliffs shimmering red, pink, orange in the dusk. 'Wow.' They hummed in the silence, a stillness here that was primeval. 'It's like we just stepped back a thousand years.'

My reservations about the adventure evaporated as I saw her childlike wonder. She rubbed her forearms, shivering. 'Goosebumps.'

'Go for a walk. Take them in.' Sally didn't need encouragement. She floated in a mirage as she inspected the cliffs, looking up at their astonishing height, the weight of time enveloping her.

I wanted desperately to grow close, to feel the excitement of a new acquaintance, the seduction of conversations beyond the banal. But could I trust her? This woman I knew nothing about.

Sally waved and I lifted my hand into the fresh breeze, waving back.

Returning was easier. The sea had stilled, sleeping in a silvered calm. As we walked towards the silhouettes of Stephen and Big Boy absorbed in a ritual of stick throwing, three tiny birds, grey with black hoods, stick pink legs so fragile it was a miracle they held up, fed timidly at the shoreline. I gestured to Sally to move away up the beach and she followed, mesmerised by the birds.

'Our hoodies,' I whispered. 'Hooded plovers. They're terribly shy and nest right on the beach.' I indicated further ahead a small area that had been fenced off. To our left the hoodies took off momentarily, only a few inches from the ground, then settled back in the glistening sand by the water and continued feeding. 'Two parents and one baby.' Sally stared at the young bird that was so delicate he looked like he might break. 'The hoodies have no concept of self-protection,' I continued as they fluttered along, stopping again to snap insects in the heat. 'They're endangered. Only a handful of them left along these shores. We all try to watch out for them.' I pointed to the fence. 'It doesn't do much but it's something. All it takes is one dog or fox and the entire brood is lost.'

Sally turned to me with an expression so intense her hazel eyes seemed ablaze. 'That one's hurt.' The largest bird was doing an exaggerated limp away from its family.

'To take attention from her baby. She figures a predator will attack her rather than the young one if it thinks she's wounded. That limp's for us. Quickly.' I led on to allow the birds their world again.

'You seem to understand them,' said Sally and I had the eerie feeling that she meant this with more depth than was necessary. Whether or not Sally felt it, I did have an instinct for self-preservation. In that moment I decided not to ask her for help, at least not until I knew her better.

That night Stephen and I abandoned our Sunday ritual of television crime drama and went straight to bed.

'You may as well skip the silent treatment, it's driving me crazy.' Stephen shut his book. 'You're acting like I sacked them.'

'You betrayed all of us who've been fighting – but particularly them.'

'There are economic realities and you know it.'

'What made you change your mind?'

Stephen frowned. I waited but he didn't reply.

'Great. You can't even say!'

'It's hard to pinpoint exactly. I wanted to discuss it with you but it all happened so quickly.'

'Why?'

Again Stephen was silent, unusually so. 'I was preoccupied,' he said slowly. 'I'd let a few things slip.'

'Like what?'

'The departmental budget had a few errors, which were spotted higher up.'

'That's not like you.'

'Let's just say I lost bargaining power.'

I seized the moment. 'I've noticed you've been a bit absent here lately too.' I waited for what seemed like hours but Stephen didn't look at me. 'What's going on?' My question hurled through the air like a grenade about to explode. Part of me wanted to take it back.

'Nothing,' Stephen answered calmly. 'We're just so chronically overworked. A situation that's going to get worse once the others leave.'

He looked across so openly I could see his black irises full and rich in his deep brown eyes. Relief surged through me. He smiled. 'It's okay, my love. I haven't suddenly changed into a monster. It really hurt me convincing them to go. I looked at every alternative, and each was more awful than the one before. Anything else would have been much worse, and would have affected a lot more people. In the end I inflicted pain where it would be most efficient.'

How like Stephen. Here was the person I knew after all.

'If it makes it any better they chose to go. The packages are quite lucrative.' He fixed me with a stern look. 'In the end we have to take responsibility, Bec. And if we can't, they'll find someone else to do our job – and probably should.'

'My God, you sound like Priscilla!' The thread of conciliation was torn apart. 'That's just bullshit!'

'No it's not! Where are the funds meant to come from?'

'From growth not cuts. What about all the plans for new income sources that we've spent hours talking about?'

'In this environment that's impossible,' he replied. 'If I didn't take action the situation would have been dire. You need to think about that in your department too. We can sit down together if you like?'

'No need. I can just sack everyone Priscilla wants me to and we'll all be happy. Until we try to run subjects and there's no one left to teach them.' I was up and on my feet, had already reached the door. 'And I'm sure Pam and Josie will be thrilled, just like winning the lottery – except once they've spent their packages they'll have no careers and few options other than part-time mums snatching piecemeal work. Great deal, Priscilla. Oh sorry – I mean *Stephen*,' I finished sarcastically.

I turned and walked slowly back to him, aware my expression had become that of a madwoman. 'And by the way, are you having an affair with Priscilla?'

Stephen's gaze was so full of disbelief and contempt I had to look away.

'I can't talk to you when you're like this,' he said. 'You're insane.' He flicked off the light.

I stood for what seemed like an eternity, my senses humming so loudly I felt like a vibrating disc, tethered but desperately needing to be airbound, to float back to when my husband was the dependable, stalwart, amiable companion I had shared my life with for twenty-five years.

Eventually Stephen started snoring and I moved down to the family room, where I lay on the sofa, Big Boy sprawled heavily across my feet. The image of Stephen leaning towards Priscilla at the birthday party spun into my brain. Was I inventing the whole thing?

By the time I woke the next morning, Stephen had gone, as quietly as the summer zephyr that brushed the leaves outside with an invisible hand.

9

'For what it's worth, I'm as shocked as you, Bec.' My good friend Rachel's eyes brimmed with sympathy. I had emailed her asking urgently to meet, and she'd raced over after giving a Jewish Studies lecture. 'It doesn't seem like Stephen to force voluntary redundancies,' she continued. 'Not at all. But in this climate it's hardly a surprise.'

'I can't stop thinking it's because he's having an affair. Maybe the woman's influencing him? Everywhere I look I wonder if it's her.' I indicated a pretty young academic in a tight slip of a dress, 'Or her, or her.' I pointed to two women nearer my age who were lean and bright-eyed with intelligence, hunched forward gossiping over lunch. 'Or a student, for that matter. What an awful cliché that would be if he ran off with one of his PhDs.'

'If Stephen's seeing someone he's managing to keep it very secret – which I would have thought is a complete impossibility in this place,' said Rachel.

But deep down I was beginning to think that Stephen was far better at keeping secrets than I could ever have imagined.

'I asked him point blank last night if it was Priscilla.'

'Rebecca!'

'Well, it's possible.'

'That's truly ridiculous.'

'Years ago, when we were friends with Priscilla, Stephen always found her good fun.'

'Yes, but she's not anymore. Hasn't been for a long time.'

'She wears clothes well, still has a figure. If you ignore the poison flowing through her veins.'

'Which Stephen wouldn't.' Rachel paused. 'No, try as I might, I can't conjure them together.'

I felt a deep sense of relief but kept going. 'Then maybe whoever he's seeing is off campus.'

Rachel gave a look of disbelief. 'Unthinkable.'

I snorted. 'I guess. Neither of us has a life outside work. Pathetic. Except . . .'

Rachel leaned forward with anticipation.

'I'm also worried he's been investing in the stock market.'

She sat back. 'He is an economist.'

'But we'd agreed that he wouldn't. Just after we were married he lost his shirt in some bad trades. It's the reason I've always insisted on keeping a separate account as well as the joint one. I think when pressed, there's an element of the gambler in Stephen.'

'And there's also a rock who you've been devoted to for

many, many years. It's natural to feel paranoid when we're under so much pressure. You're just tired.' Rachel waved her hand like she was fanning everything away.

'You're always right,' I said gratefully.

'If only that were true.' She laughed so loudly the gossipers at the next table turned and smiled. Then Rachel grew solemn. 'You know, in this instance, I think I *am* right,' she proclaimed and stood. 'Classes to run, minds to corrupt. Call me any time.' She kissed me warmly and bustled off, waving hello to people at most of the tables.

It was unfortunate I didn't have anything pressing for the next hour. It was still lunchtime and I couldn't stop myself from wandering across to Stephen's building. The glass edifice of Economics glowed steel blue in the early afternoon. I slipped inside and climbed the sleek timber stairs to the second floor and walked down the long corridor to Stephen's corner office. He wasn't there. I fished around the papers that were scattered on top of his desk. Nothing of interest. I tapped the bar of his keyboard and his computer sprang to life. Checking that no one was coming, I quickly scrolled through his emails. Nothing obvious there either. If Stephen was having an affair he was covering his tracks well. Would I find answers on his mobile phone? But how would I check it? He always had it on him. I walked briskly back to my office, trying not to allow focus to become obsession.

'Thanks for coming over,' I said to the dapper man sitting opposite me.

'That's okay. I know how sensitive this is.' Peter Carlisle, the union lawyer, was sweating lightly in the heat and looked decidedly uncomfortable.

'Oh God, you don't think I'm guilty?'

This raised more sweat and a deep blush in his usually kempt appearance.

'Peter, I'm not. Nor is anyone in my department. I don't know why the Athens 2 account was created but it's obviously just another mix-up.'

'Because I'm representing you they've let me see a few of the discrepancies,' Peter said, passing across a printout. 'Bec, there's quite a bit of money missing.'

I was looking at a monthly statement for an Athens 3 account that had started with three hundred thousand dollars and was now reduced to fifty dollars.

'What's this account?'

'It was set up by you.' Peter passed across a form with my signature.

'That's impossible.'

'Isn't that your signature?'

I scrutinised it. 'It can't be mine, even though it looks like it.'

'You don't remember setting up the account? Your signature's been tested forensically by two handwriting experts at the university. Both say the signature authorising all the Athens accounts – 1, 2 and 3 – is yours.'

I sat back, my head whirling, trying to piece things together. 'I don't understand.'

'It's better to come clean,' he said gently in his deep, musical voice. 'There's also a lot of money in your own miscellaneous account – your X account.'

'Well, that's from my consultations outside Coastal – museums and universities.'

'They must pay well.' He passed across a sheet that displayed my X account as having over five hundred thousand dollars in it.

'This just isn't right! There's obviously been a clerical error.' I scanned the entries. 'There must be an explanation.'

Peter passed me more papers. He leaned across and scribbled with a red pen, tracking some of the withdrawals from the Athens 3 account straight into my X account – a total of two hundred thousand dollars, in parcels just under ten thousand dollars each, had been deposited.

I blanched, my mouth going dry. 'I would never do that.' I looked up. 'And do you think I would have been that obvious if I was going to embezzle?'

'The Athens 2 and 3 accounts were well hidden. And no one would normally question your X account. Scientists and medicos can easily have that much.' He paused and looked down at his feet. 'I can help, Bec, but I can't do it without you.'

'Can I please take a copy of these?'

Peter handed me a manila folder that he'd already filled with the heinous evidence. He stood. 'Go through them. Take your time. But the clock's ticking.'

My legs were so wobbly I couldn't rise. I wished Melinda were here. She could probably work the whole thing out in ten minutes, expose it as some massive administrative 'cock up', as she'd say.

I focused on the signatures. They all looked identical to mine. I authorised dozens of forms every day and wouldn't necessarily remember the minutiae of them all, by any lengths, but I would remember the general overview. I knew I'd signed off on Athens 1, but I'd never approved any Athens 2 or 3 accounts. Nor would I transfer vast sums into my own university account. My heart thumped out of my chest as I realised that whoever was behind this had gone to a lot of trouble to point the finger at me.

I had only ever felt so completely alone once before in my life. When I had swum to shore and lived, forced to leave my dad to disappear behind charcoal mountains of waves, grasping on to a sinking boat.

I sprinted, leaving Big Boy lagging far behind. Ice-green surf crashed, sending misty plumes of ivory spinning high into the air. The sand had been sucked away revealing bare brown rock.

A strong undertow pulled at my legs as I ploughed into the shallows and challenged fate, refusing to watch where the sea floor dived away and water swirled into the hollows, danger-ous and swift. Sweat drenched my clothes even with the cool water surrounding me.

When I finally headed home Big Boy was straggling, a black dot in the distance. For once I didn't wait for him.

As I reached the final bend a kangaroo and its joey – a tiny mass of long limbs and soft fur – suddenly shot out from a thicket of gums and hopped towards me in the middle of the road. I could just make out the writing on the red collar of the mother roo – BONNIE. The sight was uplifting, playing as it did into the hoary myth of kangaroos in the streets of

Australia, an absurd conflation of town and bush, civilisation and nature.

Without warning, Big Boy came racing through the thickening gloom and went straight for the kangaroos. In one swift movement he snapped the joey between his massive jaws. Instinctively Bonnie whipped back on her tail and struck Big Boy with her powerful hind legs. Big Boy leaped away, not taking the full force, but refused to let go of the joey, who was emitting a thin, high-pitched squeal. Bonnie attacked again, boxing forward and scratching deeply with needle-sharp front claws. Big Boy buckled, yelping in pain, momentarily releasing the joey. Blood flowed everywhere, a dark gelatinous river emanating from the joey mingling with the brighter blood of the injured dog, who now, ignoring pain and reason, attacked the joey again, plucking him up and running away. Bonnie pursued frantically. It was happening in slow motion. I yelled for Big Boy to stop. He fled and I followed, narrowing the distance even as Big Boy raced like a creature possessed, claws clacking fiercely on the tarmac. Wet, hot, pungent metallic blood met me as I grabbed his collar and tried to wrestle him off the joey. In a frenzy, Big Boy whipped around and plunged his teeth, hard and unyielding, into my arm. I swore as my flesh pulsated like burning ice and he let go, snapping again into the joey. I tried with all my force to extricate the limp, bloodied mess of hair and bone from the dog's frothing, scarlet jaw.

'Big Boy!' I roared. 'Drop!' Alarmed by my fury he backed off, growling, and the tiny joey lay squealing with ever-decreasing volume at my feet, life sapping away. Bonnie was hovering. I couldn't think properly from the pain. Bonnie leaped forward again and I wasn't swift enough to avoid her hind legs belting my side with a sickening crack, the force lifting me off my feet. Long claws razored down my face and chest as I was pinned to the bloodstained ground. The air was sucked from my lungs and a splintering agony confirmed my fears: ribs were broken.

Big Boy returned, now stalking Bonnie, barking fiercely. Amid the mayhem I managed to pick up the joey. He was limp but there was a vestige of warmth. Blood dripped into my mouth, which hung open slackly. With the little strength I had left I carried the joey, heading for the house, calling Big Boy to follow. Bonnie was coming at us again, but this time Big Boy attacked as she lunged. I tried to run but the pain was too severe. Lurching like a wounded hobgoblin towards my stairs, looking back I saw Big Boy locked in mortal combat.

'Big Boy!' I called desperately. 'Big Boy! Come! Here!' Everything was a blur. 'Clarkey! Clarkey! Help!' With a thud I saw that his car was not there. No neighbouring lights shone through the gloom in any direction.

'Help! Help!' I shouted into the empty shadows as I took the stairs one by one in aching grinds and heard Big Boy fighting with Bonnie below, a cacophony of pain and brutality, growling and shrieking, the sounds intermingled into one hellish song.

It took all my effort to slide the glass door open, my body erupting in flames. I staggered inside and put the limp, blood-soaked joey on the floor. I moved as fast as I could into the kitchen and snatched a towel. As I came back, Big Boy slumped down onto the deck outside. 'Thank God,' I exhaled. Big Boy watched exhausted through glazed eyes, his body a dark mess. I grabbed the phone and called Ian Sinclair, our vet.

Forcing myself to remain conscious, the joey lying weakly in my blood-red lap, I reached my broken ribs upward and slid the door wide enough for Big Boy to limp inside. Without a glance at the joey he dragged himself into a nearby corner and fell into a sickly sleep. He looked like a can-opener had ripped him apart. A thumping made me turn in alarm. Bonnie had come around the back and was staring inside, one ear hanging torn and loose, her throat a fuchsia gash of blood and pale, exposed bone. She wailed, a high, reedy cry of despair as she leaped forward and began scratching at the glass with her powerful claws. She moved along the window, tail thumping, her high keening growing more urgent. Big Boy staggered up, barking furiously. I looked at the joey; it was desperately in need of care. Why did I think I was more capable of helping than its mother? Just then a car roared up the drive and moments later Ian raced inside.

'Bec!' He rushed to tend to me first.

'No, no. The joey and Big Boy and the mother.' I indicated outside to Bonnie.

'You should see yourself.' His confident hands gently felt my ribs. 'You're a mess. Have you called an ambulance?'

'Don't think so,' I murmured, suddenly beyond rational thought as a deep tiredness overwhelmed and blackness rushed up, extinguishing light and pain. The last thing I heard was an unearthly howl from Bonnie and a volley of raw, strangled barks from Big Boy as my world collapsed around me.

10

Something was weighing me down. Tears sprang, salty and sharp, as I saw that it was Stephen holding my hand. Outside, the long rays of sun on the hill were mellowing to evening.

'Hey.' Stephen's brown eyes, dulled with concern, came alive. 'I'm so sorry,' he said as I gently touched my bandages, white with yellow seeping through, and my skin flared like an inferno beneath my prying fingers.

'Big Boy?' I rasped, my throat parched.

'Ian stitched him up. He's keeping an eye on him.'

'And the joey and Bonnie? Will they be okay?'

'Ian has them. They're doing well.'

I sighed with relief and my body ached. The grotesque bite on my arm from Big Boy throbbed.

'You have four broken ribs,' said Stephen gently.

'I guessed as much.' I scrutinised Stephen – there was something different about him and he seemed tense.

'What have you been up to?' I asked and he bolted upright as if I'd just shot him.

'Nothing. Here with you.'

'Did you go to work?'

He nodded. 'Just a couple of meetings that I couldn't get out of. Clarkey came over. And Sally Chesser came when Clarkey had to go.'

'But we barely know her.' *Or do you know her better than I think?*

'She rang to thank us for the barbecue and wanted to help. Oh, and Priscilla sends her regards.'

'What are you doing talking to Priscilla?' I tried to sit up but the pain knocked me down.

Stephen sighed. 'I told her you wouldn't be in.' He paused and squeezed my hand. 'And no, I'm not having an affair with her. What goes on in that head of yours sometimes?' Said with so much warmth that more tears seeped out. I prayed I could believe him as he kissed my lips softly and I tasted his sweet breath.

'You should rest, the doctor gave you a heavy painkiller.' As he stroked my brow sleep nibbled at the edges of my mind, even as I tried to resist.

The morning was fresh and cool, with the promise of autumn. Big Boy walked shakily into the room and for the first time I felt fear as our eyes met. The dog lowered his head, about to growl. Tentatively, I reached out my hand, ignoring the fire running up my arm from his deep puncture wound. For a moment nothing happened. Stephen stood quietly behind, watchful. Then Big Boy's tail started frantically beating from side to side, he let out a yelp and came stiffly dancing over, crabbing about, twisting like a worm as he barked happily. He was bandaged in several places. We looked like twins. Stephen lifted him up onto the bed and the three of us lay together, listening to the raucous laughter of kookaburras rippling through the bush.

I nestled into Stephen as best I could with my aching ribs and Big Boy pushed gently against my body, stretching to his full length so he was almost as long as me.

'The gang's all here,' I murmured, and fell back into the deepest sleep.

'My god, Mum.'

I woke to Erin gently touching the wounds on my face. 'The kangaroo sure made a mess of you.' She picked up my arm and I winced. 'And is this what Big Boy did?' The dog lay looking up at Erin, grinning. 'You both look terrible.' She gently stroked the soft white hair on Big Boy's belly.

'I don't know what got into him. He went berserk.'

'He is a dog. It must have been some sort of instinct. Not to bite you, though.'

'He didn't mean to do that,' I said.

Every time I moved, my ribs flared in agony. 'Is Dad here?'

'He's at work. It's three in the afternoon.'

'The painkillers knock me out.'

'You're awake.' James stuck his head through the doorway. 'Cup of tea?'

'You're here too? Or am I dreaming?'

'I'll make you a cup of tea.' James disappeared and Erin tucked the sheet around me, her impish face lined with concern.

'Don't you have pressing deadlines? You shouldn't be wasting time with me.'

'We're just staying for dinner, Mum. I'm cooking. Then James will drive us home.'

'When was it you grew up so fast?' I said gratefully. 'Are you still seeing Jeremy?'

Erin shrugged. 'A bit. Not much.' She started fussing with the wound on my arm, clearly not wanting to talk about it. 'I just can't imagine Big Boy doing this. And that poor joey and mother.'

'Thank goodness they're all right . . .' My voice trailed off. I felt guilty. 'Big Boy probably saved my life,' I said.

'Even if he was the one who put it at risk in the first place,' said Erin.

Big Boy barked twice, tail flying back and forth.

'I should have had him on the leash,' I said. 'It was my fault.'

'Don't be so hard on yourself, Mum.' James deposited the tea and sat at my feet. I rested back into the pillows and gave them a blow-by-blow description, wondering if I was inventing things; shock had blurred my memory of the evening, except for the moment when the dog I trusted implicitly had turned on me.

*

One week later I could get up, dosed on painkillers and anti-inflammatory pills. It felt like knives slicing through me as I walked, but once Stephen had left for the day, I went to my computer and trawled through the accounts.

I approached the task as I would a dig – carefully sifting through all that was there in the hope of discovering what had happened. There was a maze of different lines in the accounts – 'strings' as we called them. After several hours I found a disturbing trend, hidden deep in the files. I'd missed it before because it was lying within sections of other accounts. Some of the strings had shadow strings in which money meant for the first account had been deposited into its twin or triplet. The original Athens account was the simplest to unravel. Half the students who had gone on the most recent Athens intensive had deposited the money for their trip into this account set up by Pam and signed off on by me. The other half had deposited their money into the Athens 2 account – which seemingly had been authorised by me too. But where Athens 3 had got its money from remained unclear.

Alarmingly, portions of my colleagues' grants had also been siphoned into the Athens 2 account, and also into other shadowy accounts that stalked legitimate ones. I was sickened to see my own X account had colleagues' money in it.

Other sums had gone back into legitimate accounts making up the lost amount, like a complex Ponzi scheme. No wonder Alison had picked up irregularities. I could see now why she had to cover her own position. Many of the legitimate accounts were ones that she would have presented to me for authorisation.

The logic of the perpetrator was elusive, as mysterious as

the gold ibex of Santorini. Who could have done this? I was intrigued to find out.

I flicked through the photocopied records obsessively, willing myself to remember signing them. But I couldn't. I genuinely believed I hadn't. But then, the investigators claimed the signature had been verified as mine, and it certainly looked like mine. A brilliant fake. And not for the first time in history. The world was flooded with fakes – even in archaeology we could be fooled. For every legitimate enterprise, there were those waiting to do the quick rip-off. I just hadn't expected it at Coastal. And I hadn't expected to be the victim.

I reached for my phone and excruciating pain shot from my ribs to my shoulder. Ignoring it, I looked through the address book and found Loris Gant's number. A professor at Melbourne University, Loris was a handwriting expert. He was a trusted colleague whom I knew from inter-university research committees and crucially, he would keep the matter confidential.

When he picked up, I gave him minimal information, just that I needed a forensic analysis of the signatures and would provide my own legitimate signature with them. I told him I wanted to pay the full cost, no favours. Loris said four thousand dollars was the rate. I gave him the go-ahead.

Over the next few days I made comprehensive lists of staff who could be embezzling, noting everyone who had sought authorisations from me. It read like a Who's Who of the School, everyone at senior lecturer level and higher. Even Josie and Pam were on my list. And then I had to add Rachel. Melinda too – papers were often left on her desk for me to sign. I didn't think that any of these colleagues were criminals who would perpetrate such a financial web. I kept following the strings regardless, like Theseus following Ariadne's magical thread in the labyrinth, trying to find the way out.

So far Coastal had been professional. I felt that no one outside the investigation had heard anything, including Stephen. And the further into the fraudulent accounts I went, the more I wanted to sort it out on my own, not bring him into it. Particularly if, despite his denials, he was seeing Priscilla behind my back. The thought made my ribs burn – not only at the thought of him with Priscilla, but that I didn't want to turn to him for advice – the person I'd relied on for over two decades. I took more pain-killers. Priscilla was high on my list of suspects and I wasn't going to have Stephen unwittingly feed her information if my worst fears were correct.

For breaks I would go through Stephen's computer checking his emails, scouring for evidence of an affair. There was nothing incriminating, but I did get an insight into his managerial prac-tices, which showed me just how much more corporate and conservative he had become in the past months.

I asked our phone company to supply an online breakdown of all calls on our bills. I checked for stray numbers on Stephen's phone that he dialled repeatedly, ringing those I didn't know. They were work-related people and I was deeply uncomfortable as I prattled on, apologising for getting the wrong number.

I wrote to Margaret DiStasio and informed her that I wanted to assist in every way possible and had gone through the books and found more irregularities. She sent back a short, official reply: she would be contacting me in due course. Because I had acted as an investigator on other cases, I knew she normally wouldn't approach me until she'd gathered all her evidence. Ultimately with what was being uncovered in this fraud, whomever they found guilty would be turned over to the police for a criminal investigation. If they decided it was me, I could be stripped of everything. My job. My title. In a nightmare scenario, even my freedom. I needed to ensure I gave them all the information I found to convince them I was on their side and not the perpetrator.

'Yoo-hoo, anyone home?'

Sally's voice trilled from the bottom of the stairs and Big Boy returned a volley of friendly barks. I quickly closed Stephen's computer and rose, my ribs aching from the sudden movement.

'Just a sec!' Did she mishear me? The sound of the door sliding open and the tapping of her shoes on the timber floor made me hurry.

'Hello, darling poochie babe.' Big Boy yapped back as though chatting.

'Sally, how nice.'

'Hope I didn't get you up? I feel it's been ages since I saw you and do you know I've just moved two streets away? Eagle Crescent, the other side of the golf club.'

'Really? Where were you before?'

'Geelong. Much quieter here. The air's so fresh I feel ten years younger.' She looked it too, radiant in a slip of a dress, tanned arms lean and strong. 'I didn't want to disturb you but then I thought surely there's something I can do. Perhaps some grocery shopping?'

'The local supermarket delivers everything. Even puts the heavy things straight in the fridge. So does the butcher. You've moved to a good area,' I smiled.

'How about this one? I could take him for a W-A-L-K?' Big Boy sat eagerly at her feet.

'Actually, that would be good. I can't go very far, and Stephen's so busy.'

'Done. Now, how about I make you a cup of tea?'

It was frustrating having her so close but not trusting her enough to tell her my legal troubles. I kept reminding myself it wouldn't be her area anyway. But she was smart. Why was my instinct saying keep away?

Sally passed me a fragrant mug of tea.

'I added honey. For good health.' She held a glowing golden jar to the light. 'I found it at the organic shop.'

'That's very thoughtful.'

To my surprise Sally waved a large ring under my nose, encrusted with rubies and emeralds. 'I've been wanting to ask you about this. Do you mind?'

'Of course not. It's beautiful.' I spotted the gems as fake the instant I saw them. 'Where did you get it?'

'Athens, a couple of years ago. It's about a hundred times more than I've ever spent on jewellery.'

'Well, it's a treasure.' I didn't have the strength to break the bad news. The shops in Athens were notorious for their counterfeit jewels and the well-honed pleas of the shopkeepers who hung outside, waiting to lure the next unsuspecting tourist. Another fake staring me in the face – the world really was full of them.

Sally gave me an odd look, as though she didn't quite believe me. I tried not to blush under her gaze. 'You must love it,' I continued.

Finally she smiled. 'Yes, very much.'

I wasn't sure whether I'd just passed or failed a test, and it made me uneasy.

'Well, I'd better get this fella to the beach.' Big Boy leaped up and clattered about, nails scrabbling across the floor.

'Didn't you want to ask me something about the ring?'

'Oh,' she turned, 'I just wanted to know if the rubies and emeralds were real. I've read since that Athens can be a tricky place.'

I paused. 'You could always take it to a gemologist.'

She raised her eyebrows. 'But you're an expert, aren't you?'

'At dating things. Using very sophisticated equipment. The ring's new,' I said. 'You didn't think it was ancient, did you?'

Sally laughed gaily. 'Of course not.'

'It's a Byzantine design, a lovely one.' I fetched Big Boy's leash to barks of excitement.

Sally held the ring happily to the light. It was indeed a pretty fake. 'Come on, Big Boy! Back soon.' She winked as she left.

'Would you like to stay for dinner?' I called as an after-thought.

'Not tonight, Bec, thanks anyway,' she lilted.

I was relieved when she disappeared down the stairs. Was I becoming paranoid or had there been more to the conversation than its immediate topic? Was Sally trying to catch me in a lie? And if so, why? And why hadn't I just come out and told her the gems were fake? I hadn't wanted to hurt her but now I regretted it, because it made me look deceptive. Truth was growing increasingly elusive and I was contributing; if I went down that path, I could get tangled in my own lies.

11

It was a brilliant autumn morning, the sky a deep, infinite blue. Crisp air hinted at cold nights and log fires just around the corner. I had called two days earlier and set the appointment, hoping I would be well enough to venture out alone for the first time since the attack. I was still dosed on painkillers but they were weaker and my doctor had given me the all clear to drive.

Just off the main road, the funky cafe was done up like an old-fashioned diner. Lunch was still hours away and the red vinyl tables were empty, as I'd hoped. I settled at the back of the cafe and ordered a coffee and waited, worrying as time stretched out whether I would be stood up.

Pam and Josie arrived twenty minutes late. I had wanted to see the two women individually but they had been adamant it was both or neither. They blustered in, new babies in tow. Two boys, tiny and perfect, swaddled in soft blue blankets.

'They're so cute, thanks so much for bringing them,' I cooed.

'Well, we could hardly leave them,' snapped Pam.

I was surprised by her edginess – the baby must be depriving her of sleep.

'This is Oscar.' Josie presented her little boy to me proudly and I held his miniature hand, as tiny as a doll's. 'Sorry we're late.'

'And he's Lucas,' Pam mumbled, cradling her baby and sitting as far away from me as possible. 'You know we're being investigated for serious misconduct?'

'I had no idea!' In my own self-pity it hadn't occurred to me how far the university would take things. I understood now why Pam's mood was fragile.

'I thought that's why you wanted to meet. Presumably they've contacted you as our Head? I told them you told me it was all right to set up the Athens account the way I did. But clearly it wasn't. You were wrong.' Pam bristled with hostility.

'Pammy, I said not to attack before we know the facts.' Josie sat forward. 'You're on our side, aren't you, Bec? It's so hard being on maternity leave – we don't see anyone.'

'Of course I am.' I leaned forward too, trying to sound casual. 'Were there any other accounts you set up?'

'No. Should there have been?' Josie frowned and I saw she had developed a crop of new wrinkles since we had last seen each other. I hoped it was from her newborn and not from work, but Oscar was sleeping peacefully like a perfect child.

'Both of us accessed the account in Athens and they're acting like we're thieves.'

This was news to me but it made things better. Safety in numbers.

'We're not meant to talk to each other. Or to you,' added Pam.

'Well, I certainly think it's best if no one knows we met.' I tried to keep eye contact with them both. 'What exactly are they accusing you of?'

'Don't you know?' Pam was immediately suspicious, and Josie cast her a worried glance.

I shook my head. 'I've been on sick leave.'

'Oh yes, we heard about the attack,' said Pam. 'You seem okay.'

'Four-broken-ribs okay.'

'Ouch.' Josie touched my hand gently. 'That must have hurt?'

'Only till I was drugged. I'm healing and that's the main thing. It'll just take time.' I was wearing a long-sleeved shirt to cover my wounds; the scratch on my face was hidden under make-up.

'So, why did you ask to see us? And why individually?'

'Because I wanted to catch up with you both,' I lied. 'I always find one on one better.'

'You were always happy to see us together before.' Pam wasn't about to let it drop.

'I can't disclose things,' I offered vaguely.

'So, you *did* know? Why are you being so evasive?'

I hadn't counted on them being investigated as suspects, and I tried to formulate a new plan on the run. 'I just want to support you however I can.'

'See,' said Josie, eyeing Pam, 'I told you she'd be on our side.'

Pam clearly wasn't so sure.

'I think you should be very upfront with Professor DiStasio,' I said. 'I've been an investigator myself, and it's always best when people are open and completely honest.'

'Why wouldn't we be?' Josie looked baffled. 'We haven't done anything wrong.'

'Well, evidently we shouldn't have set the account up the way we did. But that should have been picked up by you,' Pam repeated to me.

'Sorry. I seem to have let you down.'

Pam peered back, hostile. 'And you clearly *do* know what we're talking about, Rebecca.'

'I'm here to help. But I can't answer many questions,' I bluffed.

'Then, how can you help?' Josie was wide-eyed with concern.

I turned to Pam. 'So, you only set up the one account? You didn't have any need for a second or a third?'

'No. Is there more than one? If there is, it's not ours.'

If Pam was lying, she was convincing; her confusion seemed real.

I shrugged. 'I don't really know all the facts either.'

I was glad when they announced they had to get their babies home. The meeting had been a fizzer. I really didn't think that Pam and Josie were guilty of anything, let alone fraud. This should have made me feel better but it had the opposite effect. I had no idea who the culprit could be. Still, at least I wasn't the only one being accused of serious misconduct. Was anyone else at Coastal being investigated?

I would have to tread carefully interviewing my colleagues. If DiStasio found out, I could be accused of interfering in the case – that would be serious misconduct in itself.

Instinctively I felt that Priscilla should be my chief suspect.

The days were getting shorter, the weather colder. My mind was working feverishly as I steered the car to my meeting with Margaret DiStasio. I had convinced her to see me, even though she felt it was too early in the investigation. I knew if I pushed hard enough, she couldn't say no – and Loris Gant had given me his independent handwriting analysis, which I wanted to present to her.

I had seen Rachel, Robert and Constance, and not unexpectedly, I had crossed them off my list. I was reassured that they appeared to have no inkling that I was in trouble.

I had toyed with the idea of Melinda as culprit. She *had* gone on a sudden holiday, after all. But the thought was absurd. If Melinda were cooking the books she would have implicated Priscilla, not me. I wanted desperately to run things past her but she was still away and out of touch.

I worried whether Alison Wishart could be behind it – she more than anyone would have the expertise. It would be cunning to be the one who had found the discrepancies and be the perpetrator. It was a possibility that was worth full exploration and I couldn't wait to be well enough to resume work and have access to colleagues and, importantly, their offices when no one was watching.

DiStasio stood as I entered. She was a squat woman, grey-haired and overweight. Her walls were, predictably, lined with medical tomes but to my surprise there were also several stuffed animals. A wolf, a bear and its cub. The poor souls leered down, glass eyes glinting dully.

'My hobby,' she said. 'I find them on eBay. Refreshingly different to the human form.'

'I guess they can't bite back.'

DiStasio smiled and showed me to a seat in front of her desk. She had the demeanor of an animal herself. There was something almost feral in the way her sharp little eyes watched me.

'As you know, Professor Wilding, I've been asked to carry out an investigation into alleged serious misconduct.'

'I want to cooperate as fully as possible,' I said. 'I've been going over the accounts myself. I've found enormous irregularities and perhaps even some you haven't discovered yet.'

'I have to stop you there.' She held out a surprisingly bony hand. 'Is this a confession? Because it's not appropriate that we do this without a scribe present.'

'Absolutely not!' I said, blood flushing up my neck. 'Professor DiStasio I've done nothing wrong.'

'Weren't you the Head of School overseeing the accounts? Signing off on the authorisations?'

'Yes, some of them. And I have an independent expert's report from Professor Loris Gant who sees discrepancies between my signature and the one on the forms for the shadow accounts.' I produced with relish Loris's analysis, which had been well worth the four thousand dollars he charged. DiStasio took his report and scanned it.

'May I keep this?' She filed it away, scribbling the date, time and manner in which she'd come by it at the top. 'You know we have two experts who say the signatures are all yours?'

'I'm aware of that – which is why I sought my own. Professor Gant sees differences in the way the signature crawls. Very minor, but he feels the pressure of the writing is inconsistent.'

'I can read. Look, you've been an investigator yourself on alleged serious-misconduct cases. You know how the system works. Which is why I'm surprised you insisted on seeing me at this point.'

'I'm just horrified by what's happened.'

'Even if you didn't authorise the shadow accounts, don't you think you had some responsibility to pick them up?'

'Yes. And I'm truly sorry I didn't. But now I've looked over them, they're very well hidden.'

'Hmm. Your own university X account is a case in point. The amount in there wouldn't have raised alarm bells in Medicine. It was only that Alison Wishart is so thorough that she saw it in the process of investigating the original Athens account. Which you did set up incorrectly?'

I sighed. 'I take full responsibility for that mess-up.'

DiStasio gave me a stern look. 'As you know, I'll be basing my report on the balance of probabilities as they relate to the evidence. In due course I'll conduct a formal interview with you. At that time you'll be able to offer your full defence. But today I really can't go into detail and I don't think it's appropriate you say too much. I can understand why you're apprehensive, but be assured I'll be conducting myself with the highest professionalism and you will get a fair hearing.'

DiStasio stood and reached out her hand, which I shook. Her grasp was firm and straightforward. The stuffed animals leered.

'Thanks for coming in and bringing this piece of evidence,' she said.

I delved into my bag and brought out a manila folder full of accounts that I'd found with shadow strings. 'Just in case these haven't all come to light yet. They're all that I've found.'

'Thank you.' She looked me up and down.

'Am I the only person being investigated?' I asked.

'No. You're one of several.'

'Several? How many?'

'We're exploring four avenues.'

So, there was another person apart from myself, Josie and Pam. 'May I ask who?'

'No. Nor are we telling any of them that we're investigating you.'

'I'm very grateful.'

'Standard protocol, you know that.' She smiled. 'Hang in there, Rebecca. If you're innocent you have nothing to fear.'

'I wonder if I could ask you something?'

She cocked her head, at full attention.

'I'm due to go overseas with my husband. Important conferences and a holiday—'

DiStasio cut me off. 'Go. This investigation will take some time. I trust you'll be in full communication?'

'Always. I'll have my phone of course, so – emails, messages, calls.'

'Good. What are the dates?' She entered them into her computer and looked up brightly. 'I hope you enjoy your holiday.'

There was a double-edged tone – the clear inference being if I were guilty, it would be my last holiday for a long time.

At least being injured had meant an end to mediation with Priscilla. She had cancelled further sessions on the pretense that I needed time to recuperate, but I suspected it was also because of the investigation and I couldn't help thinking of that as one silver lining.

On my first day back, Rachel and I hurried across to the administration building to a full staff meeting called by Priscilla. I was short of breath from the exertion, but other than that, my body was stronger and I was definitely on the mend.

When we arrived in the airy room I glanced about. Since I had been away it was like a black hole had opened at Coastal and swallowed all the elderly professors. Old turtleneck McCall had taken early retirement, so too Oliver Yeats, who had never really coped with his downsized office. They'd both phoned me to say goodbye and the conversations were incalculably sad. There had been no official farewell and I'd been too unwell to fight Lisa Clements, who, to our collective horror, had been appointed Acting Head in my absence. And so the professors had just faded into the ether, sent off with their packages after thirty years of service without so much as a thank you.

Most of the staff from Classics and History had gathered and the room was becoming hot and close. I scanned my colleagues. Who was the fourth person under investigation?

Alison Wishart met my eye. I turned away and then realised

it would be better to meet her face to face. I looked back but her gaze was now fixed firmly on the front of the room. Was she the perpetrator?

'Thank you all for coming,' said Priscilla, rising. 'I have an announcement. We have a serious financial problem.' I held my breath.

'As a School you have seriously overspent. We are going to undertake a complete review. Changes will be made. I realise that some of us are about to head overseas to conferences and for research on semester break.' *I certainly haven't forgotten that you'll be in Paris when we're there.*

'But the consultants will need to interview you,' she continued. 'We expect your full cooperation.'

I breathed out, relieved. Consultants on anything at Coastal meant a protracted period of nothing, usually followed by nothing. And it seemed a broader context than just the embezzlement. Still, I was responsible for the School and wondered how I could have done things differently. Perhaps the consultants could get answers to aspects I couldn't? I felt humiliated, but I knew that my colleagues on the School Executive Committee shared my view that we could never see from the accounts why we were in the debt the Faculty claimed.

'So, how does that work if we're away?' roared Robert from the back of the room.

'Don't you think the start of next semester would be a better time?' exclaimed Constance. 'I thought we were supposed to travel to give papers?' She stood like a prizefighter as she talked. 'Aren't we appraised on that too?' Clearly tensions had increased in my absence.

The Lost Swimmer

'The review can't wait. Your situation is dire. Now, I won't take any questions at this point. Thanks for coming, I'll let you get back to your classes.'

'Why didn't you just email us?' called Robert loudly.

'I fear some of you don't read my emails.' A ripple of laughter spread through the room. 'Safe travels,' said Priscilla and looked directly at me. 'Even those of you I counselled to stay at home.'

I left the meeting at full speed, not looking back.

When I arose the next morning, defeated by hours of sleepless speculation as to who the unknown fourth person might be, the landscape had transformed into a magical wonderland. A heavy fog blanketed the trees, muting even the harsh shriek of a chainsaw. Downstairs in the gloom, peeking out from a pile of bills on the kitchen table, lay Stephen's phone.

I flew across and snatched it up, scrolling through his address book. There were very few contacts, mostly male professors in his department and on the Academic Board, myself, James and Erin, and a handful of friends.

I went to recently dialled numbers. Empty.

Incoming calls. Empty.

I checked his texts and emails. No record of anything of interest.

He had to be hiding something.

As I waited for the kettle to boil, the phone buzzed and the screen sprang alive.

Fingers trembling, I opened the message: a confirmation

113

order for twenty bank shares. My jaw clenched tight: so, Stephen was in the market against my wishes. But twenty shares seemed very few. I re-read the text. Actually they weren't shares at all but sell options or 'puts', each one covering one hundred shares, which made two thousand shares in total. I cursed that I hadn't paid more attention in the past. I wasn't sure what exchange traded options were. I feared they were a testosterone-fuelled product for those in the know or gamblers and that Stephen was attracted for both reasons.

He'd deceived me and here was the proof in my hand, but I couldn't be as upset as I should be. How much worse if the text had been from a woman? From Priscilla?

'Hi honey!' he called as I heard him fossicking about. I checked my computer, where I sat working on my conference paper. One o'clock.

'You're home early,' I said calmly as I came down the stairs.

'Have you seen my phone?'

'It's in the kitchen by the kettle.'

'Is that where I put it?' Stephen muttered, frowning.

'You left it on the table.'

'Right.' He picked up the phone and quickly scrolled down. He looked up at me, seemingly off-guard.

'You opened my text?'

'I thought we'd agreed?'

'On you going through my stuff?' Anger made his voice rise.

'You promised not to go into the market. And options can

be risky, can't they? Don't they magnify profits and losses?' I'd attempted to read up on them during the morning, their complexity finally overwhelming me. 'You can make a lot, but lose even more than your investment if things go against you?'

'Oh, fuck off.' Stephen stormed out, turning back only for his briefcase.

'Stephen! Wait!'

'You read my things, then this is what you get!' He was livid with rage.

In the empty house I was stuck to the spot. I'd never seen him like this before. Even the last time he'd been invested years ago when things went wrong, he'd been measured and rational. This was an entirely different side.

Tyres screeched as he sped away. Looking out the window I saw Clarkey leap to his feet and stare in surprise, and instinctively glance up at the house. He spotted me in the window and I waved.

I was so shaken by what had happened I sank back at my desk and forced myself to focus on my paper, absorbing myself in the minutiae of Macedonian gold coins minted during the reign of Philip II in the fourth century BC. I let not the slightest sliver of worry about Stephen break my concentration as I pored over the head of Heracles, his profiled eye ablaze with passion even now.

As lights on the hillside peeked out like fireflies, Stephen and I sat by the flames of an open fire, eating dinner on our laps.

The news was on but neither of us was watching. Nor were we communicating.

When I stood to collect his plate he looked up crossly.

'Oh come on, it's okay. I just wish you hadn't done it,' I said.

'I'm an Economics Professor, for God's sake. Don't you think I know what I'm doing?'

'But you should have told me.'

'What? And got your criticism? Markets are extremely volatile at the moment. It's not the best time to be in this.'

'Then why are you?' I said keenly.

'Because someone in this family has to take responsibility for seeing we have enough finances for our retirement.'

'We'll be fine. We're both going to get good payouts from our super.'

'With the way the world is? We need as much as we can get.'

'But retirement's years off.'

'Don't be so sure. In this climate, any of us could be asked to take early redundancy.'

I sat down close to him. 'Is something happening at work?'

Stephen shrugged. 'Not really.'

'But?'

'I need to publish more.'

'You've published more than most of them.'

'It needs to be more.' He stood and went to the kitchen, refilling his glass with wine.

'I'm sure you'll be all right.'

'And you? Everything fine with you?' He scrutinised me, and suddenly beneath his gaze I felt alarmed. Had he heard something?

'Yes.' I watched his face. He just seemed angry.

'Good. I'm going to work on my paper. Could you please dryclean two suits? I won't have time to do it myself before we go.'

'Of course,' I said. 'Is there anything else?'

His expression softened, his dark eyes looked vulnerable.

'No,' he said. 'That's all.'

12

Big Boy sat by the glass doors into the airport, tail swishing filthy old cigarette butts as he looked up. I bent and kissed him, wrapping my arms around his massive chest, black with a white blaze.

James held his leash. 'Don't worry, we'll take perfect care of him. Lots of walks.'

Big Boy leaped to his feet at the 'w' word and barked hysterically.

'See, he's forgotten you already,' said Klair, who was back on the scene, much to our displeasure.

'No he hasn't!' blurted James, frustrated.

'We'd better get on,' said Stephen.

'Are you sure you don't want us to come in with you?' Erin's forehead creased with concern.

'We're fine, darling.' I pinned her beneath my arm and squeezed as hard as I could. Tears welled in her eyes. I took James under my other arm and kissed him. 'Just make sure you all look after yourselves.'

Klair gave a happy, sarcastic smile.

'Come on, then.' Stephen took my hand and led me away. 'Farewell, my lovelies!' he called back, his earlier reticence about the trip having transformed into clear enthusiasm.

I looked at the cameo of my family, arms raised in the air, waving frantically. Big Boy slumped on the ground, head on paws, forlorn. Klair was already stalking off.

The plane taxied down the tarmac. Stephen was absorbed in the business pages of the newspaper, his arm touching mine. The warmth of his skin filled me with all the possibilities the trip held, to grow close again, to enjoy life. I was apprehensive about leaving Coastal while I was under investigation, but I had checked and rechecked that I had my phone, and my laptop was sitting snugly at my feet. I would be fully contactable at all times. I started obsessing again about who the fourth person under investigation might be – the mysterious, elusive ghost – and then told myself to switch off. I willed DiStasio to have better luck at finding the culprit than I had.

The plane gathered speed, its wheels left the ground and we were off. I sank back into my seat. Escape. I wanted to whoop out loud with joy.

Stephen turned to me. 'I'm sorry I hadn't told you about my investments, Bec.'

I shrugged, surprised. 'You're only trying to do what's best for us. I'm sorry I was so dismissive of the whole idea.'

He folded his paper. 'Actually things have picked up and are going well.'

'I just find it hard to understand options: intrinsic value, time value, out-of-the-money, in-the-money, put and call, buy and sell.'

'Other way round. A buy is a call and a sell is a put.'

'Complete gobbledygook. You're not doing the unsafe ones?'

Stephen smiled. 'You *have* been reading up. It's okay, I've amassed quite a few blue-chip shares as well.'

'Have you?' I leaned across and kissed him full on the lips and as I moved back I saw his eyes alight with pleasure.

'I'm acutely aware of how much we're going to need for retirement,' he said. 'And we're nowhere near that amount yet. I just want to look after us.'

I rested my head on his shoulder. 'I trust you know what you're doing.' I slipped my hand under his arm and squeezed fondly. 'And thanks for talking about it.' Stephen relaxed and hugged me. I quashed my apprehension; this holiday was the best thing that could happen and I wasn't going to let anything get in the way, particularly Stephen's investments.

'Promise you won't do anything silly?' I couldn't help but ask.

'I promise, Bec.' He kissed my forehead tenderly.

The deep indigo sea reached up yearningly as we started our descent towards Athens. It was ironic that this was the first stop on our trip. Everything had been booked and pre-paid months ago but it had turned out to be serendipitous. I'd contacted the bank about the Athens accounts and was due to meet the manager tomorrow – I just had to find an excuse to leave Stephen alone in the morning.

Beneath us, the Aegean stretched for miles, dotted with tiny rocky islands to the horizon, familiar and alluring. A part of me felt like I was coming home.

'I can't believe I've never been here.' Stephen, excited, gazed out at the dry, chalky terrain as our taxi sped down the freeway.

'That's because you were always left minding the kids. It's strange they're getting so old, isn't it?'

'No,' he laughed, 'it's very natural, Bec.'

'I hope they're okay.'

'We don't see them for weeks on end. Why's this any different?'

'Big Boy's going to miss us.'

'He'll be fine,' Stephen replied fondly.

When we reached Plaka, the streets narrowed and ancient stone buildings crowded out the light. Wherever we looked were roadworks and the shells of burned-out buildings. Although I'd been to Greece often, for the past few years I hadn't come into Athens itself, transiting through the airport directly to the islands. I was stunned by how much had changed. We passed through cobbled streets no wider than a lane, with only a handful of tourists wandering about rather than the usual throngs. The shops and stalls that used to tumble onto footpaths, overflowing with colorful earthenware, Persian rugs, tacky souvenirs and startling arrays of gold and silver jewellery, were now mostly shuttered.

Turning into an even narrower street we came up behind a tiny train on wheels, the Athena Express, a crocodile of small carts behind a fake train engine painted in the jaunty blue and white national colours. A handful of tourists sat like giants in the tiny compartments. We crawled behind, Stephen waving to kids who found our taxi more riveting than the ancient surroundings.

The train peeled off into another street and the hotel finally came into view, a beacon of hope with its line of Greek flags flapping vibrantly from its grand façade.

In our room the Acropolis faced us, lofty and mystical, its beauty as magnificent today as when it was built in the fifth century BC during the golden age of Pericles. Beneath a blue sky that was remarkably free of pollution, the Parthenon stood out white and serene as morning light played across its marble columns. For an instant it seemed to float between heaven and earth, the perfection of its architecture, its classical proportions, an enduring monument to rebirth after the city survived the invasion and pillage of the Persians. Now it was surviving the complete breakdown of the Greek economy.

I stepped onto the balcony and Stephen followed, transfixed. The song of sparrows filled the air. Even the traffic, ear-blasting in the streets, was completely banished.

I wrapped my arms around Stephen and felt his familiar contours, strong and reassuring. 'What would you like to do today?'

'Maybe we should just stay in this suite. It's the size of a small house,' he replied. 'Did you book this?'

'It's an upgrade,' I chuckled. 'I'd only booked a standard.'

'That's a relief. I was beginning to think I should have looked at the bills when you were organising the holiday.' His straight white teeth and cherry red lips stood out against his dark beard as he smiled.

'We should freshen up,' he mumbled and swept me up, carrying me squealing into the lavish bathroom, where deep red marble veined with white set off the gold taps to perfection. It seemed like Pericles' vision for Athens continued to this day.

Water spurted out in a frothy arc as Stephen turned on the shower, kissed me and left. 'Don't use all the hot.'

'Join me?' I called as I stripped off my travel-worn clothes.

'I'll just be out here,' he called back, voice full of wonder, 'watching the Parthenon.'

Golden rays lit the carpet and crossed lazily over the living room's opulent leather furniture as I awoke from a deep daytime sleep, black with jet lag. I sat up startled, momentarily disorientated, until I found Stephen snoring quietly beside me. Hunger gnawed and my favourite museum beckoned, with its magical collection of Greek vases that I thirsted to set eyes upon again like old friends. I shook Stephen gently, covering his face in kisses. He groaned.

'Let's go!'

As we wound through the narrow streets of Plaka I was surrounded by familiar sights that were now vastly different – so many places had closed and lay shuttered behind graffiti-strewn metal. A few others were bravely enduring the new austerity, holding out in hope. Homeless people were everywhere, a sight hitherto unseen in a society that had always taken pride in looking after its own.

Under the lush green arms of a plane tree we ordered moussaka and Mythos beer in my usual taverna and watched people coming and going past the towering Athens cathedral standing sentinel over the square. The soft air and dappled light flitting across tables packed with rowdy locals slowly lifted my spirits, which had been dampened by the crushed city.

Stephen leaned forward. 'So, this is what you've been doing while you were away? Living an ideal existence while I kept the home fires burning.' His eyes wrinkled with laughter as he took my hand and kissed it. 'Just as well you've brought me this time.'

'I wouldn't want to be here with anyone else.' I felt a deep pang of love.

After lunch we set off for the museum – and walked straight into a demonstration against the government in Syntagma Square. Police in riot gear made a grim sight, but the Athena Express bustled through unperturbed, children's hands waving to protesters and police alike. The crowd was chanting rowdily against job losses as we hurried around the edge. 'This is going to grow ugly any second,' said Stephen as he crooked his arm protectively through mine and led us along. 'Thank God we're not staying in one of those.' He pointed to a line of luxury hotels that were dangerously close to the rally, metal grilles down, front doors locked in spite of the hour.

We relaxed when we boarded our bus and swayed along past technicolour flower stalls and traffic chaos, feeling the intoxicating warmth of each other's bodies. An impossibly green park, leafy and mysterious, beckoned invitingly.

'The National Gardens. Can I take you there afterwards?'

'Wouldn't miss it for the world.' Stephen peered out eagerly.

Hand in hand we walked across the vast courtyard leading to the museum's grand entrance and entered the cool interior, relieved to be out of the white heat of late afternoon.

I led the way up the massive staircase to the first floor, anticipation making me flush. 'I've always wanted to show you this,' I said with barely contained excitement.

The first of the glass cabinets met us in a light, airy room, a gleaming timber floor setting off the extravagant display of pottery. 'The finest collection of Greek vases in the world,' I announced like a proud mother. Stephen stepped forward and peered at the red, black and white clay masterpieces in all shapes and sizes.

'This one here,' I pointed to a spectacular amphora decorated in geometric patterns, a central frieze of tall, thin mourners holding aloft a dead man on a bier, 'marked a grave. It dates from 750 BC. See the intricacy?' I indicated a circle of deer grazing peacefully around the neck of the vase; they had always bewitched me with their fine brushwork.

'Hmm,' Stephen muttered and my heart sank. The moment I had waited for so long, sharing these treasures with him, suddenly fell flat as his eyes glazed over.

'And here,' I swept on to the next case, where Heracles wrestled with the Nemean lion, the glossy black figures starkly beautiful against their red background. 'I feel like I'm back at Coastal with Priscilla,' I said lightly as I watched the bodies linked in mortal combat.

Stephen stared at me, hurt. 'We're on holiday, Bec,' he

retorted and stalked off, giving the sublime vases, their lives and poetry, nothing more than a sideways glance.

'Stephen?' I trotted after him.

Stephen sighed. 'Sorry. Just don't mention Priscilla, okay? I'm still annoyed how you could ever have thought . . .' His voice trailed off and he rubbed his eyes, bloodshot with tiredness. 'I'm very jet-lagged. Forgive me?'

I steered him to another cabinet of vases and drinking vessels from the seventh century BC. 'This piece is by the Nessos painter, one of the greatest artists.'

A procession of chariots and warriors pranced across a perfectly proportioned vase, their movement so vivid they seemed alive. Stephen nodded and stifled a yawn.

'Why don't you sit down?' I swallowed my disappointment. 'While I look around.'

Stephen made his way to a cool marble bench. 'My ankles are puffed from the flight,' he said as he dropped onto the bench and his phone started ringing. 'Sorry, have to take this. It's work.'

Suddenly I felt a wave of jet lag too. I passed him my handbag, which felt full of bricks. 'I'll come back and get you,' I whispered, but he was already deep in conversation. I listened for a moment – on the other end was a man's voice, confident and deep. Stephen was muttering only words of agreement. Satisfied it wasn't a woman, I left.

But how could I be happy among these treasures without Stephen by my side? Particularly with Athens so scarred. Thinking of the turmoil in the streets, I found I'd walked through several rooms and was now in the classical period of the fifth century BC. The breathtaking red-figured inspirations of the artists were so sublime that I was slowly, inexorably, drawn to the pottery. A ghostly world gently opened as heroic tales of gods and beasts that could rule and ruin swept me away. Here was the goddess Athena, winged and powerful, and Zeus, thunderous and unforgiving. A centaur, half-horse, half-man, hoisted a rock on his shoulder and armed himself with a pitchfork while a naked young girl attacked a satyr, his penis swinging back against his stomach in a roaring retreat.

Maidens danced and warriors fought, battle after battle. Men were felled by gods in myths with a spectacular cast of thousands.

On a high-stemmed cylix, an ancient wine glass, a bearded satyr caught my attention. His dark hair hung shaggily, erotically, as his massive, impossibly huge erection faced me. Suddenly I thought of Stephen. Time had run away.

I hurried back to where I'd left him and saw immediately that the room was empty. There was no sign of him in the next room either. I retraced my steps. The rooms formed a circular path and if I walked quickly I'd be sure to catch him. He must have come in search of me because I'd been gone so long. I completed a full loop and couldn't see him. Surely he wouldn't have gone to a different floor? I hurried around again, knowing I had no phone, nothing at all in my pockets except two used tissues. Being without money made me feel vulnerable – but Stephen had to be here somewhere.

After no sighting of him the third time around, I changed direction. When I arrived back at the empty marble bench and there was still no sign of him, I asked an attendant – who sat watching in the doorway between rooms – if she'd seen him.

The young woman had only just come on duty; she'd noticed me circling but couldn't recall anyone who fitted my description of Stephen.

I took the stairs to the ground floor and asked other attendants but no one could help. I had a male guard check the toilets; Stephen wasn't there. He couldn't have just vanished, I kept reassuring myself as I went back upstairs and picked my way through other collections. A golden mask of Agamemnon stared blindly out. I searched fruitlessly, the wealth of the displays now invisible.

Finally I returned to the foyer, a flush of heat burning me up.

'Can I get you some water?' A young, beautifully groomed attendant with bleached blonde hair took my arm. 'You still haven't found your husband?'

'He can't have left,' I said. 'He must be here somewhere.'

'Take a seat.' She left me on a marble bench and disappeared through a door. A few tourists wandered past, not one of them looking remotely like Stephen.

'Excuse me?' A willowy young girl carrying a sketchbook and pencils came and crouched at my feet. 'I think I may have seen your husband. About half an hour ago, a tall man with dark hair and a beard, very fit?'

'Yes, that's him,' I nodded eagerly.

'He left with a woman.'

'What do you mean?'

She shrugged. 'I am an art student. I play observational games to pass the time and because my lecturer suggests this is the way to capturing life. Through memory. Your husband is a handsome Englishman?'

'Australian. He could look English, but why would he be with a woman?'

The girl gave me a sympathetic look.

'What was he wearing?' I countered, not believing she had the right person. She shrugged.

The attendant returned with a bottle of water. 'Drink this,' she said, as the art student spoke briskly in Greek, referring to me as a poor cow whose husband had abandoned her. I was pleased the attendant whose name tag read 'Eleni' berated her for having a vivid imagination.

I gulped the ice-cold liquid and reeled as it bit into me.

'Perhaps your husband is outside?' said Eleni. 'There's a little cafe to one side of the forecourt.' She led me away, both of us glaring at the student, who muttered in Greek. I caught the words 'old fool' and hoped she was wrong.

The sun blazed white, viciously hot, as we walked towards an area of tables beneath umbrellas where waiters skimmed about with trays of beer and nuts.

'Can you see him?' Eleni asked hopefully.

I scrutinised the customers. Stephen was not among them. We walked back to the museum without talking.

'May I use your phone?' I leaned against the front desk.

'We're not allowed,' Eleni replied unhappily, dark eyes genuinely sorry.

'Is there a public phone?' It occurred to me I had no money but in the current economic climate even asking to borrow a euro might be a pressure.

Eleni gave me directions to a phone a few streets away. Before I left, I checked the museum one last time. Stephen was nowhere.

As I reached the orange phone hanging in a plastic booth my stomach was a tangle of nerves. I picked up the receiver, planning to call James in Australia reverse charge to ask him to contact the hotel and check if Stephen was there. But there was no dial tone; the phone was out of order. Cursing, I made my way on foot. It would be a scorching forty-five minutes of brisk walking amid stinking, roaring traffic.

At Syntagma Square the demonstration was still in full swing. There was a palpable tension like the calm before a storm – any minute the crowd was going to erupt. I kept walking, then broke into a run. I felt naked and at risk without Stephen. My ribs, which I'd thought had healed, started to hurt.

At the hotel I raced upstairs and bashed on our door, tearing through plans of what I would do if he didn't answer. And then suddenly, there he was.

Stephen took me in his arms and hugged tight. 'I'm so sorry. I lost you. Then I thought you'd come back here. When you weren't in the room I was going to go back but then I thought you couldn't possibly still be there. If you didn't turn up soon I was about to call the police.'

'It's all right, it's all right,' I chanted, relief surging through me.

Stephen kissed me long and deep. I could smell the sharp odour of perspiration, something he never had. The scent of fear.

'You didn't meet anyone there?' I asked vulnerably.

'Of course not,' he replied, clearly perplexed by the question.

'A young girl thought she'd seen you with someone.'

'Those attendants,' he said. 'None of them were any help when I was looking for you.'

'You spoke to them?'

'I left a message saying I was heading back to the hotel. They promised they'd give it to you if you came asking.'

'Clearly not the ones I talked to,' I sighed.

Stephen shut the door and led me out to the balcony, where he fixed a stiff gin and tonic and passed it across as I gazed at the Acropolis, trying to stop my hands from shaking. The high marble siding was plunged in shadow.

Later as footlights blazed, lighting the Parthenon an ethereal grey, we ordered room service and sat under a star-filled sky eating fresh swordfish and drinking vast quantities of sweet white wine, content in each other's company, floating above the troubled streets below.

13

Stephen sat with his coffee, reading the *International New York Times* between two huge pots of blazing red geraniums, the Acropolis glowing yellow in the morning sun. I pecked him on the cheek, feeling the soft bristles of his beard, inhaling his citrus aftershave, fragrant in the Greek air.

'So, we'll meet for lunch?'

'Enjoy your shopping,' he replied. 'Do your best to help the economy.'

'You'll be okay?'

'With this view?'

I ambled through the tiny cobbled streets of Plaka, past a makeshift market of the unemployed selling tack, looking for something to purchase among the toilet paper, tissues and cheap souvenirs. Finally I bought a cheery red apple from a stall laden with fruit outside Monastiraki station and bit into its hard, white flesh, trying to quell my apprehension about the forthcoming meeting.

The bank had double security doors and I was stuck moment-arily between them, fighting claustrophobia. My punctual arrival was met by the news the manager was running late and had yet to arrive for the day. In Greek a young assistant brightly informed me to come back later. I tried to get a specific time but she couldn't oblige.

An hour later I was back, now expecting the moment in no-man's-land trapped between the thick security glass.

'I'm sorry, he's still not here.' This time, the assistant spoke in English with an American accent.

She led the way into a small cramped room lined with timber filing cabinets and sat down beside me at a large desk, empty but for an old computer. She chatted about her studies at Harvard in Boston. Back in Athens, she could find no work in finance other than as a lowly assistant, and she felt grateful even for that. She hadn't worked at the bank long, so I couldn't ask her anything about who set up the accounts that bore my signature.

I was getting edgy about running late for Stephen when finally, two hours after the allotted time, the manager strode in and sat down opposite me. Strong and wiry with a swirl of dark hair, he swiftly dispatched the assistant for coffee, lit a cigar-ette in spite of the no-smoking sign and spoke pleasantly about his recent visit to Australia. As soon as was polite, I asked him about the Athens 2 and 3 accounts.

'But it was you who set them up, no?' He inhaled slowly on

his cigarette. 'You're the signatory and have sole access. Madam, I think perhaps I don't understand your question?'

'Could I see the paperwork I filled out?'

I knew they would have needed my passport to activate the accounts and was desperate to see how this could have been furnished, or whose image was beside my name and supposed signature.

His eyes clouded with suspicion and the smoke-filled room seemed even smaller, its drab grey chairs and walls hemming us in.

'I've been in a car accident and have lapses in memory. My therapist suggested I try to piece things together,' I said rapidly in Greek, hoping it would lend greater authenticity.

It sounded weak but the bank manager nodded sagely and tapped another cigarette from his packet. He leaned across and offered one to me, which I declined with good humour as the assistant came back with two tiny white china cups. I drank the sweet coffee in a single gulp, which pleased the manager, who swiftly ordered more.

'Professor, we have a problem,' said the manager calmly. 'I must request the papers from archives. This will take time. I will need you to fill in, please, this form?' He rose and went to a filing cabinet, where he spent several minutes flicking through until he found the required piece of paper. He sighed, sitting down again wearily, as though this was sapping all his energy. 'In these times, with our austerity measures, it is hard asking people for extra work because we do not pay them. How long are you here in Athens?'

'We leave tomorrow for Crete.'

His thick black eyebrows rose and met in the middle. 'This paperwork may take months to obtain.' He shrugged and stretched his lean torso over the back of his timber chair like a balancing act. Being used to Greek bureaucracy, I was frustrated but not surprised. I burrowed through my handbag and made a show of pulling out my wallet. He watched with patient interest. I took out a wad of euros and placed them on his desk. He smiled, full lips moist with delight as he held out both hands, palms towards me in a gesture of pushing away. He shook his head and made clicking sounds with his tongue.

'I'll see what I can do,' he said finally. The money sat on the desk between us, untouched. 'Come this afternoon at two p.m. sharp.'

I bit back a smile at his sudden punctuality.

'Thank you, sir,' I said formally in Greek as I stood, leaving the cash on the desk. 'You are a good man.'

'My wife doesn't think so,' he replied with a grin as he showed me to the door.

Stephen was sitting, waiting, at the taverna beneath the plane tree. 'Where's your shopping?' he asked, surprised.

'I couldn't find anything that fitted. Never mind.' I sat down and hungrily attacked the Greek salad that was set in front of me, biting into the juicy fetta cheese and savouring the sweet tomatoes.

'It would appear that I've been far more successful, my dear.' With a flourish, Stephen produced a tiny velvet box that he flipped open and passed across. A gold ring gleamed out furnished with a large ruby flanked by two sapphires.

'It's the most beautiful creation,' I lied, except for the creation part. The gems were fake – the ruby was heat-treated and infused with glass that hung in suspended globules as I turned the ring this way and that in the light. The 'sapphires' were just bits of blue glass.

'I fell in love with the sapphires,' Stephen said. 'They're the colour of the Greek sky.'

His attachment to the ring was so genuine, the antithesis of the cynicism the shopkeeper had peddled.

'Aren't you going to put it on?' Stephen leaned forward.

With pomp, I slipped it on the middle finger of my right hand.

'That looks great. It really suits, doesn't it?' His face blazed with pride.

'This makes up for that small diamond wedding ring,' I joked. 'I can finally say I'm happily married.' Leaning across our food, I kissed him full on the lips. 'Thank you.'

I held his face between my hands, trying to avoid looking at the fake gemstones, gazing into his shining eyes instead.

'It was worth every cent,' he said and I was appalled. How much had he paid? I would have to wear it everywhere and I dreaded what my colleagues would say; most would spot instantly the vileness of the ring's charade.

But this piece of jewellery implied something far more complex, revealing as it did Stephen's love – as well as one of the reasons Greece was in a mess.

'Shall we go back to the hotel?' Stephen asked meaningfully and I glanced at my watch. 'We've got all day!' he laughed.

My mind fluttered. It was the first time he'd suggested such intimacy since the night of the comet. That seemed like years ago and I desperately wanted to race straight back to our room and tumble into bed with him.

'I ran into a friend this morning and promised I'd have a coffee at two o'clock.'

Stephen didn't hide his disappointment. 'Can't you change it?'

'I would if I had her number. You could come if you like?' I held my breath.

'No, it's all right. Come home quickly afterwards, though?'

'You bet.' I meant it.

For the third time I entered the first glass door and waited impatiently for the second door to buzz open. Anticipation was making me perspire and my lunch was sitting uneasily in my stomach.

The assistant greeted me cheerfully and announced the manager was waiting. I followed her to the same cramped room and tried not to choke in the smoke that reeked by this time of day. The manager stood, his demeanour stiff and unwelcoming.

'Sit down,' he said. There was no offer of coffee and the assistant, surprised, took her leave with a hesitant smile.

'So, these are popular accounts?' His voice was heavy with cynicism.

'Pardon me?'

'Another person has come today after you, wanting to know all sorts of things about these accounts.'

'But how can they? My business is confidential, surely?'

'Perhaps,' he shrugged, 'depending who that person is.'

'What do you mean?' Fear made my voice rise and I tried in vain to keep calm.

'A person of some authority might have a claim to see the accounts,' he replied archly. 'Someone official.'

'I don't see why. I've done nothing wrong.'

He shrugged again, a sly smile lifting the corners of his lips. 'My duty is to the bank and the bank's duty is to our customers and to the law.'

He watched me with the stillness of a cat waiting for its prey to move.

'Are you trying to accuse me of something?' I asked forcefully.

'No,' he replied. 'But if you have done something wrong, then you would know this in your heart. It is not for me to judge; that I will leave to others. However, I cannot help you carry out something that might be unlawful.'

'I'm the signatory and I want to see how those accounts were set up.'

'Professor, I cannot help.' He stood abruptly and almost shooed me to the door, like a man herding geese.

My heart was racing and my legs were moving as if I were walking in quicksand.

'Did you get the paperwork I requested?' I turned and looked him in the eye. *That I paid you for handsomely*, I felt like saying but didn't.

'That is not something I can discuss.'

'Why?' I asked.

'Regulations,' he shot back.

'Then I'll be making a complaint higher up.' I prayed this might make him re-think his strategy.

'Do so,' he replied, too calmly.

'And I wonder what they'll think about your taking a bribe,' I said in Greek.

He laughed loudly. 'I have no idea what you're talking about. Good day, Professor.'

He shook my hand roughly and pushed me out into the main area of the bank, where the assistant was watching with alarm.

'She knows her way out,' he spat. 'Come, I need you.'

Casting an apologetic glance my way, the assistant disappeared into the smoky den and the manager shut the door with a bang.

I walked through the bank avoiding the gaze of the tellers, who had picked up the tension. Between the main doors I had a sudden wave of panic as I waited for the second one to open. Perhaps they might not let me out, trap me there like an insect behind glass until the police arrived to arrest me for fraud.

After what seemed an eternity the green light above the door lit up and I was free to stumble out onto the street. For a moment I was caught up amid a Japanese tourist group thronging the footpath and as I was swept along I had the uneasy sense that I was being watched. Was it the person who had come after me asking about the accounts? Were they police?

I turned but could only see Japanese tourists on either side, hemming me in. By the time I managed to extricate myself the narrow street was empty.

The entire way back to the hotel I couldn't shake the sensation that someone was following. But no matter where I looked,

I saw nothing out of the ordinary. The walkway was frequented by Orthodox priests in ornate purple and golden robes. I felt I'd slipped back centuries, but certainly none of these learned men walking purposefully could be my stalker.

I breathed more freely as I reached the expansive marble foyer of the hotel and took the lift, but then I considered that something sinister might already be waiting in the hotel room. I had given the bank manager the details of where I was staying.

I slotted the keycard in the lock, trying to decide what I might do if police were inside.

'What's wrong? You look like you've seen a ghost,' Stephen greeted me warmly, wearing only a white towelling robe with the crest of the hotel emblazoned on it.

I glanced back over my shoulder into the long passage and saw the fire-exit door swinging shut behind an unseen person. I wanted to run in pursuit but Stephen was already reaching his arms around me, drawing me into the warmth and attention of his body.

I accepted Stephen's amorous advances but couldn't stop worrying. Was I under investigation in Athens? It was the only plausible explanation for what had happened at the bank today. Would the university have enlisted the help of the Greek police? It seemed far-fetched for the sort of money I'd seen in the accounts. Was it worse? How deep did the fraud go?

I'd never faked arousal before with Stephen, in twenty-five years of marriage, but now I found myself being drawn deeper, inextricably, into a tissue of lies.

14

My ring's fake gemstones sparkled merrily as they caught the light beaming through the windows of the clean, modern plane to Crete. Stephen was wearing loose shorts and a T-shirt, thoroughly in holiday mode. After yesterday, his toned leg touching mine didn't go unnoticed. He was incredibly sexy, virile and generous.

Why couldn't I tell him my problem? Now we were physically close again, the mistrust I'd felt at home was fading. I started to plan how I'd break the news of the alleged serious misconduct charge, suddenly eager for his help.

The deep blue Aegean stretched seductively around a spattering of fabled islands that glided beneath us. I was in my own Odyssey. Who had been at the bank?

'Already?' Stephen's face clouded with surprise as the seatbelt sign lit up and the announcement to prepare for arrival rang through the cabin. 'We've only just taken off.' He quickly folded his newspaper and stowed it away. I was preoccupied with what lay ahead – I was about to meet up with friends, and needed to ask a favour of one in particular.

Our hotel in Heraklion was a small boutique overlooking the port and old fortress, whose pale stone edifice dominated the view with its cannon parapets and vast bulk built centuries ago by the Venetians to protect the city. Katina, a slim, charismatic girl in her early twenties, dark eyes radiant beneath fair hair, led us to our room.

'You're new here?' I asked.

'Mmm. I came back to Crete about three months ago. No work in Athens anymore. I'm a trained school teacher and now I must do this.' She sighed and gazed at Stephen.

'These things are cyclical,' he said. 'I'm sure one day you'll get to teach. What subjects do you take?'

'Maths and science.'

'Come to Australia, there's always a shortage in those areas,' said Stephen and Katina visibly melted under his charm. She unlocked a door and we entered a small, cramped room, not like my usual one. I walked to the French doors and opened up the view for Stephen, but the blast of traffic noise was so fierce I had to quickly shut them again. Katina noticed our disappointment.

'Perhaps I show you another room?' she said brightly to Stephen and led us through passageways that smelled deliciously of sea air. We made our way to the uppermost tip of the hotel and Katina swung open a door. On entering, it was like we were in the prow of a ship, looking out across the fortress and harbour and beyond to the deep blue Sea of Crete. A breakwater snaked out from the fortress, disappearing in a vanishing line. On the tiny balcony we could see for miles and the only sound was the hushed murmur of the wind.

I turned, delighted, and Stephen was already grinning at Katina.

'I'll leave you to freshen up,' she said flirtatiously to him, ignoring my presence entirely.

'This is great. Thanks.' He passed her a fistful of euros, which she acknowledged with a demure dip of her head, brown eyes flashing up and gazing directly into his.

I was glad when the door shut behind her.

Stephen chuckled. 'Youth.'

I wanted to call her something else but refrained. 'Hungry?' I asked. 'There's a delicious taverna just down the road.'

Half an hour later the saganaki prawns sizzled on our plates, covered with cheese and tomato.

'Wash it down with this.' I poured yellow gold into Stephen's glass. 'From Santorini. You'll never taste another wine like it. Nectar of the gods.'

We drank and ate as if we hadn't seen food for years and at the end of the meal we could barely move.

'I need a sleep,' announced Stephen, yawning lazily and looking out upon the brightly coloured boats anchored in the harbour.

I glanced at my watch. 'Better go.' Pecking Stephen's cheek I left him with the remnants of the wine.

I caught the bus, crowded with eager tourists, to the palace of Knossos. As the motley cafe and souvenir shops came into view, Burton Bennett, sea-blue eyes wide with anticipation, blond hair neatly cut, was waiting in the shade of a tree. His twisted legs in his wheelchair sent a pang of sadness whipping through me. Burton had always been the most athletic of us at university, the keenest and strongest member of the digs we visited as students, and true to form he hadn't let the accident diminish his passion; he was the only one of our crowd who still spent his time on location year round. An eminent scholar, he had not wasted his enormous talent like so many. He published and excavated with a force that left the rest of us far back, muddling around in the world of academia and domesticity.

I had often wondered if I'd stayed that day on the island of Lefnakos and been trapped with Burton in the collapse whether I would have had his capacity to survive, to keep alight the dream of discovery when my career had just robbed me of my mobility. I doubted I'd have been as brave.

'My dear, it's really you!' he exclaimed as he wheeled towards me. We kissed and hugged, and then he hugged some more.

'You'll crick my neck,' I laughed, managing to extricate myself.

'Sorry. We don't get a lot of good-looking girls around here.'

'I doubt that,' I snorted, wanting to send him straight down to our hotel to distract Katina.

Burton's electric wheelchair zoomed in the opposite direction to the way I turned.

'There's a new dig behind the palace,' he called. 'Come and see.'

My body sprang alive as the pegged-out pit came into view, a roped-off area full of dirt rich with possibilities from millennia ago. 'What have you found?' I asked like a kid in a lolly shop.

'Only a bit of old gold,' Burton replied mischievously. 'A cup and a ring.' I followed him excitedly into a tent, where photographs of the finds were neatly arranged on a table. Hammered into the side of the gold cup was a leaping bull, its muscles straining as it tore through a veil of netting, breaking free.

'Minoan,' I whispered. 'Much more intricate than the Vapheio Cups.'

'And the Vapheios were found on the mainland,' said Burton. 'Not here on Crete.'

I found it hard to speak. 'Where are . . . have they gone to Athens?'

Burton wheeled next to me. 'I knew you were coming, didn't I?' He leaned so close I could feel his warm breath on my neck. 'Later,' he said happily.

I picked up a photo of the ring, my hands trembling with anticipation. It was a signet ring, used to imprint a mark of its owner into wax. It depicted in even finer detail two leaping bulls with ladies in flowing robes dancing around them in perhaps a fertility ritual.

'Can we go back to your place for tea?' I said, more as an order than a question.

'In due course. But I want you to clamber through the palace first because a dear friend awaits.'

I had to walk fast to keep up, my head spinning from the beauty and richness of the site's finds.

'The chair's new,' Burton said. 'I buzz around in it ten times faster than I used to. Which is necessary. We've had massive scale-backs here in the past few months. The Brits have sent two-thirds of their lot home, and the Yanks are almost invisible they've been cut so badly. Sometimes I fear I'll be the only one left standing. Well, so to speak.' He grinned.

'Things are bad at Coastal too.'

'How's that Dean of yours? Priscilla?'

'That's one of the things I want to talk to you about.'

The sun was bleaching the landscape in clear white light laced with tones of honey. It was piercingly hot and wonderfully familiar.

'The sun has teeth,' Burton quipped in Greek.

'I enjoy being eaten,' I replied in Greek. 'It's so good being back.' I reverted to English. 'I miss Crete, I wish all this wasn't halfway across the planet.' I breathed in deeply. 'I love that chalky smell, and the silence that seems to seep out of the rocks. And I can't believe what you've found.' I tapped Burton's strong arm.

'My team can't either. We're very lucky,' said Burton as we went through the upper floor of the palace that archaeologist Arthur Evans had excavated in 1900. He'd named it 'Minoan' after the mythical King Minos, imagining that beneath was the labyrinth home of the Minotaur, half-man, half-beast, a hungry devourer of virgins.

We moved through a small stone room in which a reproduction of a famous fresco, a leaping bull with a man jumping over its back, was not dissimilar to the ring I'd just seen. Tourists crowded around but the original had been taken long ago to Athens for safekeeping. I peered through to the mural, looking at it afresh today.

'Similar but different,' I noted. 'The bulls on the ring have much more detail.'

'Earlier?'

'Definitely.'

Burton grinned, basking in his find, and whirred down a ramp.

'Do you think Stephen could have an affair with Priscilla?' I asked.

Burton snapped to a stop. 'Has he?'

'I don't know. You haven't heard any gossip?'

'No. Troy and Richard know Priscilla well. They've not said anything. And I Skype them regularly.'

'Could you ask them next time? Don't say it comes from me, I've spoken to virtually no one about this.'

'I'll try tonight before dinner if you like?'

I paused.

'Are you sure you want me to ask them?' said Burton, concerned.

'I'm impossible, aren't I? I promised myself I'd get away from everything on this trip but as soon as I see you it comes out. Perhaps I don't want to know. Well, not now.'

'Why didn't you ask me before? When you were home.'

'I didn't want to upset you. I know how you worry.'

Burton took my hand and I noticed how baby soft his skin still was, unlike mine, which was showing its age.

'Thank you,' he said. 'I would have been beside myself

thinking of that hairy bastard hurting you. You know I've never trusted Stephen.'

'Why is that?'

Burton studied me like something he'd just found in a dig. 'You've never asked me that in all these years. You've only ever defended him.'

'Well, perhaps I'm ready to listen.'

'You know I'm blunt.'

'Fully aware – and I'll probably disagree with everything you say.'

The light seared our eyes as Burton headed under a fir tree, where he wheeled to face me. I sat down in the baked dirt, looking up at him like an acolyte to Plato, surprised I had let it get to this.

'I've always thought Stephen would make a good spy,' said Burton. 'He's the type MI5 would have recruited at Oxford in the thirties. You never see all there is with him.'

I swallowed my instinctive reaction to rebut Burton. 'He retrenched staff recently,' I said, and my voice trailed off – I didn't want to speak ill of Stephen, even if I was encouraging Burton to do so.

'Really? And I bet he only told you after the event?'

I didn't reply, which he knew meant yes.

'I can imagine him having an affair with Priscilla because they're quite alike.'

'Oh, please don't say that.'

Burton shrugged. 'They're wolves. Opportunistic and hungry. I know this is harsh but I suspect Stephen would get a kick out of sleeping with your immediate superior. A sort of warped power play. Do you still have sex?'

Burton's eyes were shining like an animal's. He had taken on a rat-like quality, but I let him continue.

'You don't have to answer that but I would surmise no or not very often. "Damned whores and gods' police" as Anne Summers once said. The virgin and the call girl. I've known Stephen longer than you and as teenagers he played that out over and over. He'd two-time the prettiest girls: one would be a slut and the other Mother Teresa.'

My mouth was drying up. Burton wouldn't stop without me telling him to. He might have known Stephen longer, but surely I knew my husband far better?

'What's always annoyed me is that Stephen pretends to be so moral and everyone thinks he's the Great Man. When he talks the rest of us shut up, as though we mere mortals could never come close to his wisdom. It's complete bunkum. If I looked like him and came from his privileged background, I guess colleagues would treat me like that too. Instead, I churn out books and research and never come close to receiving his accolades.'

'That's not true.' I finally found my voice. 'And you went to the same school, so you both came from privilege. Stephen's parents weren't wealthy. They devoted their lives to medical research but they earned next to nothing. I think that's why Stephen became an economist.'

'Anyway, as I was saying,' interrupted Burton testily. 'To answer your question, there's a lot more to Stephen than you've ever realised. And none of it pleasant.' Burton sat back, almost licking his lips. 'I've been wanting to say that for years. Sorry. I don't know how to sugar-coat things anymore. I spend too much time alone.'

'I asked.' I sat rubbing my fingers in the dust, unable to move.

'I think you're ready for a bit of truth, Pollyanna.'

'Burton, I've been accused of fraud.'

We sat for an hour talking through everything that had happened and, in the end, a very startled Burton promised he'd use all his extensive contacts to find a way to get an introduction to the Athenian bank manager or failing that, the young assistant or another member of staff. He would make it his mission to discover who had set up the Athens 2 and 3 accounts and who had followed me to the bank.

'Here you are! I've been looking everywhere!'

I almost jumped out of my skin but was delighted to see Maria Kelikarkis, who was the size of a doll and well into her eighties. The tour-guide identification dangling from her neck was an ingénue shot of a bee-hived young lady from over half a century ago. Today Maria was dressed in a beautifully cut fire-engine-red suit finished off with a flamboyant blue scarf. Although she was decades older than her photo, her eyes still held the vibrancy of youth and her hair, dyed a rich black, was cut in a contemporary style. She made all her clothes herself and lived off the tips from tourists, but to the outside world Maria bore the appearance of a wealthy woman – and one who was heart-warmingly vain.

'Burton told me you were coming. I couldn't wait to catch up!' she cried.

I leaped from the ground and she stood on tiptoe, kissing both my cheeks as I leaned down to embrace her.

'Maria, I've missed you!'

'She's missed everything about Crete,' Burton said drily, annoyed by the interruption even though he'd arranged it.

'I had a dream about you the other night. Is everything all right?' Maria asked.

'Sort of,' I said.

'No, it's not,' said Burton. 'It's not all right at all.'

Maria had been our den-mother on the digs long ago when she'd been the Greek liaison. I burst into tears as I absorbed the pervasive warmth of her tiny hand tucked into mine. She sat down and proceeded to wrap me firmly under her wing.

'In my dream you were in the labyrinth,' she gave a little squeeze.

'Theseus or the Minotaur?' asked Burton.

'No, she was following Ariadne's woollen ball but she wasn't Theseus. He was behind you.' She turned to me. 'You were in between the ball and the man. The follower and the followed.' Her eyes pierced mine. 'The investigator and the investigated. That was what I felt as I woke. Are you in trouble, Rebecca? I tried to telephone you and you can imagine my surprise when Burton told me the next day that you were travelling here. Maybe I've spent my life reading too many Greek myths but I have the strangest sense that you need help. My dear, what is it?'

The shock of her insight halted my tears. Drawing a deep breath I stared at the tiny woman, so perfectly groomed she looked like an exquisite museum exhibit.

'Promise you're sworn to secrecy? Only you and Burton can be in on this.'

'Of course,' she said matter-of-factly, switching to Greek

as a group of American girls sauntered past. 'They call me the vault.'

Burton cut in, outlining the whole situation, punctuated by gasps from Maria, who clapped her bird-like hand to her mouth on several occasions, eyes widening to heavily made-up full moons.

'I have a cousin who works in that bank. Sofia,' she said when the story had been told. 'We've always been close. With your permission, I'll speak to her?'

'That would be wonderful,' Burton and I replied together, and Maria laughed gaily.

'You must take this seriously,' said Burton.

'Sorry. I've always loved espionage.' Maria's eyes twinkled.

'When can you contact her?' I asked.

Maria checked her watch. 'She'll be home cooking dinner by about seven and it's best to reach her on a full stomach. She's from the large side of the family and is an angry bear when hungry but a lamb once full.'

'Would I have seen her at the bank?'

'Did you notice a giantess with a mane of black hair?'

I shook my head. 'I'd certainly remember that. How old is she?'

'Much younger than me. Young enough to be my niece.'

'I'd like to meet her,' said Burton.

'Well, you might,' replied Maria. 'I'll play it by ear. Sometimes it's better to do these things face to face.'

'I'm happy to pay your airfare,' I said. 'In fact, I'd insist.'

'Then that's settled. I've been wanting a trip to Athens,' said Maria. 'I can stay with Sofia. That way if she's evasive I can pin her down. Burton, have you any business to do in Athens? It might be useful having you there.'

'I'll pay for you too, Burton, of course,' I said.

'That won't be necessary,' he replied. 'I need to get that gold to the museum. God knows I've run out of excuses for keeping it here. They're starting to pressure me.' He paused dramatically. 'So, anyone for a viewing?'

'He told me I'd have to wait till you came,' crowed Maria. 'Let's go!'

As we headed through the long shadows cast by the palace ruins I was grateful to Maria for turning my misfortune into an adventure. For a moment it helped give the nightmare a fresh perspective.

'There must be a solution,' she announced. 'Together we'll get to the truth.'

Burton passed us white cotton gloves and donned a pair himself. He punched in the combination to the safe and with all the care in the world lifted out a tray on which sat the treasures. He passed me the cup, about the size of my palm, its gold gleaming with a rich warmth, a lustre formed by centuries. I turned it carefully, holding my breath. The flexed muscles of the bull were so realistic it seemed incomprehensible they were formed by the precision of hammer blows.

'Around 1900 BC,' I whispered in awe. 'Much older than the Vapheio Cups.'

'The work of a genius,' Burton replied and Maria turned white.

'I don't think I dare hold it,' she said as I went to pass her the glittering cup. I was happy to keep it in my hands, greedy to absorb every detail that pushed out in high relief in the pure gold.

After what seemed like a brief time but Burton pointed out was almost half an hour, I handed back the cup and was given the signet ring. This, too, was the work of a craftsman at his absolute peak. The two leaping bulls were captured so finely in a golden bezel it seemed they would burst from the ring and into the very air surrounding us. The finery of the ladies dancing with the bulls was beyond anything I had ever seen. The photographs had not revealed the way the gold was almost embroidered, its detail was so intricate. A master goldsmith had captured a world from millennia ago that was alive even now. Maria took the ring with trembling hands and gazed upon it with so much love it seemed as if her heart was breaking.

Two hours passed in Burton's room, where we stood in an oasis of calm amid the clutter of his existence. We had been transported deep into the Minoan world and it tore us to wrench back to the present.

As Burton returned the golden treasures to the safe, reality was suddenly mundane. Burton and Maria promised to make their phone calls on my behalf, and we agreed to regroup at eight-thirty for dinner, where we would meet other friends in what promised to be a rowdy night. Stephen would be there too, so we would have to find a chance to slip away to discuss any possible leads that were uncovered.

15

Travellers talked too loudly and bumped hard against me as the bus descended into Heraklion. Dust and sweat were nauseating as Burton's assessment of Stephen rang in my ears. Granted, Burton had a jealous streak, but he was astute and passionately believed what he'd said. I was angry with myself for raising it, when Stephen and I were getting on so well. And now I couldn't ignore it. Why couldn't I just take Stephen at face value and be happy?

The bus cleared out at the main square and I took a seat as we chugged down the hill to the harbour. Alighting, the air was salty and vibrant; a sea breeze rocked the boats moored along the wall. I climbed the steps to the hotel and ordered a fresh orange juice, procrastinating before going to the room.

As I sat on mounds of Turkish pillows, I gazed down to the Venetian fortress. People on its flat roof looked like ants but one ant in particular was familiar. I peered closely – it was definitely Stephen's walk. He must have changed his clothes, to dark trousers and a white shirt. But what perplexed me was his companion: a blonde-haired woman with a neat figure. My heart froze. She could have been Priscilla, but for a lighter, more carefree movement.

I rushed out of the hotel, passing a curious Katina who had just come back on duty. Darting through traffic, I made my way to the entrance of the fortress, its massive wooden doors half-shut.

'Sorry, we're closed.' A girl was in the process of locking up, switching out lights in the gloomy, yawning space that was the main area of the ground floor.

'Would you mind if I find my husband? I just saw him up on the roof.'

'But he's probably left by now,' replied the girl, glancing at her watch.

'Promise I'll be quick.' I raced past, chancing she was too young to challenge me.

'Please hurry!' she called, making no attempt to follow.

It was cold and damp inside, distinctly creepy. I glanced into the rooms off the hall; the walls were so thick you could scream until you died without a soul hearing. Ancient iron weaponry lay about as decoration, torturous chains and cannons. I rushed on, not wanting to be locked in but feeling certain I would have seen Stephen come out with all the other tourists as I was making my way down. I'd had a clear view except when I was avoiding traffic.

I arrived at the grand staircase that led upwards and stopped in shock. Sitting to one side of the stairs was a pair of blue and white sandals, neatly laid side by side, awaiting the return of their owner. They were like the sandals that Priscilla wore – their image had been burned into my brain as I stared at them during our mediation sessions: the unusual cornflower-blue, the fine leather. And these were identical, except for one strap hanging loose and a thin layer of dust. I blinked, not trusting my eyes. Could it be that Priscilla was upstairs with Stephen?

Or coming down. Noisy footsteps started tramping towards me from high above. I crept to hide in the shadows of the staircase, and soon a little boy came tripping along, followed by his mother, father and older sister.

'How come they can stay and we can't?' he whined in an English accent.

'They're coming too. The man told them,' replied the mother patiently.

'It's not fair!' the boy screeched.

'I want to go back!' cried his sister, bursting into tears.

The mother picked up the blue and white sandals and slipped them onto her bare feet. I wanted to hug her. She was dark-haired and stocky, nothing like Priscilla. The only thing they had in common was their footwear.

After the family left I ran up the stairs as fast as I could, my ribs twingeing, slowing me down. By the time I reached the top, far above, and pushed out on to the roof, I was so short of breath I could barely keep going. There was no one in sight. The sea was choppy and tiny white horses pranced across the caps of the dark waves. The cannon parapets stood ominous in the light. A cloud passed in front of the sun and the area was plunged into cold shadow.

'Excuse me.' I jumped in fright as an elderly man creaked towards me. 'You can't be up here. You must leave.'

'I'm looking for my husband and a woman he was with. He's tall and dark with a beard, she's slim and blonde. Did you see them?'

The man shook his head. 'You must go. Now.'

From past visits I knew that there were enclosed spaces that led to smaller stairwells. I wanted to look in them, determined to catch Stephen.

The elderly man followed my gaze and flapped his hands at me. 'You must leave, please.'

I had no choice but to retreat the way I had come. He followed one step behind until I was back at the main entrance, where the girl was now dressed in leathers and motorbike helmet.

'I have to meet Alexandros!' she moaned to my companion. 'You know what he's like when I'm late.'

'I'll close up,' he said kindly. 'But take this one with you.' He gripped my elbow and flung me at the girl, then closed the heavy fortress doors behind us, locking me firmly out.

I made my way to the hotel, perplexed. Perhaps there would be a perfectly plausible explanation as to who the woman with Stephen was.

I opened the door to our room and was stunned to see Stephen sitting on the balcony wearing the same clothes I'd left him in, the T-shirt and shorts in which he'd flown over.

'What were you doing at the fort?' he asked. 'All the people had left and then I saw you up there.'

'I was looking for you. I saw you when I was having a drink downstairs.'

A strange expression crossed his face as he replied calmly, 'But I haven't left the room.'

I thought of what Burton had said, about MI5 spies and how easily Stephen would fit. I felt sick to be thinking this way about the man I'd been married to for decades.

'You didn't go out at all?' I asked.

'No. I had a good sleep and then read the paper.'

'I thought you'd already read the paper?'

'Not all of it,' he said, confused.

'Where is it?' I looked around but there was no sign. I thought he'd left this morning's newspaper on the plane.

'In the bin. I didn't think you wanted it.'

The bin was empty.

'They did a turn-down service and tidied up. What's wrong, Bec? You're being weird. How was your day – did something go wrong?'

'No, it was fine. We need to get ready for dinner,' I replied.

Burton's words haunted me again. Could there really be a part of Stephen I didn't know at all? Had my eyes deceived me today or had Priscilla been up on the fortress roof with him? What if she wasn't in Paris but had detoured here to surprise Stephen? My stomach churned as I changed into my cherry-blossom dress for the evening.

The long table in the courtyard overhung with vines was full of colleagues from around the world: our mini United Nations.

Although I had sat Stephen as far away as possible from Burton, they had managed to end up together in the middle of the table, such was the loudness and disarray caused by so many vocal people catching up.

As I heard how hard things were in the harsh economic climate I began to think of Coastal as a haven amid global doom. My head swam from horror stories of redundancies. One English university was closing its entire Classics department and no one had jobs to move on to. Stephen caught my eye more than once during these discussions.

'Maybe now you can see that the action I took was minor and necessary. Think how much worse things could have been,' he said in a soft voice as soon as there was a gap he could squeeze into.

'You're right, as always,' I replied morosely. 'But I don't think it's appropriate to point score when we're hearing these awful things, do you?'

Stephen refilled our glasses then set the bottle neatly back on the paper tablecloth emblazoned with a map of Crete.

'You need to learn from this, Bec,' he said with intensity. 'Things are changing fast. If you don't adapt you'll end up in real trouble.'

'Listen to him,' Burton cut in loudly, drunk. 'World's bloody expert on everything, Professor Stephen Wilding.'

'Shut up, Burton,' Stephen muttered. 'Don't ruin a good night.'

'Cut other people's jobs but keep your own,' continued Burton. 'Did you get a bonus for that, Wilding?'

Stephen called for the waitress. 'Could we have coffee here, please?' He reached over and removed Burton's wine glass, placing it on the other side of the table, out of his reach. 'You've never been able to handle your grog, Burton.'

'You have no fucking right to tell me what to do! At least you can't sack me!' Burton flailed his arms wildly, sending wine splashing a red gash over Stephen's shirt.

Stephen leaped up, furious. 'You idiot!'

I tried to wipe the stain with the tablecloth but Stephen brushed me aside. 'I'm going to have to change,' he said brusquely.

'Shall I come with you?' I asked.

'No. And I'm not sure I'll be back.'

'That's okay,' I said softly, catching Maria's attention. 'Just stay at the hotel.'

'Jesus,' Stephen turned on me, eyes flashing with fury, 'I'm only here for you and now you're sending me home?'

'You said you weren't coming back!' Burton chimed in unhelpfully.

Stephen reeled around and, for an instant, it seemed he might hit Burton.

'Yeah, go on,' baited Burton, 'slug a guy in a wheelchair, that'd be right. Dare you, Wilding. Here, let me turn my other cheek.' He did an exaggerated movement with his face, opening one side up to Stephen. 'Go on,' he pointed at his jaw, 'try to break it.'

With great effort Stephen regained his composure. Ignoring Burton, he stood and walked around the table shaking hands, making small talk and saying goodnight to everyone.

Maria approached as soon as Stephen left. 'I really like him,' she said. 'But what was that ruckus about?'

'I thought you'd have better instincts, Maria,' snapped

Burton and wheeled away. 'I'm going to make those phone calls – I couldn't reach either of them earlier.'

'I've made mine,' whispered Maria excitedly.

'Hang on.' I touched her arm and raced after Burton. 'Burton, remember not to tell them the question about Priscilla came from me.'

'No worries,' he slurred.

'Perhaps you'd better wait?' I held the back of his chair. He looked up at me. I stroked two strands of wayward hair off his forehead and he took my hand and kissed each finger.

'I miss you,' he said.

'I miss you too.' I extricated my hand. 'Shall we get another drink?' I wanted to tell him about possibly seeing Priscilla today but he was too intoxicated. Like a mother, I ordered him lemonade and he drank it obediently while we listened to Maria's story.

'Sofia hates her boss. She's worked with eight different bank managers over the years, each worse than the last.' Maria glanced around, making sure no one but us could hear. 'This one's a common crook. He's always taking bribes, which isn't unusual in itself but the size of them evidently is. Staff are forced to do things they feel very uncomfortable about. Of course they get no extra.' Maria rubbed her fingers together. 'Only him, which is why he's loathed.'

'So, it's more than possible someone bribed him to set up the accounts in my name?'

Maria nodded firmly and Burton nodded exaggeratedly, too drunk to notice what he was doing.

'Sofia remembers you and the way he slammed the door on your heels,' said Maria with gleaming eyes.

'I'm surprised I didn't notice her. I must be growing unobservant if I missed a giantess.'

'She was sitting down behind the counter and wasn't serving. Having a cigarette and keeping out of sight of customers. Sofia remembers you well, she was curious what your business was.' Maria held up a finger momentously. 'Now, here's the thing. Sofia didn't go out – she'd brought her lunch with her – and she doesn't recall the bank manager seeing anyone but you all day. So, if someone really did ask about that account, they must have phoned, which Sofia considers unlikely as the manager rarely bothers to take calls. And he told you someone came in, didn't he?'

'Yes, but why would he make it up? He could have just asked me for more money. He went so cold. It doesn't make sense.'

Maria shrugged. 'Who knows, maybe he thinks you'll be back and will pay more now you've been sent away the first time?'

I nodded but wasn't convinced. 'Your cousin surely went to the bathroom sometime. Maybe she missed the person coming in?'

'And go out as well?' Maria shook her head.

'She makes a good point,' slurred Burton.

'I'll interrogate further once I see Sofia. And she's promised to get the original paperwork from when the two accounts were opened. That should shed some light for us.'

I hugged Maria's little body and she returned the embrace, surprisingly strong for such a sparrow.

Burton threw his arms around both of us and promptly fell asleep. Maria gently lifted his head and settled him in his chair. She took off her coat and wrapped it over his knees.

'If I were twenty years younger,' she sighed. 'He needs some-one to look after him. Perhaps if you ever leave your husband?' A full twinkling grin caught her lips. 'But I have to say again I like Stephen. I didn't get the feeling he was a two-timer, Rebecca. He felt solid. And apart from a clear rivalry with Burton, he behaved impeccably. Perhaps he's not having an affair at all? We can all let our imaginations run away.'

I pondered Maria's words through a restless night as Stephen lay beside me snoring gently. Could I be inventing his infidelity? Being accused of something I hadn't done could be making me paranoid. But my worries about him had started before the fraud had surfaced. Could Burton be right – was I the nun to Priscilla's high-class whore? Was that how Stephen viewed me: dutiful and sexless? Despair seeped in a sigh from my lungs, emptying me; the air in the room was suddenly stifling. I'd always thought Stephen found me attractive – he'd said it so often I believed him, or wanted to. Although others said I had a good figure and a pretty face, I never could see it myself, and now I realised maybe Stephen thought like I did. Perhaps for him, the intimacy I found so deeply reassuring was just his putting up with the fumbling rhythms of the plain and boring? If he was with Priscilla or another woman, was the sex extreme? What would they be doing? Stabbing pains shot through my gut.

But Burton always had been melodramatic.

I turned and watched Stephen's chest moving up and down, his pyjama top unbuttoned in the heat revealing his strong tanned chest with a few wisps of dark hair. I laid my hand lightly on him and could feel his heart beating in soft, rhythmic throbs.

I stayed like that for a long time until, in the scorching salty air, I finally fell asleep.

Burton, clean and neat and remarkably clear-eyed, welcomed us at the airport after we checked in.

'Come to apologise?' Stephen asked gruffly.

'Whatever,' said Burton, grinning.

Stephen bit back a reply and headed off. 'Getting a paper.'

'Thank God he's out of the way,' muttered Burton, 'I'd been worrying about how I'd see you on your own. I made those calls last night. Don't worry, I waited till I was sober.'

I braced myself for what was coming next.

'It's okay, Bec. Neither of them had noticed anything different about Priscilla. They certainly don't think she's having an affair with Stephen.'

I let out my breath, so relieved I felt light-headed.

'Not that they'd necessarily know,' Burton pointed out.

'I've been starting to imagine things,' I said. 'Yesterday, I could have sworn I saw Stephen with Priscilla on top of the fort.'

Burton took this in with an intensity that darkened his features. 'There *is* one thing, Bec: Priscilla is out of the country at the moment. They said in Paris doing research. But that wouldn't mean she couldn't be in Greece for a rendezvous.'

'I had the same thought. I know about Paris. Oh Burton, don't feed my paranoia.'

'Well, it's logical. But do you think Stephen would really go that far? It seems a bit desperate.'

'I shouldn't have opened my big mouth. Now your good news isn't helping,' I replied, frustrated. 'And in the end, I don't think it was him I saw up there anyway. I was a long way away.'

'And he does look quite generic. Tall bearded alpha male. I often see tourists around here who remind me of him. Speaking of which, your Greek god's returning,' warned Burton. 'I must make tracks.' He flung his arms around me and I buried my face into his soft, warm neck.

'Visit again soon?' he asked sadly.

'Why don't you come and see me? You're always welcome to stay.'

'Let me know when Adonis is away and maybe I will.'

'That's a deal,' I said and we hugged again.

'I'll keep in touch,' he whispered. 'We'll phone you as soon as we have more about the bank. We're heading off tomorrow.'

I kissed him gratefully on the cheek. Behind us, Stephen made a grunting noise. We turned but he was absorbed in the business pages of the *International New York Times*. Burton left without saying goodbye to him. Nor did Stephen look up and offer a farewell.

16

'They say it's only sleeping.'

Stephen craned his neck for a better view as the plane banked close to Mount Vesuvius. 'It's still alive.' The volcano that had sown death and destruction over the centuries was a beast in waiting, hungry for more.

The car I'd booked online wasn't ready. Flavia, wafting a heavy floral perfume, clicked and clacked behind her screen, trying to find a replacement. She tossed her mane of dark hair dramatically, flashing long fingers adorned with huge rings through it. The air of the tiny office was thick with humidity, and the roaring traffic of Naples made the space even more claustrophobic.

Stephen ambled away, tapping into his phone, while I focused on the road we were about to encounter, the winding horror above the ocean that my mother couldn't cope with, the one I now planned to conquer. I hadn't told Stephen about the significance of this leg of our trip; I didn't talk much about that time at all. The memory of my father coming home stole into my mind – blue eyes bright in his leather-brown face, calling me over as he put his bucket of gleaming snapper on the back porch, telling me the fish were running – would I like to go with him the next day? Of course I would. Then thoughts flooded in of the boiling sea and Dad disappearing with his boat.

I sat down on a sticky vinyl chair and forced myself to think of the calm blue water that our hotel room promised to look down upon.

Stephen returned in a dark mood. 'How long can this possibly take?'

'Shh, she's trying her best,' I muttered. 'What's wrong?'

'What do you mean?' he erupted defensively.

'Who did you text?'

'I'm just finalising some bond charts for my conference paper.' He wasn't making eye contact.

'Who's helping you?' I asked casually.

There was a slight but telling pause before he replied. 'Frances Yong – my new research assistant. She's on a steep learning curve.' He stalked away, absorbed in his phone, leaving me to wonder who was really receiving his messages.

'I'm so sorry this is taking so long,' said Flavia. 'Per favore?' She passed across a dog-eared brochure of a huge van.

I shook my head. 'Not on these roads. Something smaller?'

'Piccolo?' She moved her hands together.

'Si.'

'Un momento.' She disappeared behind her computer, tapping more fervently, clearly annoyed.

I turned to find Stephen but he had disappeared. Flavia swore loudly. I'd just stumbled into the Bermuda Triangle of foul moods.

After an hour had passed I was hungry and impatient. 'Surely you have something?' I snapped. 'If not just tell me and I'll go somewhere else.'

'Un momento, signora!'

I sighed and walked towards the door. Where was Stephen? Flavia misunderstood my movement as leaving, and suddenly cried out. 'Ah, bellissimo! Pronto.' She slapped a much glossier brochure on the counter and I hurried back. A shiny red sports car beamed up. A convertible. Flavia shrugged. I grinned.

'Perfetto, Flavia, grazie.'

'Prego.' She groomed her hair with red-knife fingernails and summoned the car with a phone call. 'I close now for lunch,' she announced, dropping a *Chiuso* sign onto the counter.

I wondered how, after decades of successful travel through Europe, I had managed to choose such a dysfunctional company. There had been no other customers the entire time. I prayed our hire wasn't a lemon.

Stephen met me as the gleaming beast pulled up in front of our luggage. 'About bloody time.'

A young boy alighted and indicated for Stephen to take the wheel as he walked around to the boot and stowed the bags.

'I'll drive' I said quickly.

'I think I've earned my turn. Half the day's gone,' Stephen replied, and before I could argue he slumped into the driver's seat. 'Where did you find this place?'

He pressed a button that sent the roof whooshing away and moved through gears in a throaty roar, navigating into the flow of Neapolitan chaos. Disappointed and deflated, I told myself that there would be many more opportunities to take the wheel in the week we were staying on the Amalfi coast.

Stephen started weaving through lanes, narrowly missing other cars. He accelerated with relish, snapping on the radio to unleash a girly pop song that soared into the air. I studied him as he concentrated on the road: his dark hair, tousled by the wind, was growing long; his skin had already developed a deep tan and his teeth flashed white as he floored the accelerator and we tore up the Autostrada. Behind the wheel he was as free as a bird.

'Slow down,' I cried and he chuckled, decelerating slightly.

'It's like driving a work of art,' he tossed into the wind.

At the Castellammare exit we turned off the freeway and left the bustle of Naples far behind as the vegetation grew thicker and the scent of lemons filled the air. The road narrowed and a hazy blue coastline caught us by surprise, its transcendent weightlessness floating to meet the sky. A fine mist hovered, muting colours and lending a deep serenity. All conversation ceased as we glided through unreality, sea on one side, mesmerising in subtle layers of blue, tiers of lemon groves scrambling up the hills in lush profusion on the other. As the sun beat down my olfactory senses were blown open with a riot of citrus and herbs. I inhaled deeply and felt years fall away. I put my hand on Stephen's leg and started to dream of how we would spend the coming week together.

The road narrowed further and became the treacherous stretch I remembered as a teenager, hanging in mid-air above cascading cliffs that reached hundreds of metres down to the sea below. Hairpin bends were impossibly tight and motor scooters tore along like crazed wasps in both directions, their young drivers seemingly oblivious to the threat of lost limbs and road rules. My stomach kicked with anticipation.

'My God, I hadn't realised,' said Stephen, pale with shock as he navigated the bends.

'Would you like me to take over at the next town?' I checked the map, determined not to be afraid of this road, not like my mother. 'Positano.'

'I can't pull over.' Fear made Stephen's voice rise.

'I said the next town.'

'Yeah, right, and you'd be okay with this?'

I nodded, although I was apprehensive as we came around a hairpin bend and saw a huge green monster barrelling towards us. Stephen braked to a stop as the bus blasted its horn. A stream of motor scooters shot through.

'Jesus!' Stephen shifted the car into reverse and looked behind; already a line of cars was banked up. He waved at them to reverse, and slowly we all snaked back, with the exception of another pack of youths on scooters who roared up and past, narrowly missing the bus. Panicking, Stephen went too fast and almost collided with the car behind as the giant bus rumbled forward again then suddenly stopped and reversed.

'It's doing a three-point turn, I don't believe it.' Stephen rubbed his eyes, as though making sure they were working.

A tiny wall was all that separated the road from the death-drop to the sea. The faces of terrified tourists came close as the green leviathan turned a three-point turn into a five-point.

As the bus bore down again Stephen was forced to man-oeuvre our car hard against the wall. Finally our tormentor trundled past tooting and Stephen looked up wanly and waved. Stricken passengers stared down.

'You're doing well,' I said. 'And it's so sweet you've still got your good manners, even when you're terrified.'

'How much further to the next town?' he snapped and slowly proceeded around the bend, pressing the horn as though our lives depended on it – which they probably did, as we couldn't see a thing. After narrowly avoiding two oncoming motorbikes, we were safely through.

I checked the map again. 'About fifteen minutes.'

'We can swap then.' Watching Stephen's white knuckles gripping the wheel, I suddenly felt sympathy for my mother. As a teenager I'd been furious that she'd cancelled our plans to visit Pompeii when she'd refused to drive back along this road. We'd left the hire car in Amalfi and caught a ferry straight to Naples instead. In my young misery I hadn't realised how truly terri-fying it must have been for her to navigate these blind corners with the lethal drop to the sea, especially when she'd just lost her husband, and her entire remaining family was in the car.

It seemed more like an hour by the time we glimpsed the colourful houses of Positano cascading down the hill in muted tones of pinks, greens and vanilla.

'I'm hungry,' I announced. 'Let's have ice-cream when we stop.'

'Ice-cream?' Stephen steered around another bend and turned sharp right past a blaze of purple bougainvillea towards the sea. Motor scooters roared down beside us.

'Well, gelati. Gelato.' I laughed. 'Whatever you want to call it.'

Stephen sighed, spent, and miraculously found a park. With finesse, he slipped into the tiny space, then turned and kissed me. 'I'm sorry I was short. That was horrible.'

'Well, I'll take the wheel now.'

'Are you sure you'll be all right?'

I nodded, smiling. 'Looking forward to it.' He had no idea how much.

'You're joking?'

'No.'

I swung out of the car and made a beeline for a nearby gelateria. Inside was deliciously cool and the jewel-like colours of the fresh gelato dazzled. I ordered amareno, with huge chunks of fresh cherry. Stephen had an espresso, then ordered a second.

'What I need is a stiff drink,' he muttered.

'Go ahead. You won't be driving again today.'

He pondered for all of five seconds, and we wended our way in the balmy heat down the hill into a narrow laneway full of ultra-stylish clothing stores. We found a tiny bar and moved through to its terrace. A spectacular view over the Tyrrhenian Sea to the isle of Capri, squatting invitingly in the misty aqua haze, stretched before us.

As Stephen drank beer I gazed at the famous island. 'Just think, we'll be there soon,' I mused.

'I'm going to have to do a lot more work on my paper,' said Stephen. 'Sharpen it considerably. With so much loose monetary policy continuing in America and Europe my model needs adjusting.' He frowned at Capri as though the island were to blame. 'Are you going to be okay with the ferry?' He turned and looked directly into my eyes.

'It's a little late to ask, isn't it?'

'Well, I figured as you made the bookings ... I'd been meaning to.' He leaned across and touched me tenderly. 'How's your conference keynote going, anyway?'

I sighed. 'It'll only make me nervous to talk about it.'

Stephen smiled. 'You sure?'

'I'm covering a broad topic. I hope I won't be superficial in trying to do too much.'

'I can read it, if you like.'

I was pleased that he was finally taking an interest. Before we'd left he'd asked nothing about my paper. 'I could read it to you?' I offered.

Stephen grinned. He knew I loved doing that, enjoyed every moment of having his full attention. 'Promise I'll be gentle,' he said mischievously and then paused, growing serious. 'And let's hope things pick up on all fronts from now on.'

'Hey?'

'Between us. We'd got a bit, I don't know, taking each other for granted.'

'I never took you for granted. Did I?' I asked vulnerably.

'I think you assume my life's always fine.'

'But it generally is, isn't it?'

He gazed at me intently. 'Not always.'

My mouth went dry. 'Is something wrong?'

Stephen turned and watched a ferry wash in from the sea, stopping with a thud against the pier. Tourists disembarked, ant-like, and a queue of others slowly snaked aboard.

'Stephen?' Blood pounded in my ears.

Finally he turned back and gave a slow, relaxed smile. 'It's nothing, really.'

'Are you sure?'

He downed his beer. 'Come on, let's get this over with.'

He stood and headed for the entrance. My body tingled with relief that he hadn't confessed something awful.

Back in the shiny car, I gunned the engine and purred out onto the steep road that swung at the top to meet the horror stretch. I willed myself not to look down to the sea that was again far, far below, a sheer cliff tumbling to join it in silent reverie to the force of nature that had created such brutal, beautiful terrain.

'How can this road exist?' said Stephen, gripping his seat as we reached the first of what threatened to be many more hairpin bends, alive with dodging motor scooters.

I tooted, held my breath, dropped down a gear and accelerated slowly, breathing out only when we were back on an open stretch. My eyes yearned to look across to the tiny wall and the death-dive, but I planted them firmly on the road ahead, until I heard a honking horn and, checking the rear-vision mirror, saw a car of youths behind. I was travelling not much faster than a crawl, and the tooting and hand-waving from my followers left me in no doubt they wanted me to speed up.

'Just ignore them,' said Stephen, tight-lipped.

'I'll let them pass as soon as I can pull in.'

The youths accelerated close to our bumper bar. I waved at them to move back. 'They mustn't be local,' I muttered. 'Anyone with half a brain knows not to speed along here.'

'That would exclude the scooter riders,' said Stephen.

The beeping became a crescendo, and I couldn't make eye contact with the driver because he was wearing sunglasses that were as black as pitch. He looked about sixteen. His mates started dangling through the windows, using creatively obscene gestures.

'Idiots.' Stephen rose in his seat and threw them a frustrated gesture that merely stirred them up.

'Sit down!' I hissed as they zoomed unnervingly close.

Two cars came crawling along from the other direction. After they passed, the youths pulled out and tried to accelerate around us. Stephen and I gasped as a bus and three motor scooters came through a bend and the youths ducked in again. As the next hairpin bend loomed in front of us, I was just about to go around when I heard the loud honking of an oncoming vehicle. I stopped. The youths rear-ended our car with a sickening crunch, propelling us in a kangaroo leap before we halted abruptly.

'Jesus!' Stephen jumped out like a furious lion while the youths backed up frantically and kept reversing down the road. Stephen followed for a few steps then turned to inspect the damage.

'How bad?' I called. 'Be careful!' A large campervan coming from the opposite direction missed him by inches. 'Get back in, please? Now.' It was becoming a nightmare.

The youths were already a distance away, still reversing, until another car came up behind them and they were forced to stop.

'I'll wait for them,' said Stephen.

'Get in!' My voice tightened with fear.

Stephen looked between me and the youths who were approaching as slowly as they could, the car behind them now honking, and quickly joined by another. A trail of scooters zoomed up and sailed past them all.

'I'm begging you,' I said. 'We're insured, just get their number plate.'

Finally Stephen climbed in and I moved off as quickly as was safe, tooting loudly and praying no one was coming the other way.

'It's a chicken run,' I breathed.

'Kamikaze.' Stephen pulled out his phone and took photos of the youths' car when it came around the bend. 'We'll get them when we can stop somewhere. Our back's completely stoved in.'

'That's all we need.'

'I'll demand the driver's name and licence.'

Good luck, I thought, and before I could speak another bus appeared around the upcoming bend. It stopped, roared, reversed and disappeared, then swung again, its rear hanging over the tiny wall that separated it from oblivion. I crawled to a stop and waited while it shrieked back and forth like a tangled rhinoceros. The youths behind stopped well away, and the stream of cars now behind them set up a cacophony of horns.

'Not so bold now,' Stephen said. 'I feel like sprinting back to them.'

'You're going nowhere.' I grabbed him, just as the bus roared close. In the nick of time I leaned out and pulled in my side-view mirror, whipping my hand back as the bus came so close I thought it would touch us. It had huge dents right up its side. The tourists inside looked ill with fright.

Just as I was about to take my turn in the Russian roulette around the cliff, the youths shot past. They were quiet, no obscene gestures or hanging out windows. Stephen took more photographs. I prayed the idiots wouldn't crash into an oncoming vehicle that was as yet unseen. But there was no sound other than their receding engine. I carefully followed around the blind corner and the road ahead was clear. I sighed, exhausted, but nevertheless exhilarated. I was finally conquering this extra-ordinary terrain.

'Got their plate and make of car. Let's hope that's enough.' Stephen put his phone away. 'How much longer can this be?'

And then, around the next turn, a hotel perched over the cliff at a ridiculous angle came into sight. *Della Mare*. It was ours. And it was in the middle of nowhere. There wasn't even a path at the side of the road.

Stephen followed my shocked gaze. 'Don't tell me this is it?'

I turned into the tiny space for cars by the wall. Beyond, the sun broke through and the sea twinkled a rich blue, dancing in the light.

'It's just a cliff!' said Stephen.

'Sorry. I think I stuffed up.'

Stephen shook his head. 'Well, I'm not going anywhere. I don't plan to be on this road ever again.'

'Look, there's a ceramics shop and little cafe at the top.'

Stephen, dismayed, glanced at the colourful building that had seen better days, and then gazed around. There was no way in or out except for the sliver of road. Opposite, the hill was brown and bald. No sweet groves of citrus grew there. Below us was nothing but a spine-tingling drop to the sea.

'I thought this was in Amalfi,' I groaned. 'Anyway, I don't mind driving, that's the good news. I'm quite happy to take us anywhere. I haven't felt this alive in years. Where shall we go tomorrow?' I added.

'Let's just check in and have a drink,' Stephen replied gruffly. 'And I mean it – I'm not going on that road apart from when we leave.' With difficulty he forced the smashed boot open and grabbed both bags, almost getting hit as a massive tourist bus trundled past.

'Careful!' I called, alarmed.

He wheeled the luggage into the ceramics shop, which was lined with shelves of garishly painted bowls and jugs, and garden ornaments in startling blue and yellow. 'We're looking for the hotel check-in,' he said to an unusually handsome man in his late twenties who, lithe and tanned like a panther, leaned against the marble counter sipping a fresh orange juice. His eyes were dark liquid, his slim body toned in the peak of youth.

'Let me take those. I'm Marco Romano, your host. Welcome,' he drawled in a soft accent.

Stephen introduced us and Marco took my hand, giving my fingers the lightest squeeze.

'What a lovely place,' I said, confident and buoyed from having driven the road.

'We'll go to reception,' he purred. 'I'll get these later.' We had no choice but to leave our luggage in the empty shop, vulnerably unattended. 'It will be all right,' said Marco as he guided me into a stone passageway where steps funnelled us down into the belly of the cliff. 'So, you're the hero who drove?'

'Of course.' My smile split from ear to ear.

'You must be tired?'

'Exhausted,' said Stephen. 'Do you have a bar?'

'Precisely,' replied Marco. 'But first, your room.'

My stomach rumbled and it hit me we hadn't eaten all day, except the gelato in Positano. I glanced at my watch.

'You're not too late for lunch,' said Marco, reading my thoughts. 'I can fix you something in our restaurant. There's a beautiful sea bass on the menu today. You will love it.'

His old blue jeans clung in all the right places, his fine cotton shirt the colour of the ocean billowed lightly, and when we came into the blasting sunshine of reception, situated by a terrace that looked across the sea for miles, the silhouette of his torso through the fine cloth sensually matched the mood.

'You made it!' A tall, raven-haired woman, Italian to the core but with an upper-class English accent, came shooting from behind a desk and hugged us as if we'd been friends for years. 'And your eyes are dry! You know the famous John Steinbeck wept in his wife's arms as he was driven along the Amalfi coast. You two must be bravehearts!'

'That makes me feel a lot better,' said Stephen and the woman laughed, even though he hadn't been joking. I did indeed feel like a victorious warrior.

'Thank you for bringing our delightful guests,' she said to Marco. 'Leave them with me.'

'I will see you in the restaurant,' Marco said, giving a little bow as he left.

The woman announced dramatically that she was Adriana. 'Later I will get you to fill in the registration. But for now, your passports, please?'

She held out a long, olive-skinned hand. Stephen obeyed, placing his blue booklet into her palm. I dug into my bag and retrieved mine, and she slapped both onto the desk.

'Perfetto! Now we go.'

She led us down a long corridor, leaving the passports sitting alone near a display of sightseeing brochures. Stephen and I both flinched at the passports being left in the open, but neither of us dared raise it with Adriana.

She stopped by a lift and stood aside for us to enter. 'You start your stay with us in Paradise!'

Do not use elevator if broken, a sign in the tiny space announced nonsensically. Stephen and I both stifled a smile.

'Don't let the sign frighten you. It rarely happens.' Adriana flicked her thick hair to one side and pressed a button, sending us whooshing down into the bowels of the mountain. When the doors opened, she led us along a cold, gloomy corridor and finally stopped at door 37, which she flung open dramatically without using a key. 'Pronto!'

The immaculately decorated room, ochre walls, white-tiled floor and spotless white furniture was framed by a dazzling azure sea that dashed away to meet the watery sky. As we stepped out onto a huge balcony, replete with padded lounges and a little table with two tall glasses, ice and a jug of freshly squeezed orange juice, Capri floated on the horizon, beckoning us again.

Adriana clapped her hands like an excited schoolgirl. 'Yes, that's Capri,' she said, as if seeing it for the first time. 'A millionaire's view, just for you. And now, I leave you to enjoy. Please ask for anything, anything at all, that your heart desires.'

Stephen tried to slip her a tip but she waved him away. 'We are family!' she cried, shutting the door gently behind her.

Stephen turned away from the view. 'I'm going to have to finish my paper or that island will haunt me. It's like it's hunting me down,' he chuckled, wrapping his arms about me, lowering us onto the vast expanse of the bed. His skin glowed against the pearly sheets as he kissed me softly. My fingertips burned as I ran them over his shoulders and dug in, massaging, feeling the tautness evaporate. Stephen groaned and tipped over, 'Keep going, Bec. Don't stop.' I straddled him, pummelling his flesh, fighting off my fears about him. After all, I was a road conqueror. I could feel Dad's pride. Surely, then, I could vanquish any threat to our marriage? 'Ouch, not that hard!' cried Stephen.

'Sorry.' I lightened my strokes; I'd made his skin glow red.

He rolled over, grabbed me, and flipped me onto my back, where we lay cuddling in the mellow heat until, after a brisk rap on the door, Adriana barged in with our luggage.

Marco brought the plate of sizzling fish and a huge bowl of salad to our table, perched on the cliff-face above a mighty drop to the diamond sea below. Uncorking a bottle, he poured pale-straw liquid into our glasses. 'Buon appetito.' His torso swayed sensuously as he headed back inside and we drank the wine.

Stephen cursed. 'I just remembered we have to report the car.' He rose, taking his phone from his pocket.

'But eat first, darling?'

'I don't want trouble because we waited too long.' He perched on the squat stone wall that separated us from the drop to infinity.

'Careful!' I cried. Stephen smiled but didn't move.

'What's the name of the company again?' he called.

'Speedi.' Stephen rolled his eyes and looked up the number. When the phone finally answered he spoke quickly, flapping his hand at me to start eating.

The sea bass was sweet and salty, as fresh as the ocean. I could taste the tidal currents and for a moment felt panic as I envisaged the sea floor and its treachery. I washed it down with more wine.

'Flavia says we must report it to the police.' Stephen sat down heavily, reaching for his knife and fork, slashing a huge piece off the fish and lifting it deftly onto his plate. 'Such a bore. It's going to mess up the rest of the afternoon.'

Marco appeared with a jug of sparkling water. 'Everything all right?' he asked and Stephen explained our predicament. 'Ah, you'll have to drive to Amalfi or Positano.' Marco shrugged. 'Positano is further but it's probably the best. But, please, you must do it today.'

'We can't, we've both been drinking,' Stephen said. 'The police will have to come to us.'

Marco replied softly. 'There are not many. They can't. What if someone needs them?'

'But *we* need them.' Ice crept into Stephen's voice. 'The boy hit us. We're not at fault in any way.'

'I have an idea.' Marco's eyes lit up. 'I can drive. In your car, of course, so they can see the damage.'

'Marco, you're a godsend,' I said.

'Thanks,' Stephen said, after a long pause. 'I guess you know the road pretty well?'

'Usually I go by boat. But not today.' Marco grinned, a perfect set of teeth flashing in the sunlight. He was the essence of summer. The wine had gone to my head.

'That was delicious.' I pushed my plate away. 'I'll need a walk after all that food.'

Stephen snorted. 'What, along the road?'

'You can go down to our beach,' said Marco excitedly. 'And then when you get back, I'll be ready and we can go.'

In our room we put on walking shoes. 'Honey, I can go and report it with Marco, if you like. You could stay here?'

Stephen tapped my arm gratefully. 'Thanks, but I'll cope.'

My phone bleeped. I hurried out onto the balcony and flicked up the text.

In Athens already. Sofia had the day free, so we changed our flight. Await further news! Love Burton. PS: Hope you're managing to relax in spite of all this.

I smiled as I deleted his words. For a brief moment the Amalfi coast had taken me further from my worries than I'd been since my troubles began. This area was fabled to be the home of the sirens. I could hear their sweet songs serenading as Stephen and I left the room and made our way along a tiny path that zigzagged down the cliff-face.

I pushed the alleged fraud far away as we moved among wizened olive trees, groaning in unnatural shapes from fierce storms and the rigours of age. Cicadas screeched in the heat. The breeze smelled of fresh rosemary, lemons and salt. Suddenly a high, rusty gate cut off the path. Locked, barring our way. Beyond and below, the sea was turning a deep blue, fringed with clear, bright emerald.

'Damn,' Stephen said. 'I want to see this beach.'

'I can't imagine where it will be. It all looks so rocky,' I muttered.

184

'Come on, I'll give you a leg over.' Stephen grabbed me playfully, lifting me off the ground. I was worried how my ribs would cope but I was feeling mellow from the wine and bold from conquering the road.

'When you reach the top, just drop down,' said Stephen.

The top of the gate wedged into my chest and I hung suspended like a fish on a hook, then Stephen gently pushed my legs and I toppled over onto the other side, where I lay laughing in the soft dirt, amazed my body didn't even hurt. Stephen hoisted himself up, scrabbled like a mad ant and flung down beside me. We kissed like teenagers and I caught a furtive look in his eyes.

'Is everything all right?' I asked, alarmed.

'Yes, of course. This place is magical. It's taking my mind off this looming road trip.' He stood, brushing dirt off his shirt. 'Come on.'

He pulled me up and hand-in-hand we continued down the hill, the sea bobbing in and out of view as if we were playing hide-and-seek. Birds called in the still air, their cries haunting and foreign. The heat baked into us and I imagined myself as Odysseus on an enchanted island, expecting Circe to appear at any moment to whisk me into a den of forbidden pleasure.

Hotel Della Mare was casting a spell.

We passed under a spreading plum tree laden with fruit, and a single plump orb dropped onto the path behind us with a dull thud, breaking open to reveal its bruised, purple flesh. A blackbird flew down and gorged on it.

'Can't spy the lido yet,' said Stephen craning his neck over the cliff as we came into an opening. Below, the water swirled, cool and inviting. A breeze fluttered my light cotton dress and I felt a thrill of excitement.

We scrambled down to the next section of path, which was steeper and covered in tiny pebbles. I lost my footing and one leg shot out in front. Stephen grabbed me and held me up. 'You okay? Don't hurt yourself, not down here.'

I glanced back to the steep slope and realised just how far we'd come. I tested my leg. 'It's fine. Good catch.' Pecking him on the lips, I led on.

As the ground fell away and the roar of the sea drew us onward, the temperature dropped suddenly. We rounded a bend and a flat rocky ledge came into view, gripping the side of the cliff and ending with a two-metre plunge to the water. There was no beach, no sand: only this thin wedge of stone.

'Is this it?' Stephen stood with his hands on his hips, disappointed.

'I guess so.'

A wave rolled in and exploded high into the air as it hit the rock, then sucked back down in a greedy, roiling mass.

'This isn't a beach, it's a blowhole!' Stephen gazed in disbelief. 'I'd really been looking forward to it too.'

He paced along the stark ledge, staring forlornly out to sea as another emerald wave crashed in, soaking us, before slurping into itself in a roar of froth. I leaped back in fright and slipped on the wet surface. Again, Stephen caught me.

'Please God, let there not be a third time. You might not be there, like in a fairy tale,' I joked.

'Of course I will.'

Stephen folded me in his arms and bent to kiss me. Then we both felt a presence and turned. At the far end of the rocky ledge, two sets of eyes lay staring at us: a mother and her teenage daughter, both topless. They were as surprised as two deer caught in headlights, their respective aged and nubile bodies slicked with oil, exposed and vulnerable. Neither moved, as though hoping we might not see them.

'Hello,' Stephen called, neutrally friendly.

The mother nodded, the teenager rolled over and put her head to the stone, sunbaking.

'Do you think they locked the gate?' mumbled Stephen. 'Their own private beach.'

'Come on.' I waved and turned away. 'You won't be swimming here.'

But Stephen's attention had focused on a string of white buoys about fifty metres from the blowhole, and as we walked back we noticed an old rusty ladder dropping down into the water from the ledge.

'Wow, people really do swim here!' He bent and touched the ladder. 'It's firm. Properly attached.'

A huge wave rolled in and he jumped back, but not quickly enough to avoid another drenching.

'You are *not* swimming here,' I repeated. 'Don't even think about it.'

He grinned and grabbed me, transferring salty water in a sharp blast. I squealed.

He took my hand and we moved off, laughing, to the other end of the ledge where it widened enough to allow a thatched hut and tables to be tucked against the cliff-face.

'My God, they must have functions down here!' Stephen looked around. 'Is there a lift? How would they get stuff in?'

It made an eerie sight, like a wedding with no guests. Some of the thatch had torn off the roof and flapped crazily in the breeze. Stephen clapped a damp hand to my head and I squealed again in fright.

17

From the tiny back seat of our car I watched Marco's neck, as slender as a swan's, as he steered us effortlessly to Positano. The erratic wasp-trails of the scooters and the buses with their snorting turns didn't seem so bad with Marco in control. Beside him, Stephen's body was a rigid block of nerves.

As the blazing bougainvillea at the turn-off came into view I was sad that we had reached our destination. Marco roared down and stopped beside a pink building marked POLIZIA.

A tall, thin man in a smart blue uniform, Giotto, pulled faces dramatically as he inspected the damage: the crumpled red boot and curled bumper bar looked like a giant had punched his fist into it. Giotto brought forth a small notepad, looked at Stephen's photographs and took the details of the offending youth's car along with our own. Then we went inside to an atmosphere of convivial bonhomie and sat in a neat, windowless, whitewashed room. Giotto typed up his report while two other young police-men joked with Marco and asked where we came from, insisting on making us espresso coffee, hot and sweet.

Finally Giotto handed over a copy of his report, shook Stephen's hand then my own, and told us how sorry he was that this had happened. 'Definitely not locals,' he concluded.

'That's what I thought,' I replied and he grinned, clapping me on the back. 'You could be a local,' he said and Marco agreed so enthusiastically I blushed.

'The police are lovely,' I commented as we headed off, leaving the sparkling blue water of Positano behind.

'They are good men,' replied Marco. 'I went to school with most of them. They even like their Commissario, the district boss. One big, happy family.' His eyes twinkled. 'The Amalfi coast is a very inviting place. Perhaps you will stay longer?'

By the time we sat down it was almost ten o'clock and the terrace was filled with well-dressed diners surrounded by strings of fairy lights beneath a star-filled sky. The nights here had an old-fashioned feel, like a charming ristorante from the fifties. The clientele ranged in age from early twenties through to elderly couples who were chattering animatedly in Italian.

'Clearly a favourite spot for the locals. Always a good sign,' said Stephen but the comfortable tone in his voice didn't match his face, which was lined with worry.

'Hungry?' I asked, watching him, concerned.

'Famished.'

'Then you must have the sea-a bass.' A waiter who looked like he'd walked straight out of *Night of the Living Dead* loomed above, flesh grey and eyes sunken, in a formal black suit. 'I'm Alessandro,' he said curtly, glaring down at us with disdain. 'Two sea bass and two salads? Primi has finished for the night, so we'll go straight to secondo.' He left as quickly as he'd arrived, giving us no chance to choose something different. After shouting our order through to the kitchen, Alessandro slunk back to attend to the mother and daughter we had seen sunbathing earlier. He fawned upon the young girl and we were close enough to hear her effusive replies to his questions. She had a thick Russian accent and they spoke together in English while the mother looked on, quiet and intent. Alessandro was in his late sixties, the girl no more than seventeen. My neck stiffened, as the mother seemed to be encouraging Alessandro's attention to her child, which was in no way fatherly.

'I reckon he locked the gate,' whispered Stephen wryly. 'Probably heard Marco tell us to go down.'

'I wonder why Marco has him here?'

'Bad taste?' Stephen shrugged. 'A shocking judge of character?'

'Marco's just gone to a great deal of trouble for us.' My phone bleeped and I casually pulled it out of my handbag and onto my knee where Stephen couldn't read the text: *Sofia was blocked when she tried to access the papers. She thinks something fishy is definitely going on. Has a plan for tomorrow. More then, love B.*

'Who's that?' asked Stephen.

'Just Burton with some gossip. What's for dessert? I need a sugar hit.'

Sfogliatella, the local specialty – flaky pastry filled with sweet ricotta custard – was served bitterly by Alessandro. His slate grey eyes met mine. 'Did you enjoy your sea-a bass?' he quizzed intently.

'Yes, very much.'

His expression was cunning. I couldn't fathom why he had taken such an extreme dislike to us, but suddenly I wondered with horror if he had slipped something awful into the dish. He turned and left the table, disappearing into the shadows to resume staring at the young Russian girl. He reminded me of a big black spider viewing its prey.

'Creepy,' said Stephen in a low voice. 'I hope our door locks.' But my attention was taken by Marco, who had changed into a white linen suit and now made his way from table to table chatting animatedly with our fellow diners, most of whom he knew well. An elegant woman and her husband laughed gaily at his jokes and the woman clearly found Marco attractive. Her eyes followed him jealously to the next table, where two middle-aged women melted under his attention. At the subsequent table, a husband glowered while his well-built wife told a long and boring story about her day's sightseeing. Marco hung off every word, occasionally passing comment, and the woman reached up and touched his hair, running her plump bejewelled fingers through in a highly charged manner.

'Ten quid the husband will punch Marco's lights out if that goes on much longer,' said Stephen. I wanted Marco to visit us but a startling burst of singing in a striking soprano suddenly took all our attention. One of the guests, a chic, immaculately groomed woman in a tight silver dress, had risen from her table of friends and, with a heaving chest, flinging her arms around wildly, was performing from *Madame Butterfly*. Her voice soared and dipped magnificently as she waited loyally for her beloved Captain Pinkerton to return. Marco beelined for her, pulling up a chair at her table, resting his delicate chin into his hands and watching captivated, like a small boy.

He didn't move for the rest of the night, as the singer sang one famous aria after another, peppered with wildly enthusiastic, deeply reverent applause from the adoring Italian crowd. Finally the diva indicated that she had finished, and amid deafening cries of 'Brava, Brava!' diners raced to beseech her for an autograph. A man at a nearby table playfully picked up a napkin and passed it around, soliciting money from us all, which he placed cheekily at the soprano's feet. We applauded again until our hands stung and finally, with mock reluctance, the grande dame sang again, her voice soaring out across the water, floating towards Capri, as she died, heart-breakingly, in *La Traviata*.

The next morning at breakfast there was no sign of Marco or the diva, and as Alessandro came to take our orders, he kicked a poor mangy cat hanging around the tables.

'Hey,' I cried as the cat moaned and hid under a chair.

Alessandro scowled and muttered something in Italian that I couldn't catch. A man at another table threw a scrap of bacon to the forlorn creature whose ribs stuck out at right angles through its sparse coat.

'Please do not feed the vermin,' spat Alessandro and turned to stand over us. 'What do you want?' he said sharply.

'For you to not hurt the cat,' I replied. Alessandro rose like a cobra about to strike and a death-look flashed through his eyes.

'I will bring you eggs and bacon.' He stalked off furiously and Stephen burst out laughing. Alessandro reeled around. 'Is there a problem, sir?'

'Eggs and bacon will be fine,' said Stephen. 'I think the cat could use some too.'

Alessandro froze, and everyone assembled turned to watch.

'I beg your pardon, sir,' said Alessandro, walking slowly towards Stephen.

'Please just go and get the breakfast,' Stephen waved a hand dismissively. 'If you're cruel to animals don't expect us to give you the time of day.'

Alessandro looked like he might spit. He came close to Stephen, who suddenly stood up.

'Stephen!' I called, alarmed. Stephen walked up to Alessandro, who was now backing away.

'Yeah, kick me. But I'm bigger than the cat.' He loomed above Alessandro, not only younger but much stronger. 'What are you waiting for?' Stephen asked.

Alessandro scowled and left. The cat rubbed around Stephen's legs, purring loudly. Stephen bent to pat it and was nearly hit by a huge steak, which came flying from the kitchen. It was raw and bloody and the cat bit into it with a pleasure so intense it brought tears to my eyes.

'Satisfied?' Alessandro glowered beneath the eaves of the building, then disappeared inside.

'Jesus.' Stephen rose and came back to the table. 'That guy's a lunatic.'

I took his hand and kissed it. 'I love you.' Stephen's phone bleeped. 'Sorry, I have to take this.' He walked rapidly to an overgrown path and his body deflated as he spoke to the mystery caller. When he finally returned he was sombre.

'What on earth's wrong?'

'Nothing.' Stephen sat heavily and briefly met my gaze, which was fixed nervously on him.

'Are the kids okay?' I couldn't stop my voice from trembling.

Stephen sat back. 'Oh, Bec, it's nothing like that.'

I waited. Alessandro shoved plates laden with egg and bacon under our noses and slunk off. Stephen put some of his food onto a napkin that he placed gently in front of the cat. The cat ate noisily, purring.

'Please tell me what's happened?' I asked. 'I can see it's something serious.'

Stephen's body heaved in a long sigh. 'It's nothing to bother you about.'

I wondered yet again whether he was seeing someone, but his mood didn't seem that of a jilted lover. I took a stab at the vice I knew. 'Is it to do with your investments?'

Stephen laughed spontaneously. 'I do leave some things behind on holidays, Bec. It's just a work thing, don't worry about it.'

He ate quickly and as soon as I'd finished too, he scraped back his chair.

'Let's go,' he said.

As we walked through the fecund gardens alive with birdsong in the fresh coolness of the morning, I pressed my body into his.

'Just share it? Please?'

Stephen stopped and took one step away. 'Then tell me what's going on with you and Burton? You suddenly seem very close.'

I felt a pang of guilt that I was hiding things too. 'You know what it's like when you've just caught up with someone,' I replied. We stood in silence, our secrets hanging between us in a gossamer web as strong as steel.

'Come on. Let's hit the road before I change my mind,' said Stephen.

I peeled out behind a bus packed with tourists. Stephen held his breath, trying to appear brave. A surge of adrenalin rushed through me as I navigated the crazy scooters and winding, hairpin treachery.

By the time the bustling cafes and souvenir shops of Amalfi came into view I was thoroughly enjoying myself. Stephen had been silent the entire trip. 'That was the worst fifteen minutes of my life,' he said as we crawled along looking for a gap in the endless line of parked cars.

My memory jolted as I glanced at the white jewels of houses bustling up the hill. 'There's a cathedral here with a lot of steps.' I smiled slowly as connections jostled in my mind, overwhelming with nostalgia. There was my mother standing far away at the top of a flight of stairs, blonde hair tied in a scarf, a few escaped wisps blowing in the wind. She was the most beautiful woman alive, even more beautiful than Grace Kelly. Her face was lean with sadness but that only accentuated her deep blue eyes and generous mouth. My brother John was beside her, pulling one arm at a right angle; a lanky thirteen year old, impatient for the dark passages and secret garden inside the cathedral. I'd held my tiny instamatic camera aloft and clicked. Where was that photo now, faded orange with age? Did I still have it? That cameo revealing the awful gap left by death, the overseas holiday to take our minds off things that focused us all the more on being three not four, a single-mother family where just months before we'd been a solid unit, our dad the fisherman always looking out for us, his humour crackling as we laughed at his bad puns and ribald jokes. And coming to the Amalfi coast because it was where Dad had always wanted to take us. A place by the sea where fish were caught in abundance and where he'd fit like a glove.

A space opened up as a campervan pulled out and I shot in. My eyes drifted again to the houses. Subtle colours were emerging, muted yellow, soft terracotta, faded green shutters, the occasional slash of deep marine blue. As I followed Stephen onto the footpath, the sparkling harbour bustling with fishing boats and pleasure craft gave off a fresh breeze full of promises. A ferry ploughed in.

'Come on!' I grabbed Stephen's hand and we ran flat out to a small booth on the wharf. In the nick of time we bought two tickets and joined the last stragglers aboard. I led the way to the top deck where the sun scorched down.

'You sure you're okay with this?' asked Stephen worriedly.

'Yeah, it's a ferry. Not a small boat.' I sounded much braver than I felt, but I was determined to take this trip. It was the only way, given Stephen's fear of the road – and he, after all, had ventured back in the car to at least come here.

The engines churned into reverse and the sun caught the cathedral high on the hill. It glowed like molten gold. Stephen peered into his phone, having difficulty seeing the screen in the bright light. He tensed, frowning.

'Something wrong?' I asked.

He shook his head as he quickly tapped out an email, then turned his phone to photo mode and rose to stand behind me, goading me to turn around. As he snapped a photo, Amalfi framed my tentative grin. Old memories and new.

I hooked out my own phone, switched places and filled the frame with Stephen, the colourful houses jostling behind. I took photo after photo, Stephen mugging and finally looking directly at the lens with a haunted quality that made my heart jolt.

I sat down heavily. Salt and foam sprayed up in a white mist. Stephen, surprisingly, turned his phone off. I watched him closely, taking his hand in mine. It was hot with a thin bead of sweat. He smiled. 'So, we're off to Pompeii?'

The ferry sailed high on the waves, plunging into cool troughs before soaring up again like a giant seabird. I tried to adjust to the roll and swell of the open sea, my stomach lurching. I kept reminding myself over and over that a ferry wasn't a tiny dinghy and sought to find pleasure at being back on the water, with Stephen beside me.

Thoughts of the last time I'd been on this boat as a teenager flooded in. I swept away the sadness, brushing my mind clean.

We donned sunglasses and gazed at the rugged coastline where spectacular cliffs fell into the deep blue sea and houses clung on for dear life. A few tiny beaches lay at the foot of the sheer rock.

Beneath the ferry, a frothy white path cut into the intense indigo, a colour so completely different to my own aqua ocean back home. I tried to distract myself with detail to quell my fear.

'I think that's our hotel up there.' Stephen pointed.

'I don't think so. How about that one?' I indicated another that seemed to be suspended in mid-air.

'Not the right shape.'

'That one!' we cried together. The hulking, sprawling Della Mare was unmistakable. 'There's the beach!' Stephen waved excitedly at the row of buoys marking out the swimming area. The blowhole's massive wall of spray was clearly visible.

'No way are you swimming.'

'We'll see about that.'

A small distance on was a proper beach, small and pebbly with a few shacks along its shore. 'That's where we can go,' I said with certainty.

Stephen chuckled. 'See the stairs?'

With dismay I absorbed what must have been well over a thousand steps snaking up the mountain.

'I'm going to find *somewhere* to swim in this gorgeous water.' Stephen sat back, hair whipping in the wind as he surveyed the coast like a sea eagle.

Positano came into view as the ferry churned through choppy waves, heading for the wharf. I tried to relax. Stephen put his arm around me and gave me a supportive squeeze. 'I'm fine,' I said, leaning into him and feeling his body warm against mine.

As a crowd clambered off and more filed on, crew dangled homemade fishing lines into the pristine depths. Silver fish darted about. I thought of my father as Stephen ambled down and chatted to a sailor whose bronzed face was etched deep from storms and salt. Dad's face had been like that; so different to Stephen's, which was soft and unlined. Laughing loudly, the sailor offered Stephen a cigarette and for a moment I thought he was going to take it. Stephen hadn't smoked since the kids were born.

Then the ferry roared to life, the sailor deftly flipped up his line, and Stephen came back beside me. 'You're doing well. I'm proud of you,' he said as he entwined my hand in his. I sank into him again and wrapped my arm around his back. I placed my head on his broad chest and felt his heart beating. Did I imagine it, or was it running fast?

He bent and kissed me, chaste and warm, on the cheek.

By the time we arrived in Sorrento, where lemon and white hotels with soft terracotta roofs perched on a cliff-top, merging with the sky, our skin was burned to a crisp from the sea glare. In blistering heat we trundled up a steep, narrow footpath to the train station, avoiding being crushed by a bus only through a miracle. I was terrified, but Stephen was strangely complacent.

A fresh breeze burst through the windows as the train took off, vibrating up to speed as it shot through dense lemon groves heavy with fruit. With rattling ease it brought us to Pompei Scavi, where we disembarked and wove through hawkers touting tours and cold drinks, through a wide new arch, to join a concertina-queue beneath the baking sun.

Finally we passed through the turnstile and walked up the cobbled path to the Marine Gate, a salty breeze ruffling our backs. Stephen stopped and turned to look at the sea, twinkling on the horizon beyond a snarl of new houses. I photographed him within the vast hole of the ancient stone entrance. His craggy white smile was his usual but his stance was tense. I sucked in my breath. How could I reach him if something was wrong? And was he concerned for me too? Picking up the tension I was trying to hide?

We walked through streets crowded with tourists scurrying to keep up with their guides, until we found ourselves alone between silent buildings where life had stopped so suddenly in the summer of 79 AD. Ruins of shopfronts huddled together brought forth the once-bustling world, skeletons of villas still exuded calm and luxury – everything captured in that frozen moment when Vesuvius erupted and spewed ash and molten lava, setting the vibrant city alight as it buried it, with those forced to stay behind, guarding the wealth of their masters, dying in writhing agony. Pompeii was vast, much bigger than I expected. Even in the height of tourist summer you could still get lost.

As I stood at the side of a villa, in what were once slave quarters, I reluctantly drew myself back to the present and flicked on my phone while Stephen was a distance away studying frescoes in faded reds and pinks. Birdsong filled the air as I registered with disappointment that there was no news from Athens. I clicked the phone off, impatient, impotent, wishing I could be there investigating. The desire to discover who had set up and accessed the Athens accounts burned with a fury. I double-checked my phone, just in case I'd missed something. Scrolling through I found, to my horror, an email from DiStasio.

Dear Professor Wilding,
I have received information that alleges you visited the branch of the bank in Athens where the accounts were set up. We view this matter very seriously and request that you phone or reply in writing as to what you were doing. Please do not try to access the accounts.
Regards,
Margaret DiStasio

'Let's go to the Basilica?' Stephen called and my phone dropped skittishly as I rushed to put it away. Picking it up, brushing off dirt, I wondered if the bank manager had alerted DiStasio. Or was it the second visitor that day, the person who had come after me?

Our footsteps echoed through the cobbled streets as I thought of what I would say to DiStasio. Who had told her about my visit? I was caught in a web that was being drawn tighter but I had no idea who was doing it. I fended off panic, feeling helpless. In the distance the chatter of tourists bubbled like a stream but nearby there was no other human life. Behind us, Mount Vesuvius rose on the horizon.

We entered the Basilica, where a few pillars cast long shadows on the packed earth.

'Is this ancient graffiti?' Stephen's voice made me jump.

He was peering at a line of faint Latin script carved roughly into the stone wall.

'"Chius, I hope your haemorrhoids flare up in pain, and may they burn worse than ever, forever!"' I translated and Stephen roared with laughter.

'The Pompeians were straightforward,' I said. 'I wish we could be too.' I felt I was becoming as bad as him. I looked over but he kept staring at the graffiti. We returned to the streets, Stephen searching for more graffiti etched into the ruins.

"'If you bugger the *accensus*, you burn your prick,'" a voice echoed through time. I thought of graffiti I could write, filled with fears of Stephen's infidelity.

"'I wish I could be a ring on your finger for an hour, no more,'" I translated, and turning to Stephen, I saw sadness in his eyes.

'Maybe that's all we get. An hour, in the scheme of things,' he said, taking my hand. 'Come on, we've got a train to catch and one of us needs a swim.'

Cicadas screeched in the oppressive heat as we made our way back along the cobbled streets to the Marine Gate. Stray dogs trotted behind, ribs sticking out of lean bodies, watchdogs for the ruins once dusk settled. Dust burned our noses and the sense of loss and destruction grew deep until it swirled in our veins. By the time we caught the train, neither of us felt like speaking.

As soon as Stephen dived into the deep indigo water I picked up my phone from the warm, rocky ledge where I lay on my towel. Marco was swimming in languid strokes towards the line of white buoys and Stephen followed. The horizon was misty blue, Capri a pink smudge, the sea calm in the evening torpor. The wind of the morning had disappeared and now the private beach was friendly, peaceful.

I'm on the Amalfi coast, not in Athens, I wrote to DiStasio.

Apologies for stopping by the bank, but of course I'm concerned as to who set up those accounts.
Regards,
Rebecca

The less said the better. I held my breath and pressed send, heart thumping as I heard the whoosh of its dispatch.

The phone bleeped. How could DiStasio be so quick?

But it was a text from Burton. *Call me.*

'Come on in?' Marco had swum back to the ledge and was looking up like a sleek, friendly seal.

'Don't have bathers,' I smiled politely.

'You do not need them. We are all grown ups.' He grinned cheekily. 'And the water is beautiful. Like a warm caress!'

'Then you don't need me.'

'But of course we do, Rebecca!' He said my name like a warm caress itself, his dark eyes crinkling with laughter giving him the look of a water nymph.

'Bec doesn't swim,' Stephen called, lolling about, gazing at the clear sea floor metres below.

'Let me teach you?' replied Marco, astonished.

'My father drowned,' I said abruptly, and from the corner of my eye registered Stephen's amazement. 'I don't usually talk about it,' I added.

'I'm so sorry.' Marco looked genuinely sad and came smoothly up the tiny ladder, throwing himself onto the baking rocks beside me. 'How long ago?'

Stephen followed Marco out with a splash.

'I was a teenager. Fifteen,' I replied.

'An awful time to lose your father.'

I tried to keep my emotions in check but I couldn't stop thinking about it. Being on the Amalfi coast, where Dad had always wanted to come; sitting here by the sea. 'He was a fisherman.' I met Marco's gaze – he was so understanding I found myself continuing. 'I was with him. In his boat, in the place we'd been a thousand times. The fish were biting and we were reeling them in. Then suddenly the change blew in.'

Stephen sat on my other side. I could feel his cool body as he leaned close, protectively.

'We didn't know there'd been a flood upriver. Water rushed into the sea like a tidal wave from the wrong direction. Everything went dark.'

I stopped.

Marco's eyes were shining pools of sympathy. Stephen put his arm around me.

'I lost my parents in a car accident,' said Marco quietly and my gaze of surprise met his raw vulnerability.

'On this road?' asked Stephen.

'No, just outside Naples. They were driving home after my sister's first performance. That was my sister Bianca last night. She's a soprano with the Milan Opera. My parents had flown up and were coming back from the airport. I was meant to be with them but I'd decided to stay on with Bianca.' Marco paused for a long moment and no one rushed to fill the silence. Birdcalls echoed hauntingly through the trees on the hillside. Waves lapped calmly against the rocks.

'It changes things,' said Marco.

'My father told me to swim to shore and get help. He'd been hurt when the boat capsized and didn't think he could make it.'

My voice cut starkly into the mellow evening air that smelled ever more strongly of lemons as the sun dropped and shadows spread. 'I wasn't fast enough. I couldn't save him. I took too long.' It was strange to hear the words that I berated myself with every day drift out across the water. 'My mother never got over it. She died six years later from cancer.'

Stephen's arm gripped tightly. He knew what I wasn't saying: that my brother John had been nineteen when my mother died. He'd blamed everything on me and run off to America. In that year, when I was twenty-one, my family had simply vanished. I'd met Stephen shortly after – and my life had changed again.

Our gaze reached to the sea, as if trying to find my lone father bobbing in the gentle swell. The buoys rose and fell, and further out a ferry cut a white swathe into the deep blue as it made its way to Positano.

18

In the restaurant that night Marco introduced us to his older sister Bianca. Up close I could see a resemblance, but where Marco was lean, Bianca was full-bodied. She was bolder, with an ego that matched her talent.

After a short, polite conversation, Marco and his sister went off to a table near the bar as a bleak Alessandro led us to our place.

'How are you feeling?' Stephen asked worriedly as we settled in.

'Okay.' I shrugged. I'd surprised myself opening up to Marco; I had so much on my mind, things were seeping out unexpectedly. I was desperate to contact Burton but Stephen was sticking close like a supportive limpet.

I ran through excuses I could use to leave the table. A huge plate of grilled squid drizzled with lemon was served, and as we ate, Stephen received a call that he felt compelled to take. When he disappeared down the gloomy overgrown path I pulled out my phone and rang Burton, who picked up immediately.

'Bec, I'm so glad you called. We've managed to sight the paperwork. It was amazing – your passport and photo, your signature. If I didn't know you I'd think you were lying. It all looked thoroughly official and correct.'

My heart started thumping. 'Burton, it wasn't me.'

'Then it's fraud on quite a big scale, isn't it?'

'How could anyone have had access to my passport?' I desperately tried to think if someone could have taken it from the drawer in my bedroom, used it, and then put it back. Who visited our house? Friends and tradespeople.

'Who'd want to do this to you?' quizzed Burton.

'Priscilla hates me but I doubt she'd go that far. Would it need to be someone who knows me? Could it be organised crime or something? Maybe they got the details through Customs or Immigration?'

'Was your passport ever stolen?'

'No. I wish it had been. It would make all this seem more plausible.'

'We're going to try to make copies. We couldn't today because we almost got caught. I'll scan them and send them to you.'

'Please be careful, Burton. I couldn't live with myself if I got you and Maria into trouble.'

'There's no stopping that one now. It's taken about twenty years off her life doing this.'

My nerves swelled at the thought of the intrepid Maria, a tiny ant next to her giantess cousin. With Burton in his wheelchair completing the trio, they'd hardly disappear into the woodwork. They'd be as obvious as a beacon.

'Are you all going?' I asked, hoping he'd say no.

'We travel as a pack.'

'Can't the cousin do it alone?'

'She needs us to keep lookout. Sofia's bribed an administrator to let us into the archives. But there are others who come down and that's who we have to be careful with.'

'Promise me you won't get arrested?'

Burton's nervous giggles echoed down the phone. 'It's not in our game plan, Bec. And I certainly don't fancy doing time in a Greek prison.'

'I wish I was with you,' I said plaintively.

'Me too,' replied Burton. 'Bec, we're going to sort this out. I promise.'

'Please take care,' I said. 'Have to go, here comes Stephen.'

'Stay in touch.' I barely caught Burton's last words as I dropped the phone into my handbag.

Stephen sat heavily, eyes glistening with intensity. Burton's news rang in my ears. I would have to tell Stephen now – the fraud had gone far beyond anything I would have thought possible. My thoughts raced as I tried to decide how to raise it, but Stephen barely seemed to register me. He picked up his cutlery and ate the squid as if it were warm and delicious, not appearing to notice that it had gone cold and rubbery.

'Is everything all right?' I asked. 'Who was it?'

'Doesn't matter, everything's fine. Just a colleague.' He kept eating mechanically.

'About your conference paper?'

'Hmm. Which now needs even more rewriting.'

'Should we cancel going to the Grotta Verdi tomorrow?'

Stephen shook his head. 'Marco and Adriana say we mustn't miss it. It's okay, I'll get an early start and write before you're up.' His eyes softened. 'And then tomorrow afternoon I'll hear your paper.'

'Okay,' I smiled, 'that sounds great.'

Stephen rose stiffly. 'I don't feel like dessert, do you?'

'Saves another table visit from Alessandro.' The man in question came out on the terrace and glared.

As we headed down the path, tiny lights guiding us like fireflies, I knew I had to tell Stephen about the fraud allegation tonight; just let it all come out. It would be a great relief sharing my predicament with him once we were through the recriminations that would surely come from having kept it from him. But as soon as we were in our room Stephen flicked on the television. Channel surfing, he grew ever more intent, finally stopping on an English-language news service.

I stripped off and let my tired limbs stretch out on the bed, a numb throbbing in my feet from the hard cobblestones of Pompeii. My ribs twinged with a dull pain. Waiting for Stephen's attention, I felt sick with what I was about to reveal: that I had let Burton and Maria know before asking for his help. That was the awful problem with secrets – the longer you kept them, the worse they became when you finally told the truth.

Insecure, I reached for my phone and sent a quick message to James and Erin, checking how they were and if Big Boy was coping. Then I tried again to decipher the riddle. Who could have copied my passport?

Stephen tensed as the stock market report came on. The refined tones of a BBC announcer stated that it had been a good day in Europe and the United States. They did a quick summary around the world: stocks had shot up in Asia and Australia too.

'That's good,' I said – at least something was going in the right direction. Stephen pretended he hadn't heard. 'Stephen? You said you had some shares, so that's a good thing, isn't it?'

He turned and his face was drawn tight, his eyes black burning holes.

'What on earth's wrong?' I blurted.

'I wasn't even watching. What was it?' He glanced back at the television; the news broadcast had raced on to the weather. I didn't believe him. 'Looks like it'll be a fine day tomorrow,' he muttered. 'That's good for the grotto, it needs to be calm, doesn't it?'

He switched off the television, flicked off the lights and walked into the bathroom to clean his teeth. I wanted to quiz him further – something was definitely disturbing him – and now it didn't seem wise to raise my problem tonight after all. In the darkness, exhaustion suddenly overwhelmed me.

I dreamed I was in Pompeii, struggling through pitch-black streets as pumice and ash rained down and collapsing buildings flamed bright, consuming me. I woke choking at first light, my mind aching with images of tortured bodies found in the ruins, brought to life in their death throes through concrete casts. It struck me we hadn't seen these yesterday. We hadn't taken in much at all. We had each been lost in our own world. The lost among the lost.

A movement on the balcony distracted me. Stephen sat tapping into his phone. Quietly I slipped out of bed and tiptoed towards him, desperate to see to whom he was communicating. Instinctively he turned.

'Morning,' I said and my voice caught. Stephen was as white as a ghost.

'Hope I didn't wake you. I've been up half the night. I think Alessandro slipped something bad into our food. How are you?' he asked.

'I'm fine. That's strange, we both ate the squid.'

'You have a stronger constitution,' he smiled. 'Mind if I miss breakfast? Call me when you've finished and we'll meet?'

He went back to his phone. I wouldn't be able to tell him my problem just yet. I needed to find the right time – and perhaps later today I'd have a scanned copy of the application. Things might be clearer.

There was a queue at the elevator that took tourists down to the Grotta Verdi. Stephen had wandered off, still tapping into his phone, as soon as he'd arrived. 'Sorry, I'm right in the thick of changing my conference paper.' He still looked fragile and drawn.

I texted the children and replied to their overnight assurance that Big Boy was missing us. I had a deep desire to be back on the beach with him.

I wanted to call Burton for an update but the working day had only just begun; there'd be no news yet. At breakfast I'd tried to work out who could have accessed my passport but there were just too many people who'd been through the house;

we'd had parties with so many academics and friends. Nothing made sense.

The massive elevator doors opened and people poured out. I couldn't see Stephen and we needed to enter. I phoned him and was directed straight to his message service; I texted, standing back to let others pass, a happy throng of travellers.

Stephen ran up, breathless and strangely flushed, and we were the last admitted. The doors clunked shut and we shot down the mountainside in a stomach-churning drop. The air was thick with the scent and sweat of too many people in an enclosed space. I fought off claustrophobia, the dread of being trapped in this stifling tomb with no air. But finally the doors opened and I was jettisoned out into a fresh breeze.

The sea lapped calmly a little way below and we followed other tourists along a rocky ledge that led, enticingly, to a narrow entrance in the cliff-face. The bright sunlight was quickly extinguished as we stepped inside and were swallowed into a world of darkness.

Fine translucent stalactites the colour of parchment dangled elegantly from the ceiling, and submerged knobbly stalagmites, thick and ancient, thrust up from the sea floor.

We were in a cave. Blinking like newborn kittens, we waited until vision in the low light was restored. A huge subterranean lake glowing with the colours of every green imaginable slowly formed.

'Come this way. Prego. This way.' A tiny wizened man, hunched forward as if into a prevailing wind, herded us towards small rowboats as he took our money. The water was a pale lime at the edge, the colour of milkshakes I'd drunk in my teenage years. There was an odd thickness to it.

'Deutsche?' guides called. 'Française? English?'

I stared apprehensively at the boats lined up like death traps: insignificant bits of wood glued together in feeble defiance of the strange water. I wanted desperately to run.

'We don't have to do this, Bec,' said Stephen.

'We've come this far,' I replied, taking his hand and leading us to the English tour.

Stephen leaped aboard, causing the craft to sway and receiving a swift reprimand from our captain, a tall, gaunt, string-thin man with an unnaturally broad smile that did not convey happiness. His skin was such an unearthly pallor it seemed he had lived his entire life underground. He reminded me of albino spiders found on the ocean floor in the deepest depths. An underworld twin of our waiter Alessandro.

'You will have to-a swim if you do that again,' the White Spider said in a thick accent to Stephen. Around us people chuckled and I fought to control my panic.

'It looks inviting in,' replied Stephen. As I glanced further out the water did seem a more pleasant green, like new shoots in spring. The White Spider laughed, a grim, hollow sound like the brittle crack of ice. I held my breath as he started to row, gently and confidently, transporting us as if on a thread of silk across the smooth water and further into the darkness of the cave. I tried to imagine I wasn't on a boat.

We drew away from the tour behind, whose guide was singing *O Sole Mio* in a rich tenor, serenading his passengers. His voice bounced around, magnifying. I kept reminding myself I was in a cave, not in the middle of the ocean. It didn't make me feel better.

'I am-a Charon,' the Spider announced, his voice echoing off the smooth limestone walls, 'and if you wanna return from your trip today, you give me a coin. Or many coin.' The group dutifully laughed. 'Anyone who is-a bankrupt must wait forever there.' He stopped dramatically and pointed to a thin rocky ledge. Stephen froze.

'It's okay, honey,' I whispered. 'I'm doing fine.' I stroked his arm, silently fighting the impulse to scream in the dark enclosed space.

'You are a beautiful woman,' the Spider said suddenly to me. I looked up into his pale grey eyes with alarm. 'You will-a be my princess.' Stephen put his arm around me and Charon grinned, a cruel, lopsided smile splitting his face. 'Look-a!' he cried and plucked his oar from the sea. A thousand tiny emeralds, an intensely vivid green, cascaded with the richness of iridescent silk. They trailed into the water that now gleamed a clear, pristine emerald. 'See-a what I give you, my darling?' He dipped his oar and brought forth more brilliant jewels. Around us people thrust out their hands to catch the droplets, mesmerised. Even I was taken by the illusion.

'I'm a rich-a man.' The Spider flipped his oar a third time and the tiny gems distracted me as they tumbled merrily through the black until they merged with the glowing water. These sparkling treasures – shining so briefly and then gone – struck me as a microcosm of civilisation's quest for wealth. A mortal could hang on to an emerald no longer than this droplet existed, its fall to the sea as inevitable as death.

'Beyond-a here lies Erebus,' Charon continued, 'where lives the Furies. They hear-a complaints. Have you done wrong in the world above?' Charon fixed Stephen with his pale stare. 'They will punish you, sir.' He poked Stephen with his foot and Stephen flinched. 'They will-a chase you relentlessly, with their snakes-a for hair, wings of bats and devil eyes. Victims die. Horribly, pain-a-fully.'

Stephen's jaw tensed.

'It's just an act. Don't let him get to you,' I whispered.

'Still,' Stephen squeezed my shoulder.

'Maybe you are a guilty man! A fool!' roared Charon.

'Leave off,' said Stephen forcefully. 'Enough, Charon. How was this grotto formed, anyway? Why's it so green?'

'Yes, we'd love to know that,' said an American lady sitting in the stern.

'Me too,' said another.

'There's an underwater opening that allows-a this light,' said Charon, clearly bored with the change of topic. 'Sinner!' he denounced, pointing at Stephen.

'Leave him alone,' said the lady.

'Silenzio!' boomed Charon.

'He's unhinged,' whispered Stephen hotly in my ear and the hair on my arms stood on end.

'Do good in the world, sir, or you may-a be back here for life!'

'Yeah, right, mate,' said a man behind us. 'How big is this grotto?'

'You have eyes, look-a,' snapped Charon and turned the boat abruptly.

'Thank goodness we're heading back,' I whispered to Stephen. 'I'm feeling trapped.'

'Silenzio! Or I'll drop-a you in the water!' Charon glared at me and Stephen stood abruptly. The boat rocked wildly and everyone gasped. A boatman on another tour stopped his singing and called, 'Bene?'

I pulled Stephen back down. There was a frightened silence as Charon rowed us smoothly, staring at Stephen. 'A guilty man,' he whispered in a hiss of stale air. Stephen looked away as the man behind us called out angrily, 'Aren't you going to point out formations in the cave? You know, Garibaldi on horseback, that sort of thing?'

Charon glowered. 'I am an artist. I read-a the future.' Reluctantly he shone his torch on a formation that looked like a horse and cloaked rider. 'George Washington,' he said flatly. 'Thank-a-you for your company today.' He rowed swiftly to the ledge, where we alighted. 'Ladies and gentlemen, I hope-a you enjoyed your tour to the Underworld.' He held out his hand for tips. Not many people obliged. To my surprise Stephen passed him a twenty-euro note.

Charon smiled cockily. 'Trying to tell-a me you are not guilty, sir? Charon cannot be bribed.' But he pocketed the money swiftly and turned to help an elderly woman off the boat.

'Why on earth did you tip him?' I asked as we emerged into the delicious sunlight, and warm air brushed over us like a reassuring blanket.

'Everyone has to make a living.'

'But he mocked you!'

'I'm made of sterner stuff.' Stephen laughed unconvincingly.

'It was a terrible tour. I'm so sorry I chose it.'

'You're not to blame. We just got the wrong guide. Luck

of the draw. Everything's luck of the draw, Bec. Shall we have lunch? I need to line my stomach after that.'

Cool, white wine calmed our nerves as we gazed from our balcony towards the misty silhouette of Capri. Stephen was extremely attentive, quizzing me about my keynote address as we ate salad fresh from the hillside, aromatic tomatoes, orange and capsicum dancing on our tastebuds. He encouraged me to air areas I thought might be weak, and offered his ideas. I felt comforted that he was so much better.

I opened my computer and made the changes we'd discussed, and then read my paper aloud, keenly watching Stephen's response. At the end, he was fulsome in his praise.

'Really? You don't think it needs more refining?'

'It's absolutely ready.' He kissed me tenderly on the forehead. 'I wish mine was half as good.'

The heat of the afternoon was upon us and we lay down on the bed. The crisp sheets soothed my tired limbs and Stephen rolled close, his breath caressing my skin as he fell into a light sleep. I started to drift off, pleased to stop my mind from worrying about news from Burton, and I promised myself that later, when I'd had an update, I would tell Stephen everything.

As the warmth rose in the stillness, Stephen lapped an arm across me.

'I love you,' he said, kissing me tenderly on the lips. I tried to wake and respond, but the wine was strong; I couldn't lift my head.

I love you too, so much, I thought as my dreams carried me far away.

By the time I woke an hour later, Stephen was not in the bed. I yawned, momentarily sprawling in comfort then grabbed my phone and checked my messages. Nothing from Burton. I flicked through emails from work, replying to a few.

Robert and Rachel had sent messages hoping I was having a good time. Things in the department were getting worse and there were rumours that a wave of forced redundancies was about to hit.

I panicked and phoned Burton. I'd be the first one out if I didn't find the answer to the fraud.

'Can't really talk, Bec,' he whispered. 'We're at the archive. I'll phone you.' He hung up abruptly.

Someone was trying to destroy me. But why? And who? The more inexplicable the activity in Athens became, the more I began to wonder whether I even knew the perpetrators. Academics weren't known for their espionage skills. Well, at least not at Coastal in this day and age. It was possible I was a random target of organised crime.

The air in the room was stifling as I slipped into a sleeveless cotton sundress. I pulled a jug of orange juice from the fridge, filled a glass with ice, and carried them down the mountain to a refreshing glade that looked out to the Tyrrhenian Sea, cobalt blue now, rich and deep. As I drank the sweet, cold juice I craned my neck to see the beach below, where I assumed Stephen was swimming. I had only a partial view: the sea was glass calm; the white buoys bobbed gently, tiny specks. The afternoon was so hot the birds had stopped singing. I debated whether to send an email to DiStasio enquiring how things were going. I knew she'd see that as unprofessional.

I read a book instead, one I'd picked up at Naples airport about the lost civilisation of Pompeii. I'd meant to look at it before we went, but at least now it held more immediacy. I became quickly absorbed.

Cicadas shrieked in the forest above, and after a while my eyelids grew too heavy to prop open.

By the time I wrenched myself awake it was growing dark, so I hurried back to the room.

'So sorry, you must be starving!' I called into the gloom.

In the silence there was no trace of Stephen. I glanced around for his wet bathers, expecting to see them hanging off the balcony rail. A thick mist, an ethereal pale blue, had settled over the sea. But the balcony was empty.

I dressed quickly for dinner, hurrying to join Stephen in the restaurant. I waited for the lift but it didn't arrive, so I went outside and climbed the steps. I was still putting on my lipstick as I crested the hill and walked onto the patio full of noisy diners beneath the cheerful fifties fairy lights – I couldn't see Stephen among them. I approached Alessandro, the only staff member in sight. His chilly reply was unequivocal. 'Not tonight, signora. He has not been here tonight.'

I went down to reception and rang the bell. No one appeared, but I did see a pile of German and Russian passports sitting unattended. I rang the bell again, its tinkle echoing thinly against the walls.

'Marco? Adriana?' I called. Finally Adriana appeared, a little dishevelled. 'So sorry, my dear. Can I help you?'

'I can't find Stephen. Have you seen him?'

'No. You were together?'

'I think he went swimming. There's nowhere else he could have gone.'

'Have you checked down at the beach?'

'How stupid of me. No. But wouldn't it be late for him to still be there?'

'It's a beautiful night.' Adriana shrugged. 'We have the lights on. Marco was thinking of going down later with his friends.'

'Oh, I see.' I wasn't convinced.

Adriana picked up the telephone and spoke rapidly in Italian. Moments later Marco appeared, dressed from top to toe in white. He'd had his hair cut, short and stylish at the sides, longer on top. It made him look even younger and more handsome.

'I've just come back from Napoli. I had business. So, you can't find Stephen?'

'I'm going to look at the beach. He was sick this morning. Do you think he might have got into trouble?'

'I'll come with you.' Marco extracted a heavy torch from behind the counter. 'Come,' he said and took me through a series of rooms to a private staircase that led down onto the mountain-side. 'So, Stephen was unwell?'

'Early on. But he felt better later. He thought perhaps it was something he ate.'

'But you ate here.' Marco was concerned.

'It was probably just a slight virus. I've been fine.'

'No one else was ill. What did he eat?'

'The squid. So did I, and I'm okay.'

Marco nodded, relieved. 'My friends arrived, I think, perhaps while I was out? On a hot night they hurry to the sea to cool themselves. Stephen's no doubt chatting and lost track of time. Have you tried phoning him?'

'I'm not thinking at all, am I?' I pulled out my phone and dialled but it went straight through to his voicemail.

Bile rose as my lips went dry. It seemed so unlikely that Stephen wouldn't come back as dusk fell, knowing I'd be waiting to eat. I tried not to give in to the panic that was taking over my body, thinking of my father engulfed by waves. The sea today was calm. Stephen had eaten lunch, he'd been fine. *I mustn't worry*, I chanted internally all the while fearing the worst. Another loved one lost to the ocean.

Stephen's a strong swimmer. Stephen's fit and clever. Stephen would never go anywhere dangerous. Whatever stomach bug he'd had overnight was out of his system. He really had been healthy at lunch.

I remembered the blowhole in action the first day we saw the private beach and my body wrenched. Marco turned. 'We'll hurry. It will be all right, I promise,' he purred in his rich, warm voice.

A plum dropped heavily onto the path behind us and I started. Marco grabbed my hand and led me on.

'No one has ever drowned here. It will be okay.'

If I lost another, if I couldn't save him, I didn't know how I would survive. Stephen loved me – he'd told me so just this afternoon. An emotion so strong it almost tore me apart ripped through and tears sprang into my eyes.

Marco looked at me, alarmed.

'Sorry,' I muttered. 'It's just the sea . . .' My voice trailed off in a sob. I breathed in deeply and angrily brushed away the tears that were salty and hot and stinging my eyes.

We scrambled down the hill, faster, Marco caught up in my panic as I now led the way. Pebbles rolled noisily underfoot, I could see only a blur as the tears and sweat fogged my vision. An overhanging branch tore at my face and blood gushed out. Marco stopped in concern.

'It's okay, keep going,' I barked. Marco pulled out a linen handkerchief and dabbed my blood. I grabbed the handkerchief and applied it tightly to the wound. 'Marco, I can't hear anyone talking, can you?'

'We wouldn't necessarily expect to, we're still too far away.' He looked worried, though, and I was sure he wasn't telling the truth. We were almost at the bottom of the path. A plum fell on to me, staining my shirt purple as the rocky ledge came into view and I ran flat out.

'Stephen?' I roared at the top of my lungs. 'Stephen?' I cast my eyes in every direction: the sea, flat, calm, was devoid of people; the rocky ledge was empty. There was no sign of him – or any clothes or towel.

'Stephen?' I called again, even louder. The quiet hush of the Tyrrhenian Sea answered, sighing against the cliffs.

We hurried to the tables and chairs under the thatched roof. Deserted.

'Where are your friends?'

'They mustn't have arrived yet,' said Marco quietly. He walked back to the rusty ladder that led to the water and stood stock-still, squinting out to sea.

The line of white buoys bobbed in the gentle swell.

'Stephen? Stephen?' It was all I could do, a hopeless bleat. Night was closing in and a heavy mist was forming, thickening the indigo twilight.

'Are you sure he came down here?' Marco was calm and rational.

'He must have. There's nowhere else. He wouldn't have driven anywhere – and certainly not gone on a bus. He wouldn't go without me anyway.'

'No,' agreed Marco hesitantly.

I sank onto the ledge, not taking my eyes from the sea. Shuddering violently I gripped my knees, rocking back and forth, praying fervently.

A school of fish shimmered and glistened in the clear water below. They flashed away as quickly as they'd come. In the tranquility the ring of Marco's phone made us both jump.

'Pronto.' Marco listened. 'Si, si.' He hung up. 'The elevator's stuck. Adriana can't get it going and the emergency phone isn't working. We think Stephen's inside,' he finished with relief.

Hope hit me like a brick. Stephen was not lost at sea, but simply locked safely away in an iron cage halfway up the mountain. That's why the lift hadn't come when I waited earlier.

Marco was pulling at my hands. I hesitated, gazing at the flat, silky surface, checking once more that Stephen wasn't swimming in through the buoys.

'Come,' said Marco. 'He's not here. There's no towel. No clothes. I don't feel he's been here.'

*

A small crowd of guests and technicians had gathered outside the lift near reception. Adriana was loudly leading proceedings.

'It's your husband who's trapped inside?' asked an elderly Italian lady dripping with diamonds.

'I hope so,' I replied abruptly.

'I'm sure Stephen is in there,' announced Adriana. Beside her Marco was in rapid conversation with the main technician, who stood at an open control box fiddling with circuitry.

'When did it stop working?' I asked the crowd at large. The elderly woman shrugged dramatically. 'Adriana, how long has it been?' she called.

'There's plenty of oxygen.' Adriana marched over and flung her arms about me. 'He won't suffocate, my dear. We've had others trapped. We always get them out alive!' The crowd laughed, but I couldn't.

'Caro, we need to get you cleaned up. Look at you.' Adriana fussed over the blood and plum stains on my shirt.

'It's the last thing I'm worried about!' I snapped but Adriana was not deterred. She dragged me to the public bathroom and washed the stains with warm water. It just made them mingle and spread. She bathed my face like a mother and tears started to seep out. 'I need to know what time the lift stopped working.'

'We don't know,' replied Adriana matter-of-factly. 'Come, come, my love. It's all right, it's okay,' she soothed, rocking me in her strong, slender arms. A shout from the crowd filtered in. We ran back, just as the lift rumbled to life.

An eternity passed as the iron beast rose. Finally the doors creaked open and I rushed forward.

Empty.

The lift was empty. My knees buckled, but Adriana held me up. 'We'll check your room again.' She led me quickly away.

The room was dark. And when we turned on the lights there was still no sign of Stephen.

Adriana flew into the bathroom. 'Check if his bathers are here,' she said and I scurried to Stephen's suitcase, trying to think where they might be if he hadn't gone swimming. I rifled through his neatly packed clothes, then hurried to the wardrobe and searched.

'I can't find them,' I called. 'They're not here!'

I tipped the suitcase upside down. Clothes scattered. Adriana dropped to her knees beside me and we sorted through. There were no bathers.

'There's a towel missing from the bathroom,' she said finally and moved to hug me. I went completely still. This was it, the moment I'd waited for. Losing the man I loved for a second time.

'We must go back,' I said.

Strong searchlights blazed through the inky blackness. Two police boats plied the waters, large cruisers with rumbling engines; above them a helicopter emblazoned GUARDIA COSTIERA roared like a warzone, shooting a dazzling white arc across the waves. On the rocky ledge, lights brighter than daylight had been set up; police cast long shadows as they hunted along the cliff-base. I sat with Adriana and Giotto from the Positano police station. Someone had placed a rug around my shoulders. Above me, the tatty thatched roof let in the night air that was growing colder.

'Perhaps you had a fight?' asked Giotto.

'No. We were having the perfect holiday. But his illness this morning – I'm so worried it came back. If he's too weak to swim he'll be out there treading water. We must find him.' I stood abruptly.

'They were always happy.' Adriana backed me up like she'd known us all her life.

Voices of men and women shouting in Italian echoed around the high stone walls that stretched up forever. I was finding it hard to focus; I wanted to be searching with the others.

'And you don't think he could have just gone into town? To Amalfi or Positano?'

'He hated that road, he wouldn't go without me.' I thought suddenly of the time he left me in the museum in Athens. I wouldn't have expected he'd do that either.

'What is it?' Giotto was staring hard.

'I really think it's unlikely. There'd be no reason. He wouldn't have left me alone for dinner. He'd be back by now.' My voice cracked. It was after midnight. Then a thought struck. 'Stephen's due to speak at a conference on Capri next week. Maybe he was called across?'

I scrolled through my phone and found the hotel where the conference was being held and where we were due to stay. I dialled, hands shaking, and reception picked up immediately. Rapidly I outlined my problem – was Stephen there? After a long minute the helpful man came back: no, he certainly hadn't checked in, our booking wasn't until next Wednesday. I asked if he could check if Stephen was in the building, perhaps meeting with someone in the bar. I waited for what seemed an eternity before the reply came: no, Professor Wilding was not there. I left my number, and he assured me he would contact me if Stephen turned up.

'Perhaps he went to shop in Amalfi or Positano for a surprise for you and got lost?' Adriana was trying to be helpful, but it didn't make any of us feel better.

'Could someone check there?' I asked, in spite of thinking it was stupid. Where would they even start to look?

Giotto shrugged. 'All of us are here. I'll see if the Commissario wants to send someone.'

A commotion rang out along the rocky ledge.

'Over here! Over here!'

Marco stood at the front of the crowd. In a tiny crevice, a white hotel towel was rolled up. Marco pulled it out and the Commissario, a tall, lean man in his forties with the look of a sleek wolf, took it and unfurled it.

Stephen's shirt and shorts fell to the ground.

The world went black.

19

I woke in the small lounge off reception. A shell-pink dawn was creeping across the sea.

My limbs were as heavy as anchors as the night's events slowly came back.

'Have you found him?' I slurred and Marco rushed to my side.

'Not yet.' He handed me a glass of water. I touched my lips but couldn't feel anything.

'The doctor's given you a tranquilliser,' said Marco, gently rubbing my shoulders.

Adriana came in with the Commissario, who in the daylight looked even less friendly. 'You remember Commissario Napolitano from last night?' I nodded like a rabbit frozen in headlights.

'Do you have his passport please, Signora Wilding?' Napoli-tano's voice was cold with suspicion.

'It'll be in our room, in the safe.'

'We've looked,' said Adriana apologetically. 'Yours is there, but not Stephen's.'

I blinked mutely.

'Did you always keep them together?' asked Marco.

'I can't even remember getting them back after we left them at reception.'

'Of course I gave them back,' said Adriana, offended.

I thought hard but had no recollection. 'When?' I asked.

'That day or the next.'

'Who did you give them to?'

'You or Stephen, I'm not sure.'

'I'm sorry, I don't remember getting them,' I repeated. All I could think was how passports were left lying around unat-tended at reception.

'Well, clearly I did because yours is in your room safe,' said Adriana. Marco frowned and went to reception, where he shuffled about behind the counter.

The Commissario called Giotto over to take notes. 'I'd like to go through the last twenty-four hours you spent with your husband, please? Every detail.' He sat down in a deep sofa that sighed with his weight. 'Firstly, please, you need to tell me if you had a fight?'

'No, we had a lovely day. Stephen was unwell in the morning but then he was much better by lunchtime.' I flashed to how generous he'd been about my keynote address; my leg jittered uncontrollably. 'I'm so worried his illness came back. Please, can we go down to the water?'

'We have our boats. There's nothing you can do,' said Napolitano.

The drugs were numbing my brain; it was difficult keeping a train of thought. If Stephen's passport had disappeared, was that good or bad? I struggled to make sense of anything. The sea had taken another man from me. I'd asked Stephen never to swim there. Adriana, the Commissario and Giotto were staring at me. I'd just spoken my thoughts aloud.

'He's a strong swimmer and the sea was calm,' I continued. 'Are there rips?' No one understood. I made a movement with my hands and twisted my body, trying to imitate getting caught in turbulence. I felt like I was swimming through molasses. 'Dangerous water? Strong currents?'

Finally they nodded.

'Perhaps,' said Napolitano.

'There can be,' muttered Adriana sadly.

'We grew up here. We know how to read the sea,' said Giotto, looking up from his note-taking. 'Last night was calm. It would be unusual. But then, you can never take the sea for granted.'

'I know that,' I said grimly. 'Are there coves? Could he have swum somewhere and not be able to get back?'

'We're checking everywhere,' replied Giotto, 'and we have divers.'

Tears rose uncontrollably, forming into a tight sob that I tried to suppress. When my father drowned, divers had gone in, but his body had washed up further down the coast the next day. My mind grasped slowly the concept that Stephen's passport had gone.

'Anything?' I called to Marco.

'It's not here,' he called back. 'Stephen's passport is not here with us.' He looked at me sympathetically.

The image of Stephen's clothes hidden in the crevice flashed back. 'Do you think he's met with foul play?' My voice cracked.

'How?' said Marco, 'It's a private beach.'

'One of the guests?'

'That's highly unlikely,' said Adriana loudly.

Napolitano watched us.

'Sir, is it possible?' I asked.

'It is completely improbable,' he snapped, 'that a guest or a stranger would be down there. Your husband was the only one who asked for the key to the gate that day.' He stared at me. 'I am wondering, did he leave his wallet and phone?'

Napolitano led the way to our room. Marco picked up my phone from the bedside table, and I listened to the messages. Burton had left five, growing increasingly urgent. There was nothing from Stephen. Napolitano's eyes remained fixed on me.

I couldn't see Stephen's wallet anywhere; it wasn't in his bedside drawer or the safe, so I rushed to the wardrobe and found the trousers he'd worn to the Grotta Verdi yesterday, feeling in the back pocket. Pain as sharp as a knife cut through me as I pulled the wallet out. With trembling hands I opened it: there were gaps where some plastic banking cards had been but I had no idea whether he might have just left them in Australia. I'd left a lot of mine at home. Stephen's main credit card was there but I knew he had others that weren't. My head spun as I stared at the black leather wallet that Stephen would normally always have on him in the outside world.

In his jacket pocket was his phone. I turned it on and it immediately died. I went to the charger still plugged into the wall and slotted it in. I tried to turn it on again but knew it would take a few seconds to kick to life.

Napolitano observed like a hawk as I propped on the edge of the bed and waited impatiently for Stephen's phone to fire up.

There was a message from his stockbroker Phillip Bradley in Melbourne, asking to call him urgently. I flicked through Stephen's emails – a few from work needing his advice even though they knew he was on holiday and hundreds of other emails he'd deal with upon his return. They looked typical and uninteresting as I scrolled frantically.

There was nothing from Priscilla in any medium.

The Commissario coughed. 'May I?'

I handed him the wallet and phone, which he quickly inspected, flicking through the small amount of cash Stephen had.

'I can't tell if anything's missing,' I said. 'He has more banking cards but he might not have brought them on holiday.' I was desperately frustrated I didn't know.

Napolitano eyed me as if I were an insect, then turned his attention to the phone and rang through to the messages, listening to Phillip Bradley.

'Who is he?' Napolitano asked as he hung up.

'Stephen's stockbroker.'

'Ah.' The Commissario's eyes lit up. 'May I keep these, please?'

I didn't want to relinquish the wallet or the phone in case they held clues I could decipher and they were Stephen's – they were part of him.

'We will return them. When we can.' Napolitano strode out, giving me no say in the matter.

The sun's rays cut strong white lines across the tiled floor. Rolling over, I saw the empty bed. I sat up and looked around, eyes heavy, mouth desert-dry with a sandpaper tongue.

'Stephen?' There was birdsong and the soft lull of the sea. A ferry echoed through the stillness and I could hear a low throbbing of slow-moving boats. Reality hit.

Stephen was gone.

Vaguely I recalled Adriana giving me a strong sleeping potion this morning. I hadn't wanted to take it but in my disorientation I must have acquiesced. Or did Adriana only tell me after I'd drunk it? My memory was blurred.

I rushed to the balcony. Two police cruisers crawled through the water. Further out, the helicopter was a small dot in the sky, swooping along the horizon. I checked my phone, hoping against hope there'd be a message from Stephen. There wasn't.

I threw on my clothes and ran to reception, taking the stairs as the lift now bore an OUT OF ORDER sign.

Marco met me. He had clearly not slept.

'Any news?' I asked. He shook his head and led me into another tiny sitting room that didn't look out to sea.

Police and other guests mingled in the reception area and I was glad to be away from their sight.

'There's no sign of him. My friends the police are checking other towns, the railway stations and airports. I will bring you something to eat.'

'Just water,' I said, my head aching. As soon as Marco left I phoned Burton, who picked up immediately. 'Where have you been, Bec? We've been worried. And we have the most explosive news.'

'Burton . . .' I said shakily.

'What's happened? You sound dreadful.'

'Stephen's disappeared. He may have drowned.'

Burton was silent. Far below, the police boats thrummed as they swept the coves.

'Bec, are you there?

'Yeah,' I croaked.

'Stephen's a strong swimmer. He knows the sea. Why'd he go in if it was rough?'

'It was calm.'

'Were you there?'

'No. And he hadn't been well in the morning.' Tears spat from my eyes. 'Burton, if only I had been with him. I was sleeping. If I'd gone down this would never have happened.'

'We'll come immediately. Where are you?'

'Between Positano and Amalfi. Hotel Della Mare.'

'How are the kids taking it?'

'I'm hoping Stephen will turn up. Walk back in the room like nothing's happened and tell me off for overreacting.' My lips split into an involuntary smile. 'Like in Athens. He was safe all the time.' I wept silently.

'So, the kids don't know?'

'That's right, Burton,' I snapped.

'Hang in there, I'm booking tickets as we speak. We'll see you in a few hours. Damn, I hope Maria brought her passport. I always travel with mine. Maybe it'll just be me.'

I took a breath. 'Burton, Stephen's passport's missing.'

'Well, that's strange . . .' Burton paused. 'Bec, I'm on my way.'

I went back to my room to put on shoes. I needed to get down to the beach. The image of Stephen's clothes falling onto the stone was nightmare-vivid.

Before I could leave, there was a loud rapping on the door. Commissario Napolitano, Giotto and two other policemen stood in the corridor. Marco was a distance behind, his brow deeply furrowed.

'Please, Signora Wilding. We need to take you to Positano for questioning,' Napolitano said gruffly.

'Can't we do it here? I don't want to leave in case Stephen comes back. Or if he's found,' I added, my voice barely audible by the end.

'We go now.' Napolitano took my arm in a pincer grip and started to lead me out, but I planted my feet firmly on the ground and forced more strength into my voice than I felt.

'I'll answer anything but I'm staying here.'

The Commissario's cheeks blazed. 'But you will please come?'

Marco sidled up. 'Rebecca,' he said firmly, 'do what the Commissario asks. I'll come with you. Adriana will let us know immediately if there's any news.' He cast a quick glance at Napolitano, who stepped aside to let Marco take my arm. 'You'll make things worse if you don't oblige him,' Marco whispered hotly into my ear.

I grabbed my phone and handbag and accompanied the tall gaggle of men up to street level and into a small blue car with a white stripe, POLIZIA emblazoned on its side. Giotto and I squashed in the back while the Commissario positioned himself in the front beside a young driver. The other police led the way and Marco followed in his car.

At the hairpin bends the sirens whooped and lights flashed. The cars sped along, stopping for no one.

'What's the rush?' I whispered to Giotto.

He shook his head. Napolitano turned around, glowering. All I wanted was to be down at the private beach waiting, searching for Stephen, looking for—

Suddenly I silently cursed; Burton had mentioned at the start of his call that he had explosive news. Were Stephen's disappearance and the fraud somehow connected? And if so, how? Whichever way I juggled them, the two pieces of the story didn't fit. Nothing was making sense.

The purple bougainvillea blazed in the sunlight at the turn-off. How much had changed since the day I'd first seen it. Stephen had been moody then. I needed to sit and retrieve the past, sift through it layer by layer and build a picture. My time at the police station must be brief. I vowed to myself to answer everything quickly and efficiently.

Inside the pale building Giotto seated me in a stiff, upright chair in a cavernous room that had a view down to the sweeping bay where ferries plied the water and colourful tourists queued wharf-side, filing on and off the boats. A happy scene, carefree and playful. Had Napolitano chosen this space on purpose? Pleasure craft dotted the horizon. I watched a handful of boats, rainbow sails full of wind as they skimmed the white-capped surface. My mind flashed back to my own beach at home. Like two paintings, one on each side of the world. What was wrong with this picture in front of me?

'You have financial problems, Signora Wilding?' Napolitano moved swiftly between me and the water, his bulk casting a shadow as the sun poured in behind.

'No.' I frowned, panic churning my stomach as I willed myself to keep calm.

'But I think you do.'

How could he possibly know about the university investigation? It was internal, there was no way he could find out, surely?

'I phoned your husband's stockbroker, who was most obliging. He was not surprised that Stephen Wilding has disappeared.'

Now he had my full attention. I sat forward on the edge of the hard vinyl chair, barely breathing.

'His stock market bets have gone sour,' Napolitano announced imperiously. 'In the past weeks, the market has been volatile. Every time it plunged or rose, your husband went the wrong way. He had, is it called, a loan of the margin? And options. He lost everything. Signor Wilding now owes a great deal of money. But you know this, no?'

I shook my head as it drained of blood. I tried to stop the floor spinning.

'You will lose your house,' Napolitano continued matter-of-factly as he scrutinised me. 'It was mortgaged against his loans.'

'Don't be ridiculous,' I snapped. 'Our house is in joint names. And I certainly never approved anything like that.'

The Commissario shrugged. 'I talked to his broker and then to his banker, who is in the same firm. They were both very eager to hear from me. They'd like to talk to you, too.'

My heart was beating so fast it was like I'd just sprinted uphill. 'If any of this is true, I'll be more than talking to them. They have no right to be having these conversations with you. Anything between them and my husband is confidential.' Stress rose tight through me as I thought of the bank revealing these awful things to Napolitano, and I started to wonder if they could possibly be true.

The Commissario raised his shoulders and dropped them. He reached to a table and poured a glass of water. My throat was parched.

'Could I have a drink please?'

He ignored my request.

'You were perhaps very angry? Wives have killed for less.' His manner turned from frosty to glacial. 'How handy it would be for you if he disappeared.'

My mind was grasping for facts. Could Stephen have bankrupted us? He had my power of attorney, something our solicitor had advised when making our wills years ago. It was just conceivable that Stephen could have put the house up without my knowledge. It would make sense of his strange moods of recent times. With horror it struck me that perhaps he hadn't drowned accidentally. If he had lost everything . . .

'There is life insurance with him gone, no? You could save the house. Your family home.'

'No. No. You're wrong,' I blurted. 'But what if Stephen killed himself?' My hands and feet jittered, unable to keep still.

'Was he the type?' asked the Commissario softly, looking like a lion about to pounce.

I shook my head. Stephen would be devastated and ashamed and certainly wouldn't want to face me. If it was as bad as Napolitano said, he might have panicked. I sat back as I saw a whole world opening.

Stephen might have run away. Not been taken by the sea like my father. He could just need space.

The Commissario was watching me and I didn't care. Let him accuse me of whatever he wanted. Let Stephen lose everything – but if he was alive I would hunt him down. And I would take him in my arms and tell him it would be all right. All of it. As long as we were together, we would find a way to fix everything.

The sea had changed to a deep indigo and a mist was rolling in, heavy and opaque. Napolitano had gone for a break – we had all been here several hours – while Giotto had stayed to keep an eye on me.

I debated whether to request a lawyer or to contact the Australian embassy. But that might make me look guilty. I prayed Napolitano wouldn't learn of the accusation of fraud against me. I was astonished at how innocent I was and how terribly it could all be portrayed. But I was also jubilant. Stephen's worst news had been my best: a disaster from which he'd run. As the minutes ticked by I became ever more convinced that Stephen had not drowned.

Somewhere, perhaps, he had left me a note or a sign? Perhaps it was the clothes wedged in the rocks? I caught myself. The sight of Stephen's blue shorts and white shirt tumbling from the towel flashed again before me. Surely they were the clothes of a dead man? But if he had just gone swimming, why had he tucked them away? Normally he would leave them lying on the rock. Casting my mind again for possibilities, I had a horrible realisation.

'Giotto, I need to see the Commissario.'

*

'Yes?' Napolitano peered down his aquiline nose, thick black eyebrows rising.

'The day we arrived, a car full of youths hit us from behind. We put in a report.'

'With me,' chimed Giotto.

'What happened about that?' I asked, turning.

Giotto frowned. 'I'll have to check.' He bounced out of the room.

Napolitano walked to the window and stared out into the twilight. 'A soft night,' he announced. 'Bellissima.'

'Couldn't it be possible these youths came back and attacked Stephen? Took his passport? It seems strange to me that Stephen left his clothes wedged in the rocks. It's like someone hid them there. And we haven't found his body. Stephen is alive. We need to act,' I finished, panic rising.

Napolitano turned slowly, silhouetted against the sky. No one had switched on the lights but in the gloom I could just make out a thin smile on his lips.

'I thought for a moment you were going to accuse the boys of murdering your husband. That would be,' he paused and walked close, 'novel.' He pulled up a chair, swivelled it around and straddled it, his face inches from mine. I could smell his rancid breath. 'Let's get real. I want to be home for dinner. My wife is cooking lasagne. I'm glad you mentioned the towel and the clothes. I, too, found them odd. But I think that you put them there, Signora Wilding. To take us for fools. We've checked and your husband hasn't accessed his bank accounts.'

My heart froze.

Napolitano leaned closer. 'Where is the body?' His eyes

burned into me, like those of a salivating dog. 'What did you do? I know you want to tell me. That is why you are still here.'

'I stayed to try and help!' I yelped. All I could think was that Stephen hadn't accessed his accounts – my hope started to fade. They were words I'd read so often when people went missing, later found dead. But occasionally, abducted – and saved. 'There may have been a kidnapping. I'm going to the Consulate.'

'Perhaps he had a lover? Is that why?' Napolitano blocked me as I stood. He registered my pause. 'I think Stephen Wilding was seeing another woman, yes? You waited until there was an opportunity to make it look like a drowning.'

I shuddered at the word and headed rapidly for the door, waiting for him to stop me. In a flash I was through into the next room.

'Giotto?' I called loudly. 'What did you find?'

I could feel the Commissario behind but I didn't look back.

'The driver has a record but when the polizia de Napoli went to his house he was not there. They want to talk about several matters; one is theft.'

'So, he's a criminal?'

'A small-time thief,' Giotto nodded enthusiastically.

Marco came towards us from the back of the room. 'Can she go now?' he asked Napolitano.

'Marco, I'm worried that the youth – what's his name?' I turned to Giotto.

'Carlo Lotti.'

'What if Carlo Lotti is involved in Stephen's disappearance? That he made Stephen get his passport while I was asleep?'

'But if it was kidnap wouldn't they have made contact?' said Marco.

'Perhaps it's something else?' My mind strained to connect the pieces. Could the Athens account be involved? Or was I losing all perspective?

The Commissario walked up beside me, grinning. He clapped. 'Brava, brava. A stellar performance, Professor.' He laughed sarcastically. 'Perhaps Carlo Lotti is a debt collector?'

'If you won't help me, Commissario Napolitano, then I'll find people who will,' I said and strode out. Marco trailed behind.

'That man's insane. He's completely incompetent. And he thinks I murdered Stephen!' I was shouting.

'Shh, shh,' Marco waved his hands.

We hit the night air, cool and fresh compared to the heavy atmosphere of the police station. 'I have to get to Naples,' I said as my head spun and a lump of bile rose in my throat.

'The Commissario's a hero. The last thing you must do is put him offside,' said Marco, glancing back nervously at the police station. Nobody had followed us out.

A wave of nausea belted me and I bent and vomited into the gutter. 'I have to find someone who'll help.' I vomited again, as if my stomach were heaving out of my body. I tried to focus. 'Could you please take me to a bus or somewhere I can get to Naples?'

Marco handed me a handkerchief, uneasy. He chirped his car unlocked. 'Come on, I'll drive you,' he murmured.

'Thank you.' My heart was racing, my head pounding as I hurried into the car.

'This is a very small place,' Marco said as he fired up the engine. 'You must be careful.'

But careful was the last thing I intended. I would do whatever it took to find Stephen. At the turn-off where the bougainvillea shivered and bounced in the long twilight, I wound down my window and tried to breathe, fighting a deep fear.

20

In a cramped office in the central Naples police station, Marco was explaining the situation to an officer in her late twenties. Stylish and commanding in a crisp blue uniform, she cast a sceptical glance my way.

'Professor Wilding?' she asked as though it were in doubt. 'My name is Nina. I am a good friend of Marco. So, I am at your service.' She shook my hand with a firm grasp. 'I am very sorry to hear about your husband.' Her English was assured and she rolled her r's with a slight American twang. 'I am also sorry to say that Carlo Lotti is known to us here in Naples. In fact, it was I who went to his house to enquire about your car accident. We also wanted to question him for robbery. He wasn't home but we met up the next day as he tried to board a train to Roma. He has been our guest ever since. We caught him red-handed with stolen goods.' She gazed at me with concern. 'Unfortunately this was the day after your accident. Carlo Lotti could not possibly be involved in the disappearance of your husband.'

I felt hollow as the news sunk in.

'I am sad to hear about Signor Wilding's gambling problem,' she purred gently.

'Nina, don't you think it's strange that no body has washed up? And the sea was so calm that night? Could he have been murdered?' I asked, the thought unbearable.

'I find that very unlikely. You were in the hotel and it's not the most accessible of places.'

Had the road that Stephen hated protected him? I longed to hear his voice complaining about it.

'But it's possible?' I pursued.

'Random killings in this area don't happen.' Nina shook her head with certainty. 'Professor, until there's a body, you're free to go where you like, but of course you won't leave the area?'

'No.'

'We have checked that he hasn't used his passport or accessed his accounts, but there is only so much we can do. I am very pleased that Marco has offered to help. I would suggest you ask around. If your husband has run away because of his bad debts, someone must have seen him somewhere. He might have hoarded cash and planned this.' She gave an unsettling smile – but she had also reignited my hope. Stephen would, of course, build up cash if he intended to run away.

'A pleasure to meet you,' said Nina, standing. 'I am sorry it had to be under these circumstances. We will do what we can.

Good luck.' She disappeared into the loud, bustling bowels of the station.

Marco and I found our way out, past a seedy group of shuffling humanity, victims and abusers, and a large contingent of police.

'Nina is a professional. She keeps an open mind,' said Marco once we were in the street.

'I think Stephen's alive,' I said intently, checking my phone; nothing from Stephen but a message from Burton popped up. He and Maria had just arrived at Naples airport. I called him immediately, relieved. 'We'll come and get you.'

Marco's face dropped in disbelief when he saw my dynamic duo. Burton was sitting stock still with anticipation in his gleaming wheelchair. Maria stood beside him, Burton's coat wrapped around her. She looked ancient.

'My dear, my dear, you poor thing, how are you?' She ran up. 'What a terrible, terrible tragedy! Have they recovered the body?'

'No, and I'm not sure he drowned, Maria.' We kissed each other on both cheeks as she wrapped her tiny wings about me.

'Whatever do I make of that?' she exclaimed as Burton took my hand and squeezed tightly.

As we drove back to the hotel I filled them in on Stephen's disappearance.

'We'll start canvassing tomorrow,' said Burton. 'Between us, if Stephen did run away, we'll find someone who saw him.'

'And I'll take friends and scour the coastline in my boat,' said Marco. 'We'll check every cove again, in case the police missed something.'

As we arrived at Della Mare it glowed silver beneath a moonlit sky, perching like a Cubist eagle on its cliff. Marco hurried inside to check if the lift had been fixed, and came back relieved. 'It's working,' he said confidently, and proceeded to wrestle Burton's wheelchair around to the side of the car. 'I'll see your friends to their rooms, Becca. You get some rest.'

Maria darted about, trying to help Marco, trying to soothe me. 'Are you sure you don't need company, Rebecca?' she asked, looking spent, a feverish tiredness driving her.

'Thanks, Maria, but you must sleep.' The words stuck in my throat. Under her kind gaze the muscles of my face suddenly gave way to tears. Maria flung herself against me and hugged me so hard I gasped for air. 'It's just so unbelievable. Stephen's debts, his disappearance, that foul Napolitano accusing me of killing him,' my voice rose to a wail as sobs shook my body. 'Please help me find him.'

'Of course we will, of course we will.' Maria rubbed my back with a firm, warm hand.

'Don't worry, Bec.' Burton wheeled close, his voice soothing and authoritative. 'Together we'll get through this. Let's come to your room and go through everything again. Just like a dig: we'll sift through and look at every tiny detail.'

We opened the balcony doors for air but sat inside, not wanting anyone to hear us. Our voices low and urgent, we circled around everything again. Once Marco had brought coffee, handed out keys to neighbouring rooms for Burton and

Maria and then gone to bed, we could finally add the fraud and suspected affair to our deliberations. How did it all fit?

'Bec, when I was ringing you earlier,' said Burton, 'I wanted to tell you what happened at the bank archive. When we went back to photocopy, all the paperwork had vanished. There's no record of it anywhere.'

Maria nodded, wide-eyed. 'And the accounts have been blocked now, so Sofia can't access them.'

'We were sure no one had seen us – well, no one we didn't trust or hadn't bribed,' continued Burton, 'but someone was looking and they'd taken everything. Do you think there's a connection?'

I rested my forehead into the palm of my hand and it felt like lead. Thoughts snapped in an electrical fizz. My head swam and I felt sick. I couldn't make sense of anything. Maria took my hand.

'There's nothing more we can do at this moment,' she said gently. 'Burton, you go to your room. Rebecca, I'm here with you. Sleep. All of us. That's an order.' With that she kicked off her shoes and lay down on my bed. Stephen's side of the bed. My face crumbled again. Burton, dismayed, moved close.

'Thank you,' I whispered, kissing him on the head. His blue eyes looked up, filled with sympathy. I moved him out the door and then fled to the bathroom where I drenched my face in cold water and silently wept, my body racked with pain, until I was so exhausted I could barely make it back to the bed, where I collapsed beside Maria. Still my mind wouldn't turn off. I lay thinking haphazardly, my brain a stew of nightmare scenarios and a fierce attempt at logic that went nowhere. And I worried desperately how I would tell James and Erin their father was missing.

*

The day was fresh and crisp, the sea lapped calmly beneath a startling blue sky. I rose quickly, not wanting to wake Maria.

I looked over the balcony, scanning far along the coast, but I couldn't see the helicopter or police boats. My stomach wrenched. Had they given up the search already? Gratefully I remembered that Marco was going out with his friends today.

I phoned reception and Adriana confirmed he had left at dawn. Maria sat up, stretched her tiny wings, then quickly bustled into action, throwing on a bright red sundress and wrapping a rainbow-coloured scarf around her head, pinning it into her black, perfectly-styled hair.

After setting Burton up at a table overlooking the sea, Maria and I struck out for the beach. I wanted to see everything in the daylight. Burton immediately started tapping notes into his computer, making a list of possible people who might have seen Stephen.

'We'll eat after!' called Maria. I marvelled at her agility as she flashed along, balance-perfect as she navigated the loose gravel path with ease. I quizzed her for more details about the bank, desperate to know everything in case it might help us discover a link.

'Sofia had never seen anything like it, Rebecca. The first day we went to the archive, she bribed the man in control and he was fine – he went off for a cigarette and we were away. It took us a while because as you can imagine, nothing was well ordered. Files plonked here and there, boxes of stuff that had never been dealt with. They're all chain smokers and the air was thick with cigarette odour, quite revolting. Sofia and I gathered anything that looked promising and Burton sorted through it. If it weren't for his meticulous eye we would never have found the papers. They'd slipped between two other files.' Maria flung her arms in the air in a gesture of prayer. 'There was your passport photo, and Burton swore it looked like your signature. To all intents and purposes, if we didn't know better it just all looked above board – like you'd opened the accounts, no big deal.'

We were suddenly stopped by the gate, which was locked. I groaned. How would I get Maria over? I felt a stab of memory for Stephen, the day he'd tossed me up, how much we'd laughed. Had he been desperate even then? I fought back tears, my eyes so sore and swollen they'd close completely if I cried again.

'It's all right, dear.' Maria's focus was on the barricade. She pulled a hairpin from her scarf and proceeded to twist it expertly from side to side in the lock until there was a loud click and the gate sprung open.

Maria hurried through. After I followed, she suddenly stopped, then scurried back to the gate and, hairpin in hand, locked it again. 'Just in case,' she mumbled, then bustled on. I struggled to keep up.

'Now, where was I?'

'My passport photo.'

'Ah, yes. So, we scrutinised the application. Sofia said it was very standard – and definitely the sort that was set up in person.'

'Set up in person? I thought it was authorised from Australia?'

'No. Set up in person, in Athens,' Maria replied firmly.

'I know the date it was set up from the university records. April twenty-ninth,' I cried, elated. 'I wasn't in Greece then – I was working at Coastal. It was first semester. That means I can prove it wasn't me.'

Maria stopped so abruptly I bumped into her, nearly tumbling us both into the dirt.

'But it wasn't April, Rebecca. It was February second. And I know exactly where you were. You were travelling home – you'd just been to the conference in Crete.'

'But I didn't even go into Athens that time. I just changed planes at the airport. And the bank statements I've seen clearly show the accounts were set up in April.'

'I don't know. Possibly the bank moving slowly? It was only an application.' Maria's brow puckered. 'But now we don't have the paperwork, so we can't check anything.'

I felt a chill – whoever was doing this had checked I was in Greece in February last year and knew that it would be hard to prove I had waited at the airport for the flight back to Australia. I would have had plenty of time to go into the city.

'So, tell me about how the paperwork disappeared?' I asked as we moved off down the hill again.

'The main boss came back from lunch.'

'The one Sofia had bribed?'

'No, that was the guy in control of the archive, Vasson. Not the boss. This is Greece, don't forget. Lots of excess layers. So, it's hard to hide Burton, and the boss starts asking questions. But Vasson, God bless him, makes up an altogether different story for why we're there.'

'Couldn't you just take the papers with you?'

'That would be a criminal offence. Sofia felt it best to return at lunchtime the next day: Vasson would let us in, and we'd photocopy everything.'

'And that's not an offence?'

'Evidently not as bad,' Maria shrugged. 'But when we came back, the papers had gone. Burton was positive he knew where he left them. And not in the official file, of course. Which makes it creepier. If someone from the bank branch had come for them, they were misfiled so they wouldn't have found them.'

'Vasson?'

'Sofia thinks not. Vasson certainly seemed to be as surprised as we were when we returned and couldn't find them.'

'That might have been an act.'

'For sure. But he'd been smoking and talking on the phone in a different area. I don't think he'd noticed exactly where we'd been, let alone the file Burton hid them in.

Sofia thinks there is only one explanation – someone was watching us. Someone who Vasson didn't know was there.' Maria scurried ahead, leaving me to ruminate. The day I went to the bank in Athens someone had come after me. It was conceivable this was the same person. Who were they? Police? I shuddered. I wasn't favoured by the police here in Italy. It would be a nightmare if the Greek police were after me too.

Suddenly the forest parted and the sparkling sea lay just ahead. There was an unreality to everything and the sharp contrasts of colours in the clear air by the water mocked and danced. Murky and misty would have fitted, not this image of Paradise that unfolded before us.

Maria bent and shook the rusty ladder that plunged into the sea. 'Firm, could be slippery though,' she muttered.

I stared at the row of white buoys bobbing on the crystal waves. If Stephen had manufactured his exit, how could he have chosen such a cruel way? He knew how my father's death had affected me, and he had always been so supportive. Was this all a fantasy I was constructing? Surely Stephen wouldn't have been so callous as to fake my worst fear? Or was it perhaps some cryptic clue? I turned and began searching for the crevice in the rock where his clothes were found. Everything looked different in the daylight and it took a while to ascertain where it was. There was no tape, no official marking, which bothered me. It was like the police had just stopped investigating, which I knew couldn't be true.

I plunged my hand into the deep crack, hoping it wasn't home to spiders or scorpions. I could feel only cool rock. I swept my hand around, frisking the mountain. There was nothing but air. A soft crunching of gravel sounded down the hill and the hair on the nape of my neck stood on end; I looked rapidly back up the path. No movement. Were we being watched?

Maria stood. 'What's wrong, Rebecca?'

'Shh!' I strained my ears. All birdsong had stopped. All I could hear was the splash of the sea gently washing against the rocks and sucking back out. Turning, I shrugged. 'It's nothing.'

Maria sighed and trotted towards the broken thatch up the other end, where she picked around the tables and chairs.

Finally I walked to the water's edge and looked down. The sea was so translucent I could see the sandy floor. Was it the grave of a dead man? My beautiful husband?

I bit my cheeks hard to try to stop the tears but they came, incessant, out of control. Through blurred vision I imagined Stephen swimming out. Had he ducked under the line of buoys, holding his breath, opening his eyes and letting the salt sting, adjusting his vision to the underwater world in all its vibrant life deep below? Had he marvelled at a school of fish, small sardines glistening, brushing against his cool skin as they passed? Had the currents swept him away, unsuspecting? Or had the anxiety that he had held at bay for so long gushed up, reaching through his veins like tentacles until he finally let go, allowing it to drive him onwards into the swell, darker now, indigo water so infinite it looked like night?

As I had slept on the hillside, had he kept swimming, wondering how it all could have happened, how an Economics professor of his pre-eminence had lost everything, bankrupting his family? Costly mistakes, stupidity, lies, his complexity of emotions so strong he couldn't hold on to a single one.

I looked out and imagined Stephen increasing his speed until his breathing was ragged, the sea starting to swamp his body, his strong frame now tiny, sucked into the vast ocean current.

If I had sat up that day and glanced down the mountain, would I have seen him swimming away forever? Disappearing into the blue mist that wrapped gently around him until he was gone.

21

'D on't worry, I've done this before!' cried Burton, leaning backwards, bumping his wheelchair down step after step in a long flight as we headed into the heart of Positano. Maria was already way in front, hopping like a sparrow. I'd gone into Amalfi and hired a van to make travelling for Burton easier, but the steep mountains along the coast were still going to cause problems whenever we got out of it.

We passed the bar where Stephen and I had sat gazing at Capri; where he had vowed to be closer to me, to not take me for granted. They didn't sound like the words of someone who planned to take his own life, yet his stock market gamble must have been awry even then.

At lunch I'd emailed Erin and James and asked them to be together so I could phone them tonight. I ached that I would not be there to hold them when they heard the awful news. I'd give them my credit card details and get them to fly straight over. 'Hang on, I'll meet you down there!' I called, suddenly realising I hadn't checked my own bank accounts. Burton waved, unable to stop. I leaned into the shade against an ancient wall and quickly flicked on my phone and logged into my bank. The joint account had been drained, one week ago. I opened my personal account, where most of my savings were held: it too had been drained, four days ago. The only money left was my most recent pay, which had gone in yesterday. I slumped down into the dirt, ignoring the tourists who thronged past. A cool white rage enveloped me.

Was it cash Stephen was stockpiling for his disappearance? Or was he trying desperately to pay his debts? I checked the time; it was too late to call the bank in Australia, so I sent off an email. Where had the money been paid? How had it been allowed to happen? In my fury I still hoped that it had been transferred to Italy for Stephen's escape. But how many days had we been here? I couldn't think clearly.

All our money was gone. Our life savings. I had studied wealth in civilisations for too long not to know the chilling effect of poverty. I had a job – just. For now that gave me an income, I quickly reminded myself, as I fought off panic.

I did some quick calculations as I eyed the balance on my two credit cards. I would only just have enough for my children's airfares. I rose and continued down the steps. How could Stephen have done this? I'd read stories of people living with someone who turned out to have a double life. I'd always thought the aggrieved party was naïve. As my anger boiled over I vowed to track him down – and bring him to account for what he'd done to us.

The tall, rotund sailor dangled his homemade line in the translucent sea, its baited hook visible, surrounded by a school of fish. 'The crewman you describe, signora, he could be anyone.'

'He was working the Amalfi–Sorrento ferry three days ago. The ten-oh-five that connects with the train to Pompeii.'

'Perhaps try head office?' He shrugged dismissively.

Burton drew his wheelchair close. 'Signor, we want to speak to your fellow crewman because we need to find a man – a gentleman, fit, tall, about fifty – who has disappeared.'

'Missing?' The sailor grew interested.

'Si, si. Vanished. We wonder if he came on the ferry. Perhaps the evening before last?'

I held out my phone and showed a photo of Stephen standing inside the Marine Gate at Pompeii. It was a good likeness, capturing him vividly.

'Hmm. No.' He took another look. 'Perhaps maybe?'

'Were you working that night?' asked Burton.

'Si, si.' The sailor took my phone and scrutinised the image. 'It's possible.' He tipped the phone one way and another, as though trying to make Stephen come to life.

'There are other photos.' I quickly showed him. He squinted hard, screwing up his weathered face. The ferry's horn blasted, making us jump and the sailor pulled up his fishing line.

'No. I have not seen this man.' He handed back my phone and moved to stow the gangplank. As we hurried to dry land I passed him a flier that Burton had printed, the photo of Stephen at Pompeii with our contact details. It was captioned 'Missing'. My mouth went dry and a sour liquid rose.

Everything that was happening was impossible.

'Where to next?' sighed Maria.

'We'll call the main office,' said Burton, dialling. But we had no luck there either.

We walked back to the small crescent of beach and, with Burton quizzing the bartenders and shopkeepers, started pasting the fliers of Stephen. 'Missing'. I stood glaring at Stephen's soft, sensuous mouth and kind, brown eyes creased with laughter lines. The few times I'd seen posters of the missing I'd found them tragic. Haunted faces frozen in time. The unreality of the situation swirled about me. Stephen's vibrant face was far too handsome to be on a poster of the lost. Men like Stephen didn't just disappear.

Or perhaps they did when they'd ruined their family's finances.

A short while later we were back in the van navigating hairpin bends. I had so little money I would have to return the other hire car. My lips quivered. The sports car was inextricably linked with Stephen. A carefree, happy image burned into my brain. That first day, driving from Naples, the world had opened with freedom and possibilities.

I pulled the van over and parked in a tiny dirt space on the side of the road, and, dodging buses, hauled out Burton's wheelchair and helped him manoeuvre into it. We headed for the elevator that would take us down to the Grotta Verdi.

Tourists made way for the wheelchair as we edged closer to the lift doors. 'I'm good for something,' muttered Burton.

Maria took one hand and Burton my other as we plunged down.

When we exited at the bottom, Burton's face dropped. The rocky path above the swirling sea was narrower than I remembered.

'We won't let you fall,' said Maria, grasping the wheelchair handles.

'Don't, please,' replied Burton. 'It's best if I steer alone.'

'I'm right behind you,' said Maria.

'Me too,' I said, thinking if he were to slip there was nothing we could do. 'Maybe we should go back?'

'Nonsense.' Burton kept moving ahead. 'Please be careful,' I called. Soon we were halfway to the entrance, and in a few more minutes we were waiting in line to enter the grotto.

'Wow.' Maria stepped inside and stopped to let her eyes adjust to the gloom.

'Amazing.' Burton gazed around, transfixed by the massive limestone stalagmites thrusting up from the sea. 'Poseidon's den.'

A ruckus broke out and from the corner of my eye I saw the wiry little man flapping his arms and running towards us. 'No, no. No wheelchairs!' he cried in a thick accent. 'No, no, you cannot come in. Too dangerous!'

Burton replied in Italian that we were here to speak to a guide and that it was of crucial importance.

I scanned the boats as the rowers sang loud bursts of opera that bounced wildly off the cave walls. My heart sank when I couldn't see the White Spider.

'His name is Charon,' said Burton wryly and the wiry man laughed.

'They're all Charon, all of them!'

'Then we need to talk to one Charon in particular,' I said and pointed, relieved, as the White Spider came gliding into sight, his boatful of distraught passengers clearly eager to disembark.

'Buongiorno,' he called, tipping his cap. 'The signora has-a returned. Where is your husband?' He gave a sly smile.

'That's what we're here to ask,' replied Burton in a friendly tone.

'We were wondering if you'd seen him?' I said.

'In the village? No.' The Spider alighted from the boat and stepped aside to let on the next load of hapless sightseers. 'But why do you ask?' He loped towards me, a cruel, eager smile lighting his face. 'Have-a you lost him? Have-a you lost your husband?' He brushed a cold hand against my arm and I recoiled.

'Si, he's disappeared,' replied Burton while Maria scrutinised the Spider with a stern look of disapproval.

'I would expect it,' the Spider shrugged. 'Those men are all-a the same. He's missing? Very-a interesting. Fascinating.' He looked me up and down. 'But it's-a strange, you know?' he said merrily. 'Now I remember. Recently I saw-a him in a boat. I thought, *Charon, what's he doing with a blonde woman who is not-a his wife?*' The Spider watched me with pale, eager eyes. 'It was the evening before last. I was visiting friends at Praiano and we went-a fishing. Along came-a your husband in a speedboat and imagine my surprise when you weren't-a with him? He had his arm around another woman. Bella.' He thrust his long, thin arms into the air and traced a quick outline of her shape: a perfect fantasy woman.

261

His eagerness repulsed me; I couldn't trust him.

'How old?' asked Burton.

The Spider shrugged. 'Not-a young. Mid-forties? Maybe older? She had beautiful blue-a eyes. Too good-a for him, I thought. Better with Charon.' He chuckled cruelly.

I held the Spider's gaze. He grinned, revealing stained, tombstone teeth. 'I must take-a my next tour. You wanna come?' He waved provocatively as he thrust off into the limegreen water.

'He made that up,' muttered Maria disdainfully.

'But the woman. Blue eyes, blonde hair, well preserved. Remind you of someone?' asked Burton.

'A cliché?' said Maria.

'Priscilla Chiton,' he declared. 'It's conceivable he's run away with her. Sorry to be blunt, Bec, but I didn't think Charon was necessarily making it up. And the timing fits. Evening. Stephen could have swum and met her in a cove. Praiano's between your hotel and Positano, isn't it? And we know that Priscilla's not in Australia at the moment.'

My stomach contracted.

'Breathe,' whispered Maria, stroking my back. 'Deep breaths.'

Tourists were pushing past, talking loudly, their voices echoing against the cave walls. I fought back panic and claustrophobia as I rushed to the exit, grateful to be back in the sunlight and away from the revolting Charon.

'I don't think I believe him,' I said as we navigated the path. Anger was taking over: anger at myself for coming, anger at Charon's games, anger at Stephen for putting me in this position. I wanted to hurl rocks and scream.

'He was fabricating it for effect.' Maria shook her head. 'I saw him embellishing as he watched your reaction.'

'I'm not so sure,' said Burton.

If Stephen really was with Priscilla my rage would be unstoppable. My head spun.

'He was utterly loathsome. Let's get to the hotel and see if Marco has found anything,' said Maria.

Cameras pointed at my face as I alighted outside Della Mare's ceramics shop; microphones were thrust forward. Television presenters with big hair and higher heels thronged towards us.

'Signora Wilding, did you murder your husband?'

'How does it feel to be accused, Signora Wilding?'

'Professor, are you denying any involvement?'

'Rebecca, Rebecca, you must be distraught that your husband is missing?'

Startled, I darted back to the sanctuary of the van.

'Good God!' Burton stared at the reporters in shock.

'Someone's setting you up,' said Maria angrily.

A scrawny olive-skinned hand, bejewelled and young, wrenched my door open.

'Professor Wilding, do you deny murdering your husband for his money?'

I laughed cynically as I struggled to pull the door shut. 'Drive off!' cried Burton. I locked the doors and slammed the van into reverse, about to force my way through the pack when Marco came running from the shop.

'Rebecca! Rebecca!' he bellowed and then spoke sternly to the press.

'What's he saying, Burton?' His Italian was too rapid for me to understand.

'He's telling them to piss off, basically. In no uncertain terms.'

Reporters started a stream of conversation in return.

'And they're telling him it's public property where they're standing. They're not leaving,' Burton sighed.

Marco ploughed through the crowd. He ran around to the back door and I quickly undid the locks. I snapped them shut again as soon as he flung himself inside.

'A pack of wolves!' he cursed. 'Rebecca, I've been trying to phone you.'

'Did you find something?' I pulled out my phone and saw that the battery had gone dead. I focused on it, terrified by what Marco was about to say.

'Somehow it got reported in Australia. And now the press here are all over it.'

'Marco, has he been found?' My voice sounded far away, as if someone else were speaking.

'No, no. It's okay. We didn't find anything. There's nothing new.'

I let out a long breath.

'Sorry,' Marco leaned forward and squeezed my shoulders. 'I didn't mean to frighten you, Becca. But your children have heard. They've been phoning.'

The blood drained from me and Maria leaned quickly across to take my hand in hers.

Burton passed his phone over. 'You must call them and explain.'

'Too late. They're on their way,' said Marco. 'They were heading straight for the airport.'

I tried to think what time it would be there. 'When was this?' I muttered.

'About four hours ago. Then the press started arriving here.'

'But they couldn't get a flight that quickly, surely?' I dialled Erin's number. It rang out.

Everyone watched as I stabbed in another number. Cameras outside were pointed at me, lights pierced my eyes. I turned my back on them as Klair picked up.

'Is James there?'

'Rebecca, is that you?

'Yes,' I snapped. 'Can I speak to James?'

'He's not here. He left his phone with me at the airport because it won't work overseas. Erin's going to try ringing you when they get to Singapore.' Klair paused. 'Are you all right? Is Stephen really missing? They're saying you're under suspicion for murder.'

'Of course I'm not,' I roared. 'Look, I've got to go.' I hung up as she kept babbling. 'I must charge my phone. What if Stephen's tried to call?' I wrenched open my door.

'Rebecca, wait!' cried Marco but I was already running towards the small gate at street level that led to a flight of stairs cascading down the mountain to the hotel reception. Maria came after me, beating off reporters with tiny whirling arms, like a hummingbird. Marco moved to retrieve Burton's wheel-chair; they'd have to battle their way inside to the lift. A reporter screeched. Maria had kicked the woman's shin. We reached the gate and fled downhill.

Adriana greeted us with hugs and despair. 'Caro, caro! Come quickly away from those monsters!' She ushered us into the small sitting room. 'Vultures.' Adriana drew the curtains shut, plunging us into gloom. She switched on a lamp that cast a reassuring golden glow, and came and sat beside us on the white leather lounge.

'I cannot tell you how sorry I am, Rebecca. The police have been here looking for you.'

'What on earth has happened?'

'They won't say. Even Marco could get nothing from them.'

'Do you think they've found him?' My voice cracked and my legs went numb. 'I must call.'

'Caro, perhaps we might find a lawyer for you?'

'But I haven't done anything wrong!'

'Rebecca, maybe it would be a good idea?' Maria said, eyes wide with fear.

'If you think so,' I mumbled, aware I might not be making the best decisions at the moment. 'I'd like to ask Burton.'

'Coming!' he called and wheeled in like the cavalry.

'We think she should get a lawyer,' said Maria, and Burton nodded. 'Who knows one?'

'I do,' said Marco as he followed Burton into the room. He went to a small ceramic table and picked up a phone. 'Is this okay?' He looked at me.

'I guess so.' I was wondering how I'd pay for it.

Marco spoke quickly into the receiver and hung up. 'He is the very best. A friend of my late parents. A criminal lawyer.'

'Can we call the police?' I asked. Marco obliged, summoning Giotto. After a hushed conversation, Marco turned to me.

'There's nothing. But the Commissario thinks you're hiding something. Evidently my waiter Alessandro has been aiding them in this view. Are you?' Marco looked at me directly.

I sat back, overwhelmingly relieved that I wasn't hearing Stephen confirmed dead. 'No, Marco, I'm not. The Commissario can ask me whatever he wants. Once my lawyer arrives.'

22

Signor Vitale was model-thin with a full head of glossy black hair. Immaculately groomed in a white linen suit, blue silk tie and soft leather slip-on shoes, he exuded expensive. His English was perfect, spoken in a deep, commanding voice. I was glad that he was on my team and not batting for the opposition.

He ordered everyone else to leave the room and once we were alone he turned casually, leaning in ever so slightly as he held me in his hypnotic gaze. I kept a surreptitious lookout on my phone, wishing I'd asked Klair what time my kids were arriving in Singapore. I'd played and replayed their heartbreaking messages saying they were on their way, pleading to know what was going on.

'Professor Wilding, I must put to you one question. Did you do it? Did you murder your husband? I promise I will tell no one, but I need to know.'

'Of course not!'

'If my wife had ruined the family finances I could be violent,' Vitale shrugged. 'Anyone could be.'

'We didn't even fight. He said he loved me, I went to sleep and he went for a swim. Well, I think he swam. I didn't even know about the finances until later.'

'When he said he loved you, was this unusual?'

'It didn't seem so at the time.'

'So, you often say this to each other?'

'It's not rare. Although in recent times it was perhaps a bit unusual.'

'Why?' Vitale snapped.

'We'd both been preoccupied. In hindsight, I can see that Stephen was sick with worry about his investments.'

'And yet he told you nothing?'

'We both had secrets,' I sighed.

'And what are yours?'

Immediately I regretted speaking. 'Nothing relevant,' I replied firmly.

'I'll decide that.' Vitale stood and walked to the window, lifting a curtain back slightly with one finger and glancing out. 'Tell me everything. It's the only way I can protect you.' He turned back dramatically. 'Were you having an affair?'

I shook my head. 'But I wondered if Stephen was.' I hoped this would occupy the conversation and I wouldn't be quizzed again on my secrets, which I had no intention of revealing.

'We'll come back to that,' said Vitale smoothly. 'What were you hiding from him, signora?'

'Please, if we're to work together, I must stay focused on Stephen. The boatman from the grotto, Charon – I don't know his real name – told us he saw Stephen with a blonde woman fitting the description of a colleague, Priscilla Chiton. It's possible Stephen contacted her and asked her to help him disappear. I've worried for months if he was seeing Priscilla. And I might have stumbled upon her sandals in Crete.'

'Her sandals?' Vitale frowned.

'In the Venetian fortress in Heraklion. I thought Stephen might have met her there.'

'And the sandals?'

'She wasn't wearing them. She'd left them on the stairs.' I stopped and rubbed my temples, remembering that I'd seen the Englishwoman put on the sandals. 'Sorry, I'm a bit . . . I saw a woman, from a distance. Forget about the sandals.'

'And you thought the woman looked like . . .' He checked his notes. 'Signora Priscilla Chiton? Have you told the police any of this?'

'Not yet.'

'Then please don't. It's very confused. You'll whip up the Commissario. He's a man who runs on instinct. Our problem is he's convinced you are guilty.'

'Without a shred of evidence, because I'm not. Don't they know how to conduct an investigation down here? And that waiter Alessandro is a maniac.'

'We all know each other very well. It doesn't pay to be rude.'

'I'm not being.' Impatience rose. 'My husband's missing

and every minute the police stand around presuming I'm guilty is time wasted from the investigation. Surely you can see my problem?'

'If he has gone missing, how do you propose we find him?'

'For a start I'd like the boats and helicopter to keep searching. And for the police to interview all the crews on the ferries and check any closed-circuit-television footage. What about the wharves in Sorrento and Naples? The train station? The airport? Although I doubt Stephen went to the airport because he couldn't use his passport without the police knowing.'

Vitale stared at me like I was something quite repulsive – something that could be squashed.

'His passport's missing,' I added.

'And you don't think he met with foul play?' Vitale's voice was quiet, his dark eyes bright with suspicion.

'It can't be ruled out, can it?' One of my knees started jittering of its own accord, beating out a tattoo. I put a hand on it firmly to pin it down.

'I hope for your sake that your theory he ran away is correct,' said Vitale, suddenly gentle. 'I think perhaps our instincts about our loved ones are also worth listening to. And I get the strongest feeling speaking with you that you think your husband is still alive.'

I bit my lower lip to try to stop the quivering. I nodded but couldn't find any words.

Vitale crossed the room and took my hand. 'I shall ask the Commissario to keep looking. But now, take me through moment by moment the day your husband disappeared.'

*

Two hours later Vitale was satisfied that I was ready to meet the police again. He organised for Napolitano to come to the hotel, not wanting me to have to run the gauntlet of the press. Before the Commissario arrived, I called Erin's phone but it kept ringing out.

Maria bustled in with a plate of food. It was dinnertime and I found I was surprisingly hungry. I devoured the spaghetti marinara and salad gratefully but refused the wine. Burton watched without saying a word.

'You're unnerving me,' I finally said.

'I've contacted the Australian consulate in Rome. They're sending someone as soon as they can but they're short staffed, particularly as you haven't been charged with anything yet.'

'And she won't be!' said Maria.

Burton took my glass of wine and gulped it down.

'Careful,' warned Maria, 'we need you on board, Burton. Rebecca, what's Vitale like? If you're not happy we'll find someone else.'

'He's good. He's on my side, I think,' I added vulnerably.

Minutes later, Vitale led Napolitano and Giotto into the room. Maria quickly cleared my plate away and she and Burton were asked to leave.

'We have discovered something unpleasant,' said Napolitano, pulling up a chair that grated on the tiled floor. 'You have something to tell me about Coastal University?'

For the first time that question made me flood with relief: at least it wasn't Stephen's death he was announcing. 'It's where I work.'

'Something else?' He waited as both Giotto and Vitale took

notes. Vitale looked like an animal waiting to pounce. I hoped he really was on my side.

I said, 'I don't know what you mean.'

'Does fraud sound familiar?'

I tensed and fell silent.

'Does it, Professor Wilding?' Napolitano raised his voice a notch.

'You'll have to be more specific.'

'You're under investigation for misappropriating a very large sum of money. In the millions of dollars.'

'No, not millions.'

'I believe it is. I spoke to Professor DiStasio.'

'I would have thought that's confidential. And it's only alleged. Several people are under investigation.'

'There's a pattern, though, is there not?'

How had the Italian police managed to find out university business? Had Coastal referred the matter to outside authorities since I'd been away? What was Priscilla's role in all of this?

'Where did you get the idea of millions of dollars?' I desperately hoped to get a clearer picture.

'From your local police.'

My stomach cramped. The matter had gone further and was vastly more serious. I would have to contact DiStasio as soon as I'd finished with Napolitano. Was the fraud somehow linked to Stephen's disappearance?

'I ask you again,' beat on Napolitano, 'to tell me about the fraud. I can only assume you needed the money to cover your husband's gambling debts?'

'Stephen didn't gamble. He invested money and the stock market went against him.'

Napolitano smiled. 'Did you use the money you stole to help him?'

'She's confessing to nothing,' roared Vitale and thumped the little ceramic table so hard it rocked wildly. 'Say no more, please, Rebecca.'

'But I never did any such thing!' I was suddenly in the middle of an Italian soap opera.

Vitale leaped to his feet. 'I need to talk to my client,' he said.

'No,' replied the Commissario. 'We will continue. There are many millions she has hidden away and if we get to the source of the money trail, I believe it will lead to the answers we need.'

'I wish you *would* get to the bottom of the money trail. But first you need to find my husband.' The mood around me was pure testosterone. 'Please?' I added.

'Tell us where you dumped the body?' whispered Napolitano and Giotto's eyes widened as he looked up from his notes. Vitale gazed at me. I opened my mouth to again profess my innocence.

'No, no, no!' Vitale shouted. 'She is saying nothing. You have no proof that there is a body and until you do, this meeting is over. The alleged fraud is in Australia and it has nothing to do with your jurisdiction.' Vitale grabbed me under both arms, lifted me up and led me out on jellied legs, shutting the door on a fuming Napolitano and an alarmed Giotto.

Marco, Maria, Burton and I sat around my room. No one had spoken for the past few minutes. I was drained but needed the company. The police and Vitale had left the hotel over an hour ago, Napolitano vowing to return as soon as he had more proof.

Finally Marco shuffled in his chair as if he were about to speak. Everyone turned. He sighed and shook his head.

'I've known Rebecca nearly thirty years, Marco,' said Burton. 'And I promise she never would have stolen money, not a cent.'

'Then, who is setting you up?' asked Marco quietly. 'Might that person have something to do with your husband?'

'I don't know. But why would they? That's what I can't work out.' My blood ran cold.

'To make everyone think you're guilty,' replied Marco.

'It's possible, isn't it, Rebecca?' Tonight Maria looked her age, her face creased with worry.

'Anything's possible,' I sighed. 'Including that Stephen drowned or committed suicide.' I felt the familiar tears gush up.

'But could Stephen have stolen the money and faked his disappearance?' continued Marco.

'It would be completely out of character. He's not like that.' I shook my head tiredly. I didn't know what to think anymore.

'Is that because you don't want it to be true or because it's impossible?' quizzed Marco.

'I'm sure he could forge your signature, Bec,' said Burton, and Marco sat forward.

'Well, he'd never been to Athens, so he couldn't have set up the accounts,' I said.

'But Sofia says the bank manager takes bribes. He could have mocked it up to look like someone went physically to the bank, when they didn't,' said Maria.

I gave a long exhale that sounded like a moan. 'Give me

some credit for knowing my husband. Put it this way – Stephen played the stock market. I didn't know about his losses but I'm not surprised. Horrified. But not in any doubt it's true. On the other hand, Stephen manipulating university accounts and using my name? I honestly don't think so.'

'But he would know you think that,' said Burton gently. 'Unfortunately it gives him the perfect opportunity.'

'Someone's set you up, and Stephen has a motive,' echoed Maria.

'Gamblers who lose all their money can get desperate,' said Marco.

'He's not a gambler,' I mumbled tiredly.

'Bec, you need to face this.' Burton wheeled close and dipped his head, trying to catch my eyes, which I averted to the ground. 'It doesn't seem like coincidence that you're accused of fraud, Stephen loses all your money and then disappears. Think like a professional.' Burton's blue eyes were vibrant and pleading. I lifted my head and he followed my gaze, locking mine into his. 'Reason this out like the leading archaeologist you are. If we found those three threads in the dirt – missing public funds, lost savings and the disappearance of a key person – what would we hypothesise?'

I leaned away and broke eye contact. I wanted to retreat, but I had nowhere left to go. 'All right, I get where you're heading,' I replied. 'But I'd also keep an open mind. I'd form another hypothesis to test against it.'

'Which would be?' asked Marco.

I paused, racking my brain, angry at all of them.

'Why don't we make a list?' said Maria, sensing my distress. 'Let's draw up columns. If Stephen's alive and if, God forbid, he's not.'

We worked into the small hours and were still batting out ideas, going round in circles, as the pink dawn crept into the sky and brightened. It was Monday morning. As soon as it reached nine o'clock I phoned the organisers of Stephen's conference on Capri to check if they'd heard from him. They were from an English university and had only just arrived, with the conference due to start on Wednesday. There had been no messages from Stephen. My heart sank. They were sympathetic and worried and promised to get in touch immediately if there was any contact. As I hung up, a wave of despondency hit. Maria took my hand. With great effort, I went back to working out scenarios of what might have happened, determined to cover every possibility, fighting back nausea.

It turned into a sunny afternoon. I was struggling to keep awake when a bustling in the corridor outside distracted me. The door burst open. I blinked, standing, not believing my eyes. It was Erin and James.

'My phone ran out of battery and we couldn't find anywhere to phone in Singapore,' cried Erin, flying into my arms.

'Mum, tell us everything,' implored James as he kissed me. I could smell acrid sweat. 'Dad's missing, isn't he?'

'Yes, I'm so sorry. He is. That part's true,' I replied awkwardly, hugging them tight, pinning one under each arm, never wanting to let them go.

'But obviously you didn't murder him?'

Erin was clinging to me like a baby possum.

'Of course not. And we don't know he's dead.' The last word stuck in my mouth.

'Those lying reporters said he was.' James blinked back tears.

277

'The press do that,' said Burton. 'And God knows how they got onto the story in Australia. They're making everything up.'

'Not unusual,' said Maria.

'So, what happened, Mum?' pleaded James.

'Your dad went swimming,' I frowned, trying to think if it was two days ago. It was hard to keep track of time. Sickened, I realised it was longer. 'Three days ago. On Friday. And he never came back.' This time my own tears didn't well. In the presence of my children I found a sudden stoicism.

'We have to fear the worst, that he may have drowned,' I said. 'But – there were a few other things going on. He might have run away. Just for a bit. Just to sort himself out.'

Both kids peeled off and stared at me like I was a nuclear bomb.

'Like what?' asked James.

'Your dad took a hit on the stock market. He was trying to make money to look after us but things went the wrong way.'

Everyone in the room was watching the children.

Erin shrugged. 'Doesn't that happen all the time?'

'How bad?' asked James. 'If we're in trouble I can help cover things. I've saved a bit from my part-time jobs and I've still got some money left after paying for our tickets over here.'

'I can help, too,' said Maria and my lips quivered and tears tried to flow. Maria was as poor as a church mouse and James's casual jobs paid appallingly – he couldn't possibly have put much away.

'I've already offered,' said Burton proprietorially.

'I would if I had anything. I could get a job,' said Erin.

Again tears welled.

'You're all terribly kind and I'm very grateful but that won't be necessary,' I replied, knowing none of them could help given the extent of our perished finances and Stephen's massive debt.

'But if Dad did run away we need to tell him we're here to support him,' persisted Erin.

'Get word to him that it's okay,' added James.

'Honestly, your dad may have drowned and we need to understand that,' I announced, more honestly than I'd planned.

'But he may not have,' said James emphatically.

'If he'd drowned, wouldn't his body have turned up like Granddad's?' Erin hugged me.

'Usually. Yes, I agree,' said Marco. 'We would expect a body to float to the surface. We've looked in all the coves, from my boat. And we've dived. The police have too.'

'They found his clothes in a crevice at the private beach here,' I added. James and Erin went very still. 'But one ray of hope is that your dad's passport is missing.'

'What does it mean that they found his clothes?' asked Erin.

'I don't know. But I think it's good that his passport has gone.'

'What if someone stole it and got rid of Dad?' asked James. 'The mafia or something?'

Marco was affronted. 'This is a very safe part of the world. No one would do that here. We all know each other,' he said, pride tinged with anger.

'Then, I can see why you think Dad's done a runner,' concluded Erin. 'Have you any idea where he might go?'

I sighed. 'Well, nowhere he needs his passport at the moment, because the police would be flagged.'

'Mum, in Australia they said on the news that you were under suspicion for murder. Why would they say that?' James blinked vulnerably.

'Because . . .' I stopped to choose my words. 'Because they're trying to work out what happened. They don't know me. I guess they have to keep all avenues open.'

'That's right,' Marco agreed fulsomely. 'They're just doing their job.'

'But how can they say it? Isn't that defamatory?' pursued James, aggression biting into his words.

Marco shifted uneasily. James glowered.

'You must be exhausted,' I said. 'James and Erin, why don't you sleep in here with me?'

'I'm not tired at all, I slept on the plane.' James was clearly lying.

'We'd like to go diving ourselves,' said Erin. 'I want to see where Dad went swimming. And we want to make sure no one's missed anything. Sorry, no offence, Marco, I'm really grateful for all you've done. But I'd just like to check for myself. I can't really think until I've done that.'

Marco looked to me for permission. The kids were experienced divers, having received their qualifications years ago. 'I'm coming on the boat too, then,' I said, and they reacted with surprise. 'I'm not going to let anything happen to you.'

'And, Burton, would you be able to set up a social network site asking people for help, see if anyone's seen Dad?' asked Erin.

'Good idea,' replied Burton. 'Onto it.'

'Do you really want to do that?' said Maria worriedly. 'You'll get a lot of nutty people.'

'But we have to, it'd be crazy not to have a site,' replied Erin firmly.

I knew it was going to be a long day – but I would never have guessed how long.

23

Lack of sleep made my head thick and lumpy as I gazed out at limestone cliffs plunging into the indigo sea. On any other occasion it would have been a sight of inspirational beauty. Now in a haze I watched for a corpse, bloated and savaged. The remains of Stephen.

Marco was behind the wheel of his long, sleek boat. My children, as black as seals, were perched astern in wetsuits, their eyes intent on the water and rocks that stuck out like jagged teeth near the base of the mountain. Every so often there was a tiny, pebbled beach in a cove and Marco would carefully guide the boat towards shore. He was patient and thorough as he continued down the coastline.

'I'd like to go in now, Marco, if I could, please?' James's voice was brusque with exhaustion.

'Why here?' questioned Erin. 'I would have thought further back?'

'The current's going this way, isn't it, Marco?'

'Yes, this is the prevailing current.'

'And three days ago?'

'The same.' Marco cut the engine and we started to drift, surprisingly quickly for what appeared to be a calm sea.

'Then, wouldn't he be further away by now?' reasoned Erin.

'He could be snagged,' said James.

Clearly they were in deep shock, talking about Stephen as casually as if they had lost a flipper. I was devastated they'd found out through the media and astonished they didn't seem remotely angry with me for not telling them sooner. But it was a great comfort to have them here now; in spite of how difficult it was, it felt right to be searching as a family.

'I'm going in,' James announced.

I stood and held him, the wetsuit rubber cold and unyielding to my touch. 'Please be careful.'

'Help me get this on, Mum?' I took the air tank while James fitted his arms into the harness. I tightened the belt. His cheeks were pink and eyes wide with adrenalin.

Erin walked up, having quickly donned her own scuba gear. They sat in silence as they squashed their feet into flippers. Marco dropped anchor and came back and stood over them.

'No more than fifteen minutes, okay?'

They nodded.

'I'm coming in with you,' continued Marco and quickly slipped on a scuba tank. 'You'll be all right?' He turned to me.

'I'll be expecting you all up in fifteen.' It was hard to keep my voice from cracking. It hadn't occurred to me I'd be alone on a boat. I tried to quell my fear, attempting to convince myself it was insignificant compared to everything else that was happening.

As they splashed into the sea one by one I wanted to grab them, make us all return to dry land. Instead, I sat on my hands and pressed my lips closed, praying for their safe return.

Erin waved and then their masked faces submerged. The surface retracted back to a glassy calm and they were gone, black bodies swimming out of sight down into the dark blue depths.

I watched the clock. The first five minutes were an eternity. I paced up and down the deck, forcing images of my father the day he drowned out of my mind as quickly as they came bubbling up.

Ten minutes. The late afternoon was still, as though the day were holding its breath. I fought back claustrophobia: even though I was in the open I felt a crushing sense of enclosure. I wished for a breeze, to move the oppressive air that sucked like warm tar in my lungs.

Twelve minutes. Still no sign of them. Panic rose, irrational, uncontrollable.

'Erin? James? Marco?' My voice flew mockingly back off the cliffs.

I forced myself to sit down. Still three minutes to go. I welded my eyes to the sea, straining for visibility. It was very deep here. I wondered with dread why James had chosen this spot. Did he have a sixth sense about his father's resting place?

Thirteen minutes. Still no sign. Fourteen. I resolved to dive in myself and look for them. I hadn't swum since I was a teenager but I used to be strong.

Fifteen minutes. Bile stuck like glue to the sides of my mouth.

Sixteen minutes. I'd trusted them. How could they have let me down?

Seventeen. I called again, my voice echoing forlornly.

Eighteen. Two more minutes and I was going in.

Nineteen. I saw a black shadow rising, then another, and just as Erin broke the water a third diver rose into view. Marco surfaced and seconds later, James came up with a refreshing splash. They swam to the boat and I hauled them in, my precious, glistening catch of the day.

'Nothing,' announced Erin as she dropped beside me and peeled off her mask, her cool body touching mine.

'Thank God,' said James, sitting close on my other side.

Marco smiled. 'Okay, Becca?'

'Okay.'

He padded to the prow and lifted anchor, clanking the tri-forked monster on board and stowing it away. He gunned the engine and we glided further along the coast. I dreaded the moment they would be underwater again but the kids' faces were alive with hope. It was helping them; the best thing they could do.

With each dive they grew more elated. Every time we stopped I had to battle my demons all over again while they swam into deep caverns, searching everywhere for clues.

There was a growing sense of euphoria. No body meant that Stephen could be alive.

Finally we all agreed it was time to head home.

'I just don't feel Dad's here,' said Erin suddenly.

'Me neither, I know what you're saying,' echoed James as he

sat looking back at the white, churning water behind the boat. 'You think that too, don't you, Mum?'

'I want to.' They stared, shocked by my tone. 'We mustn't rule anything out,' I sighed tiredly. 'It's easy to convince ourselves of anything at the moment.'

'Are you trying to tell us you think Dad's dead?' said Erin as tears sprang hotly.

'Shh, no, no.' I wrapped her into my arms. 'All my instincts tell me your father's alive, but I don't want to lead you on and give you false hope.'

'Why not?' said James. 'It couldn't make it any worse than it is.'

We were all sunburned, and salt stung our skin as we traipsed up the mountain from where Marco had harboured his boat at a tiny beach at the base of the cliff. At a fork we went left and silently, like a line of goats, scrambled along a thin dirt track to come out finally at Della Mare's private beach. The line of white buoys bobbed rhythmically in the gentle swell and a fine blue haze was forming on the horizon. James put his hands on his hips and pulled himself up to full height. 'So, this is where Dad went swimming?' He stared at the sea like a beast he was about to conquer.

'It was hotter than today and even calmer.' My voice rang high and hollow in the still air. I took Erin's hand, her fingers slick with sweat going limp in my grasp. I desperately wished I could say something to make her feel better.

James strode to the rusty ladder that plunged into the water.

'When it's rough, this whole area blasts,' I said, turning to Marco. 'Is it still dangerous when it's calm? Can it suddenly fire up?'

Marco thought for a moment. 'Not usually, but I suppose it's possible.'

'Like a rogue wave?' asked James.

Marco squinted at the glassy sea, silver in the evening light. James kicked the ladder, which held firm.

'It's very unlikely,' Marco finally declared. 'No, it was calm that day. That's why it's so unusual that a strong swimmer might have drowned.' His last words were almost lost beneath a cacophony of barking dogs. Within seconds, enormous German shepherds bounded down the mountain, running fast, their howls building to a crescendo as they reached me and dropped to their haunches. Erin ran squealing in fright and James and Marco moved quickly to stand between me and the dogs, whose powerful jaws hung open revealing gleaming fangs. Two uniformed police stumbled forward, breathless. They stopped abruptly when they saw the dogs at my feet.

Erin stood stock-still at the end of the rocky ledge.

'We're looking for a man,' the shorter policeman said, perspiration slicking his upper lip. He turned and stared at me.

'Signor Stephen Wilding,' said the taller cop, who was thickset and toned like the dogs.

'He's not here,' said James, giving a wild look.

'Rebecca must have his scent,' said Marco calmly. 'Are you wearing something of Stephen's?'

I looked at my clothes, surprised.

'Mum, you're wearing Dad's watch,' said James.

'Of course!' I quickly unbuckled the leather band.

'Was he not wearing this when he disappeared?' quizzed the taller policeman, taking the watch and holding it to the dogs, who barked, tails wagging. He handed them small dark biscuits of reward.

'He'd left it by the bed.'

'Why had you not mentioned this before? I take it that you are Signora Wilding?'

'I hadn't thought to.'

'If he'd run away as you told the Commissario, would he not have been wearing it?'

That hadn't crossed my mind, but it now seemed of vital concern. 'He didn't take anything else,' I reasoned, as much to myself as to the cop.

'Except his passport?' added James.

'If he was trying to make it look like he drowned, wouldn't he leave his watch?' asked Erin, walking back to join us.

'You should have told the Commissario you were wearing your husband's watch,' barked the shorter cop and both dogs looked up at him then back at me, tails wagging. I went to pat the closest and it growled.

'Don't do that, signora,' snapped the taller cop, and I muttered an apology as I pulled my hand to safety.

'Shall we head back?' Marco spoke pleasantly but authoritatively.

'We'll be staying here,' said the short cop.

The hair rose on the back of my neck as we left the police. If they had sent out the canine squad, they really believed that Stephen was dead.

*

'Here she is! They're back!' A vision dressed in white from top to toe stood dramatically at the top of the hill then tore down to meet us.

'Rebecca!' Arms were flung around me in a bear hug. 'I'm so sorry. It's just awful.'

'Sally Chesser, what on earth are you doing here?'

'Didn't you get my messages?'

'What messages?'

'I called when I saw it all over the news. If they're accusing you of murder you're going to need a good lawyer.' She draped a tanned arm across my shoulder and walked me up the hill. 'You must tell me everything, Bec. I've heard a bit from your friends up here, but I need to go through it with you. Every detail you can think of.' She nodded to my children. 'You must be Erin and James? I'm Sally Chesser, a mate of your parents.'

They greeted her shyly, overwhelmed.

'Did you fly from home?' asked James.

'As luck would have it – not that luck's the right word – I was in Rome for a conference. I left several messages for you, Bec, because I didn't want to turn up unannounced. But when I hadn't heard back I thought I'd better come down.'

'It's strange I didn't get your messages. I've been checking my phone all the time.' My stomach lurched. 'Sally, can you tell me exactly when you rang, because if I haven't got your calls, then maybe I've missed Stephen.' In a fog of tiredness I realised I didn't have my phone.

'Meet you all in the restaurant,' I called back and ran to my room, which was engulfed in long shadows. I snatched up my phone and checked the calls. No messages from Sally. And nothing from Stephen.

If Sally was telling the truth, and I had no reason to doubt her, then my phone service wasn't working properly. My heart pounded as I re-checked everything. Still I found nothing from Stephen – but there was a new email from DiStasio.

Dear Professor Wilding,

I have now completed my initial investigation and strongly believe that you have a case to answer on the matter of alleged fraud. At this point you need to be aware that there appears to be extensive evidence of activities undertaken by you that constitute serious misconduct. If you cannot give evidence explaining how your conduct fits within university guidelines, I will be recommending to the Vice-Chancellor that your employment with Coastal University be terminated. The police have been advised that substantial fraud has allegedly occurred and been asked to take the matter further.

I suggest that it would be in your interest to have your lawyer present when we meet. Given the serious nature of the allegation your interview cannot wait until your return from overseas. We will need to organise a time to have a telephone conference and perhaps a visual link-up. Please contact my assistant in the next forty-eight hours to set up a time.

Yours faithfully,

Professor Margaret DiStasio.

I raced out to the balcony, desperately in need of air. I forced myself to breathe deeply as I perched on the edge of a sun lounge and re-read the email.

My head spun. I needed sleep.

I knew the others were waiting.

Quickly I tapped a reply, requesting an extension of thirty days to organise the interview, given the circumstances of my husband's disappearance.

'Yoo-hoo?' Sally was outside my door.

'I'm coming,' I snapped, rising, but Sally was halfway across the room before I'd even stepped in from the balcony.

'Just wanted to check you're okay?'

'I didn't get your messages. What day did you leave the first one? Can you tell me what time?'

'Let's see.' Sally whipped out her phone and retrieved the details of her calls. I checked against the times and dates.

'I haven't received a single one. Should I try calling my phone company? Will they be able to tell me everyone who's phoned?'

Sally thought for a moment. 'I think so.'

'Can you explain to the others that I might be a while?'

'Shouldn't I stay with you? We can phone up.'

Sally went to the house phone beside the bed and put in the call, while I tried to contact my telco provider back home.

I listened for an hour to bad music and frustrating announcements that I'd been moved up the queue while Sally sat quizzing me, taking notes. I told her everything that had happened – except for the alleged fraud at Coastal – feeling weary going through it all again.

Finally I hung up. 'I'll try later. Let's go.' I kept my phone on me. I wouldn't leave it out of my sight from now on and cursed that I ever had – I needed to be more aware.

And I needed to eat and rest or I'd cease to function.

'Just a quick dinner, then I'm coming back here,' I said tiredly.

Sally grabbed my shoulder. 'You look exhausted. You stay here.'

'But the kids?'

'They probably need sleep too. I'll bring you something to eat.'

I lay on the bed and tried to reply, but my eyes flitted shut and I'd drifted off before I'd formed the words.

It was pitch black when I awoke to a babble of voices. I panicked, disoriented. Then someone flicked on the lights and I sat up blearily as James and Erin led Burton, Maria and Sally into my room.

James closed the door and locked it.

Burton wheeled across and closed the shutters to the balcony.

Maria, Erin and Sally sat down on the bed. 'The police are on their way,' whispered Maria. 'We've called Vitale – he's on his way too.'

'What's happened?' I asked, horrified.

'Marco was talking to Napolitano, asking about that dog squad and Napolitano let slip that he thinks your wearing Dad's watch is significant,' said Erin.

'Hugely so,' said James. 'Marco was being politic, but even he suggested to us that he thought Napolitano was going overboard.'

'They think the watch is some sort of trophy,' said Erin, her face lined with worry.

'Mum, you have to leave,' announced James.

'It's best to go now before things get even more serious,' said Sally. 'This is the least worst option. No one can stop you at this point. But there's not a minute to lose.'

'But won't that make me look guilty?'

'Perhaps. But at the moment they have nothing concrete and they haven't charged you with anything,' replied Sally.

Maria rose and started quickly throwing clothes from the wardrobe into my small carry-on case.

'Remember that American boy in Sienna they arrested for killing his roommate?' said Burton. 'It took years before they admitted they'd made a mistake and set him free. You don't want to end up like him.'

I froze at the thought.

'Marco hinted to us that Napolitano is under a lot of pressure to solve this because of the international coverage it's getting.' Sally took my arm and urged me up.

'The rest of us will stay here looking for Dad,' said James.

'I'd like to go with you but I'd only slow you down,' said Burton miserably.

'They won't let me go either,' called Maria. 'Unless you need me?' she added hopefully.

'You'll be fastest on your own,' said Erin.

I tried to think, overwhelmed. I'd driven through Europe many times but where would I go now?

'We'll keep in touch. Take my phone.' Erin handed it over, eyes glistening with fear and excitement. She pulled her charger from the wall and passed it to me. 'You're to call Burton. You'll just need to get a new SIM card. Don't under any circumstances use your own phone or they'll trace it.'

'I can't just run!' I finally said.

'Mum, you don't have a choice.' James pinned my arms and looked at me so seriously I was reminded of Stephen. My heart melted.

'What does Marco think?' I grabbed a few of Stephen's clothes from his case and threw them in with mine. In case I found him. In case I never saw him again.

'Marco doesn't know,' Sally replied firmly.

'Quickly, Mum. Please?' James implored.

'We'll form a better plan once you're safely away,' said Sally.

'Are you sure this is sound legal advice?' I turned to her. 'It seems dishonest. Cowardly.'

'Mum, if they arrest you, God knows what might happen.' Erin's voice rose in distress. 'They're already out of control even to be thinking it's you. They could fabricate evidence.'

'But no one's arresting me.'

'Yet,' said Sally. 'After further questioning they might.' 'Mum, can you please stop arguing? Sally says you're not breaking the law, so trust her.' James picked up my bag.

'What are you going to tell the police?'

'You're following a lead of your own but you rushed out without saying where you were heading,' said Sally. 'We're hoping Vitale will take our side and convince the police that your behaviour is valid. That you'll be back soon. After all, we're still here.'

Burton's blue eyes were wide with fear. 'You must go now, Bec.'

'Please, Mum?' James's face was flushed. 'For us. For Erin and me?'

Maria opened the door and looked out rapidly in both directions. 'Coast's clear,' she whispered and James hurried out with
my luggage. I grabbed my handbag.

'My passport!' I rushed to the safe, stabbed in the code and
pulled out my valuables.

And then I scrambled out into the corridor and ran. We
couldn't all fit in the lift and in the confusion Burton went in
with Maria and James, and the rest of us raced up the endless
flights of stairs to the road.

'Can't I at least say goodbye to Marco? Thank him?'

'No!' they replied in a collective grunt.

'Buy a SIM card and be in touch,' ordered Erin.

'It's best we don't know where you'll be for now,' Sally said,
'and when you do call keep things vague so no one has to lie.'

James was peering fearfully up the darkened road. 'Can you
just get going, please, they'll be here any minute!'

Sally stuffed a wad of euros into my hand. 'Don't use your
credit cards or ATMs for now. You can pay me back when we're
home,' she said.

I barely had time to hug my children as they thrust me inside
the red sports car and slammed the door. Maria and Burton
looked on with deep concern, clearly desperate to come. I didn't
want to leave any of them.

'Don't worry, Bec,' called Burton, 'we'll look after James
and Erin.'

'As if they were our own,' added Maria, eyes tearing up.

'Hurry!' cried James.

'Where are the keys?' I called in alarm.

'In the ignition,' James and Erin yelled. I gunned the engine and roared off as I saw lights coming from the direction of Positano.

I flew along the narrow road, heading towards Amalfi. It was the middle of the night and the road was mercifully empty. After I rounded the first hairpin bend I didn't see the lights behind again. Shuddering, I realised they must have been the police.

I floored the accelerator and went at breakneck speed, slowing only at the corners where I tooted the horn incessantly and kept going. At the turn-off to Ravello I had to make a quick decision whether to advance along the coast road or head up into the hills. I took a sharp left and began the steep ascent.

I wanted to turn around and go back, but they'd all been so insistent. And I couldn't afford to get arrested. I hurtled through the night, roaring up the mountain, taking hairpin bends with dangerous bravado. It was hard to believe I was the same person who had always been so fanatical about ethics, so responsible for my children. Now I'd left behind my family and friends to face the wrath of the police alone. And where on earth was I to go? To Florence, tracing the steps of our holiday? Might Stephen have gone there? Could he be walking through the Boboli Gardens like we always did, getting lost on the vine-covered paths? Perhaps I should check, ask around our favourite haunts. And yet my instinct didn't feel that this was right.

Maybe he had run to Venice to hide among the throngs of tourists, disappearing in the tiny alleys along the waterways, living a secret life in a city of mystery. I could ask my glass-blower friends on Murano to help me look.

Then it hit me. A blast of clear sight spliced through my sleep-deprived brain. If Stephen had fled, the obvious place would be Paris. He was a creature of habit and he loved the City of Light. And Priscilla was in Paris on study leave. What if the White Spider had been telling the truth after all? I hadn't wanted to believe it but Priscilla could have picked Stephen up from a cove near Praiano in a boat, and then they could have driven to Paris.

Suddenly I felt sick, and foolish – of course that's what he would have done. If they travelled by road and stayed in the Eurozone, there would be no border checks to interrupt their journey. Priscilla must have already hired a car and had it waiting.

I had to get to Paris as quickly as possible, but how? My car could well have satellite tracking, and I couldn't hire a new car because Napolitano could easily get wind of it. I made a split-second decision: I would detour en route to Paris, and I would find another vehicle.

I sped through the night with resolve. But was I now not only fleeing the law but chasing an improbable phantom? I wondered about my sanity.

24

I reached the large car park I knew in Mestre, just outside Venice, and quickly abandoned the car. With my carry-on bag I hurried to the wharf and called a water-taxi; a vaporetto, the large waterbus I normally travelled on, would be too slow and too public.

Dawn was breaking tentatively through ragged clouds as the water-taxi cut cleanly through the shallow waters of the lagoon, and the buildings of Venice floated into view in shades of muted ochre, white and palest pink.

As we entered the Grand Canal the boat slid easily between gondolas and churning vaporetto. Celadon water lapped gently at the foundations of crumbling palazzos that grandly, slowly sank into the marsh. I found the familiarity reassuring: here was

Ca' d'Oro, the House of Gold, Venetian Gothic at its most lux-uriant, there Ca' da Mosto, a palace that had survived the tides since the thirteenth century, its crumbling arches standing proud as we washed down the canal beneath the Rialto Bridge. Soon we came to the wooden beauty of the Accademia Bridge and passed Stephen's and my favourite pizza restaurant, not yet open for the day, its umbrellas closed, its pink geraniums bright in their waterfront boxes. I pictured us eating there – it was why I'd asked the boatman to bring me this way, to try to feel Ste-phen's presence, use my archaeologist's intuition. Had he been here recently? To my disappointment, I couldn't sense anything.

As we floated out again into the lagoon, the Lion of Venice on his pillar golden in the dawn, I remembered with shock that I was due to give my keynote address here next week. How could I get in touch with the conference and send my apologies?

As we swept past Giardini della Biennale, the lush gardens alive with Venetians and their dogs of all shapes and sizes taking the morning air, I searched for Stephen – but he was not among them. We picked up speed as we skimmed away, and I could think only of him, feeling a volatile mixture of hope that I would see him again and anger at what he had done. A fresh salt wind blasted into the cabin. I threw my head back, breath-ing in deeply, remembering the many times Stephen and I had made this journey together. *I will find you soon*, I promised.

Venice disappeared like a half-remembered dream as we ploughed on until Murano rose suddenly on the horizon. The water-taxi tore past the large brick edifices of glass factories, some of which had their own small wharves jutting out into the water.

We slowed and turned into a narrow canal that split the small island, and puttered along until we stopped at a wharf of silvery timber, where I disembarked.

The shops that lined the path were shuttered, hiding their glassware of all descriptions. Locals sat in the small cafes. I kept my head down as I rolled my bag along, wishing it was later in the day when the place would be full of tourists.

I was all but running, my ribs starting to ache, as I moved through a wide sunlit square spotted with shade trees, feeling dangerously on display. Finally the door that looked tiny in the massive brown stone building came into view, its huge lion's-head knocker glowing like gold at the end of the rainbow.

I rapped loudly. After what seemed an eternity the door swung open and Guido, a giant with arms the size of tree-trunks, peered out blearily. 'Rebecca? Come in, come in. You're in trouble, no? I was so hoping you'd come – I've been trying to reach you. You're in the news again this morning. They want to question you further about Stephen's disappearance.' He squeezed me tightly in a bear hug and I crumpled into his body. My old friend.

The smell of wood smoke hung in the air as Guido led me to his private quarters. Beyond was his glass factory, where workers were starting for the day, firing up the kilns. I knew most of them, had spent many drunken nights in their company. I prayed no one would come to ask Guido a question as he sat down beside me on a huge leather lounge.

'I know that Stephen is alive,' Guido said suddenly in his deep, melodious voice.

My breath caught in my throat. 'Have you seen him?' I cried.

'My nephew Ludovico saw him in Paris.'

Time stood still.

'Where?' I asked, my heart thumping.

'In the Tuileries Gardens. Ludovico has an exhibition in Paris at the moment. He went for the opening.'

'Ludovico saw Stephen in Paris?' I echoed like a ghost. The world had stopped spinning.

'Two days ago – Sunday morning. He was clearing his head after the previous night and went for a long walk, ending up at the Tuileries, where he sat at a cafe beneath the trees. To his surprise Stephen was a few tables away. Ludovico called, but Stephen looked right through him. Then Ludovico wondered if he was mistaken. The man seemed like Stephen but he had no beard, he was clean-shaven, so he did look a little different. And he was with a blonde woman, about your age but definitely not you.' Guido stopped and plucked his massive fingers into the leather lounge. 'Sorry if I'm being indelicate,' he said.

'Not at all. I think I know who the woman is.'

'Ah,' said Guido.

'Please continue?' I implored.

'Well, there's not much more to add. The man dropped his voice and mumbled to his companion. The woman, Ludovico thought, seemed frightened and jumpy that Stephen had been recognised. But the man was as calm as the lagoon on a still night – and that convinces me it was Stephen,' finished Guido triumphantly. 'It's exactly what Stephen would do in that situation.'

It hit me like a rock. How could Stephen do this? To think of him sipping café au lait with Priscilla made me furious. But if it meant I would see him again and my children still had a father . . .

People had affairs all the time. Couples survived. Hope rose, a balloon of warmth and wellbeing suffusing despair. My body was shaking uncontrollably.

'It's so out of character for him to disappear,' said Guido quietly.

'The Tuileries Gardens are a favourite place,' I said. 'It's him.' My eyes bubbled with tears of relief.

'I tried to email you but I have a new computer and didn't have your address.' Guido wrapped me in his massive arms. 'So, I called my local police station. I assured them you were no murderer, Becca, and that Professor Stephen Wilding was very much alive.'

Guido's words sang. *Alive*. Surely the best word in the human language.

'Our Commissario spoke to his colleague Napolitano. Unfortunately the police on the Amalfi coast will not be persuaded. They are adamant that Stephen is dead.'

'Did they tell you his passport's missing?'

'No.' Guido frowned.

'Do you think Napolitano's been bribed?' I shifted awkwardly, the very thought making me flush with anxiety.

'It's possible, of course.' Guido watched me carefully. 'It wouldn't be the first time. But why do you think so?'

'They jumped to the conclusion that Stephen's dead with no body and no evidence. And then they started blaming me. It was all very quick.'

'You think Stephen paid them off?' Guido's voice went high with incredulity.

'Priscilla. The blonde woman, his companion.' I sighed, exhausted, my head spinning with relief that Stephen was alive.

'Becca?' Guido took my hands in his giant paws, his black eyes burning into mine. 'You must find Stephen. Get proof. Without that, it's dangerous for you. The police around Naples,' Guido cast his eyes heavenwards, 'they are not like us Venetians. Their morality is different.' He gripped me tightly. 'When you have proof, call me and I'll speak to the police here.'

'Guido, can I use your computer? I must tell James and Erin.' He sprang up, unusually quick for someone so large, and led me through into his small cramped office that smelled of leather and paper.

'Becca?' he said softly. 'If there is anything else I can do, anything at all?'

I sat in his huge chair and clicked on the computer, rapidly typing my message in code. I couldn't send it from myself. I used a secret language we'd invented when the kids were small; I prayed they would remember. What I did know was that they would recognise Guido's name. As I heard the whoosh of my dispatch I imagined my children's elation and wished I could be with them. *Soon*, I told myself.

'Here's Ludovico's address,' said Guido, passing me a slip of paper. 'He's in Saint Germain. I'm sure you want to hear for yourself.' He smiled. 'And now we eat. You look wrecked.'

I followed Guido to the cavernous kitchen, absorbed with the news that Stephen was all right and happily ensconced in Paris. That he'd abandoned me seemed suddenly immaterial. Somehow I would set things right: all I needed to do was find him. Surely he'd had some sort of breakdown and needed help? I wouldn't leave him behind, like I'd left my father, that terrible day in the storm. This time, I was staying.

Guido's strong arms worked like machines as he flung slabs of bacon into bubbling oil and cracked huge eggs into a saucepan. The glassblowers of Murano were special. I had never doubted that Guido would support me in my hour of need.

I fell upon the food: Stephen being alive gave me an enormous appetite.

'I want you to take my brother's van,' Guido said solemnly. 'It's parked at Mestre. I'll load it with glassware. If anyone asks, you're taking a delivery for me, but obviously don't give your real name. They can phone and I'll back it up. I'll program in the safest route for the border crossing on the van's GPS. Places aren't patrolled these days, except recently the coast road – and they're only looking for dark-coloured people.' He shook his head disapprovingly.

I thanked him profusely but worried police at this very moment might be tracing the email address I'd just used.

We crammed down the last blissful mouthfuls and Guido led me into an adjacent room where a long table displayed vases of exquisite beauty: swirls of aquamarine, rich deep blues, ghostly grey and all the colours of the Venetian lagoon danced through clear, pristine glass. The vases were alive as sunshine breathed into them, through them, sparkling and enriching their lustre. At any moment it felt like they would heave and sigh with the tide. Guido picked up a vase in the hues of sunset and dawn across the sea. It glowed as if lit from within. He wrapped it and passed it across like a swaddled baby.

'For luck. I will come and see where you put it at home,'

he said. Then we went into another room filled with crates of Ludovico's glass, which we carried to Guido's boat.

The sky was crystal-blue as we sped smoothly across to Mestre. In the vast car park we rapidly loaded the anonymous white van – I didn't know whether the police had located the sports car and were watching the area – and I couldn't get away fast enough.

Without speaking Guido pulled me into a bone-crushing hug. For a moment I wished he could come with me but I reassured myself that I'd driven from Venice to France before, and no one could trace me now. Guido put my carry-on bag on the passenger seat and I hauled myself into the van and fired up the engine, blowing heartfelt kisses to him as I circled past. He was still waving as I left the endless aisles of cars and set off for Paris.

The GPS led me easily on a back road across the border, past an old guard hut, long abandoned. I sailed through. Even though I was in the unmarked van, I took minor roads the whole way. It was just after dawn when I reached Ludovico's place on the Left Bank of the Seine, in a narrow street in the sixth arrondissement. I found a park directly outside the gracious nineteenth-century building. Beside the sleekly painted door, Ludovico's name peered out among the tenants; I buzzed up.

'I'll come straight down, Becca,' he purred in a rolling Venetian accent.

He hugged me so solidly I felt instantly reassured, his slender body strong from breathing life into glass the traditional way. At twenty-five, Ludovico had not yet developed the thicker build of his uncle. His glossy black hair and dark eyes above generous lips and friendly smile made Ludovico popular.

'Quickly, I don't want you to be seen,' he whispered. 'You're in the news.' He stole a furtive look around; it was too early for many people to be on the street.

'It's a very local area,' he murmured. 'The walls have eyes.' He ushered me through to a small courtyard with a bubbling fountain at its centre, and took my hand as he led me hurriedly up three flights of stairs.

The apartment was small with massive windows that stretched to the ceiling. Ludovico's glass creations glowed in rich colours of the rainbow. As he went back to unload the van I used his computer to look up the news online.

There was a short article in the French press saying I was wanted by the Italian police for questioning and had not returned to my hotel on the Amalfi coast. My photo was posted, along with a request for anyone who saw me to contact police. There was also a picture of the red sports car, and I consoled myself that it was miles away in Mestre.

When Ludovico came back with my bag I set about making myself as unrecognisable as possible. I plastered on make-up and swirled my hair into a bun. I donned clothes that looked the least like those I was wearing in the photo – a much more formal dress and shoes – and I borrowed a stylish straw hat from Ludovico. If I kept my sunglasses on at all times I might just go unnoticed.

'It was here.' In the Tuileries Gardens, Ludovico led me to a wrought-iron table beneath a plane tree. We sat down, and Ludovico ordered us coffee and croissants. In the distance a circular boat pond glistened in the sparkling light and Parisians and tourists were already draping themselves on the elegant slatted seats that surrounded the water. A few children floated replica sailing craft, poking them around with long sticks.

I was momentarily overwhelmed with relief to think that Stephen had been here so recently but then I felt sick – he'd been here with Priscilla.

'It's going to be a perfect day,' said Ludovico, trying to surreptitiously glance at his watch.

'When do you need to get to your exhibition?'

'Soon. I'm sorry, will that be all right? I need to display some of the new pieces that you've brought.'

'Of course. I'm so grateful to you. But before you go, would you . . . Could you tell me every detail about Stephen?'

Ludovico ran long fingers through his matt of hair. 'So,' he leaned close, 'Stephen was sitting here with a blonde woman. About your age. Thin, blue-eyed. Well dressed. Sexy. They were deep in conversation when I called out. I was over there, closer to the kiosk.' Ludovico scrunched his eyes, recapturing the scene in his mind. 'Stephen had his back to me. When he turned, I saw that his beard was shaved. He didn't respond at all; stared like he'd never known me. Then I started thinking it wasn't him. He seemed intimate with the blonde woman, and that felt wrong.' Ludovico cleared his throat and shifted uncomfortably in his chair. 'Sorry, Becca, but I'm going to tell you everything in precise detail like I'm making a vase.'

I nodded and waited, trying to hide how difficult I was finding it to hear every word.

'I realised they'd been holding hands.'

I gritted my teeth and forced myself to keep listening.

'After I waved, the woman let go as if he'd burned her but he just mumbled calmly. He put money on the table and they walked off. That way, towards the fair.' Ludovico indicated a Ferris wheel and sideshows that squatted along one side of the gardens near the Rue de Rivoli. 'I followed them, curious to see if it really was Stephen. Perhaps I'd been mistaken?'

'But you know what he looks like. You've met him lots of times with me at your uncle's place.'

'Si, si. That's why it was so strange. Anyway, they soon stopped and bought frozen drinks.'

'Can you show me?'

'Of course.'

We called to the waiter to tell him we would be back and then Ludovico led me to a multi-coloured granita stand, where banks of orange, lime, pineapple and strawberry concoctions were stacked one on top of each other in giant dispensers.

'It's not like Stephen to want one of these.' I frowned as I surveyed the garish frozen drinks.

'Perhaps it wasn't him?'

'Or his tastes have changed. Was it hot?'

Ludovico shrugged. 'Maybe humid.' His long eyelashes fluttered up and down. 'It was, you know, morning. A sunny day.'

We walked back to our table past cheerful sideshows, carnival clowns with open mouths sitting ready to take the small white balls and spit out numbers so every child could win a prize the world over.

'We've always loved this carnival. It's Erin and James's favourite.' I looked up at the giant replica ape waiting to beckon the evening crowds to his roller-coaster. We passed the dodgem cars, silent now. 'They'll be raucous tonight,' I said, remembering our family visits on warm summer evenings that stretched until eleven o'clock when the gardens shut. It would still be light, a long, exquisite twilight, the moon hanging like a prop in a school play. I shuddered at the thought of Priscilla sharing such a moment with Stephen.

Back at our table in the cool shade of the trees we ate quickly, in silence. Ludovico gulped his coffee and kissed me lightly on the cheek. 'Good luck today,' he said with a smile as he strode away through the dappled light.

Now I could move – but in my exhaustion I couldn't think where. I looked around through the shimmering trees. Might Stephen take a walk here today? Where else could he be – the Musée D'Orsay, or having breakfast in a cafe in the Latin Quarter? Would he lunch with Priscilla in the Marais beneath the gracious arches of the Place des Vosges? My heart shrank. Rage surged through me, clearing my head.

I reminded myself to think like an archaeologist. Narrow the possibilities. To find Stephen would take a random search through his favourite haunts, in the vast arrondissements of Paris, relying on chance. On the other hand, Priscilla was here on study leave and I expected that even in the flush of romance she would be far too driven and ambitious to waylay her research. I'd been to archives in Paris and I knew from talking with colleagues which ones held the best resources for French historians. Research the researcher. It was far more likely I could find Priscilla.

I would follow her and let her lead me to Stephen.

25

I made my way to the twirling art-nouveau sign on Rue de
Rivoli that signalled the entrance to the Metro. I hurried
down the long flight of stairs, bought tickets from the
automatic machine and was soon on my way to the Archives
Nationales in the Marais, a logical place for Priscilla to do her
research.

I walked past Hôtel de Soubise, the imposing building that
used to hold the archives, and through a verdant garden to
where a new building housed the collection. I went upstairs
to the long reading room, peering like a hawk for its prey. Green
lamps proliferated like a field of flowers above timber desks.
Scholars had their heads down, working hard. There was no
sign of Priscilla.

I thought rapidly. Another possibility was the new Bibliothèque Nationale – I wasn't sure where it was, having only been to the old one in Rue du Richelieu, but I'd heard French historians complain that a vast majority of the collection had been moved there. I hurried to a taxi stand, and thirty minutes later through heavy traffic the driver dropped me on the street beside a vast flight of steps in the thirteenth arrondissement. At the top, a forecourt stretched far and wide, with monolithic buildings on each of the four corners rising up to the sky. I walked through the stark concrete landscape to an elevator that took me down to the library, where rooms were spaced around a wild, tree-filled courtyard bigger than two football fields. For admission I had to show my academic credentials, which I always carried with me in my wallet, and then wait for a day ticket. My stomach tightened as I handed over my photo ID, which didn't look particularly like me and today less so with what I was wearing, but I was terrified that my name might be recognised from the news. To my relief the girl behind the counter didn't give me, or my card a second glance.

I sat impatiently, planning where I would go next if Priscilla wasn't here. Then I paced up and down a corridor with a wall of glass giving views to the forest that had been transplanted here. The place felt odd – too new, its subterranean rooms looking out into the strange greenery, displaced. When I finally got into the reading rooms it took an inordinate amount of time to search, and by the end I was weary and deflated. Priscilla was nowhere in sight.

In desperation, I caught a taxi back to the first arrondissement to the original Bibliothèque Nationale. Inside, I paced around the circular, colonnaded edge of its stately room. And suddenly, there she was: Priscilla, wearing a chic, sleeveless pale-lemon dress, sitting in the centre at one of the long tables, a stack of ancient manuscripts piled high in front of her.

Standing against the rows of bookshelves a distance away, I waited. The normality of what she was doing disgusted me. Soft light glowed a pearly blue through the stained-glass dome as Priscilla tapped notes into her tablet. Every so often she would photograph a page with her phone. I noticed every detail. Had Stephen wound his arms around her this morning? She looked light and summery. Bile rose and I forced myself to stand still and not run and rip her limb from limb. She and Stephen were here, living a life together.

Finally she stood. I held my breath. She boxed up the papers and carried them to a nearby returns shelf, then retrieved her handbag, stowed her tablet into it and sauntered out of the building. I was quick to follow, a safe distance behind, my heart pounding. Soon I would be with Stephen.

Priscilla moved quickly on the street, and descended into the Metro. On the hot, howling platform I waited until she was on board and then leaped into the back of the carriage, from where I had a good view. At Gare Saint-Lazare she hopped off the train and I followed like a bloodhound.

She went into the country ticket office and bought a fare. I hovered in the queue, trying to ascertain which train she'd booked, but she was too far away for me to hear. She and Stephen must be staying out of Paris. I found this odd – but, then, Stephen was behaving so strangely it was fitting.

As soon as she left I pushed my way to the front. Speaking French, I asked the man who'd sold Priscilla her ticket where she was heading. I finished with an embarrassed shrug. To my eternal gratitude he obliged. 'Vernon,' he grinned, clearly thinking we were lovers who had just had a fight.

I jumped onto the train as it was pulling out. The landscape swept past and half an hour later I alighted in a tiny, picturesque village in Normandy. In the distance Priscilla walked purposefully towards a bus that heralded Giverny as its destination. My breath caught in my lungs. Monet's garden in Giverny was a favourite haunt of Stephen's whenever we were in France. She was going to meet him.

Another bus rolled up behind the first, also headed to Giverny. Tourists thronged and I mingled with them, taking the second bus.

I tried to think what to say to Stephen, but my mind went blank. In what felt like seconds we pulled in beside a field of scarlet poppies bobbing and shimmering in the breeze. I let Priscilla get ahead along the tiny cobbled streets of the town, where roses and hollyhocks soared against mellow walls. At the ancient stone building that housed the ticket office, the queue was long to enter the artist's garden. I waited a distance behind Priscilla, my legs jittering, refusing to keep still. I wanted to see Stephen, to demand an explanation. But most of all I wanted him in my arms to feel his warmth and strength, to go back to what we'd had; wipe the slate clean. Start again. A second chance.

Once inside, I lost sight of Priscilla. I walked past the dusty pink walls and green shutters of Monet's house, shrouded in roses, red geraniums in front, a scene that framed Stephen's smiling face on my study bookshelf at home. *Home*. The house that we may not have for much longer, the house that he'd gambled away. Quickening my pace, I raced past the arches of the Grande Allee, with its nasturtiums in gaudy splashes of red and orange overflowing onto the path.

A riot of scarlet roses scrambled up a fence as I strode down into an underpass that swept beneath the road. On the other side, the fecund lily pond, the scene of Monet's famous paintings, came into view. Stephen would be here, on the bench we always shared, gazing at the tiny wooden boat moored beneath a weeping willow. As a gardener, Stephen had felt it a spiritual journey to walk the gravel paths, immersed in the shimmering plants that morphed into an impressionist painting wherever the eye was drawn.

I looked for him among the spellbound throngs of visitors hustling quietly about. People of all nationalities lingered on the Japanese bridge gazing at the pale water lilies below, posing for photographs, but neither Stephen nor Priscilla was among them. I headed around the pond, past tourists ambling by cascades of pink roses that dipped into the water.

Every step took me closer to the wooden bench – Stephen's bench. But when I reached it, I stopped abruptly. The bench was empty.

One more time I went around the lily pond, pushing through the tortuously slow crowd of sweaty bodies, their rank perfume hanging sourly in the air. Rounding a bend I saw Priscilla standing at the path's edge gazing at a patch of water lilies. Her expression was glazed, her mind far away. She was alone.

I bit my lip so hard droplets of blood beaded as I strode towards her.

'Rebecca!' She reeled back as she focused on me, a look of disbelief changing to acknowledgement that I was actually here. My disguise hadn't fooled her.

I walked up close. 'Where's Stephen?' I asked forcefully.

She blinked, confused. 'I'm so sorry, Rebecca, to hear what happened. I didn't realise you were in France. Are you here to see Melinda?'

Now it was my turn to be confused. 'I've come for Stephen.'

'You don't think he's with me, surely?' she said, her voice shaking.

'The game's up, Priscilla.'

She took my hands and I flung her off. 'Whatever he's done isn't enough to drive me away,' I said. 'I know you picked him up on the Amalfi coast and brought him here. I've come to take him home.'

Tears welled in Priscilla's eyes, unnerving me.

'I'm in Paris doing research for my book. The only person from work I've seen is Melinda,' she said gently as if I were a wounded animal that needed calming. 'I called to her but she slipped away. On purpose, I'd say. I'm sure she saw me.'

'Melinda's in America,' I snapped. 'I need to see Stephen now. The kids are desperate. Let us know he's all right. Please.'

Priscilla's expression was full of alarm and pity but she did not speak.

'Oh God, he *is* here, isn't he?' My body began to tremble uncontrollably.

'Rebecca.' Priscilla moved to a bench and sat down heavily, indicating for me to join her. 'Rebecca,' she sighed, 'you must know that Stephen loved you more than anyone in the world.'

She fixed me with startled cornflower-blue eyes. I sat at the other end of the bench, as far away as possible.

'Stephen and I did have an affair. It ended just before he went overseas with you. He was the one who chose to finish it.' Her voice was now no louder than a whisper. So, I'd been right all along, but the moment fell flat, hollow. There was no victory in having guessed the truth. I was so shocked I couldn't yet even feel anger – only cold, grey numbness and a rising nausea.

'You were sleeping with my husband while you were monstering me?' was all I could say.

Priscilla leaned forward and I reeled back as if from an adder. 'I miss him dreadfully,' she said. 'Did he really lose all that money? If I'd only known I would have helped.'

Fury rose in me as she played her game.

'Don't try to fool me, Priscilla. Take me to him.'

'My darling, it must be a terrible shock.'

'Where are you staying?'

She blinked. 'In Paris.'

'Take me there.'

Priscilla slumped back. 'He's not with me.' Her blue eyes misted over again. 'But perhaps you should come and see for yourself.'

'You'll just ring ahead and tell him to disappear. I have a better idea.' I pulled a scrap of paper from my bag and scrawled down Ludovico's address. 'Bring Stephen to me. Tell him I have to see him – to talk about the children at least. Seven o'clock. Be there or you'll regret it. You've been harbouring Stephen while the police think he's dead. You've wasted everyone's time and I'll contact them if you're not there sharp at seven.' I knew she wouldn't agree; I would wait for her at the station and follow her back.

Priscilla took the paper and reached out towards me but I yanked my arm away. 'Seven o'clock,' I called as I strode away. 'Or I'll phone the police.'

A bus was waiting in the car park, and I caught it back to Vernon. Priscilla's confession roared through my head, and I cursed myself for not asking how long their affair had gone on. Was it weeks, months or years? I tried to work out when it might have started, but I had no idea. A bitter liquid flooded my mouth. Priscilla had seemed alarmingly to be telling the truth about Stephen not being in Paris with her, but she couldn't be; it wasn't possible.

As I stood in the searing heat waiting for the train, another thought rushed into my mind: would Priscilla instead turn me into the police? If she had bribed Napolitano, I was now in a truly vulnerable position. Suddenly I realised I was stupid to have given her Ludovico's address. I glanced around: every man and woman looked like undercover police. I paced up and down the platform, unable to keep still.

When the train pulled into the station in a burst of boiling air I looked everywhere for Priscilla. Hordes of tourists pushed into carriages, but Priscilla was not among them. Had she rushed back to Stephen in a taxi? Why had I left Giverny when perhaps Stephen was on his way to meet her by the water lilies? I wasn't thinking clearly at all. Thoughts jumbled one on top of each other.

I retreated to a drink vending machine near the ticket office and clunked in coins for a bottle of water. I drank slowly, looking everywhere for Priscilla, imagining her in bed with Stephen. Now I'd heard her confession, the truth was too hard to deal with, a giant lump of betrayal that trapped my mind in a lead veil. Suddenly claustrophobic, I went back out into the explosive heat.

I'd made such a mess of things. Was it my fault that Stephen had run into her arms? How could he have lied to me? While I was in mediation with Priscilla he was slipping between sheets with her. Why did I even want him back?

But what if I never had the opportunity to talk to him again, to make him explain why he'd lied, why he'd done such terrible things? I tried to hang on to Priscilla's admission that Stephen had ended the affair. He must have had a vestige of conscience before he went running back to her when his world collapsed. But perhaps Priscilla was just tricking me and he had never ended it.

With every thought I was more desperate to speak to him.

I chided myself to hold firm. He was in Paris in some bolthole with Priscilla, and I would make him come to me. I would make him explain.

And then suddenly Priscilla came clipping out of the ticket office and onto the platform. She stood waiting patiently, her face flushed, her expression distracted.

When the next train arrived I held back until she was seated and then I stepped aboard the carriage behind. As soon as we left the station I moved and stood swaying in the space between carriages, where I had a good view. She sat gazing out at the scenery, eyes bloodshot with tears. I hoped that meant she was planning to deliver Stephen, but I doubted it. Why was she crying, then? She didn't look like a lover going back to her man.

At Gare Saint-Lazare I hopped off the train seconds after Priscilla and followed her through busy streets, almost losing her in the crowds outside the department stores Les Printemps and Galeries Lafayette, picking her up again as she crossed Boulevard Haussmann towards Palais Garnier, the Paris opera house. I studied her body, the way she walked, the flow of her blonde hair, imagining myself as Stephen, seeing through his eyes. I tried to visualise what I looked like to him, how he had lost interest in me. Or had he? Did he need us both? The virgin and the whore.

Priscilla turned down a small street and made her way into a plush hotel. I hovered in the foyer, as if waiting for a friend, and heard her ask for the key to room 212. A large tour group was arriving and people were milling about, and among them Priscilla was swallowed into the lift.

I sank into a deep leather lounge and waited until the reception staff were so busy checking in their new guests that no one noticed me slip into the elevator, where I pressed the button for the second floor.

Room 212 was at the end of a long corridor of red carpet so deep I left footprints. Anticipation rose as I walked closer. At the door I stopped, ran my fingers through my hair, neatening it, drew in my breath and rapped confidently. Silence. Moments ticked by. I wondered what conversation they might be having. The walls were soundproof, I couldn't hear anything. My heart beat fast; I was about to see Stephen. Finally, Priscilla opened up. I pushed her backwards and barged in as she squawked in alarm.

She was alone. I moved around the room seeking evidence of Stephen. I flung open the wardrobe, expecting to find new

The Lost Swimmer

clothes he'd bought in Paris – but there was only Priscilla's high fashion. I hurtled into the bathroom – a single toothbrush, make-up, perfume. Nothing male.

'Where is he?' I demanded hotly as I re-entered the main room, which was decked out luxuriously in thick velvets.

Priscilla stood by the neatly made bed, tears flooding her cheeks. 'Darling, he's not here.' She hugged me, so tightly I couldn't breathe. 'I really haven't seen Stephen. You must believe me. Tell me everything that happened.'

She drew away to look at me and I slapped her face, hard. In my shock I felt like I had released a valve that had been stuck tight. She flung a hand to her reddened cheek, eyes wide in surprise and pain. As I went to slap her again she grabbed me, twisting my wrist into a grind of nerves.

'Listen. To. Me. Stephen drowned, Rebecca, didn't he? You're going to have to come to terms with it. We both are, God knows how. Either that or you murdered him, as the police think.'

I lunged at her, desperate to force the truth out, but she caught me and held me back.

'You must go now and calm down, Rebecca. Contact me when you're ready to talk.' Her face crumpled as she propelled me to the passage in a grip so tight I could do nothing other than obey. Pain seared my arms. She threw me out and locked the door.

I stood breathlessly, arms hanging limp at my sides. A happy-looking couple approached, staring curiously as they entered the room next door. I heard their door click shut and, in a daze, I found the lift.

In the foyer I pushed through the milling tourists who were still checking in. Once in the street I tried to process Priscilla's

319

reaction. I was certain she was lying. It was typical and cruel of her to pretend that Stephen had drowned like my father. How could I get to him?

I walked fast and soon passed through the clipped gardens of the Palais Royal with their startling green lawn and headed through the traffic on Rue de Rivoli, going towards the Louvre. I turned right as I reached IM Pei's glass pyramid, where tourists posed ludicrously as statues on little coloured blocks. I crossed the road into the Tuileries Gardens.

My feet propelled me to the table. Stephen had been here recently. I found comfort in that, despite knowing that he had been here with Priscilla.

'Back again?' said the waiter as I sat and ordered a café crème. I obsessively watched every passer-by, tapping my fingers on the table to try to calm down, thrumming out a tattoo until people nearby threw looks of annoyance. With difficulty I tried to sit still. I reminded myself I needed to remain invisible but my leg started bouncing up and down. My body refused to obey commands. I threw down a handful of euros, not waiting for my coffee, and fled.

Walking up the wide tree-lined path I tried desperately to form a plan but my mind was blank. All I could hear was the crunching of gravel echoing loudly underfoot.

I passed through the gardens and out into the chaos of Place de la Concorde. Cars roared by as I crossed the River Seine over to the Left Bank. A crowd had gathered outside the Musée D'Orsay, queuing in the wide forecourt beside the old railway building with its giant clock. It was open late tonight. Had fate led me here? Another place to which Stephen and I had always come. Perhaps today would be no different? I joined the queue, forcing away my doubts. It was in Priscilla's nature to mislead; she did it with relish, along with her theatrics.

I glided through a special Impressionist exhibition including our favourite painters – Monet, Manet, Renoir, Sisley, Pissarro – more of their work than I had ever seen hung along the vast walls. They appeared different today, my sleep-deprived mind taking in every brushstroke. I saw the detail rather than the picture, the fine beads of paint. It was unnerving and yet exciting. I looked everywhere, expecting to see Stephen poring over a masterpiece as he waited for Priscilla's all-clear. I wasn't fooled for a minute that she wasn't with him. They must have carefully packed away his belongings. She would have expected me to follow her.

When I couldn't find Stephen I hurried upstairs. Still no sighting. I rushed into the restaurant, forcing myself to slow to an amble beneath the grand chandeliers. I stared at the tables of diners eating in the sumptuously decorated rooms. Outside, Paris was beginning to twinkle, the parks and rooftops floating.

I took in everything and everyone. My mind was a computer.

'Can I help you, madame?' An officious man in black and white stood close. Not a policeman, only a waiter.

'I'm looking for someone. He's tall, fit, dark-haired with a beard.' I paused. 'Actually, he may be clean-shaven. He's a little older than me but you wouldn't know it.' As if from a distance I heard myself give a silvery laugh. The waiter eyed me with concern.

'Perhaps you'd like a glass of water?'

I shook my head and walked away, knocking into a group of diners, hearing the quiet tones of people's reactions.

A guard approached. 'Can I help, madame?'

'I'm leaving,' I called.

'Then let me show you the way, madame.' He took me gently by the elbow and propelled me down to the exit. I blinked into the soft night air, confused, disoriented; where should I go now? In the long queue to enter the museum, I felt someone staring and glanced up.

'Melinda?'

I was certain it was Melinda but she looked so different. Years younger, happy. Stunningly beautiful. Parisian. And she'd died her hair blonde.

'Melinda, you're in Paris!'

But she was already out of the queue and moving rapidly away.

'Melinda! Mel?'

Suddenly she was running. Hadn't she recognised me with my extra make-up and formal clothes? But surely Mel, of all people, would know me. A horrifying thought occurred – could Stephen be with Melinda? She was blonde now. And she certainly wasn't pleased to see me.

She flew down a narrow street lined with tiny homewares shops and cutting-edge art galleries. I knew I was quicker, but I pretended to be breathless, doubling over feigning a stitch, keeping a firm eye on the street she turned down. As soon as she was out of sight I pursued, trying to absorb the possibility of her with Stephen. How could either of them do that to me?

For several blocks I stalked from a distance, hiding in shop doorways or behind crowds of pedestrians whenever Melinda turned to check she wasn't being followed.

But all the time I felt that someone was behind me, too.

The stalker being stalked.

I turned back abruptly. 'Stephen?' But I recognised no faces in the mass of tourists and locals chattering happily as they headed out to dinner.

I hurried after Melinda and saw her open a heavy blue door with a lion's-head handle. She was soon swallowed into a shadowy courtyard as the door swung shut. I ran and slipped my foot in the crack just before it closed, then waited a few moments before I poked my head inside. Melinda had climbed a long set of stairs and was unlocking an apartment adorned with red geraniums. As soon as she disappeared, I followed.

I climbed the stairs, making sure my feet made no noise. The apartments looked expensive, far beyond Melinda's budget. Had Stephen used our money? The betrayal was deeper than anything I'd thought possible. My arms reached out to a pot plant and I hurled it through the window. The glass was old and gave way easily. The red geraniums flew into the gloom inside and Melinda, furious, opened the door.

'Get away, Rebecca, or I'll call the police.' She looked around but no neighbours had appeared.

'Let me in. I need to see Stephen.' My voice cracked. I wanted desperately to hold him. To have him envelop me and tell me how sorry he was.

'Stephen?' Melinda was icy, her face pinched with rage. 'He's not here. I wouldn't have anyone here from your lot.'

I tried to push past but she blocked the door. There was terror in her eyes.

'How did you find me?' she asked.

'I must see him. Please!' Everything was unreal.

'I've told you he's not here. Why on earth would he be, Rebecca?'

Melinda seemed genuinely confused. But why had she run? Her hands were shaking violently.

My mind ticked over, slowing down as I watched her, trying to work out what was going on, grappling to understand. There was something... And then it hit me. I had trusted Melinda with my passport once. I had been frantically busy preparing for an overseas trip and I had asked her to check me in online.

'You're the fourth person under investigation, aren't you?' I blurted.

Melinda stepped closer.

'They've figured it out,' I bluffed. 'You accessed my passport.'

Melinda's fury was palpable. I'd guessed right.

'I thought we were friends,' I said, shocked, realising I should leave. I glanced around, trying to work out how I could get away. I was between her and the stairs and I didn't want to turn my back.

'At least I rob honestly,' she replied angrily. 'Not like you, on your fat salaries while you whine about how bad things are. Do you realise how little I made when I worked harder than any of you? And now you've hunted me down.' She pitched forward suddenly with alarming speed and I lost my footing, tumbling backwards. I tried to grab hold of her but she pushed me away. The gaping stairway flew beneath until I crashed to the courtyard and my head struck the unyielding stone. Blood flowed into my eyes, wet and gelatinous; my nose went numb. The kangaroo attack roared back but this time there was no dog to save me.

Flashes of Stephen and Erin and James scarred my mind as Melinda stepped down towards me. She was wearing sparkling red Parisian stilettos and they were coming fast, flickering like the images in a silent film, and that was the last thing I saw.

26

I awoke with a start and gazed around a sterile hospital ward. Nearby were two other patients, both asleep, both elderly. The snowy-haired man snored loudly. The breathing of the other, a slender woman, was so shallow she might have been dead.

How had I come to be here? I looked around expectantly for Stephen, then realised with a thud that I was alone.

'My children?' I said aloud to the indifferent room.

I rolled onto my side to reach the telephone sitting on a night-stand but the drip attached to my arm made movement foolish. I yelped as my ribs erupted in pain. The man woke, flapping about, and pressed an emergency button. A nurse came running and he pointed to me, speaking rapidly in French.

The nurse shifted me onto my back. 'Shh, shh, madame, vous êtes malade.' She stroked my brow as she fiddled with the drip. After a few moments I drifted away again.

It was hot and bright when I opened my eyes. The ward was bustling. I had more neighbours in beds and everyone had visitors.

'How are you going?' Sally Chesser sat in a corner of the room. She came over and squeezed my hand.

'Sally?' I wasn't yet ready to believe she was real.

'You must feel pretty sore?'

'Like I've been run over by a bulldozer. What happened?'

'You can't remember?'

I shook my head and gritted my teeth in pain.

Disjointed images flashed slowly back.

Melinda running into the distance.

Melinda's angry face, snapped tight and foreign.

'How did you know she was the one who embezzled the money from Coastal?' Sally asked piercingly.

'I didn't.'

'But you accused Melinda. You know it would have been better if you hadn't. You were lucky I was there.'

Why were *you there*, I thought, my mind a jumble.

'Sally, what were you doing in Paris?'

Sally paused, went back to the chair, and lifted it across to plant it near the head of my bed. She was wearing the same white linens she'd had on the first time she came to our home and she looked more like she belonged on a yacht than in a hospital. She sat so close I could see the pupils in her hazel eyes and feel her breath hot on my face.

'I want you to know you're in the clear,' she whispered. 'Melinda's in custody. She'll be extradited back to Australia. She'd bought apartments all over Paris with the money. We'd found other accounts that you hadn't seen. All up, it amounted to over twelve million dollars. She'd been doing it for years.'

I felt sick. 'All in my name?'

'You and others,' said Sally. 'At first it was just small amounts so no one noticed. Then she grew bolder and more ambitious. She bought some real estate in Australia and then branched out over here. She used her maiden name. It took us a while to work it out. And we had to see if you were involved.'

'I don't understand.' I scrunched two fists into my eyes, rubbing them as if it might help my head make sense. 'I trusted Melinda with my life.'

'She resented all of you. And she was an obsessive real-estate investor. The university will actually make a profit once it's all sold.'

I peered at Sally. 'What's your role in this? Who are you? Is anyone who they seem?'

Sally smiled crookedly. 'I'm working for Coastal. I'm sorry I had to be so deceptive.'

'You're an investigator?'

She nodded. 'A lawyer and a cop. Well, ex-cop. I run forensic investigations. I was hired to track the money.'

'How did you know where I'd be?'

'I didn't. But I knew where Melinda was, so I went to her apartment and followed her around, waiting to see if you'd turn up. After I'd visited the bank in Athens and heard what you'd been asking, and then found out you'd sent your friends to the archived records, I thought you might be trying to destroy evidence, and that you could be in the whole thing with Melinda.'

'Did she set up those accounts?'

Sally nodded. 'She's admitted to bribing the bank manager so it looked like you'd been there in person. For the record, Bec, my instincts never felt you were guilty.'

I massaged my aching head. 'Can I see Stephen?' I sat up hopefully, my eyes bright with expectation, my pain suddenly gone. All I wanted was to touch his soft, fresh skin and inhale his salty, soapy aroma. 'Is he here?'

Sally stared awkwardly. 'No, Stephen's not here,' she said gently.

I sighed so deeply my ribs started to hurt. 'So, he's not been found? I'm sure he's in Paris with Priscilla.'

'Rebecca.' Sally stopped and drew in her breath. 'Stephen's been found.' She took my hand and gripped it tightly.

'Stephen's body washed up further along the Amalfi coast,' she said suddenly. 'He drowned.'

Sound fell away. I could see she kept talking but I couldn't hear a thing.

Stephen's body washed up.

Stephen's body.

My mouth quivered, the muscles moving uncontrollably. I tried to ask a question but nothing came out. Surely I was hallucinating? Sally wasn't here and Stephen hadn't drowned. Taken by the sea. Never to return.

Sally pressed her hand around mine. I felt the warmth and the weight of her. She was beside me.

And Stephen would never be again.

His bloated corpse had been dressed and bathed in formaldehyde. His hair had been brushed smooth, his beard trimmed. His eyes were closed, as if he were only sleeping. He had been kept cool as he waited for me to fly from Paris.

A local fisherman had found him washed onto rocks in a tiny sea cave. There, Stephen had been saved from the sucking mouths of hungry fish, preserved in the salt air, hanging like a weary angel.

Now, in a small room in a Naples funeral parlour, he lay patiently, his flesh white and powdered, lips rouged.

They told me his body had been autopsied. I unbuttoned his shirt to see the pallid flesh, huge stitches holding together the long V-shape where the medical examiner had cut.

I ran my fingers along it and drew the shirt closed, buttoning it up with clumsy hands.

Erin and James, Burton and Maria were waiting outside, but I wouldn't rush. I bent forward and kissed Stephen's lips, lurid, not cherry red as in life. They were cold, a different cold than I'd ever felt before. Unnatural. A dead expanse of dry, chalky ice. A wedge dropped through my heart as his bristly beard stubbed into me, familiar yet alien.

'I'm so sorry,' I whispered, fighting back the feeling that Stephen wasn't here, that his spirit had flown.

I wanted to hear his voice, to see his chocolate eyes, the way they'd blinked and shone and smiled at me for all these years. Talk everything through. Stephen would know how best to take his body home.

But Stephen had drowned and there was no evidence of foul play. He had gone swimming, a perfectly natural thing to do on the Amalfi coast. He'd run into trouble.

I prayed fervently that it was an accident and had not been intentional. I felt frantic that I didn't know but there was nothing I could do.

I sat beside him for hours, asking him why he'd had an affair, why he'd ended it. Did he really love me more than anyone in the world? Had Priscilla spoken the truth about that?

I loved you more than anyone, Stephen. You and our family. Our small, shining gang. If only you'd shared your problems, not always been the alpha male, coping.

You lost our savings because you wanted to make a better life for us, make us financially secure. You tried. I know you always tried. But the money was unimportant, my love.

I wondered again why he left his clothes in the crevice, not on the ledge. Was it a message? His superannuation and life insurance would more than cover his debts.

You saved our home. But without you, it's meaningless, you fool.

Were you saying goodbye to me on the bed that afternoon?

The neatness of it seemed chillingly like Stephen. He'd made a mess and he'd cleaned it up.

I covered his freezing hand with my own, trying in vain to let the warmth seep into him but his coldness drained the warmth from me instead. I left my hand there; I couldn't let go.

Finally Burton came in to lead me away. I didn't resist, although inside I wanted to scream and rage. Erin and James needed me and I promised myself that no one in my family would ever suffer again like Stephen had. In spite of all my love he'd died alone, unreachable.

The next morning was already steamy at dawn, a damp, thick heat. A gossamer blue mist shrouded the Tyrrhenian Sea, as though the whole world were holding its breath. My family made our way in silence, single file, down the mountain to the private beach at Della Mare. I looked back up at the baking cliffs where I had sat, and slept, while Stephen drowned.

My eyes felt like they were stung by bees, and Erin's were worse. She broke down at the water's edge and I ran to her. The sea lapped calmly against the rusty ladder as we held each other. James stood silently behind us, pale and stoic. One by one we threw flowers into the water: two red geraniums and a small, bright bunch of bougainvillea from me. They floated out towards the string of white buoys, until a wave rolled gently in and drenched them. They disappeared and Erin wailed. I clutched my children to me as I forced away images of Stephen with Priscilla, swallowed the anger that rose like a hungry shark. At least the children would never know of that. But like me with my own father, they had to farewell Stephen when their lives lay ahead of them. A wave sighed and sucked itself back into the sea. How could I ever leave this place?

Marco drove us along the winding coast road to Naples airport. I remembered vividly Stephen's fright the first time he'd seen this road, and my own exhilaration when I conquered it.

'Maybe you will return one day?' said Marco.

'Or you'll come and visit us?'

Marco smiled shyly. 'I would love to see the kangaroos.'

'Until then,' I said, kissing him on both cheeks and then walking away, not turning back.

I held Stephen through the flight, his ashes locked tight in a bright ceramic urn. If only I could love him as I always had. But his infidelity dragged me down. Was Priscilla the only one, or had there been others? Would I ever know? Did I really want to?

He had always been my rock, but in the end it was Burton who had been right: Stephen was as duplicitous as a spy.

The ashes sat heavy in my lap. On one side, Erin slept with her head on my shoulder; on the other, James stared out into the black night, roughly wiping back tears. Across the aisle, Maria and Burton were asleep, nestled into each other. I reminded myself how lucky I was to have this small pack of people as I battled a thick fog of depression that left my limbs heavy and my throat aching to scream.

I'd entered a new club, one I'd hoped never to join. A widow, whose loved one's death had been sudden and terrible. I was haunted by the vast mess of Stephen's life: his gambling, his affair, his seeming rekindling of his devotion to me if Priscilla was telling the truth. It sickened me that I'd have to see her every day at work – although it would give me the opportunity to force out of her how long the affair had gone on, and how it had started.

I floated between rage and despair. Who was I? A grieving wife, a victim, a fool? Or somehow the person responsible for everything? Perhaps if I'd been a better communicator Stephen might have known I loved him far more than money. I would have stuck by him through financial ruin. I needed only him.

I flicked obsessively through the photos on my phone from the day we'd gone to Pompeii. On the ferry, he smiled, dark eyes twinkling, but there was a haunted look too. What if his death was not an accident? Had he kept swimming in the misty sea until there was no point of return? Or was it just distraction and bad luck that led him into the swirling force of hidden currents?

Why did he say he loved me on that hot, calm afternoon, as we sank into the crisp white sheets and I drifted off to sleep?

The air was soft and clear when I went out, Big Boy at my heels, past the pointed quills of the grass trees that Stephen had nurtured like babies, and climbed halfway up our hill. Inhaling the fresh eucalypt, to a chorus of kookaburras raucously heralding the morning, I opened the urn, made in the shades of the Amalfi coast, vivid blues and yellows, swirls of lively colour that housed the ashes and bones of Stephen. I looked inside at the grey waste, and slowly, deliberately, trying to think of Stephen but with my thoughts flying away, I emptied half the ashes. They fell heavily and I scattered them with my boot, kicking them around until they mingled with the soil, my movements growing more savage as Big Boy backed away. Two kangaroos hopped down silently, stopping as they saw me – a maniacal middle-aged woman taking revenge on her pathetic life. They stood stock-still, and I read the collar of one: BONNIE. One of her ears hung raggedly, stitched and scarred, but otherwise she was strong and healthy. The roo beside her must be her joey, now a robust young buck. Big Boy growled half-heartedly and I grabbed him, but he just hunkered down and put his chin on his paws, exhaling all the air in his ramshackle frame. The kangaroos bent and grazed on the sweet emerald grass. We'd been through so much since that day Bonnie and her tiny joey had come to our hill for the first time. We made a strange vignette. Survivors.

I sat down wearily beside Big Boy and teased the white blaze on the top of his head around my finger. He settled into my lap with a sigh. I thought of my father. The first of all those I'd loved who hadn't survived. I'd always felt responsible, but in my tired fury today I viewed it differently. Dad was a fisherman, he knew the sea and that a storm was forecast – we all knew it, just not how bad it would be, certainly not that the river was flooding upstream, the river that spewed destruction from its mouth when it mixed with the south-westerly gales and churned the waves into a deadly maelstrom. None of us ever questioned Dad; his judgement was infallible. But if I were placed in that position today, would I take my children out in that forecast? In a flash I thought, *No, not ever.*

Dad knew the risks and had made a wrong call. Neither of us should have been on the water that day. In a surge of anger I realised with astonishing clarity that it wasn't my fault at all.

Stephen and I hadn't discussed what to do with our bodies if one of us died, but after an overwhelming tide of business and organisation had been worked through, we held the funeral. I had decided a marker was important, if only so someone could chance upon it, dig it up centuries later to try to make sense of our lives, of how we'd lived. Perhaps they could understand it more than I ever would.

I'd spent my own life unearthing other people's worlds, piecing together a jigsaw of the past. Now it all seemed completely meaningless. I'd noticed nothing of importance, hadn't understood the signs that must have been there mapping Stephen's despair, hadn't been able to reach him.

As archaeologists we imagine history, based on the secrets of discovered artifacts. We interpret and find meaning, always expecting that there is a story to tell. But what we say, how we say it, depends on us, not the people whose lives we dig up.

We tell stories of change, creating order out of chaos. A mirage, a panacea. I'd so desperately wanted Stephen alive, to rescue him. Grief pushing to the edge of reason, shredding rational thought even as I was trying to squeeze everything into a pattern. We can think we recognise someone, only to be wrong. In the twilight of unfathomable loss and exhaustion I'd grasped each report and used it to stand firm in my belief.

In the end we make up what we want to see, and potentially are blind.

Burton and Maria sat beneath a towering, twisted ironbark, holding tight to each other. Maria looked old, like an ancient civil-war veteran. Greek civil war, US civil war, Indian, Chinese revolution . . . My mind flew wildly.

Where was Stephen's passport? Had it been stolen at reception where they never guarded anything? Why couldn't I remember Adriana returning mine? Would the passport turn up one day, having been mixed up in paperwork or fallen down somewhere to be found much later, like an artifact in a dig?

Why had Stephen left his clothes in the crevice?

I glanced at the fake ring he'd given me: it shone brightly and my heart swelled.

James read a beautiful eulogy, and Erin sang a solo like an angel. I said nothing. All I could think was that I would never see Stephen again. And never be able to shout at him – and then forgive him – for his infidelity.

Maria had asked to speak.

'I only met Stephen once,' she began, her voice rising into the still air, 'although I've known Rebecca since she was a young archaeology student on digs around the Greek islands. What I do know is how much Rebecca loved him, and what a good father he was. I heard all about everything he did for Erin and James, how he'd ferry them everywhere when they were teen-agers and how well he'd look after them and play mother and father while Rebecca was away on her many trips. Stephen was an unusual academic in that he cared so much about his wife's career as well as his own, and encouraged Rebecca to flourish.'

My body was shaking so hard it felt like a seizure. How could I go on without him?

'Not only was Stephen extraordinarily handsome, even to someone of my age, but I could see he was a charming listener and an astute thinker and someone so generous he would do anything for those he loved.'

And those he was sleeping with, I thought.

'Stephen can never be replaced in your lives but his memory, his influence, his scholarship will live on. And what I will say, is we're all going to try to fill the gap and do everything we can for you: Erin, James, Rebecca.'

I attempted to meet her eye but I was crying too hard, a wrenching sobbing, cocooned between my two children, whose hot arms wrapped about me. They were desolate; we would all be haunted, never know the truth. I squeezed them tightly and vowed I would forever try to fill the void.

'Stephen cared deeply about the future of his family; that was obvious from the first moment I spoke to him. I'll treasure that time. I'm so glad we met.' Maria's birdlike body stood at attention, like a tiny soldier. Had Stephen cared too deeply about our future? Had he been terrified? How could I have understood him so little? His demons were buried deep beneath his virile alpha armour. For an awful moment, it felt like Maria – who had met him once – knew him as well as I did.

Stephen had chosen not to trust me with his secrets, wrapping them up so tightly they crushed him.

I glanced around at our large gathering of family, friends, colleagues – and a new friend, Sally Chesser – the sparkling sea behind them. Even Burton was crying.

*

When I was ready, a few weeks later, I tore myself out of bed and returned to the campus at Coastal. There was no Melinda to welcome me. She was on remand in a low-security prison.

Burton and Maria accompanied me, having carried out their threat to stay for a while. We had lunch with Sally and Rachel on campus, overlooking the diamond-bright bay. Spring was just around the corner, and there was a perfume and excitement in the air. When I entered my office, I found an email from the Vice-Chancellor.

'Welcome back, Rebecca,' said Patrick, waving me over to a plush leather chair. His office was even higher up than Priscilla's glowing den in the silver tsunami building on the coast.

'I want you to know how sorry I am. Stephen was a very decent man. I was in Sydney, otherwise I would have been at the funeral.'

I nodded, trying to stop from welling up. *And Stephen was not as decent as you thought, Vice-Chancellor, or did you know? Secret men's business?*

'Priscilla has decided to stay in Paris and take up a position lecturing at the Sorbonne.' Patrick paused. I tried to plaster a neutral smile on my face, angry at the very thought of her – and deeply relieved she wouldn't be back.

'Priscilla says you've shown a great deal of courage and integrity and that your colleagues think highly of your leadership. She's suggested that you'd make an excellent Dean.' *So, Priscilla was trying to buy forgiveness.*

'I agree with her,' Patrick continued. 'Just not yet. But I do hope you'll stay on as Head and work with the new appointment. I've reviewed the Faculty and identified it as an area for expansion. Your School will be in surplus once we've recovered the money from Melinda's real-estate ventures.' I imagined laughing with Stephen about the absurd irony and my throat caught.

As I walked back across campus, watching the sea dance in a shimmer of tiny diamonds, it struck me that everything was transitional, cyclical. Change comes in like the tide, sweeping everything in its path.

The evening was unseasonably warm. Late in the afternoon as the last, long rays of sun dipped beneath the hill, I drove down to the beach with Big Boy and pulled on an old wetsuit of Erin's, leaving Maria and Burton to argue about dinner in the mellow, reassuring glow of the kitchen.

Big Boy rushed headlong into the waves, chasing seagulls.

Mustering all my courage, I ran after him, wading out through the swell and then surging forward in clean strokes. I was amazed I remembered how to swim; a thrill ran through me as my body floated over the crest of a wave, its spearmint clarity cool and refreshing. I dived as the ocean crashed about me. Coming up for air, I screamed at the top of my lungs and the surf embraced me with a thunderous roar of its own.

A strong rip sucked me out towards the horizon as memories of Stephen and my father brought hot, salty tears to mingle with the salty water. For a moment I saw Stephen's vibrant brown eyes wrinkled with laughter, his white teeth catching the sun as he ducked and rose in the translucent green, his strong, tanned shoulders ready for anything. I yelled at him like a madwoman, bellowing into the heaving air.

'How could you have risked everything?'

'How could you abandon us?'

I saw my father dive to touch the sand and bring up seaweed, dark and thick, which he threw high into the deepening sky.

'Why did you go out that day? You're a fisherman – you know the sea,' I screamed over the thumping breakers.

I cursed them both, shouting foul words of fury, howling until my voice was hoarse.

I turned and swam and kicked and breathed until I'd caught a crystal wave and its force carried me with a fierce energy towards the shoreline.

As it broke I tumbled through the frothy, swirling white and emerged, eyes stinging, lungs burning, and saw Big Boy lunging at the water's edge, barking furiously, tail wagging like a demented feather duster.

I headed out again into deep water, swimming once my feet could no longer touch the sand that heaved and shifted below. I caught another wave, and then another. The misty sun dropped into the sea, blazing pink, setting the clouds alight. The surf pounded, echoing against the vivid ochre cliffs.

I swam until my skin was wrinkled, pale, and stars began to prick the soft velvet sky.

ACKNOWLEDGEMENTS

I would like to thank the entire team at Simon and Schuster UK and Australia for their commitment and hard work, which has been so crucial to the release of *The Lost Swimmer*. In London, I am especially indebted to Jo Dickinson, Publishing Director, Fiction, for her tremendous support and faith in acquiring the book, and my sincere thanks also to Suzanne Baboneau, Managing Director, Adult Publishing Division, Gill Richardson, Sales Director, and publicist Sam Evans.

My heartfelt thanks go to the brilliantly gifted Roberta Ivers, Managing Editor at Simon and Schuster (Australia), who has guided the way with her astute suggestions and insight. Without her I would not be here. Her notes shaped and improved the manuscript at every turn, and she has taught me so much as a writer. She has made the process of bringing *The Lost Swimmer* to fruition a joy. I also owe an enormous debt of gratitude to my wonderful Australian publisher Larissa Edwards, for her encouragement and belief in picking up this book as my debut novel.

Thanks, too, to editor Claire de Medici, who cleverly tightened the manuscript and focused the themes, and made it so much better. And thanks to Carol Warwick, Senior Marketing and Publicity Manager, for her amazing efforts and advice.

I would also like to thank my patient readers of drafts: Jenny Sweeney and Katie Edwards, childhood friends who have helped me on the journey through all these years and have given such skillful comments and enormous support; and Julie Wells, Carmel Reilly, Rivka Hartman, Rajyashree Pandey, Myles and Kathy Vinecombe and Mary Damousi for their feedback and encouragement. For her enthusiasm, comments, and always dropping in at exactly the right moment to really help, I thank Kerry Landman.

Annette Blonski needs a big thank you for suggesting I follow my love of literature and write novels. So too does my late father Dick Turner for making the same observation, and my late mother Margaret Turner who supported my writing efforts from my earliest years, including furnishing me with a set of *The Shorter Oxford English Dictionary*, and having the foresight to give me a teenage Christmas present of typing lessons, both of which proved to be inestimably useful.

For their professional help along the way I would like to thank Nicola O'Shea, whose feedback was truly valuable, Iain McCalman for his advice and generosity, Chips Sowerwine and Susan Foley for their help regarding archives in Paris (all mistakes are my own), Warwick Anderson for his medical guidance regarding broken ribs (again, all mistakes are definitely mine), Andrea Rizzi for his assistance regarding Italian police, Mary Tomsic for her cheerful help, and Phillipa McGuinness for her positively-fateful suggestion of editors.

A huge thanks to Mary Beard for permission to use quotes from her inspiring book *Pompeii, The Life of a Roman Town* (Profile Books Ltd, London, 2008) – 'If you bugger the *accensus*, you burn your prick,' (page 202) and 'I wish I could be a ring on your finger for an hour, no more ...' (page 114).

I also acknowledge the many bookshops that I have frequented. Many of my favourite authors I discovered while browsing, or came recommended to me by the knowledgeable owners and staff of the beautiful book-lined stores.

And finally, my love and thanks go to my fellow traveller, history professor extraordinaire Joy Damousi, for her inestimable inspiration, invaluable advice and boundless support and optimism through the writing of this book.

Ann Turner
2016

ABOUT THE AUTHOR

Ann Turner is an award-winning screenwriter and director, avid reader and history lover. She is drawn to salt-sprayed coasts, luminous landscapes and the people who inhabit them all over the world. She is a passionate gardener. Her films include the historical feature *Celia*, starring Rebecca Smart – which *Time Out* listed as one of the fifty greatest directorial debuts of all time; *Hammers Over The Anvil*, starring Russell Crowe and Charlotte Rampling; and the psychological thriller *Irresistible* starring Susan Sarandon, Sam Neill and Emily Blunt. Ann has lectured in film at the Victorian College of the Arts.

Returning to her first love, the written word, in her debut novel *The Lost Swimmer* Ann explores themes of love, trust and the dark side of relationships. Her second novel, *Out of the Ice*, a mystery thriller set in Antarctica, will be published by Simon and Schuster in 2016. Ann was born in Adelaide and lives in Victoria. Visit Ann's website at www.annturnerauthor.com.

BOOK CLUB NOTES

1   Rebecca Wilding recalls the words of a fifth-century BC Greek philosopher – 'that you could travel a thousand miles and never notice anything'. She refutes this by noting that 'surely powers of observation would eventually take hold?' How does this connect with events throughout the book and is observation purely subjective depending on situation and mindset?

2   What is the significance of the title *The Lost Swimmer*? Does it have more than one interpretation?

3   What is the significance of the landscape, both urban and natural, in *The Lost Swimmer*? The book traverses the Australian coastline, heads to Greece and Crete, the Amalfi Coast, Venice and Paris – is it a reflection of the different characters and does each place reveal a new secret about the characters as they travel? These places also have romantic connotations. Could these places be replaced with any other parts of the world or is the setting crucial to how the story unfolds?

4   The sea is an important element of *The Lost Swimmer* and it could almost be considered a character. What is its nature and does it affect the characters? If it does, how do the different characters interact with it?

5   Professor Rebecca Wilding is an archaeologist. She sifts through the physical evidence of history to piece together the past. Is she able to use her professional skills objectively to reveal what is happening with her marriage and her husband?

6   What is the significance of the comet? How does this scene set up a sense of foreboding and deepen the feeling that something is not quite right in Rebecca's usually stable world? What other events in the novel add to this sense of foreboding or suggestion that something bad is going to happen? How does this add to the atmosphere or mood of the novel?

7 The story is told from Rebecca's perspective so it is always her point of view. Can her point of view be trusted, and as a reader do you ever doubt her or feel less than sympathetic to her situation – both at the university and while she is travelling?

8 Loss of trust is one of the themes explored in *The Lost Swimmer*, but this is also juxtaposed with the theme of forgiveness. How do these two ideas play out? Does it lead the characters to some kind of redemption or self-realisation at the end of the novel?

9 What is the significance of the scene when Rebecca's dog, Big Boy, attacks Bonnie's joey and then turns on his owner? Does this scene signify a shift in the direction of *The Lost Swimmer*? Bonnie and her joey appear again towards the end of the novel – is this a symbol of another shift in the story?

10 Betrayal is another theme woven through *The Lost Swimmer*. How does this add to the thriller element of the novel? Does it feel as if all the characters have a secret to hide or are covering up their own agenda or motives as to why they are behaving the way they do? In what ways does this theme of betrayal play out within the novel?

11 *The Lost Swimmer* is an emotional thriller throwing up clues, scenarios and behaviours of characters. People and events are not always what they seem. Are some of these clues red herrings or do they all lead to the final conclusion?

12 The visit to the Grotta Verdi introduces Rebecca and Stephen to the crazed boatman, the White Spider. What is the relevance of the reference to Charon and how does this feed into the tension and mystery that unfolds?

13 Stephen's disappearance heightens the tension that echoes throughout the novel and it throws up many questions for Rebecca and about Rebecca. How do you feel she deals with the secrets that are revealed to her and her reaction to Stephen's fate?

14 The ending of *The Lost Swimmer* is surprising in many ways due to the twists and turns of the plot. Does it create more questions to be answered or considered?